LOVE LESSON NUMBER ONE

Sam clicked his tongue to the mare. The horse stepped forward; the surrey was moving now. "So that's how you start her!" Prairie exclaimed.

Sam's full-bodied laughter erupted beside her. She watched his lips as he laughed, then watched as he transferred the reins to his left hand. His right hand snaked out and touched her lower arm, sensuously stroking. She tried to focus her gaze on the folded hands in her lap. The mare trotted along. The touch of Sam's hand made it hard to breathe easily. Then, suddenly, the surrey came to a halt and Sam was facing her, taking her face between his palms. "We started something the other night," he whispered. "Something that's going to take a lot of practice if we ever want to get it just right."

His face was but a hairbreadth from hers, so close his breath tickled her lips.

"And what was that?" she asked, knowing full well what he meant.

"This," he said, touching her tingling lips with his own, very lightly, then drawing back and repeating the caress.

Prairie felt as though a fire smoldered deep inside her and his touch was a breath from a bellows. Her eyelids fell shut and her body tensed with longing.

He kissed her again, more deeply this time, then withdrew his hands from her face. "End of lesson one," he said, his voice husky.

ELIZABETH LEIGH

Prairie Ecstasy

ZEBRA BOOKS
KENSINGTON PUBLISHING CORP.

To my aunt,
Ethel Greer Hammon,
who told me the story behind "toodlum" gravy

ZEBRA BOOKS

are published by

Kensington Publishing Corp.
475 Park Avenue South
New York, NY 10016

First Printing: May, 1993

Printed in the United States of America

ACKNOWLEDGMENTS

Laura Myers—Librarian, Jennings Carnegie Public Library

Richard "Pos" Guidry—toolpusher and lifelong resident of Jennings, who took me to the original oil well sight

Michael "Tawny" Hancock—my husband, whose oil field experience I depended on for the answers to multiple questions

Norma Franklin—who assisted me with researching dime novels

Annette Womack—who described a fishtail bit

Barbara Veillon, Julia Williams, and others who lent me their knowledge and support

Historic New Orleans Collection

Prologue

Lafayette, Louisiana
1899

"I swear, you can get yourself into more scrapes than any one other person I've ever known!"

Prairie Jernigan set her jaw in defiance of her friend's allegation, but he spoke the truth and she knew it. Nevertheless, there was an addendum to that truth, and this she promptly added. "But I've always managed to rescue myself."

"Not this time. You'll never get out of this alone."

"Which is exactly why I need your help. Come on, David. I'm not asking you to do anything illegal or immoral."

"No, you're asking me to do something unethical. You should have thought it through before you sent off that story."

"I did think it through and it's not unethical! It's . . . a necessary evil, a means to an end," she reluctantly admitted, then quickly regained the offensive. "And don't lecture me about the end not justifying the means."

"I wasn't going to," he denied, but his withering glare beneath a beetled brow contradicted his disavowal. "You had this plan in mind the whole time, didn't you?"

Prairie turned her gaze to the window and the bare train tracks beyond the deep porch. "You know I wouldn't involve you if there were any other way around

7

this," she said in a voice as soft as the April dusk. "I can't do much about society's narrow-mindedness. I want to write under my own name—honestly, I do. But I could—no, I *would* lose my teaching position if I did. Then those self-righteous W.C.T.U. women in Jennings would run me out of town."

"You've always said you'd like to leave Jennings one day," he reminded her. "How many times have I heard you say nothing exciting ever happens there?"

"I'd like to be the one who made the decision," she averred, "and not have someone else do it for me. Besides, the publisher probably wouldn't give my story the first consideration if he knew a woman wrote it. For the time being, I'll escape through my writing."

"Wait, wait, wait a minute! Are you telling me you haven't heard from the publisher yet? You don't know whether they're buying your story?"

She shook her head. "I just put it in the mail today."

"Here? In Lafayette?"

"No. In Opelousas. I left it at the coach station."

"And what return address did you use?"

Prairie removed a folded sheet of paper from her reticule and passed it to David. "I wrote down everything you need to know. Here's the publisher's address, the pseudonym I'm using, and my instructions to the publisher concerning correspondence."

David unfolded the sheet and gave it a quick perusal. "Have you considered the fact that *I* could lose my job over this?" he asked. "The Board of Education's rules plainly state that 'no teacher is to engage in unseemly conduct.' I'm afraid they wouldn't consider working on the side as a dime novelist 'seemly.' "

"Yes, I thought of that, too. If anyone asks, you say you're writing a textbook. But you honestly shouldn't have any problems. Those rules you mentioned allow much more leeway for men than women. So long as you don't smoke, drink, frequent pool halls, or get a shave in a barber shop, they're not likely to question your character."

He pursed his lips and gave that a moment's consideration. "How did you manage to make this trip?" he asked. "The rules for women generally prohibit travel outside the city limits without permission."

Prairie covered her hesitation with a swallow of coffee. Obviously, David wasn't aware that Jennings didn't have an official board of education nor a set of established rules. Her supervisors were the senior teacher, Ruth Nolan; the town's commissioner of education and Ruth's husband, Doc; and the mayor, Michael Donovan, who was also her foster father. While the three gave her far more leeway than a board would have, she wasn't convinced either would sanction this present course of action. Nor was she convinced David would help her if he knew she didn't have to answer to an unyielding board of education.

Nevertheless, she'd be obliged tomorrow to explain her absence from Jennings over the weekend. Perhaps the excuse she planned to use would satisfy David. "I told them I was applying for a position here."

"On Sunday?"

"I couldn't very well come on a weekday while school is in session," she replied. "Besides, the weekend's easier if you're using public transportation. There's a coach going east on Saturday and a train going west on Sunday."

David shook his head in disbelief. "You took quite a risk coming here. Why is this so all-fired important to you?"

She leaned toward him, summoning all her persuasive powers. "Can you imagine not knowing who your parents are, David? Can you imagine not knowing where they were born or who their parents were? Can you imagine not even knowing the date of your own birth?"

Her head lowered briefly and, without any coaxing, her throat made a gurgling sound. She swallowed hard, fighting back the swell of emotion. "I don't have the foggiest notion. But I can use my writing as a vehicle to try to find my roots. If I bury the few clues I have often enough, surely some reader somewhere will catch on. I can't afford to have my efforts exposed before that end is accomplished, or all will be lost."

She paused, sipping her coffee and studying David's reaction. He was softening. She knew he was, although he seemed to be trying very hard not to give in. Not easily.

Prairie made her voice matter-of-fact, made her request sound like she was asking him for nothing more than a stick of peppermint when a pound of chocolate truffles wouldn't cover the full extent of the assistance she required. "All you have to do is pretend to be me for awhile. Accept my mail, send off my manuscripts, that sort of thing, and all in your own name. No one here need ever be the wiser."

"I don't know . . ." he hedged.

She reached across the table and laid her hand on top of his. "Please do this for me, David. It has to be a man, and he needs to live outside of Jennings. You're the only man I know who fits the bill."

"You're going about this the hard way, Prairie. Recant your spinsterhood and agree to marry me, and then all your troubles will be over."

Prairie squeezed the back of his hand. "You know how fond I am of you, David. You're probably the best friend I have in the whole world. But marriage won't solve my problems. I have to find my origins. Please try to understand."

In response, her companion rolled his eyes, took a sip of his coffee, and offered in a droll tone, "You could always hire a Pinkerton man."

"That won't work and you know it," she scoffed. "Where would he start? It's a big country, David, and I wouldn't know where to send him. Look," her voice was firm, filled to overflowing with unbridled determination, "I'm not leaving here until we settle this—and if that's not soon, I'll miss the train back to Jennings, and then I'll be in even more trouble."

The upward quirk at the corners of David Hamilton's slender lips and the glimmer in his gray eyes bespoke his amusement at her predicament. "Trouble, my dear, is your middle name. I think you revel in it."

"David—" she warned, feeling the sudden tight clench of her jaw thrust out her pointed chin and imagining how childish she probably looked.

He laughed and threw up a surrendering palm, inadvertently summoning the waitress moving among the tables in the depot. David didn't protest as the woman poured fresh coffee for him, but Prairie laid her hand over her cup.

"No more for me, thanks. I have a train to catch." The waitress nodded curtly at Prairie, then flaunted a wide smile and winked provocatively at David before turning away. "I hope I have a train to catch," she added once the waitress was out of earshot. "Please tell me you'll do it."

"Yes, I'll do it." He was grinning when he said it—probably, Prairie figured, at the waitress's attention. The sober face he pulled when he caught her grinning back failed to erase the twinkle in his dove-gray eyes, a twinkle that bespoke his amusement despite the consternation in his voice. "But I still think it's the silliest darn fool thing I ever heard of."

Chapter One

Jennings, Louisiana
September 21, 1901

Prairie Jernigan had done a lot of silly darn fool things in her twenty-two years. Recently, she'd begun to think that David had been right two years ago, that posing as a male dime novelist was the silliest darn fool thing she'd ever done.

After all, more than two years of writing pulp fiction had accomplished nothing — not unless one counted the immense popularity of a certain Pampas J. Rose as just reward, and Prairie didn't. Nor did she count the fun she had creating stories and seeing them in print. Even the fact that her writing enabled her to live out her fantasies through her characters, fulfilling an inner need that writing poetry and Victorian prose could not provide, didn't count anymore. Not when her efforts had failed to provide a connection to her past.

What she did count was the nuisance of maintaining anonymity in a town as small as Jennings. All the time and effort and risks she'd put David through unnecessarily. All the long hours she'd spent pounding away at her Remington typewriter, hours that often ran far into the night as she pushed herself to write one story after another, planting in each one the few clues she held to her past, hoping one of the stories would hit pay dirt.

And maybe, just maybe, one of them finally had.

13

Maybe all the effort had been worth the headaches. Maybe writing dime novels hadn't been such a silly darn fool thing to do.

She stood that bright Saturday morning on the front veranda of the Donovans' house, holding an open sheet of cheap white writing paper in one trembling hand and swiping with the other at a sudden misting in her eyes, eyes Wynn Donovan often said were the color of the weathered clay flowerpots adorning the porch. Prairie didn't dare risk ruining the scrawled ink strokes with a flood of tears. Nor did she care to explain the reason behind such uncharacteristic behavior to the Donovan boys, whom she regarded as brothers.

The conscious reminder of her obligation to her foster parents, Michael and Wynn Donovan, who were in Buffalo for the Pan-American Exposition, gave her pause. She listened for the sound of the boys' play and heard instead two voices raised in argument over who had touched base first while a slightly more mature and somewhat deeper voice commanded that the younger ones hush. If this quarrel followed the path of their other spats, it should keep all three occupied for several more minutes — time enough for her to sit down and absorb the contents of the letter her publisher, Beadle and Adams, had sent to David, who had then forwarded it to her.

She chose the porch swing as her perch, settled plump, chintz-covered pillows at her back, kicked off her slippers, and pulled her bare feet onto the thick cushion, resting them next to her left hip. Prairie would have preferred to sit cross-legged, Indian fashion, but the possibility of being caught in such an unladylike position, even by one of the boys, forced her to compromise. Sunlight trickled in over her shoulder and fell in dappled splotches onto the coarse white paper, softening its five-and-dime quality.

Dear Mr. Rose, she read, *I aint never rote to a arthur before but after my granson read Fiery Flora or Fallen from*

14

Grace in New Orleans out loud to me I disided I must put pin to paper and ask you were you heared about toodlum gravie. I aint never heard no one call brown gravie that ceptin my youngist sister Annie who ran off a long time ago and was never heard from agin. If you no her pleas tell her to rite to me.

The letter was signed "Mrs. Albert Byers."

Prairie squinched her eyes tight and willed the constriction in her throat away. Was it possible? Could this letter be from her Aunt Martha? She could check the penmanship against the letter Michael had found in her father's saddlebags years before, but she knew without looking that the handwriting didn't match. Yet, who else would know about toodlum gravy?

Every day of her life—at least since she'd learned to read—Prairie had taken the old letter out of her stationery box and read it, had memorized its every pen stroke, every dot and tittle. By now, the paper had yellowed and cracked with the brittleness that comes with age, and the ink had faded to a soft gray; much, she supposed, in the same way the intervening years must have treated her Aunt Martha.

Prairie tried to conjure an image of her aunt's face, tried for the umpteenth time to recall a shred of memory of the family she hadn't seen for eighteen years. But again, as always, such recollection evaded her. She saw only a wrinkled complexion and thinning gray hair, a manufactured image evoked by the cracking paper and faded ink of the one tenable link to her roots—the letter in her stationery box upstairs.

She opened her eyes and read through the letter in her lap again. Couldn't time have altered her aunt's penmanship? The letters had been formed with a hand none too steady and were larger and bolder than those of the old letter. The result of failing eyesight? A possibility.

Definitely a possibility. Prairie had never heard anyone else use the term "toodlum gravy" except her mother, about whom she remembered almost nothing. But she did remember her name — Anna. The letter said "Annie," which, though certainly close enough, still left a prickle of doubt in Prairie's mind. Ann, Anna, Annie . . . they were all very common names.

Prairie closed her eyes again, willing memories to surface that refused to be dredged up, stroking with a trembling forefinger the silver filigree brooch pinned to her bodice. Her fingertip grazed the solid body of the dragonfly, touched the bulbous garnet eyes, then moved outward to caress the lacy wings.

The brooch had been her mother's. In her mind's eye, Prairie could see it pinned to Anna's pristine white bodice, could see herself as a very young child reaching up and touching the piece in innocent wonder. It was one of the few memories Prairie was certain she hadn't fabricated in an effort to create a background for herself.

And her mother was from a place called Big Spring. Of that she was certain as well.

Prairie slipped the envelope from beneath Mrs. Byers's letter. It was postmarked Texarkana, Texas. Her spirits took a sharp nosedive, but pulled up before plummeting too deep as an idea struck her.

Never before had she had an inkling which state Big Spring could be in. Not that she hadn't searched map after map for the town. Indeed, she had — and discovered one Big Spring after another. Naming a town Big Spring was about as common, she'd decided, as naming a girl child Anna.

Perhaps there was a Big Spring near Texarkana. Perhaps Mrs. Albert Byers was her Aunt Martha. Perhaps, at last, she had found a connection to her childhood.

It was certainly worth investigating.

When Jude Langley, a farmer who lived some five miles east of Jennings in the Evangeline community, told some of the local men what he'd discovered on his land, they decided it was certainly worth investigating.

They'd been sitting in the barbershop on a Saturday afternoon in early April of that year, gabbing about the wet weather, speculating on the economic effects of the creation of the gigantic United States Steel Corporation, the future of the new automobiles Henry Ford was manufacturing, and the prospects for the oil fields opening up in Southeast Texas.

In the midst of the gabbing, Langley jerked the hot towel off his face and sat straight up in the barber chair.

"Hold on now, Jude," Dub Jackson admonished. "You made me gap your hair."

"I ain't worrit about the few locks I got left up there, Dub," the farmer barked, his sharp tone snaring the attention of the small crowd. "All this talk's put me to mind about this here seepage I found in one of my rice fields after that last hard rain."

"What kind of seepage, Jude?" Doc Nolan asked. Doc had been in Jennings since the summer of 1880, longer than anyone else except Slim Moreland, the stationmaster, and as long as Michael Donovan, Jennings mayor and resident land baron. Though sixty-six, Doc continued to practice medicine, and no one questioned the sharpness of his mind or the wisdom of his judgment.

"Bubbly, smelly stuff. Almost smells like sulphur. Really stinks."

"Probably just marsh gas," the barber said in a voice rife with exasperation. "People've been finding seepages like that around here for years. 'Tain't nothin' to get excited about. Be still!"

Doc ignored Dub's rantings. "Sounds to me like the seepages they found over near Beaumont. You think it might be oil, Jude?"

"I think I want to find out, but who would know?"

Doc didn't answer immediately, but sat pulling on his right earlobe for a moment. Finally, he said, "The Blackman brothers would."

Joe Corley twisted around in the barber chair next to Jude and asked, "Who are the Blackman brothers?"

"They're the ones brought in the Spindletop field," Doc explained.

Joe, who was a carpenter by trade, could discuss all aspects of building construction quite knowledgeably, but he didn't know squat about oil. "Spindletop?"

"Where have you been, Joe?" Johnny Perkins, manager of Donovan's Hotel, chimed in. "Don't you ever read the papers? That's the field over near Beaumont, the one that came in back in January, the first one in Texas."

"And if there's oil on my land," Jude said, "then we'll have the first well in Louisiana right cheer in Jennings. Whattaya think about that?"

"I think if you don't sit still you're gonna be awful embarrassed in church tomorrow," Dub replied. "I can't cut a bobbing head. You're worser than a little boy."

"What'll it take to get these Blackman brothers over here?" Jude asked, disregarding the barber.

"Money, more'n likely."

"How much, Doc?"

Doc pulled his ear again. "Don't rightly know. I suppose I can find out. But you're gonna have to let me in on this deal, Jude. And you'll probably need some more speculators, too, to finance the drilling. I expect the boy will want in."

The "boy" was Michael Donovan, who was nearly twice Doc's size and almost fifty years old, but they'd been calling each other "boy" and "old man" too long to change.

Jude gave a low whistle. "I don't know, Doc. Been thinkin' I'd keep it all myself."

Johnny Perkins came to Doc's defense. "You got to have money to make money, Jude. I hear tell it takes about ten thousand dollars to drill a well. You got that much?"

The farmer's face, already pink from the heat of the towel, stained a deep crimson. "I got a mite put back."

Doc's watery blue eyes narrowed, the spring-loaded gesture jutting coarse, unruly gray eyebrows outward into a menacing canopy. "Now you listen to me, Jude Langley. If you're wrong, there's no sense in losin' every dime you've got. If you're right, there's no sense in waitin' around until you can afford to drill a well — or gettin' part of it drilled and have to quit 'cause you ran out of money. Best thing to do is let some of us go in with you. It's your land. Naturally, you'll get the biggest cut."

"Well . . ."

"I can see it now," Doc interrupted, changing his expression quicker than a chameleon changes color: his face softly aglow, his voice smooth and low. He raised his right arm and arced his splayed hand in the air.

"What can you see, Doc?" Johnny asked, an impish grin playing with the corners of his mouth.

"Headlines. 'Gusher on Langley Farm.' Then in smaller print — you know how they run a teaser line underneath on a big story — 'More Derricks Going Up on Neighboring Land.' " Doc shook his head sadly then, playing his fabrication for everything it was worth. "But I don't suppose we'll ever see Jonas Richardson run such a story in the *Times*. Years from now, he'll run an obituary that'll say, 'Jude Langley, sixty-nine, died today a poor man, following a lengthy illness brought on by remorse at not having the gumption to investigate a mysterious seepage on his land.' "

Doc had spoken so softly, so seriously, that every man in the barber shop shook his head sadly and looked down at the toes of his shoes, including Jude Langley.

"All right, Doc," the farmer said in a voice heavy with resignation. "You're in. What's next?"

Doc slapped his thigh and yelped, "Yah-hoo! I knew you'd see the light, Jude. Me and the boy'll come out one day next week and give this bubbly bog of yours a look-see. Then we'll send for the Blackman brothers."

There were four of them: J.C., Myron, Wayne, and Sam, but it was Sam who'd talked the other three into becoming oilmen.

The youngest of the bunch, Sam Blackman had left home the earliest, following a wandering star that led him to the gold fields in Alaska and the oil fields in California. In the late summer of 1900, he'd come back home to Beaumont, Texas, sporting a fat bank account and driven with the overwhelming desire to continue prospecting, just a bit closer to home, with J.C., Myron, and Wayne for company. He found them content with tending the family truck farm and playing music at local dances on an occasional Saturday night.

"Dull!" Sam had declared.

"Safe!" J.C. had countered.

"Don't you ever take a chance on something?"

"Only when I know I'm holding a winning hand. Nothing as ridiculous as looking for gold in Texas. They ain't none here, Sam."

"Not gold." Sam tried to be patient, but his natural impetuosity more often than not won out. "Oil."

"There's no oil here either, Sam," J.C. argued. "Everyone knows all the oil's way off in other parts of the country, like Pennsylvania and California."

"Who's to say there isn't any here, too? Captain Lucas thinks there is."

"That old fart? What would a former captain in the Austrian Navy know about oil? Besides, I hear tell he's run out of money."

A complacent smile settled on Sam's wide mouth. "Obviously, J.C., you've never met the man."

The eldest brother wriggled his shoulders in what appeared to Sam to be an indication of sudden discomfort with the subject. "How do you know I've never met him?"

Sam leaned forward and pressed his advantage. "Because he isn't old. He's forty, tops—'bout your age, I'd guess, and he's traveled the world, J.C. He knows a lot more about a lot of things than most men." Sam's shoulders slumped then and he shook his head resignedly. "But you're right about the money. Lucas is broke."

J.C. jumped on Sam's last statement like a half-starved chicken on a fat cricket. "What'd I tell you! He's as big a fool as Patillo Higgins—a bigger fool, 'cause Lucas agreed to take over knowing Higgins'd spent years and a small fortune looking for oil here. You do what you want to, but I ain't havin' nothin' to do with no fool venture, Sam. I ain't about to lose my shirt."

Sam looked at his other two brothers, silently asking for their agreement. They both remained stoically silent.

"I want ya'll in on this, all three of you, but I don't suppose I can blame you for being skeptical. I'll make a deal with you. You don't rib me if I go bust and I won't rub it in if I'm right. You're always welcome to come in with me later."

Wayne coughed. "I, uh, I'm going in with you now, Sam. Just tell me what you want me to do."

The two proved to be perfect business partners. A clear thinker and firm negotiator, Wayne was a magician with figures and statistics, while Sam was the adventurer, the free spirit. Both possessed tireless energies and driving personalities. Together, they pooled their resources of money and talent and began combing the marshy hillock known as Spindletop, about a mile south of Beaumont, looking for surface indications that oil lay beneath.

Higgins had looked. So had Lucas—and neither had found anything, though both held fast to the belief that oil was there. Where their predecessors had failed, Sam and Wayne did not. One day, following almost a week of steady rain, they discovered gas bubbles seeping out of the ground. They hammered an old piece of stovepipe into the earth and dropped in a lighted match. The gas ignited.

As excited as children on Christmas morn, they went to see an almost broke Lucas, who agreed to give them a one-half cut in exchange for operating capital and their labor. Sam and Wayne bought the necessary drilling equipment, hired a driller, and went to work.

A few months later, on January 10, 1901, they

brought in the first well in the Spindletop Field, a well that blew in with an explosion heard for miles around and sent a spray of mud and oil hundreds of feet high, a well that spawned the oil industry in Texas and would be called "the most famous well in the world."

Sam never said, "I told you so." Nor did J.C. and Myron admit their error in judgment. Instead, the two older brothers quietly joined the two younger ones in the booming oil field and began to help out with selling oil and managing property.

The first well in the Spindletop Field was a big one, but not as large as the second one Sam brought in. The press heralded the Blackman brothers' reputation for workmanship in bringing in large wells, and soon the services of the Blackman brothers were being requested by other companies being organized.

Sam promptly went out and found two drillers who understood the practically new rotary well drilling system and convinced them to go to work for Blackman Brothers, Well Contractors, for a ten percent share each in the company. The four brothers retained the remaining eighty percent, dividing it equally among themselves.

The Spindletop Field attracted a multitude of promoters, who bought up property and sold leases in all sizes, some of them twenty-foot-square plots, the size of a derrick. Within a few short months, many of the wells on Spindletop were so close together that a man could walk from derrick to derrick and not set foot on soil. The Blackman brothers were offered more work than they could manage and found themselves either turning down contracts or scheduling equipment and crews weeks in advance of drilling.

Sam should have been happy. His belief that Higgins and Lucas had been right had paid off. But he wasn't happy. He'd met the challenge in Beaumont. He was ready to do some more wildcatting.

When he heard about Hackberry Island over in Louisiana, he took the train to Sulphur, hired a rig, and drove south to a piece of land that wasn't really an island but rather a marshy knoll surrounded by low, swampy country. Everything about Hackberry Island reminded him of Spindletop. Sam wasn't the least bit surprised when he found gas bubbles along the edge of the island. But he was surprised when he contacted some of the local landowners about leasing their property. Not only did they refuse to talk to an "outsider"—they also threatened to shoot him if he didn't "vamoose."

Vamoose he did, right back to Beaumont.

But fate wasn't through surprising Sam Blackman. A few days later, two men walked into the offices of Blackman Brothers, Well Contractors, and asked to see Sam.

"You're speaking to him," Sam said. "How can I help you?"

The younger, taller man just stared in disbelief, but the older one gasped out, "You! Why, you're just a kid. What the hell do you know about oil?"

"Probably a hell of a lot more than you do," Sam said evenly, smiling despite his irritation. "And I'm not a kid. I'm thirty-two. I've found oil before, and I'll find it again. If I find it on your land, I'll make you rich. And then I'm going to make you pay for that remark by ducking you in your own oil."

The old man grinned and stuck out his hand. "I like your spunk, young man. If you're really *the* Sam Blackman, we've got a proposition for you. I'm Enoch Nolan. Most folks call me Doc. And this here's—"

"Michael Donovan. I'm pleased to meet you, Mr. Blackman."

Sam rose slightly from his chair, reached out to accept Donovan's firm handshake, then invited the two to have a seat. Within minutes, his head was spinning with a combination of exultation and triumph. He might not bring in the field at Hackberry Island, but if these men knew what they were talking about, he'd still be the man to bring in the first field in Louisiana.

"You say there are seepages?"

Donovan nodded. "We've known about them for

years, but we thought it was just marsh gas. That may be all it is, but we'd appreciate it if you'd come back with us and check it out. That is, if you're interested."

Sam had already risen and snatched his hat off the rack, a wide grin splitting his tanned face as he settled the gray felt trilby on his head and ran his hand down the dent in the crown. "Just give me time to tell my brothers and pack a bag, gentlemen. You can answer all my questions on the way."

"But the train doesn't run again until day after tomorrow," Donovan reminded Sam.

"We're not waiting for the train. I want to get there before word of this leaks out. We'll take my surrey."

Sam Blackman and his cherry-red surrey, which was topped with yellow fringe and equipped with pull-down isinglass windows, became the talk of the town. Any man, folks said, who would drive around in such a gaudy vehicle had to be eccentric.

Any man who was that eccentric couldn't be trusted to know the difference in natural gas and marsh gas. And both Doc Nolan and Michael Donovan were crazy for trusting Sam Blackman to know what he was doing.

That's what they said in town—in all four barbershops, in clusters standing on the street corners and on the steps of both the Congregational and Catholic churches, in the pool halls and at Saturday night poker games.

Wherever the men gathered, they talked about the "Crazy Trio" who were spending ten thousand dollars to drill a hole they'd more than likely have to fill in later.

Jude Langley kept them abreast of all the details. Drilling for oil had changed things at his farm so quickly that Jude forgot about making history and getting rich. He got panicky about the drilling ruining his farm, so he tried to stop it—even went to Lake Charles to see a lawyer about it, but he'd signed a lease and the lawyer said he was stuck.

"Sam said not to worry," Jude reported later. "He can't afford to drill very many holes at ten thousand apiece, and he'll fill 'em with dirt and plug 'em if there ain't no oil, so's my cattle won't step in 'em and break their legs. 'Sides, he paid me ten dollars for only three dollars' worth of rice he's ruined. Sam's a good man."

The men said Sam Blackman might have a good heart, but he and Doc and Michael were all fools who didn't have anything better to do with their money than pour it into a dry hole. But they never uttered a word of such talk within earshot of Sam or Doc or Michael.

The women reserved judgment on the foolishness of the venture. What they said was that Sam Blackman was one of the best-looking men they'd ever laid eyes on—all the women, that is, except Prairie Jernigan. She'd heard the rumors, of course, but she'd never been close enough to Sam Blackman herself to form an opinion about his looks.

Not until that sunny Saturday in September, the day her placid, unexciting world turned upside down.

Chapter Two

"Hey, Prairie!" Jason Donovan called. "Doc and Ruth're here!"

The creaking of the screen door hinges marked the sixteen-year-old's entrance, its slam his hasty exit, the combination startling Prairie, who was attempting to draft a letter to Mrs. Albert Byers. She was having no better luck with it than she'd been having with her dime novel writing lately. The words just seemed to stick somewhere in the back of her mind and refused to come out.

"I'm coming!" she called back, blotting the paper and then opening a desk drawer and carefully stowing away the sheet before scraping back her chair.

Doc was already in the house, his short, pumping legs coming to an abrupt halt as Prairie walked into the wide front hall. Although sweat poured from his bald pate and forehead and his chest heaved from the unaccustomed exertion, his watery blue eyes twinkled as brightly as Prairie had ever seen them twinkle. He grabbed her elbow and tugged hard. She stood her ground—literally.

"Come on, Prairie, m'girl. If we don't hurry, we'll miss it."

"Miss what?"

"The well's comin' in," he wheezed, continuing to tug at her but going nowhere.

Prairie pushed down harder on her heels. "How do you know the well's coming in?"

"Because Sam said so."

"How does Sam know?"

"Because he does. I'll explain it to you on the way."

He had her elbow in a stranglehold. Prairie tried to snatch it back, failed, and attempted to justify her reluctance. "I don't care a thing about that old well, Doc, and you know it. Besides, I have too much work to do this afternoon to go off with you on some wild goose chase. Take the boys if you want to, but I'm staying here—ouch!" she wailed, stumbling forward. "Don't pull so hard, Doc!"

He stopped pulling but he didn't let go. "Come on, then. Time's awastin'." When she still balked, he added, "This is history in the makin', girl, and you *ought* to care about it, you bein' a teacher and all."

A weary sigh escaped her lips. She knew she might as well give up because Doc wasn't about to. "Oh, all right. Just let me get my bonnet."

Maybe, she mentally added, the change of scenery and country air would do her some good. Maybe she'd come home refreshed in mind and body and be able to write again.

"You sure we got a well here, Sam?"

Sam Blackman shaded his eyes against the blaring sun and fixed his gaze on the lower crossbars of the tall wooden derrick, the low thrum of the boiler and the chug of the pumps singing sweetly in his ears. "Can't you feel it, Wayne?"

"Nope. I just gotta trust your instincts."

Wayne's admission humbled him. "Thanks for sticking by me. You and Myron and J.C. could have packed up and left here a couple of weeks ago—and with good reason. I appreciate you staying."

Wayne grunted. "I just hope you know what you're doing. The people in Jennings don't think you do."

Sam smiled. "I'm glad they don't, 'cause if I'm right, we'll make a killing."

27

Before Doc and Michael had ever gone to Beaumont to get Sam, they had formed the Nolan and Donovan Company. A contract between this company and the Blackman Brothers created still another company, Southwest Louisiana Oil, which was capitalized at $50,000, consisting of fifty thousand shares with a par value of one dollar per share.

These shares were divided equally between Nolan and Donovan Company and Blackman Brothers, but Sam insisted that the contract deed to Blackman Brothers any forty acres out of the leased holdings which he designated. Doc and Michael reluctantly agreed, with the stipulation that the plot not revert to Blackman Brothers until the drilling had been completed.

Each party retained the right to sell any part or all of the treasury stock. Sam chose to sell eight thousand of the Blackman Brothers shares in order to defray the costs of drilling the first well. Wayne made quick work of it by selling all eight thousand to an investor he knew in Beaumont. Nolan and Donovan also sold several thousand of their shares to a number of Lake Charles investors who figured anything Doc and Michael initiated was a sure winner.

For a while, hopes ran high. But when Sam had drilled to 1500 feet with no favorable results, some of the stockholders' feet got a mite chilly. Southwest Louisiana Oil stock was put on the market at twenty-five cents a share, and Sam bought up every share he could get his hands on. That was when J.C., Myron, and Wayne thought he'd finally lost it. But Sam was convinced there was oil under Jude Langley's rice field.

He'd been amazed when he'd first seen the area, even more convinced after he climbed a modest grade for over a mile and looked around him. A marshy depression sat on top of the grade, and off to the east was a hill similar to Spindletop. In fact, the whole topography could have been a duplicate of Spindletop.

If his wildcat fever hadn't run high enough then, it did after he set a five-gallon can over the seepage, waited until he thought it had time to fill up with gas, then set a match to it. The explosion shot the can almost twenty feet into the air, confirming the seepage to be natural and not marsh gas. Sam wasted no time in signing the contract with Nolan and Donovan, selecting forty acres with the hill as its center for his designated plot.

But after drilling to 1500 feet and finding no indications of oil, his brothers had been ready to quit — and the stockholders eager to cut their losses and pull out.

Not Sam. He ordered more drill pipe. At 1700 feet, he struck an excellent showing of oil in a sand as fine as sugar. It took another hundred feet of drill pipe to get through the sand. With each foot, Sam's fever soared higher. He pushed himself harder, pushed his brothers and Jake Daniels, the driller he'd brought with him from Spindletop. For several days they'd never shut down the boiler and the pumps, working instead around the clock to reach the pool of oil Sam assured them they'd find.

Early that Saturday morning in September, Sam ran the bailer, examined the cuttings, and said they'd hit pay dirt. He set the casing with a gate valve for protection and sent Myron into town to tell Doc, and Wayne over to tell Jude, who lived less than half a mile from the derrick. Wayne and Jude had been back for hours; Myron had only recently returned. Doc had said to wait. He was coming — just as soon as he finished up with a few office patients.

"I wish the old man would get here," Sam said, as much to himself as to Wayne. He took his watch out of his pocket and noted the time to be nearly two o'clock. "I'm ready to run the bailer again and bring this baby in."

* * *

It was mid-afternoon when Doc stopped his buggy beside the rig. Within seconds, the derrick floor was swarming with boys.

"Good heavens, Enoch!" Sam exclaimed. "What did you mean bringing all these kids out here? They're liable to get hurt."

"Patrick, come down off that derrick!" Doc hollered. "Mickey, don't touch that boiler!" He waggled a finger in the general direction of town. "Jason, take your brothers off over there away from the rig." To Sam, he said, "They're Donovan's boys. Since he's not here to see this, I thought the least I could do was bring his offspring."

Sam wasn't listening. He wasn't watching the boys anymore, either. His scrutiny had settled on the diminutive child-woman who stood by the buggy, every feature of her heart-shaped face bespeaking wonder. It was the wonder, he supposed, that made her look like a child, for there was nothing juvenile about her figure.

A sudden breeze sailed over the field, lifting the brim of her bonnet off her wide forehead, exposing and then teasing thick strands of dark, wavy hair the color of molasses. A piece came loose and fell over her brow, and in Sam's mind it was his own hand that reached up to tuck the strand back under her bonnet. Sam could feel the soft texture against his palm, imagined himself removing the bonnet and burying his fingers in the lush tresses . . .

". . . want you to meet my wife."

Doc's voice in his ear and a sharp tug on his lower arm splintered Sam's daydream into a host of incohesive fragments. While he followed Doc to the buggy, his mind raced with questions and observations.

Could Doc actually be married to this woman? Or she to him? How in the devil had the old man man-

30

aged it? Land sakes, he was old enough to be her grandfather!

There was a wide-eyed innocence about her, a pureness that spoke of inexperience more than youth, and yet, there was a hardness as well. Sam could see it in her almost rigid posture — shoulders held squarely, spine straight as a plumb line — and in the tilt of her little pointed chin. The combination served to emphasize the outward thrust of her bosom, the flatness of her stomach, and the firm roundness of her derrière beneath a russet-colored cotton dress. In a society obsessed with hourglass figures, hers would set the standard.

Suddenly, Sam realized he was staring, perhaps because she stared back at him — boldly and with the barest hint of impertinence in her ginger-colored eyes. A man could lose himself in their spicy depths . . .

"Ruth and Prairie teach together at the Jennings Primary School," Doc was explaining.

Sam gasped at the instant, totally unanticipated craving that gnawed at his heartstrings. It was a craving to know this woman Doc called Prairie — to know her in every sense of the word. What an odd name, he thought, but a beautiful one. As beautiful as its owner.

He forced himself to look at the other woman — Ruth, the one with frizzy red hair that should be graying, judging by the collection of wrinkles around her mouth and eyes, but it wasn't. The one with big front teeth that protruded forward, ruining the shape of her mouth. Her eyes were brown, too, but a darker, duller shade than Prairie's. Those eyes gazed lovingly down at Doc, who stood a full head shorter, the difference in their heights making him have to reach upward to encircle her shoulders with his arm.

Realizing that Ruth, not Prairie, was Doc's wife sent a rush of relief sluicing through Sam, although he wasn't quite sure why it mattered to him. There

31

simply was no room in his life for permanence — never had been, never would be. And now that Doc had finally arrived, Sam was eager to run the bailer again.

The sound of Prairie's soft, melodious voice put that notion right out of his mind. "This entire operation amazes me. Doc says you're down to eighteen hundred feet. How did you ever manage to drill that far? And where did you get all this equipment?"

In the back of his mind, Sam knew that women didn't usually care about such things — didn't understand them, even if you tried to explain. That fact dredged itself up as he took her elbow and guided her onto the derrick floor, using his free hand to indicate specific items as he mentioned them and warming to the subject despite his skepticism.

"Eighteen hundred and *ten* feet, actually," he corrected. "We shipped this machinery in from Spindletop," he began. "We have a small draw works over there, which is what raises and lowers the drill stem in and out of the hole by means of that cable you see running up to the top of the derrick and down to the traveling block. The derrick is sixty-four feet high and that boiler is a forty-horse. Its power is what turns the rotary and pushes the bit deeper into the earth."

Dadburnit, but you smell good. Like a meadow full of sweet clover. And me — well, I smell like an oil man who's been out in the heat too long — all sweat and grease.

"Bit?" he heard her ask. "What's a bit?"

Sam cleared his throat and tried to concentrate on his explanation. "It works with the rotary to bore through the earth like a carpenter's drill bores through wood. The bit is attached to the bottom of the drill pipe. The boiler provides the power to turn the rotary, which turns the bit. We're using fishtail bits."

He reached into a bucket, drew out a strange-looking contraption some eight or ten inches long, and held it out for Prairie's inspection.

"It almost looks like a cookie made with a Christmas tree cutter," she said, her analogy earning her a smile from Sam, "the way the triangles flare out on each side of the bolt. May I hold it?" she asked, her willingness to take the dirty bit in her hand surprising Sam. He handed it to her.

"It's heavier than I thought it would be," she observed.

Sam laughed. "Not that heavy — just four or five pounds."

As she examined the bit, her eyebrows slowly rose to mid-forehead. "This can cut through the earth?"

"Not when the edges are all chewed up, like the one you're holding. If the formation is soft, like it is here, this is the kind we use. Those curved flanges bore right through dirt and clay. But if it was rocky, we'd use a claw bit."

"What happens when the bit wears out, like this one did?"

"It's not actually worn out. It just needs to be sharpened. When it gets dull, though, we have to come out of the hole — pull all the pipe out — and attach a new one. We keep several bits on hand, so we don't lose time waiting for someone to take a file to the dull edges. Of course, we don't need a sharp bit right now, since we're through drilling this hole."

Her eyes were downcast, her attention on the dirty piece of steel in her hands. Sam caught himself staring again, but this time he didn't look away. She seemed totally oblivious to the effect she was having on him. This woman honestly seemed to understand, honestly seemed to care about his work. Sam shook his head in amazement.

"Doesn't coming out of the hole take a long time?"

"It can," he said mechanically, his thoughts focused on the delicacy of Prairie's face instead of his speech. Without realizing what he was doing, he started explaining how to go into the hole rather than how to come out, which was a reverse process. "While one joint of pipe is being put down, someone lays another joint into the V of the derrick and starts screwing a swivel into that joint. When the first joint has been drilled to the top of the rotary, the second joint is hooked onto it and pulled into place."

Heaven above, woman! Did anyone ever tell you your lips were made for kissing? So soft and full and pouty . . . Talk, man, and be quick about it. It's the only way to save yourself from looking like a lovesick calf.

"We have to work quickly. As soon as the swivel has been unscrewed from the pipe in the hole and the new joint put in place, we start the pumps up again before all the threads of the pipe are made up, or else the formation can cave in, and then we'll be in real trouble."

She looked up at him then, intending to ask about the function of the pumps. But when she looked away from the dull bit in her fist, she found herself staring into eyes as clear a blue as she'd ever seen — as blue as the summer sky without so much as a trace of gray or green. They were blue all the way out to the edges, not cat's eyes rimmed by a darker band, but solid and vibrant and piercingly intense. They were like two pools of deep-set sapphires nesting beneath almost perfectly straight eyebrows. The lids drooped a bit at the corners, lending a lazy, devil-may-care air to a man whose entire being exuded energy and confidence. No wonder the women in town drooled over Sam Blackman!

It took more effort than she would have ever thought necessary to draw her gaze away from his. "So what do you have to do now to bring the oil out of the ground?"

"Running the bailer one more time ought to do it."

"You'll have to forgive me for asking so many questions, Mr. Blackman," Prairie said, "but I don't understand all this oil field lingo. What is a bailer?"

"Of course, you don't understand, Miss — Pardon

34

me, but I didn't catch your last name."

"Jernigan."

"I'm the one who should be apologizing, Miss Jernigan. I get carried away sometimes."

Sam smiled then, treating Prairie to a symphony of warm, throbbing feelings with the simple upward curve of chiseled lips. Unconsciously, she wrapped her fingers tightly around the drill bit.

"The bailer is a long pipe that removes water, mud, and rock from the hole. Once the hole is clear, the pressure of the gas will force the oil up the drill pipe and the well will come in."

"You make it sound terribly simple."

"It *is* simple. We do our work, then Nature does hers."

"And we're holding you up."

Sam was inclined to argue with her, but he realized with sudden clarity that she spoke the truth. She *was* holding him up from accomplishing the one final task necessary to bring the well in. This well represented a major investment of his time and money, but just as important — maybe even more important — was the investment of his heart and soul. This woman might tickle his fancy today, but women weren't worth the major investment a relationship required. At least, he'd never met one he thought worthy of such sacrifice.

He watched her glance around.

Prairie saw Doc and Ruth climbing into the buggy and the boys playing freeze tag some hundred yards west of the derrick.

"Hurry up, Prairie," Ruth called, "and you won't have to walk so far. We're moving the buggy out of the way."

Out of the way of *what?* Prairie wondered, wanting to ask Sam but sensing his eagerness to return to work. She supposed she'd find out soon enough.

"I — I'll get out of your way now," she stammered,

her tongue mimicking the flutter of her heart.

She forgot she was still holding the drill bit in her fist until she reached up to accept Doc's hand. "Oh!" she gasped. "I have to take this back."

"Keep it for now," Doc said. "We'll return it later. I don't want to delay Sam a moment longer. And, ladies," he added, "I'd take off my jewelry if I were you. Otherwise, it's liable to get ruint."

Within the next thirty minutes, half the town showed up in the rice field, or so it seemed to Prairie. Doc mumbled something about not being able to keep anything a secret in a town as small as Jennings. In buggies and buckboards, on horseback and foot they came. King Clarkston sputtered up on his brand-new, four-cylinder Indian motorcycle, causing more stir for a few minutes than the prospect of oil spewing out of Jude Langley's rice field.

The crowd stood too far away to see much of what was going on up at the derrick. They shuffled around, visiting amongst themselves, the atmosphere that of a box social. But when the earth began to tremble, Sam hollered, *"Quick!* Put out your cigarettes! It's coming in!" The crowd went wild. Like the tide rushing in, they ran toward the rig. Beneath their feet, the earth moved. It shivered and shook and threatened to open up and swallow them, but they kept running.

Prairie ran right along with them, her younger, stronger legs moving her ahead of Doc and Ruth. She heard a roar, distant at first, almost like the gurgle of a brook, but increasing in volume until it thundered in her ears. Suddenly, a column of oil and sand shot out of the hole, shot high above the sixty-four-foot derrick, then spread out like a huge umbrella and rained down in a peppery torrent upon the crazed crowd.

Some of the men—Jude Langley among them—

36

lifted their faces to the sky, lifted their hands and caught the oil sand in their open palms, and shouted for joy, while others just stood staring, dumbfounded. Some of the men hugged each other, and each other's wives — the wives who weren't hightailing it back to the line of buggies and horses, beyond the spray of oil and sand.

King Clarkston grabbed Prairie's hands and spun her around. "Oil!" he cried, his handsome face alight with pleasure. "We'll all be rich, Prairie. Rich!"

"You're already one of the wealthiest men in town," Prairie observed, the laughter in her voice a reflection of her delight over the well and not King's attention.

"Now I'll be even more wealthy!" he exclaimed. "I'm going to start my own oil company." He pulled her closer — too close for Prairie's comfort. There was something about King Clarkston that cried *Danger!* And it wasn't the sort of danger that stirs excitement, but rather fear. "Will you marry me now, Prairie?"

He'd asked her at least a dozen times before. Never had she thought him completely serious. Nor did she now. She grasped for polite words of refusal.

Doc — who, along with Ruth, had finally caught up with Prairie — saved her.

"Whoopee!" Doc cackled, taking Prairie away from King and twirling her around. "I knew it. I *knew* it! I wish the boy was here to — "

The report of a pistol cut off the end of Doc's sentence. Everyone whirled toward the sound, toward Otis Hill, who'd brought along his jug of sour mash and imbibed a bit too heavily. Otis held his gun above his head and pulled the trigger again, shooting into the oil sand.

"Stop him!" someone hollered.

"Don't he know a single spark could explode the well?" Doc muttered, his eyes popping, his face aghast.

Two of the men who stood close to Otis wrestled

37

him down and grabbed the pistol from his hand. Doc, along with Prairie and Ruth and probably everyone else who had any inkling of their scrape with danger, breathed a heavy sigh of relief. The roar, however, rendered their sighs inaudible.

After awhile, the roar subsided, but the oil sand continued to flow. People were lying down in the field and rolling in it.

Sam stood on the derrick floor, his heart pounding with the sweet rush of success. He surveyed the crowd, smiling at their antics now that Otis Hill had been deprived of his pistol, thinking he wouldn't mind rolling around in the oil sand himself.

Without conscious direction, his gaze sought Prairie. The universal drenching in oil and sand obliterated features, but there were few skirts in the crowd. Sam couldn't imagine Prairie Jernigan running away to the line of buggies. He spied someone who fit her general description standing close to a couple who, judging from their heights and the way they clung to each other, could only be Enoch and Ruth. He'd bet Enoch wouldn't label him a kid now.

"There's Enoch Nolan," he called to his brothers, having to shout to be heard above the melee. "Grab him! I owe him a ducking!"

Doc fought the four of them gallantly, but in the end, he lost. They dragged him up close to the derrick and made him stand in the stream of crude oil with them. The oil soaked them through, plastering their hair against their heads and their clothes against their bodies. They laughed and slapped each other on the back and took turns rubbing the oil into Doc's bald pate.

For more than an hour, folks danced around in the spewing oil and sand, but by dark only a few diehards were still hanging around.

"Look at us!" Prairie said to Ruth, her voice filled with laughter. "Aren't we in a mess?"

"Yep, but I don't know when I've had so much fun."

"Me, either. But we need to be heading back. I need to get these boys cleaned up and feed them some supper before it gets too late."

Ruth nodded. "I'll get Enoch."

Doc was talking to Sam. He told Ruth he didn't want to leave quite yet. "You take the buggy on home. I'll catch a ride with Sam tomorrow."

"But, Enoch," Ruth protested, "tomorrow's Sunday. And you don't even have a change of clothes with you."

"I may just miss church tomorrow, Ruth. I'm not leaving here until we've got this well under control."

"When will that be?"

"When it stops spewing sand and starts flowing pure crude."

The well flowed sand and oil for seven hours, covering Jude Langley's rice field with a lake of oil and piling up a foot of sand a hundred feet around the derrick.

Finally, around eleven o'clock, one big, bright gush of oil and gas shot upward into the star-dusted sky. The seven men who'd never left — the four Blackman brothers, Doc, Jude, and Jake Daniels, the driller — whooped and hollered and pranced around in the sand on the derrick floor like a bunch of wild Indians.

Somewhere in the middle of their whooping and hollering and prancing around, the crude oil stopped flowing. They were so caught up in the revelry they didn't notice it at first. A hush fell over the group. They all stood stock-still, lifting their heads and waiting expectantly.

"What happened?" Doc finally asked.

"It's gone and it's not coming back," Sam said. "Let's get some shut-eye." He stood at Doc's side, his gaze on the pile of sand he was standing in.

"How come? What happened?"

Sam appeared unperturbed. "The sand caved in. I've seen it happen in the oil fields in California. Tomorrow we'll start cleaning it out. When we've created a cavity, then our sand troubles will be over. You'll see. It's nothing to worry about."

It was nothing to worry about.

Prairie held the yellowed, time-worn letter in her hand, the letter from Aunt Martha. It began, "My dearest brother," thus disproving her earlier supposition that Mrs. Albert Byers was her Aunt Martha. Her mother might have been Mrs. Byers's sister— Prairie refused to let go of that particular hope, but Aunt Martha was her *father's* sister. In her desire to find her aunt, she had overlooked that fact. Although she kept telling herself it was nothing to worry about, she couldn't help feeling disappointed.

For years, she'd dreamed of Aunt Martha, envisioned her aunt's face, imagined her house, created a personality for her, manufactured a husband and children, and later, as Prairie grew older herself, grandchildren. At some point, the dream had become almost reality, needing only a moment of renewed physical contact to make it genuine.

She'd dreamed as well of her own house, her own husband and children. But just being married wasn't enough; if it was, she would accept King's or David's proposal. She dreamed of being swept off her feet by a man who embodied the stuff her own fictional heroes were made of, a man who was totally independent in thought and deed, a man who actively sought adventure and intrigue . . . a maverick.

But this dream she'd put on hold. She had to find out who she was; without that knowledge, Prairie felt as though she were only half a person.

Michael and Wynn Donovan had been wonderful

40

to her, had provided not only the physical necessities but that all-important element: love. They'd planned to legally adopt her, and probably would have if she hadn't stopped them.

Prairie leaned back in her chair and let her eyes fall shut, let memories of the past engulf her. She saw herself as a little girl, no more than four or five, waking up in Wynn's old house, the one Wynn had built when she first came to Jennings, the one Doc and Ruth lived in now. Wynn was the only doctor in town then — except Doc Nolan, who wasn't practicing medicine. Prairie had a fever. Her father had left her with Wynn and then disappeared. Later, some men had found his body next to the Mermentau River.

Jernigan was all they'd known to call him, all the name that was carved into a simple headstone. He'd been the first person to be buried in Jennings, but his death was soon followed by many others who fell victim to the disease that had claimed his life: diphtheria. Wynn almost died from it herself, had been left with a lame leg from the disease. The diphtheria epidemic forced Doc back into practice; when Wynn recovered, she persuaded him to continue.

That was in the spring of 1884. That fall, Michael Donovan had married Dr. Wynnifred Spencer, and Prairie had moved with her from the little house on the north side of town into the big, new, three-story painted lady Michael had built.

The two would have searched for her family had they known where to start, but Prairie could tell them nothing of importance, nor had her father left any real clues. All they had to go on was the contents of Jernigan's saddlebags. Years later, when Michael thought she was old enough to assume the responsibility, he gave them to her. Inside were the letter from Aunt Martha and the silver filigree dragonfly brooch. Michael had said the only other contents had been some tobacco and beef jerky.

Soon after they were married, Wynn and Michael went to Lake Charles and petitioned the court for adoption, but the judge thought they should wait to see if anyone came to claim Prairie. By the time the judge agreed to allow them to begin the proceedings, Prairie was old enough to resist. She didn't want to be Prairie Donovan, she said. The name Jernigan was one of the few links she had to her own family and she didn't want to let go of it. Couldn't she continue to live with them without changing her name?

The judge said yes. And, eventually, so did Michael and Wynn. Though Wynn held fast to the belief that Jernigan might not have been Prairie's natural father, she acknowledged the importance to Prairie of the only family name she knew. They became her legal guardians and Prairie retained the name Jernigan.

Some of these things Prairie remembered herself; some Wynn and Michael and Doc had told her about. There were so many things she didn't know, so many things she couldn't remember.

But if Mrs. Albert Byers was, indeed, her aunt, Prairie might soon know much more.

Maybe then she would be free of the bonds that held her to an uncertain past, bonds that overshadowed an even more uncertain future.

She reached toward the lamp on her desk, caught a glint of gray metal in the golden light, and stayed her hand on the globe. She moved her hand to the piece of steel she'd washed clean earlier. The tips of her fingers brushed across the fishtail bit while the memory of Sam Blackman's vivid blue eyes brushed across the inner sanctum of her heart, sweeping away the cobwebs of fatigue and leaving her with a powerful hunger.

Chapter Three

From the moment the well came in, Prairie felt as if a different person had jumped into her skin.

She couldn't explain it, wasn't even completely certain of the change at first. Initially, the excitement over the gushing oil precluded examination. Then, all the way home from Jude Langley's rice field, Ruth and the boys chattered incessantly, allowing Prairie little space to assess the glow that enveloped her.

When she did finally ponder it, she credited the letter from Mrs. Byers for the glow. But late that night, after she'd realized her mistake, when she sat at her desk caressing a piece of cold steel, Prairie felt a thrill, an exhilaration far beyond any other she'd ever experienced. Although its source was spiritual, it fueled her physically, erasing the disappointment, energizing and electrifying her, just as though she'd been a candle and was now one of those newfangled light bulb lamps.

Where before time had carried only the promise of endless repetition, now it carried the hope of change, of progress, of transformation. Before the discovery of oil, Prairie had thought that to find excitement she would be forced to leave Jennings, her beloved hometown, forced to leave behind the only family she knew. Instead excitement had found Jennings, and in doing so, had found Prairie Jernigan.

Her heart sang a zany, unstructured tune. Her head buzzed with ideas and plans. Her soul burned with the fever of excitement.

She removed her hand from the fishtail bit, rolled a sheet of paper into the old Remington, and typed:

THE ADVENTURES OF PROSPECTOR PETE,
or
Panning for the New Gold: Oil!

She didn't sleep a wink that night.

From the moment the well came in, the people of Jennings stopped calling Sam Blackman "that lunatic with the red surrey who's drilling for oil in a rice field." Suddenly, he became a "great pioneer." No one would admit to ever calling him anything else.

Jonas Richardson wrote at length in the *Times* about the first oil well in Louisiana and the man who had held on long enough to see it come in. Telegraph wires carried the news across the nation. Within a few days, Jennings was getting more national publicity than President McKinley's assassination, which had occurred almost simultaneously with the discovery of oil in Louisiana.

In the midst of the excitement, no one stopped to think about how this discovery would immediately affect Jennings—no one except the Blackman brothers, who knew what to expect. After all, they'd been right in the middle of things in Beaumont when Spindletop came in. There were plans to be made, contracts to be signed, leases to be negotiated—before the world caught on.

On Sunday, Wayne took J.C., Myron, and Doc into town in the surrey. That evening, J.C. and Myron boarded the westbound train and headed back to Beaumont, back to the offices of Blackman Brothers, Well Contractors, back to the business of running an oil company.

On Monday morning, Wayne signed a two-year lease with Johnny Perkins for the old Donovan Hotel building—the only empty building of its size available, paid for six months' charges in advance for two rooms at the best boardinghouse in town, and began the task of hiring a crew for Sam and a half-dozen office workers for himself.

He sent the crew out to the well armed with tents and a store of food and other supplies. The office workers, all relatively young women thrilled to find a job in the small town, sat around drinking coffee and filing their nails, waiting for Wayne to furnish the building and then give them something to do—and wondering in the meantime what foolishness the Blackman brothers were up to.

By the end of the week, they knew. A horde of buckboards and heavy wagons pulled by sweating oxen began streaming into Jennings, hauling men and oil field equipment. The Wednesday train from Beaumont hauled one passenger coach and two box-cars more than its normal tow, unloading scores of people and uncoupling several freight cars loaded with building materials at the Jennings depot.

Speculators and gamblers came, prospectors and drillers, investors and roughnecks, men looking for a quick profit and men looking for profitable employment. Some of them brought their families. They filled up the hotels and boardinghouses and spilled out into the streets. Thinking about how much money he'd lost for Michael Donovan on the old hotel building made Johnny Perkins sick.

Anyone who owned a vacant lot had no trouble selling it. Joe Corley put to work every able-bodied man he could find. Buildings started going up everywhere, and in the sudden furor no one bothered to ask what specific purposes the buildings were to serve or to protest their shabbiness.

Maintaining discipline with small, easily excitable children in the middle of the sudden furor proved an almost impossible task.

Ruth brought up the subject over lunch on Friday. She and Prairie were sitting on the porch of the two-room school. The children sat clustered in groups scattered across the deep front yard, their lunch pails half forgotten as they watched the construction next door.

"Wouldn't you know," Ruth lamented, "I finally got the third-graders interested in learning their multiplication tables when BAM! Before I could collect my wits, the entire group was standing at the windows, whooping and hollering. An unbalanced load of lumber had fallen off a wagon right on top of some poor, unfortunate soul, and he was screaming at the top of his lungs. It must have taken me ten minutes to get those children settled down again. I never could stir up any interest in multiplication after that."

Only half listening, Prairie frowned into her jar of buttermilk. "There's a fruit fly in here. I thought it was too late in the year for fruit flies."

"It's never too late in the year in Louisiana. You grew up here, Prairie; you know that. Isn't the noise bothering you?"

Prairie made a face, set the buttermilk aside, and bit into an apple. "Not really," she said between chomps. "Your room buffers the noise."

"They can't build on your side. Your house is in the way," Ruth observed, a trace of irritation in her voice.

"You want to swap rooms?"

Ruth puffed out her flat chest and stuck her round, freckled chin up in the air. "I've been teaching school for thirty-five years. I think I can manage to make it through a little sawing and jawing and hammering. This can't last forever."

Prairie grinned behind her apple. It had only lasted one day so far, and it wasn't bothering her a bit. In fact, she found the sudden activity invigorating. She hugged that realization close and offered only vague comments when Ruth asked for her opinion. The older woman was so caught up in righteous indignation, she never seemed to notice.

Judging from the amount of oil that had spewed out of the hole before it sanded up, Sam estimated that the well would produce 7,000 barrels of crude per day — if the sand could be controlled. That made it a gusher field. At ten cents per barrel, they were going to make a killing! Just like he'd told Wayne they would.

But it wasn't the money that interested Sam Blackman as much as it was the challenge. He'd sniffed out the field and brought in the well. Now, if he could just get all the sand out of the hole and start pumping those 7,000 barrels a day, every day . . .

And then what was he going to do? Spend a few months developing the Jennings field as he had the one at Spindletop, and then move on?

The instant the thought crossed his mind, Sam shooed it away. The future had never interested him, and he left the past behind, where it belonged. Sam lived in the present. Always had. Always would.

* * *

Prairie woke early, just before daylight, threw the covers back and bounced out of bed before she remembered it was Saturday. Her favorite day of the week. The only day she could do exactly what *she* wanted to do all day, and not what someone else either expected or required her to do. And she knew what she wanted to do that day—if the boys would cooperate. She wanted to write.

Never had Prairie felt the urge quite so keenly. It wasn't an urge, exactly, she mentally amended. It was more a compulsion, almost an obsession. Something had happened to her exactly a week before, the day she'd received the letter from Mrs. Albert Byers, the day Sam Blackman had brought in the well. Something she couldn't quite put a finger on, although she'd given the subject ample thought over the past seven days.

Since she'd sold her first story, Prairie had concocted enough situations and characters to fill fifteen dime novels and almost twice that many half-dimers. Most of her protagonists were men, with a few women, such as Fiery Flora, thrown in from time to time for good measure. She would rather have written from the female viewpoint exclusively, but she dared not risk it. Her reading public thought she was a man. She'd planned it that way and she wanted the public—and her publisher—to keep right on thinking so.

Sometimes, she even thought of herself as a man, as Pampas J. Rose and not Prairie Rose Jernigan. She'd been proud of herself when she'd thought up the pen name. No one except David, insofar as she was aware, knew her middle name was Rose.

The memory of her mother calling her "Prairie Rose" had pierced her consciousness in her mid-teens. For some reason she didn't honestly understand, she didn't tell anyone—not even Wynn Donovan—that she recalled her middle name. Later, when she'd had to come up with a pseudonym, she was glad she'd kept the knowledge a secret.

Somewhere along the way, along the two-and-a-half-year track of clandestine writing, a part of her had become Pampas J. Rose—not merely the popular male novelist, but the imaginary man himself. At first, the realization frightened her. As she considered this bit of self-knowledge, she forced herself to peel back the layers of her personality. There was a part of her, she discovered, that was more male than female in outlook.

More importantly, she realized she enjoyed writing more than anything else. It might cause her frustration. It might totally infuriate her at times. But it was the most wonderful, most completely satisfying activity she could ever have devised for herself.

Whether these two parts of her—the man and the writer—existed innately or were by-products of the role she'd created for herself she didn't know. Nor did she care. What she knew, deep down in her soul, was that she couldn't stop writing. Not even if and when she uncovered her roots. She was a writer, and if she had her way, she'd never be anything else. All the school bells and wedding bells in the world couldn't be as important, as fulfilling, as the tinkling carriage bell on her beat-up Remington typewriter.

She put that typewriter to use again that morning, as she had every waking minute for the past week. The words poured out of her so fast her flying fingers had trouble keeping up. As she finished each page, she added it to the rapidly growing stack on her desk, weighing the sheets down with the fishtail bit she'd brought back with her from the rice field. This story was, she knew, the best she'd ever written.

* * *

49

"We're in trouble," Sam told Wayne that morning. "More trouble than we've ever been in, by a long shot."

"What kind of trouble?" Wayne asked.

"Serious trouble. As in I don't know if we're going to have a producing well here or not. I'm not sure we'll be able to control the sand."

A frown so slight, so fleeting it was barely noticeable rippled across Wayne's brow. "I thought you said this was like California. You just had to clean it out and make a cavity and then everything would be hunky-dory."

Sam shook his head. "That's what I thought a week ago. Now I'm not so sure."

"I've been leasing up parcels, Sam. Using up big chunks of our capital. If you can't bring this well in, we *are* in big trouble."

"I can't make you any promises, brother."

"So? What's the next step?"

"We keep cleaning, I guess. I can't tell for sure what's going to happen until we've gotten all the sand out."

"How much longer will that take?"

"Maybe another week, two at the most — probably," Sam said. "Can we hold out that long?"

This time, the frown dug deep furrows into Wayne's forehead. "Can you keep these men out here quiet?"

Sam shrugged. "I can keep them busy. And I can try to keep outsiders away. But people are bound to find out, Wayne. We need to do something to divert their attention."

"You got any ideas?"

Sam pushed long fingers through his thick, curly hair. "If I'm right about this field and I can bring it in, we're going to need a pipeline. Can we afford to start laying one?"

Wayne's face brightened considerably. "If I have to, I'll wire J.C. for some money. You're going to make this work, Sam. Just tell me what else you need me to do."

Prairie didn't perceive her new story as being Sam Blackman's, but that was exactly what it was. Ever a storyteller in his own right, Doc had unintentionally supplied the background details long before she'd met Sam; then the wildcatter had provided an explanation of his work himself.

But there was still one minor detail Prairie needed. What had Sam said about the pumps? Prairie had racked her brain until it hurt, but she couldn't remember. She had to know what their function was. She couldn't finish the novel without finding out, and she had to find out without letting anyone know that was what she was doing. She'd come too far to allow herself to be caught now.

She was running on sheer willpower and she knew it, knew her energy would give out soon. She hadn't slept much nor eaten properly for a week, her writing providing all the nourishment she required. Her body was beginning to let her know it had been neglected, but she wouldn't rest until she gleaned this one last bit of information.

There was only one way to get it—only one person to get it from, and that was Sam Blackman himself. His name danced around in her head for a moment. Sam. A good, strong, old-fashioned name. Blackman denoted strength as well, the strength of the common working man. But there was nothing common about Sam. He certainly didn't seem to mind physical labor, but it was his brain, not his brawn that had propelled him to the top of the

51

heap.

Suddenly, Prairie realized she desperately wanted to see him again, but she couldn't just march herself up to him and say, *I came to feast my eyes upon you, and while I'm wallowing in your good looks, would you please explain to me the purpose of the pumps?* How she wished she could! How pleasant being honest all the time would be.

This wasn't merely a matter, however, of improper boldness. Even if she left out the parts about feasting and wallowing, he'd be bound to ask her why she wanted to know about the pumps, and then she'd have to concoct some plausible story.

She had to play it safe. And the safest way was to play it dumb.

What excuse could she use as cover? she wondered, absently caressing a piece of cold steel with the tip of a finger.

The frown Prairie didn't know she'd been wearing disappeared and she grinned. She picked up the fishtail bit, folded it into her fist, and went to round up the boys.

Part of the trouble Sam was into had nothing to do with the sanded-up well. It had everything to do with a woman whose delicate features and soft voice insisted on intruding upon his thoughts at the most inopportune times.

Although he'd trained the crew well and the work was going according to plan, the men still needed steady supervision and the well needed his constant attention. He was the only one of them who'd been in California, the only one who'd seen a well sand up, the only one who knew how to create the necessary cavity. One little mistake could ruin everything. The last thing he needed was a distraction.

But a distraction he had. No matter how determinedly he pushed away the intrusion, it kept coming back. Her eyes, her voice, her hair, her lips . . . God! what lips! If he'd ever seen lips made for kissing, Prairie's were. So soft and pink and pouty.

At the precise moment a situation demanded all his faculties, he'd catch himself dreaming of kissing those lips. Once, he even caught himself puckering up. The men were going to catch him, too, if he wasn't careful. Worse, the well was going to catch his mind astray, and then they'd really be in trouble.

Why? he questioned. Why did she affect him so profoundly? She was just a woman.

But she wasn't just any woman, and he knew it. Prairie Jernigan didn't play coquettish games. She didn't bat her eyelashes and play dumb. She didn't swing her hips or speak in coy phrases. She didn't play at being provocative; she didn't have to. Prairie Jernigan *was* the most provocative woman he'd ever met.

More importantly, she was a woman he could talk to. Even most men weren't interested in the process of drilling for oil, just in the money they stood to make from it. But she was interested — genuinely interested. She was bright and intelligent and . . .

Go away and don't come back! he ordered the vision. But it did come back, time and time again, as elusive and enchanting as a hummingbird, returning to drink from the nectar of his soul.

Thinking about Prairie Jernigan as often as he did was bad enough. Having her show up proved his undoing.

"What the hell —" he muttered, narrowing his eyes against the afternoon glare as he watched Prairie drive the buggy right up next to the rig.

"Isn't that — yeah, that's the Donovan kids with Miss Jernigan," Wayne supplied. "Hi, folks!"

"Hush, Wayne. I'll handle this," Sam hissed.

"What's to handle?"

Wayne was grinning from ear to ear. Sam shot him a withering glare and barked, "Just don't let those kids get too close to the derrick. I'll be right back."

Sam tried to keep from looking at Prairie, but it didn't work. She was, he thought, the most blatantly feminine female he'd ever seen. Today she wore her thick, dark hair poufed out from her face and then swirled and pinned to the top of her head in the Gibson-girl style. As she set the brake and looped the reins over it, a wayward breeze tugged playfully at the wisps curling across her forehead, in front of her ears, and at her nape.

Her high-necked, full-sleeved shirtwaist emphasized the slender length of her neck, the fullness of her bosom, and the trimness of her waistline. She stood up, revealing a skirt that hugged her rounded hips and clung to the tops of shapely thighs before falling into bell-shaped fullness. Sam watched its hem, mesmerized, as a tiny foot encased in black kid emerged, exposing a froth of scalloped, white ruffled lace. The foot set itself upon the dip in the side rail of the buggy and pointed its toe at his stomach.

Sam stared at the toe for a moment, and might have stared at it longer if she hadn't coughed. He looked up at her, watched her cupid's-bow mouth ease into a friendly smile, and felt like a schoolboy at his first barn dance.

Prairie stared down at him, into eyes as bright and keen as she'd ever seen, and the smile froze on her face. Yes, she thought, they were eyes that mirrored intelligence, and eyes that were open and honest and demanded respect. For a split second she hesitated, suddenly filled with a degree of remorse over her planned deception. But it was such a tiny, insignificant deception, she reasoned, at least it was tiny compared to the much bigger deceit she'd been practicing for several years.

She was a novelist gathering information. More importantly, she was an orphan desperately seeking her roots. If she had to employ a bit of chicanery to do it, then so be it. She had to protect herself, to protect the method she'd chosen to accomplish her goal. She couldn't be held responsible for the prejudices of a society that forced her to pose as a man with their refusal to acknowledge that women could be equally intelligent, equally capable, equally clever.

"Good afternoon, Mr. Blackman," she said, molding her voice into that of an empty-headed flirt, popping open her parasol, and then holding out a gloved hand in invitation for him to aid her in her descent. His touch set the nerves in her arm to tingling, whether with joy or fear she couldn't be sure. Nor did she have time to decide before his other hand moved around her waist and pulled her to the ground.

Their bodies were close, so close she could feel the warmth of his breath upon her cheek. For a moment, his arm held her possessively while his eyes searched hers. They seemed to say, *You don't fool me for a minute, Prairie Jernigan.*

The perception of his thoughts almost unnerved her. She pulled her gaze away from his and stepped sideways, her mind scrambling to reconnoiter its intended purpose. He let go of her, but she continued to feel the brand of his arm about her waist and the warmth of his eyes on her cheek as their crystal blue gaze followed her movement.

"What brings you all the way out here today?" he asked, his normally smooth baritone as rough as sandpaper.

"I, uh, I thought you might need this," she said, reaching behind her and removing the fishtail bit from the seat of the buggy.

Sam couldn't believe his eyes. A week before, she'd taken the dirty bit in her bare hand and marveled over its function. The bit was now as shiny clean as a new nickel, yet she held it out to him as gingerly as if it were a warty toadfrog. He plucked it from her fist, his eyes narrow slits. This was not the woman who had insisted on invading his thoughts. Where had she gone?

"You could have saved yourself a trip," he observed dryly.

"Pardon?"

"Enoch comes out here almost every day."

"I—I didn't think about that."

Truthfully, she hadn't thought about sending the bit by Doc. She hadn't wanted to give it up, wouldn't be returning it now if she didn't need to know about the pumps. How was she ever going to work the conversation around to them?

"We're kinda busy here."

Though his comment was brusque, it gave Prairie the opening she required. "I can see that. Doc says you're trying to clean out the sand."

She made a point of lifting her voice on the word "sand," almost making her statement a question, hoping Sam would volunteer to explain the process. When he just glowered at her, she tried a different tack. "The Donovans are coming home tomorrow," she said, "and the boys want to be able to tell their father everything about this well. He is part owner, you know."

"I'm disappointed in you, Miss Jernigan."

He couldn't have surprised her more. Her heart pounded in her chest as possible reasons for his disappointment raced through her mind. Oh, why did she have to pretend? He was seeing right through her. She covered her discomfort by fluttering her

56

eyelashes and laying a gloved palm between her breasts. "Disappointed in *me*, Mr. Blackman? Whatever for?"

Sam's eyes bugged. How could she possibly think he wouldn't know who his own business associates were, or that he would believe three rambunctious boys were interested in the workings of a drilling rig? Didn't he have eyes? Couldn't he see them running around the rice field chasing a moth?

Sam wanted to say, *I had credited you with having more intelligence — with having a genuine interest in me and what I'm doing — with being different from other women. But you're just as much a flirt as all the rest of your breed. And damn if I don't want to kiss you just as much now as I ever did!*

Instead, he said gruffly, "I thought you had more sense than to bring those boys out here. They don't need to be around this equipment, even if they are Donovan's kids. It's too dangerous. I'd appreciate it if you'd take them home and keep them there."

Prairie glared at him, then spat, "Of all the gall! They aren't hurting a thing! What gives you the right—"

"The fact that I own the controlling stock in this well, Miss Jernigan. Because I'm responsible for what happens out here. Because—oh, hell!"

Without preamble, he grabbed her parasol and tossed it into the buggy. She was still standing there gawking, her mind grasping for some explanation for his behavior, when he pulled her into his arms and rammed his mouth into hers.

Is this what a kiss is like? she wondered, all her preconceived notions of the act destroyed by his assault. She struggled against him, pushing against his iron-hard chest with the flats of her gloved hands, twisting her neck, refusing to succumb to the savage passion coursing through her veins.

57

Her struggles won her nothing. His strength far surpassed hers. His arms held her in a viselike crush, his length molded against hers.

What Prairie lacked in physical strength, she made up for in determination. But he seemed equally determined, which gave him the advantage. His tongue swept the seam of her tightly closed lips. His lips plucked at the corners of her mouth. His breath burned hotly upon her face. But it was his moan that finished her resolve.

Her blood turned to liquid fire, melting her bones. Her lips parted, allowing him entrance, allowing him to plunder and ravage until her world spun out of control.

As suddenly as he'd pulled her into his arms, he tore his mouth from hers and pushed her away. Instinctively, she groped for a spoke of the buggy wheel, something to hold on to until her pulse returned to normal and a modicum of strength returned to her legs. She stood staring after him, her breath coming in short pants, her eyes awash with unshed tears. He stepped back onto the derrick floor, then turned to pin her with an ice-blue gaze.

"You got what you came for, Miss Jernigan. Now take those boys and go home."

Chapter Four

You got what you came for.

Prairie rubbed her temples and willed Sam's voice to stop echoing in her head. Doggone it! Why did he have to go and kiss her? Why did he have to complicate matters? Why hadn't he just let things be?

She'd never imagined that a man's kiss could stir such feelings. His kiss made her feel beautiful and important and wanton and shameful — and made her realize she liked feeling *all* those things, all at the same time. Although she'd never set out to win his kiss, she found herself wanting another from him, and another and another.

Such yearning, however, could prove dangerous. She was too close to attaining her lifelong goal, too close to finding a link to her past, too close to discovering who she really was. The last thing she figured she needed was an emotional entanglement.

If he'd never kissed her in the first place, she groaned, she wouldn't have to deal with this emotional turmoil now. Whatever had she done to make him think a kiss was what she'd come for?

Deep down, she knew she'd unwittingly asked for it, knew now that she'd underestimated Sam Blackman, knew he was a man who should never be underestimated. She knew, too, that she would never find out what she needed to know about the pumps.

Not from Sam Blackman. His kiss had changed everything.

Well, she'd finish the book anyway. To do so would require either neglecting to mention the pumps altogether or devising her own explanation of their function. At least she'd gotten a good look at them before Sam had kissed her. Big pipes were attached to the offsides of each pump. On one, the pipes led to a pit with mud at the bottom, but she had absolutely no clue as to how or why this mud was used. On the other pump, muddy water spewed out of shorter pipes and splashed into the pit.

She took great pride in presenting her material accurately. The characters and plots might be fictional, but facts were facts, and these she refused to tinker with.

Prairie chose a middle ground. She could mention them, she decided, if she had to. She could include the noise they made and describe their appearance, but exclude their purpose, and hope no one noticed the omission. Most readers, she reminded herself, wouldn't know anything about drilling for oil anyway.

Throughout most of the night, her fingers danced upon the typewriter keys, their jangling noise sweet music to her ears. While the stack of manuscript pages grew, her own physical and mental frustrations diminished, lost somewhere in the pages of the story of Prospector Pete.

The shrill whistle of the Sunday train sliced the air, silencing the larger than average crowd gathered at the depot. Slim Moreland, the stationmaster, dug a meaty hand into the shallow pocket just below what would have been his waistline if he'd had one, removed his official Southern Pacific watch, and marked the time—5:32. Fifty-seven minutes late.

Slim could remember a time when the Sunday train never arrived before dark and was sometimes as late as midnight. The Atchafalaya River bridge had helped speed things up, but the SP had yet to construct a bridge over the wide waters of the Mississippi. That meant the train had to be ferried across. It took an entire hour for the switch engine to uncouple half of the train, back it up and run it onto one track of the ferry, then go back and pick up the remaining cars and run them onto the other track. Once the two sections were on the other side, they had to be taken off the ferry and reassembled, which took another hour.

Those two hours were, of course, built into the schedule, as was the size of the normal load—five passenger cars and a combination mail-express and baggage car. Extra cars required extra time at the ferry, plus they slowed down the speed of the little woodburner steam engine, which wasn't too fast to begin with.

While he didn't eliminate the possibility of engine trouble, Slim expected the delay that particular Sunday resulted from additional cars. He figured the throng of people who waited for the train thought the same thing and had come more out of curiosity than anything else.

Some of them, though, he reminded himself, would have been there anyway—those who were meeting friends and family and those who always showed up because watching the train come in was their favorite pastime. Too, some of the extra onlookers might be there simply because Jennings mayor, Michael Donovan, and his physician wife, Wynn, were supposed to be on this train.

Slim didn't doubt that the good people of Jennings would be glad to see the Donovans back home. But they were also eager to hear all about the Pan-American Exposition. Rumor had it that Michael and Wynn had been there the day President McKinley had been shot. He hoped the Donovans weren't too tired. Between the interest in their trip and the news of the oil boom, Slim figured the couple would be busy for the next several hours.

He shouldered his way through the crowd of people who'd been arriving since noon and took his place beside the tracks. Some distance from him to the west, a boy darted out from the crowd and raced toward the iron rails. Immediately, a woman's voice rang out, "Patrick! Come back here!"

Prairie had to raise her voice to be heard above the blaring whistle and the noisy steam engine. The effort took all her breath. She watched in horror as Patrick put his hand down on the rail. Her feet were frozen to the planking, her head swimming from lack of oxygen. She swayed dizzily toward Doc and felt his arm on her shoulders. The whistle blew again. The brakes screeched. The cowcatcher loomed dangerously close to Patrick's hand.

Several people who were much closer to Patrick than she rushed toward him. Jason was the first to get there. His arms flew out and grabbed his brother around the waist. Prairie watched the great iron wheel roll by, watched Jason snatch Patrick away, even over the commotion heard the youngest of the Donovan clan holler "Ee-ow!" It all happened so fast, she couldn't be sure which had come first, but she knew she had to regain control of herself.

She broke away from Doc and started toward Patrick, willpower fueling her movements. At the same time, Jason moved toward her with Patrick in tow, the eleven-year-old screaming at the top of his lungs.

"What happened? Let me see!" she demanded,

pulling Patrick's right arm up, steeling herself against the sight of what had been a hand but was surely now nothing more than a stub of blood, bone, and sinew.

She blinked twice, swallowed, and looked again. The hand was fine. A bit dirty, but whole. She turned the hand over and inspected the back side. Not even a scratch. Unconvinced, she snatched up his other hand. It, too, was fine. Relief washed through her, cleansing away the panic, allowing her time to catch her breath before anger boiled thick and hot within her breast.

Prairie's hands dropped Patrick's and flew up to his shoulders. She shook him hard enough to make his head flop. "What did you think you were doing! Trying to get your hand cut off? Don't you know better? Don't you *ever* do anything else like that again, Patrick Donovan!"

"Yes, ma'am," he blubbered, his eyes, pale blue like his mother's, streaming tears. "I woulda been all right, Prairie. Jason hurt me and now you're hurting me!"

Prairie stopped shaking him and pulled him into her chest. Despite the comfort she offered him, though, her voice remained rough. "Hush up that whining, Patrick. Jason probably saved your life."

A familiar voice came from behind her. "The little fool. I told you these boys were ripe for an accident."

Sam Blackman!

Slowly, Prairie turned around, dragging Patrick with her. She gritted her teeth and felt the skin tighten up around her eyes. Why, the nerve of the man to show his face to her today!

"This is all your fault!" she snapped. "If you had only cooperated yesterday—"

Prairie's brain caught up with her tongue and she clamped her jaw shut.

Sam's jaw dropped open and he looked at her as though she'd just sprouted horns and a tail. "What in blazes are you talking about? I *did* cooperate. Remember?"

Prairie felt the heat rise in her neck and face. Lord, did she remember! All over again, she felt herself go weak with longing. Immediately behind the memory, however, followed a spark of indignation. Fueled with another memory, namely that of the frustration of having to work around her lack of knowledge, the spark quickly spread into a flame and the flame into a bonfire of anger.

"Why, you—you—nincompoop!" she sputtered.

At that moment, Michael and Wynn rushed toward them. "What happened?" they asked in unison. "Let me see Patrick," Wynn added, her husky voice tight. "Don't call him a nincompoop, Prairie. He's just a child."

"He isn't hurt," Prairie assured them, turning the boy over to his mother, thankful Wynn had misunderstood. "Just shaken up a bit. For that matter, so am I." *In more ways than one!* Prairie's gaze darted nervously between her foster parents and Sam Blackman.

"I wanted to flatten a penny," Patrick whimpered against Wynn's breast, "but it kept sliding off the rail."

"We'll talk about this later, Patrick," Michael said sternly, a dark frown smoldering on his brow. For a moment, his gaze vaulted back and forth between Prairie and Sam, and he frowned harder. Then he looked at Wynn again, jerked his head toward town, and mouthed, "Get them out of here!"

What in tarnation was going on? Prairie wondered. No hugs, no smiles, no gushing "We missed you." She'd never seen these two act so strangely.

Michael turned and clapped Sam on the back.

"Good to see you, Blackman." His arm snaked along Sam's shoulders and he steered the oilman away from the tracks. "I appreciate your coming today. Come along home with me and tell me all about the well." Within minutes, the two were out of sight.

Prairie scurried along beside Wynn, who was pushing the boys along in front of them. "Move, boys. We have to get out of here."

"But, Mama, I want my penny!" Patrick whined.

"I'll give you another one," Wynn said.

"A body would think the train was fixing to explode, Wynn. What's going on?" Prairie asked.

"Glance back and you'll see," Wynn whispered.

Prairie couldn't believe her eyes. A long line of painted women wearing feathered hats and bright-colored, low-necked gowns were quickly disembarking from the last passenger car in the line.

Jason must have heard her as well. At sixteen, his hormones were going wild. He pursed his lips and let loose with a long, loud wolf whistle.

"Jason Donovan! How embarrassing! Hush!"

He grinned wickedly and jiggled up and down dark brown eyebrows shaped exactly like his father's. "My-oh-my!" he babbled. "Look at those scarlet women!"

"Jason!" Wynn admonished again, her voice sharper. "Walk!"

"Yes, ma'am." He turned his back to the train, but from time to time he glanced over his shoulder toward the tracks until the depot and the oak trees around it blocked his view.

Wynn slipped her fan out of her reticule and opened it wide. "My stars, it's hot!"

Prairie grinned. It wasn't *that* hot. "I brought the buggy," she said.

"If you don't mind, I'd rather walk. My leg's stiff from sitting on the train for hours. The exercise will do me good. I'll send Winkle back later to collect the buggy and bring our bags."

"I left a pitcher of lemonade cooling in the ice box and Marmie made a batch of tea cakes."

"Sounds good." Wynn waved the fan again, then snapped it shut and returned it to her reticule. "How is Marmalade? And Zoey and Winkle? Did they give you any trouble?"

"No, of course not—unless you count all the gallons of homemade ice cream and dozens of cakes Marmie made for the boys. I don't know why they aren't butterballs. I had trouble convincing Zoey to let me clean my own room, and Winkle puttered about in the gardens, as usual. The roses are still blooming and the mums are full of thick buds ready to burst open."

"Then we got home just in the nick of time, didn't we?" Wynn said, referring to Prairie's physical intolerance of chrysanthemums and smiling for the first time since she'd stepped off the train. She stopped walking and took a deep breath, lifting her chin and closing her eyes briefly. "Come here, you boys, and let me hug you. It's good to be home."

When it was Prairie's turn, she clung to Wynn a bit longer than was required. "I really missed you," she breathed, her voice scratchy with sudden emotion. "How was your trip?"

"Hectic, but fun."

"The exposition?"

"Wonderful."

"Were you there when the President was shot?"

"Yes, and it was awful! We'd heard McKinley speak the day before. There was a big military parade along the Triumphal Causeway, and afterwards people packed themselves into the Esplanade and the Court of Fountains to hear him speak. Gosh, Prairie, there were *hundreds* of people there!"

66

"The papers said fifty thousand."

"At least. He was a tremendous speaker, full of hope and enthusiasm, a very impressive man. The next afternoon, we were in line to meet him in the Temple of Music, but we were too far away to see what happened. Two shots rang out, everyone started talking at once, and then some men took him away in a motorized ambulance to an emergency operating room on the fairgrounds. We followed them, and I kept trying to get in, but two burly men blocked my way." Wynn's voice caught in her throat and her pale blue eyes welled up with tears.

Prairie placed a comforting arm around her foster mother's shoulders. "I'm certain the other doctors did everything that could be done to save him. Don't blame yourself for his death."

"You don't understand. I knew they'd never allow me in the operating room. But there was an X-ray machine on display at the exposition. I wanted to tell them to use it."

"What's an X-ray machine?" Mickey asked, falling back to walk beside his mother.

"I should have known when I said 'machine,' you'd come running." Wynn chuckled and reached up to ruffle his thatch of light brown hair, her tears forgotten. Her gaze seemed to measure his height. "My, you've grown some more while we were gone, Mickey!"

The thirteen-year-old grinned sheepishly. "Do you think I'll be as tall as Daddy?"

"Perhaps."

"What's an X-ray machine?" he asked again.

"It takes pictures of the inside of your body."

"Like your bones and stuff?" Mickey asked.

"Yes."

"And your heart and lungs and stomach, too?"

"No, dear. Not clear pictures. Just shadowy outlines of tissue mass. But doctors can use X-ray pictures to see broken bones—"

"And bullets?"

"And bullets."

Suddenly Prairie remembered the news stories that followed the shooting. "They didn't find the bullet, did they?"

Wynn shook her head sadly. "No. There was only one entry wound, so the doctors assumed a button or his pocket watch deflected the other bullet. They didn't know where the bullet that did hit him had lodged, and they didn't think it wise to probe his rather large abdomen in his weakened condition. So they sutured the tears and cleaned out the peritoneal cavity as best they could. Then they sewed him up."

She sighed. "They were right about the single bullet, but they were wrong to think they didn't have to remove it. He rallied, you know, and then a week later the bullet killed him. It had damaged a kidney and destroyed part of his pancreas. An X-ray would have shown them where it was, but we couldn't get in to recommend it."

Prairie said, "I can't imagine Michael letting anything—or anyone stop him. Not even two big men."

"Huh! He tried to get past them, but one of them punched him in the stomach, and before he could recover, the other one whacked him on the jaw. He was out cold for fifteen minutes! Later, they moved the President to a private home in Buffalo, but no one would tell me where."

"Didn't the other doctors know about the X-ray machine?" Prairie asked.

"I suppose. Maybe they didn't think about it—or didn't trust it to work right. But I saw it demonstrated. It's amazing!"

"Are you going to get one, Mama?" Mickey asked, his eyes shining.

Wynn smiled at her middle son. "It's on its way. But I can't use it until Jennings gets electricity and we open the hospital. Ah! Home!"

They stopped on the front walk, Sam Blackman's red surrey directly behind them at the edge of the lawn. They waited quietly, giving Wynn a chance to soak up the exterior of the house and the yard. When she started down the brick walk, Prairie said, "I didn't know you were going to open a hospital."

"You know I've been wanting to for years, but Michael was against it. Now he's finally decided I can have the old hotel building. I can't wait to tell Doc."

They were at the steps. Prairie reached out and took her foster mother's lower arm, halting her progress. "You boys run on ahead and tell Marmie we're home," she said, waiting until she and Wynn were alone to continue. "You're going to have to find another building, I'm afraid. Last week, Johnny Perkins leased the old hotel building to the Blackman brothers."

Wynn seemed unperturbed. "That's not a problem. It will take me a couple of months to order everything I need and get it all in anyway."

"No, Wynn. It is a problem. They signed a two-year lease." Prairie's chest constricted at the look of utter dismay that claimed Wynn's face. "Maybe you can talk Michael into building you a new hospital."

"Maybe," Wynn said, but there was no real conviction in her voice. "Come on," she said with obviously forced brightness. "Let's go have some lemonade and tea cakes and I'll tell you all about Steeplechase Park on Coney Island."

The older Wynn got, the more her gimp leg bothered her. Prairie let go of Wynn's arm and slipped her own arm around the older woman's waistline, supporting her as they climbed the steps to the porch. They were almost to the door when it flew open and Sam Blackman came tearing out, his face black with rage.

"Excuse me," he muttered, sidestepping the women and practically running across the porch. Somewhere inside the house a door slammed.

Wynn caught the screen door before it banged shut. "Whatever happened between those two?" she pondered aloud.

"Whatever it was," Prairie said, "It wasn't friendly."

Sam slapped the reins, setting the solid white mare in motion with a bounding leap that hurled him back against the leather seat. He righted himself, braced his feet against the floorboard, and urged Dolly ahead at breakneck speed.

Bits and pieces of his conversation with Donovan sprinted through his head with a swiftness akin to that of the horse. "Pull out before you go under . . . we'll buy you out . . . nullify the lease . . ."

Oblivious to the cloud of dust engulfing the vehicle, he turned right, taking the corner on two wheels and dislodging the isinglass windows from their moorings on the passenger side. They flopped against the vertical bars that held up the canvas roof until the surrey straightened out and plopped down on all four of its wheels again.

In the middle of the block, he pulled up in front of Miss Bidwell's boardinghouse, secured the reins, and leapt onto the wide dirt path that served as a street. He took the stairs two at a time, turned down the hall, and dashed into Wayne's room. His brother sat at a makeshift desk — a wide plank supported by twin stacks of books, his attention totally absorbed by figures he was recording into a ledger.

"Wayne!" Sam bellowed. "I need to talk to you."

"In a minute."

"Now, Wayne." When he didn't look up, Sam snapped the ledger closed.

"What did you do that for?" Wayne asked. "I would have been finished in another minute or two."

Sam paced the room, his hands shoved inside his trouser pockets. "We've got trouble."

"So? What else is new?"

"More trouble. Different trouble." Sam whirled around and glared at Wayne until he put his pencil down and angled his chair away from the plank.

"What kind of trouble, Sam?"

"Donovan trouble."

"That doesn't make sense. Why would Donovan give us trouble? He's in on this deal. Didn't you explain to him about the sand?"

"Yeah, but he thinks we ought to quit. Pack up and leave town. Says he'll buy our interest."

Wayne steepled his fingers and brought them to his chin. "What kind of deal did you strike with him?"

Sam stopped pacing and stared openmouthed at his brother for a moment. "None. We aren't selling out. We aren't pulling out. And we're not giving him back his building."

"Wait a minute, Sam. You're way ahead of me. Tell me about the building."

Calmer now, though he couldn't have said why, Sam pulled out a side chair, turned its back to Wayne, and straddled the seat. "He wants his old hotel back. Says he promised his wife she could turn it into a hospital. Says Perkins had no authority to lease it to us. Says he'll give us back all the money plus ten percent for our trouble if we'll agree to vacate by the end of the week."

Wayne smiled broadly. "Sounds good to me."

"We're not giving it to him, Wayne. We need it."

"No, Sam. We *hope* we'll need it. There's a difference. I say let him have it back."

"No."

"Why do you have to be so stubborn?"

Wayne squinted up his eyes and gave his younger brother a long, hard stare. Sam shifted uncomfortably in the chair. Then, when he couldn't meet Wayne's eyes anymore, he jumped up and started pacing again. "I'm going to show him, Wayne," he mumbled. "Come hell or high water, I'm going to show Donovan it can be done."

"Of course you are. You've weathered ridicule and skepticism before, Sam, and you've always emerged the victor. I've never known you to let someone else's doubt bother you." He paused, watching Sam pace. "There's something else, isn't there? Something you're not telling me about."

"No—yes." Sam moved over to the window and absently fingered the blue gingham curtain hanging against the frame. A long moment passed before he said, "Donovan told me to stay away from his daughter."

"His daughter? I thought he had three boys."

"He does. He says Prairie Jernigan is his daughter."

"How can that be?"

Sam planted the flat of his hands on the window sill. His shoulders slumped forward and he rested his forehead against the window pane. "I don't know. Maybe she's a widow. But she doesn't kiss like one."

"She kisses like a virgin, huh?"

Sam raised his head from the glass and shoved his hands back into his pockets. "Let's just say no one ever taught her how to do it properly."

With his back to the room, Sam couldn't see the upward quirk of Wayne's eyebrows. "And you think you might be the man to do it?"

"Possibly."

"What was Donovan's reasoning? I thought he liked you."

"I thought he did, too. What I don't understand is why he'd concern himself."

"Because you kissed her?" Wayne offered.

"He couldn't have known that. No one had a chance to tell him. I was with Prairie when Donovan got off the train, and then he and I went directly to his house. I don't know what I could have said or done to make him think I'm interested in her."

"Are you?"

Sam's reply was a long time coming. "I don't know, Wayne. I honestly don't know."

"Leave it alone, Sam. We can't let your infatuation with that little filly mess things up for us here."

"You know me better than that."

Wayne shook his head. "I know that when some-one says you can't have something, you set out to prove them wrong."

"Have you ever known me to fail?" Sam challenged.

"Nope. But there's always a first time, Sam. There's always a first time for everything — and your time's coming."

Chapter Five

"You sweet on this here David Hamilton?"

Hazel Kinnaird's question struck like a knife in Prairie's stomach. *I should have known this was coming,* she thought, but two and a half years of disinterest on the part of the mousy postmistress had lulled her into complacency. She removed the stamp from her tongue and slapped it on the package—the *Prospector Pete* manuscript, then made a face as the bitter tang of the gummed back permeated her taste buds.

"I have a wet sponge here, you know," Hazel said.

"Yes, ma'am. It's a habit."

"So's writing to this David fellow."

She might have guessed Hazel wouldn't let it lie. Not after she'd finally screwed up enough courage to ask. "He's a friend. From Normal."

"You met him in Natchitoches, huh? Is he a teacher, too?"

"Yes, ma'am. We, uh, we exchange lessons, tests, that sort of thing." The lie she'd concocted in the beginning but had never had to use before tasted far more bitter than had the gummed postage stamp.

Hazel Kinnaird bounced the package up and down in her palm. "Seems to me he's getting the bigger end of the stick."

"Ma'am?"

"His letters to you are much lighter. Two or three pages at the most."

Why, the nerve of the old biddy! She really had been paying attention — too much attention, to Prairie's way of thinking. Someone needed to put her in her place. Prairie figured it fell her way to do it.

"His penmanship is quite cramped. Sometimes I have to get a magnifying glass out to read it. But it's worth the effort, Miss Kinnaird," she said conspiratorially, leaning over the counter. "Every letter from David is an education in itself. Perhaps you'd like to read the next one he sends me. They tell me there's a way to steam open envelopes so no one knows they've been tampered with . . ."

Prairie let her voice trail away, relishing the pink stain that slithered up Hazel's neck all the way to the silly-looking hat she wore every day — a navy blue sailor with a big red pompon on top.

The woman gasped, and though her mouth worked, no words were forthcoming.

"I have to go now, Miss Kinnaird. Have a good day," Prairie called cheerfully on her way out the door.

When she was outside, she leaned against the plank wall, closed her eyes, and held her hand over her mouth in an effort to stifle the giggling fit that threatened to erupt. That ought to keep the woman's nose out of her business for a spell. She'd knocked it squarely out of joint. Despite her effort to the contrary, a smile turned up the corners of her mouth and she giggled behind her hand.

A deep, familiar voice sent her heart lurching again.

"Good afternoon, Miss Jernigan," the voice said.

Her eyes flew open and she found herself as speechless as she'd left Hazel Kinnaird — and as lost

75

in the sharp, clear blue of Sam Blackman's eyes as any red-blooded woman would be.

"It is *Miss* Jernigan, is it not?"

She nodded, her throat working convulsively.

A gray trilby rode low on his forehead, the angle of its brim rakishly askew. He leaned toward her, placing the pad of his forefinger on the tip of her nose, the edge of his hat almost touching her brow. "That's good. I wouldn't want to think I'd kissed a married woman," he whispered.

Had her hand not covered her mouth, Prairie had no doubt he would have placed the finger on her lips. And perhaps placed his own lips there as well. Right there on Main Street in broad daylight with everyone around to see.

With everyone around to see . . . He certainly hadn't hesitated to kiss her out at the rig in front of his brother, his crew, and the boys. Jason had teased her about it unmercifully, but so far, only in private. She felt no shame for having been kissed, and she refused to feel any shame for wanting it to happen again. But not right there on the porch of the Jennings Post Office for the whole town to see. It wasn't worth losing her job over — and Prairie had no doubt someone would raise a bigger stench about that than even Michael could get her out of.

Part of her screamed, "Run!" But running required control over one's lower limbs, and Prairie's knees were the consistency of oatmeal. She tested one of them anyway, determined to remove herself from his presence before the flame in his blue eyes succeeded in completely melting her. The knee refused to support her weight and she wobbled a bit. Sam's hands caught her upper arms, burning her clean through the gathered folds of full taffeta sleeves. Her gaze locked on his, begged him to understand. He grinned wickedly at her and made a kissing motion with his chiseled lips.

That gesture proved her undoing. "Why, you — you scoundrel!" she gasped. "Take your hands off me!"

He didn't comply, which didn't surprise her. "You seem to be having some kind of spell. It wouldn't be very gentlemanly of me to let you fall, would it?"

"I'm all right now," she hissed, her gaze darting toward the activity on the street. People bustled back and forth and a heavy wagon lumbered past, but no one seemed to be paying any mind to the couple who stood in the shadows of the shallow porch.

Luckily, the post office door had been set into the side of the building, near the front but off the street. The bell on the door jingled then, drawing her attention to the customer — whom she recognized as a clerk from Donovan's Mercantile — stepping through the doorway and onto the porch.

Orville Mason tipped his hat, his gaze on Sam's hands wrapped around her upper arms, his voice registering friendly concern. "You're looking a mite pale, Miss Jernigan. You need me to fetch your ma?"

"No . . . no, thank you," she said, the clerk's presence lending her strength. "I haven't been sleeping well lately." Now that she'd said it, Prairie realized that was true. She hadn't slept much — nor had she eaten properly the past ten days. Small wonder she felt so weak!

"That will tend to make a body dizzy," Mason agreed, turning his head to glance at the western sky. "If this heat will ever let up, we'll all be sleeping better, I expect. Well, if you're sure you're all right — "

She gave an affirmative nod.

"—then I'll be taking myself back to work. Good day, Miss Jernigan, Mr. Blackman." Mason tipped his hat again and strode away.

Prairie thought Sam would leave, too. He did drop his left hand, but he used its companion to steer her toward his surrey, which he'd left directly in front of the building and, therefore, out of her line of vision.

"Where are you taking me? What are you doing? Let me go!" she snapped.

"Nothing doing. You're obviously unwell, so I'm taking you home."

"You can't!" she insisted in a panic-ridden voice. "It's forbidden."

Sam's blue eyes turned to a stormy gray. "I don't care what Michael Donovan says—"

"It's not Michael, you fool," she said. "It's the whole town. They wouldn't take too kindly to my riding unchaperoned in a carriage with an unmarried man." Intolerance aside, she thought, if she couldn't rid herself of the man right there on the street, how was she ever going to manage it once they got to her house?

Sam threw back his head and howled with laughter.

"What's so funny?" Prairie asked, trying to dislodge his grasp with her free hand.

"It's perfectly all right for you to go gallivanting off somewhere with a married man, huh?"

"No. What in blazes are you talking about?" Prairie jerked away from him, but he held on tight. "I'll scream," she threatened.

"Go right ahead. Create a scene. I'm taking you home regardless." His voice was tight.

"It's just a few blocks. I can walk."

"I'm taking you home, Miss Jernigan, whether

78

you like it or not." His hands moved to her waistline and a mischievous grin lit his face. "And if there's a problem with the narrow-minded fools in this town, I'll take care of it." In one deft movement, he swung her up and onto the black leather seat.

Prairie didn't know where the idea came from. Desperation, she supposed. While he was walking around the back of the surrey, she scooted over to the driver's side, yanked up the reins, and slapped them against the mare's back. "Giddeeup!" she called.

The horse bolted so suddenly Prairie dropped the reins. She scrambled forward, caught the end of one of the leather straps and felt it slip right through her fingers. In horror, she watched people running to get out of the way, watched a man in a carriage quickly guide his horse into a side street, watched the mare's pale mane flow toward her as the horse galloped ahead. She gripped the edge of the seat, holding on for dear life.

Behind her came a shrill whistle, the kind created by placing a thumb and a forefinger between pursed lips. The mare's almost instant halt pitched Prairie forward and she hit the floor—hard. Before she could regain her senses, much less the seat, strong arms encircled her from behind and pulled her out of the surrey. She struggled against the embrace, flailing her arms and kicking her feet, which were several inches off the ground.

"Put me down!" she shrieked. Miraculously, he complied, although he continued to hold her around the waist. She twisted around, ready to do battle, then gasped when she saw who held her. Michael!

"What were you doing in that surrey?" he demanded.

She opened her mouth, then wondered how she could possibly explain without making herself look like the biggest fool, which she supposed she was, or Sam look like the worst cad, which she supposed he wasn't. The pound of running feet diverted her attention, and Michael's, too.

"Thank God, you're safe. You gave me quite a scare," Sam wheezed, slowing to a jog as he approached them.

Michael's arm tensed against her rib cage and she heard his sharp intake of breath. "I thought I told you, Blackman—"

The memory of Sam's angry face and a slamming door flashed across her inner eye. "The heat made me feel faint, Michael," Prairie interrupted, instinctively protecting Sam. "Mr. Blackman offered to drive me home. Something spooked the horse, I suppose."

"I'll walk you home," Michael said, his eyes glaring at Sam, his voice brooking no argument.

Despite Prairie's insistence that all she needed to regain her usual vitality was a square meal and a good night's rest, Michael sent Wynn over to check on her.

"He's really concerned about you," Wynn said, pressing her stethoscope against Prairie's chest. "Deep breath . . . release . . . another one. Breathe normally . . . good." She removed the ear pieces, rolled the instrument up, and returned it to her medical bag.

"Well?" Prairie asked.

"Your pulse is a little fast; otherwise, you're sound as a dollar." Wynn shot her a narrow-eyed scrutiny. "When was the last time you looked in the mirror?"

If Wynn had asked her when she'd eaten last, or

when she'd last slept the night through, Prairie wouldn't have been taken aback. But this question caught her totally off guard. "What?" she squeaked.

Wynn disappeared into the hall and returned a moment later with a hand mirror, which she shoved in Prairie's face. "Look. Really look at yourself."

What she saw amazed her. Gray shadows lay in half-moons under lackluster eyes and deep hollows disclosed cheekbones seldom in evidence. Even in the warm, golden glow of the lamplight, her skin languished a pasty white. Why would any man, Prairie wondered, especially one as handsome as Sam Blackman, give her a second glance? She'd never thought of herself as beautiful, but neither had she ever looked quite so unappealing.

"You haven't been taking care of yourself, Prairie. Since we came home, you've been wound up as tight as an eight-day clock," Wynn said, more concern than reproof in her voice. "I know something is troubling you. Do you want to talk about it?"

Prairie laid the mirror on the table by her chair. "It's nothing—really, Wynn. Just the usual frustrations at the beginning of the school year. And I'm so tired of this heat! Honestly." But she could see that her foster mother didn't believe her. Not completely.

Fortunately, Wynn didn't pursue the subject. "You know I'm always here for you, Prairie. Whenever you need me." She closed her black leather bag and stood up. "Promise me you'll turn in early."

Prairie yawned in earnest and smiled. "Don't worry. I will. I think I could sleep through next week."

Something spooked the horse, my eye! Sam grinned in spite of himself at the memory of the red surrey careening down the dusty street. Dolly *always* bolted

81

when anyone slapped the reins on her back. And she *always* stopped dead in her tracks when he whistled. Prairie had no way of knowing those things, but then she'd had no business taking off on her own in the first place.

What kind of game was she playing? Sam wondered. He thought about little else all through supper at Miss Bidwell's boardinghouse. From time to time, he'd nod or offer some pat reply when Wayne paused in the monologue he kept going, obviously expecting a response, but Sam's mind was elsewhere. His mind was on Prairie Jernigan.

"What do you think about scuttling the hole and leaving here?" Wayne asked.

"That ought to work just fine."

"I think you ought to reconsider, maybe accept Donovan's offer."

"Whatever you say, Wayne."

"How about stripping naked and dancing on this table?"

"Sounds good to me."

Wayne threw his napkin down and pushed back his chair. "I knew you weren't listening!"

"Of course, I am," Sam argued. "What did you say?"

"Come on, Sam. Let's walk down to the depot and wait for the train. The fresh air will do you good."

Dusk was quickly giving way to darkness. The night air, somewhat drier and slightly bracing, held the promise of autumn. Sam shoved his hands into his pockets and ambled along beside Wayne. They walked in companionable silence through much of the residential section, then headed toward the depot. Their route took them past the dark school house. Next door, a single light burned in the front window, its yellow glow casting a single silhouette

82

on the shade. Without conscious thought, Sam stopped walking and stared at the window.

"You've got it bad for her, don't you?" Wayne asked.

"Who? Me? Naw. I just have a lot on my mind."

"Admit it, Sam."

"She's just so—"

"Pretty?"

"That, too. I was going to say she's . . . puzzling. I can't think of a better word. Every time I think I have her all figured out, she throws me a curve."

"Why don't you go see her?" Wayne suggested.

"Now?"

"Why not?"

"She, uh, she's not expecting me. Maybe she isn't decent."

"She wouldn't be wandering around in the front room if she weren't decent, Sam. Besides, when are you planning to be back in town for the evening? If you don't see her tonight, you might not get another chance for several weeks. Go on."

"If the people in this town won't condone her riding in the surrey with me, I don't think they'd look too kindly on a visit, especially after dark."

"I'll watch the street for you," Wayne offered. "Go on."

Sam hesitated. "I don't know . . ."

While he stood in front of her gate, trying to decide what he would say to her, Prairie's door opened and a woman emerged. Immediately grateful for the cloak of darkness, Sam turned and started walking briskly away. The explosive sound of the train whistle knifed through the quiet.

When they were out of earshot, Wayne asked, "Who was that?"

"Donovan's wife."

"Prairie's mother?"

"I suppose. I'm still confused about where the Jernigan name came from."

"Maybe your widow theory was correct."

Sam told him about seeing Prairie that afternoon and the calamity with the surrey. "I made a point of asking her if she was *Miss* Jernigan, and she said yes."

"I'll bet Miss Bidwell would know."

"Don't ask, Wayne. We're having enough trouble of our own with Donovan without word getting out that we're asking questions about his so-called daughter."

"Yeah, I suppose you're right. Donovan does carry a lot of weight in this town, him being the mayor and all . . . Hey! You don't suppose she's his mistress, do you?"

"I've considered the possibility, but it just doesn't ring true. If that were the case, why would she and Donovan's wife be so friendly? And why would she be so concerned with propriety? It doesn't make sense."

They had reached the depot. The train sat on the tracks, hissing and coughing, new arrivals spilling out of its passenger cars while two men piled baggage and crates onto the boardwalk. A short, hump-shouldered man, dressed in ticking-striped overalls and wearing a matching bibbed cap, hefted a large canvas bag marked "U.S. Mail." This he deposited with Slim, who exchanged it for a similar bag. Hawkers, carrying everything from cigars to oranges, moved among the crowd.

"Do you see the one with the books and newspapers?" Wayne asked Sam.

"You'd do better on Sunday, catching the train from the East."

"Yeah, I know. But I'm out of reading material. There he is." Wayne hurried toward a man of slight

84

build who was pushing around a large wicker cart loaded with magazines, newspapers, and pulp fiction. The vendor stopped the cart under a kerosene lantern hanging from the pavilion roof.

"There's a library in town," Sam reminded his brother.

"They don't stock dime novels." Wayne selected a new Beadle's title by Bill Cody, a half-dimer from the Wide Awake Library called *Denver Dan and His Band of Dead Shots* by "Noname," and that week's Brave and Bold release: *The Lost Chief, or Gordon Keith's Adventures Among the Redskins* by Lawrence White, Jr. "Do you have one by Pampas J. Rose?" Wayne asked the vendor. "He's my favorite."

"Yours and everyone else's!" the little man snorted. "Let me help you look. He has a new one out, but I don't recollect the title. Something about a sawbones in Sacramento. Naw, sir, I don't see it. I must've sold the last one in Lake Charles. Catch me again on Sunday. I work the stations between New Orleans and Houston, you see, and replace my stock on each end."

Wayne said he'd be there Sunday and gave the man the twenty cents he owed him. After a brief discussion, the brothers decided they'd mosey on back to the boardinghouse. The two walked without talking for several minutes, mainly because Sam was having a mental conversation with himself. A name insisted on rumbling around in his head, a name that somehow meant something to him. He couldn't figure out why.

"Pampas J. Rose," Sam sneered aloud, emphasizing each syllable. "What a sissy-sounding name!"

"He doesn't write sissy stories," Wayne staunchly defended. "You ought to read them."

"How can I? The vendor doesn't have any to buy."

"I'll lend you some of mine, but you have to promise to take care of them and give them back when you're through."

"Wait a minute," Sam protested. "I didn't say I wanted to read that pulp. I have better things to do with my time."

"Like visiting Miss Jernigan?" Wayne goaded. "We're almost back to her house."

"It wouldn't do her reputation any good for me to visit her at night, unchaperoned."

"When did you ever let a little thing like a reputation stop you?" Wayne said teasingly.

"You know me better than that!" Sam snapped.

"I might, and then again, I might not, little brother," Wayne badgered.

"Verbally tormenting me will not make up for all the teasing from J.C. and Myron you've put up with, Wayne."

They came abreast of her house, then. All the windows were dark.

"Too late," Wayne clucked. "I suppose you'll have to settle for Mr. Rose's excellent company tonight. Unless you want to stop by Madame Angelique's tent. I hear tell she's got a passel of beauties under all those stripes."

Wayne referred to the multi-colored canvas that housed the group of prostitutes who had come in from New Orleans on Sunday's train.

Sam shook his head. "They aren't my kind of beauties, Wayne. I guess I'll settle for Mr. Rose."

Wayne was right. Mr. Rose's company *was* excellent.

Sam stayed up most of the night, reading one dime novel after another. He cheered for the good guys, booed the bad guys, and put each book down thoroughly satisfied and eager to see how this talented writer would rescue the next hero from the passel of trouble he was bound to get himself into.

Sam had thought all dime novels were written about real men, a good many of them outlaws depicted as swashbuckling paladins with misunderstood motives. And that was true about much of the pulp fiction being written.

But not the stories penned by Pampas J. Rose. If his heroes were patterned after actual men, Rose had successfully camouflaged their identities. But they all were men Sam thought he'd like to meet.

Sam thought he'd like to meet Rose's heroines as well, judging by *Fiery Flora, or Fallen From Grace in New Orleans,* the only one of Wayne's Rose collection with a female central character. Now, there was a woman with spunk—sassy and strong. A real spitfire. Yet, the fire was tempered with such dignity, such intelligence, such grace.

There was one thing, though, about Mr. Rose's work that bothered Sam. The author, he decided, must not keep accurate records of story details because there were a few he used over and over, from one book to another. Instead of counting sheep that night, Sam counted Rose's repetitive details: a place called Big Spring, women named Anna and Martha and Susie, characters who loved oatmeal and hated brown gravy, which they always called toodlum gravy.

And the man must have an obsession with dragonflies. The winged creatures themselves flitted through some stories, while in others their images appeared cast in gold or silver as brooches, pendants, or tiepins. In one, Rose put a captured dragonfly in the center of a glass paperweight, and in another, the novelist named a pirate ship *The Dragonfly.*

Sam wondered if Wayne had ever noted the recurring details and made a mental note to ask him at breakfast. He went to sleep pondering the familiarity of the novelist's name: Pampas J. Rose.

There was something he was supposed to know about that name . . .

Chapter Six

"Whatcha doin', Miss Jernigan?"

Prairie looked up from the atlas she had spread open on the top of her desk into eyes as green and bright as the shade the illustrator had used to color the fertile Mississippi River valley. "Studying this map, Kevin."

"Gee, Miss Jernigan. You got to study, too?"

"Of course, I do. No one knows everything, not even teachers." Prairie closed the atlas and slipped it back into its niche on the bookshelf behind her desk, disappointment running rife within her. She might as well face it, she supposed. Pouring over the map every day served no purpose other than causing her supreme frustration. There was no Big Spring close to Texarkana, at least not on the map.

She turned around and began to straighten her desk. The boy hadn't moved. "Why haven't you gone home? School's been out for almost an hour."

The boy looked down at his bare big toe, which he scrubbed against wide pine planks sanded white from the traffic of countless dirty soles moving from desk to blackboard and back to desk again. "I had some studyin' to do myself, ma'am," he said sheepishly. "I flunked my spellin' test again, so Miz Nolan made me stay and write my words a hunnerd times apiece."

"Come on," Prairie said, making sure her voice

smiled even if her heart could not. "I'll walk you to the café. I'm going to the mercantile and Louella's place is right on the way."

Kevin McCormack was one of the many new students the influx of oil-hungry settlers had brought in. Prairie didn't know where his family was living—probably in a tent, but she did know his mother had taken a job as a waitress at Louella's Café.

In the week or so the eight-year-old had been at the Jennings school, he'd gone out of his way to speak to Prairie. One day he'd brought her a handful of black-eyed Susans; another time he'd insisted she take his blue cat's-eye marble and keep it in her pocket for good luck. She supposed this was what they'd meant at Normal when they told her to be prepared for a child's infatuation with his teacher. Although Kevin was Ruth's pupil, not hers, his behavior certainly fit the profile.

They'd said not to encourage the child. She supposed that was exactly what she was doing by offering to walk him to the café, but she didn't think it was a good idea to let him go alone—not at his age. Not with the kind of riffraff roaming the streets of Jennings these days.

Perhaps, she thought as they walked away from the schoolyard, if she understood why he was so enamored of her, she could put an end to it. It wouldn't hurt to ask.

"Why do you like me so well, Kevin?"

"Because you call me by my name."

Prairie blinked, stupidly she supposed, but his answer made no sense to her. "What does Mrs. Nolan call you?"

"Noel—you know, like the Christmas song."

"Noel?" That made even less sense.

"Yes'm." The boy nodded vigorously. "The first day I come, I give her a paper from my last teacher,

90

the one I had over to Eunice. Miss Cormier must've written 'Kelvin' on the paper 'stead of 'Kevin,' 'cause that's what Miz Nolan called me after she read the paper. I said, 'No, ma'am. No *l*.' And she's been callin' me Noel ever since."

Prairie felt the corners of her mouth twitch, but she dared not laugh. "Did you tell Mrs. Nolan your name is Kevin, not Noel?"

"I tried, Miss Jernigan. Honest, I did. But she called me imper—" Kevin screwed up his freckled nose and tried again. "Impertnunt and made me sit in the corner."

Prairie patted the boy's dusty, carrot-top head. "Mrs. Nolan's been a little frazzled lately, Kevin. Would you like for me to talk to her for you? Explain what happened?"

"Oh, yes'm, I shorely would."

"Consider it done. Here's the café, Kevin. Promise me you'll study your spelling words next week."

A wide grin split his round face. "Yes, ma'am, I will. I'll make a hunnerd."

He darted toward the door, then ran back and threw his arms around Prairie's rib cage and squeezed hard. "I love you, Miss Jernigan," he said against her chest, then he broke loose and dashed off again.

The unexpected gesture warmed Prairie, filling her heart. She stood still for a moment, staring after him, staring at the snapping screen door until it settled on its hinges. Almost immediately, it popped open again. At the sight of the customer coming out of the café, any thought of continuing on to the mercantile to purchase the buttons she needed flew right out of her head. She whirled around and started back the way she'd come.

"Hold on, there, Prairie," King Clarkston called. "I want to talk to you."

Prairie kept walking, but his long legs precluded escape. He caught her by the elbow and pulled her to a halt. "Let me go, King," she stated flatly. "I'm in a hurry."

"You didn't seem much in a hurry yesterday."

Prairie didn't like the sneer in his voice. "Whatever are you babbling about?"

"You and that wildcatter, that's what I'm talking about. I saw him putting his hands on you outside the post office, and I didn't see you running away from him."

"Then you didn't stick around long enough, King. Besides, that's none of your business." She jerked loose from his grasp and started back toward the school.

Getting away from him wasn't going to be that easy. "Now, hold on a minute, Prairie. I told you I wanted to talk to you."

She didn't slow her stride. "Then talk!"

His voice softened considerably. "I just wanted to remind you about the dance Saturday night. I'll be by around sevenish to pick you up."

"I don't remember saying I'd go with you."

"But you're going, aren't you?"

"Yes, I suppose I will," she admitted, though reluctantly.

"Is someone else taking you?"

"No."

"Then you might as well go with me."

Prairie groped for an excuse but none came readily to mind. She felt like a dolt, standing there on the street with her mouth working but no words coming out.

"I'll be by around seven," he repeated, his mouth and eyes leering at her. He ducked his head in mock respect and walked away.

"I'll meet you there," she called after him, gratefully finding her voice but knowing that whether or not King Clarkston actually accompanied her made little difference. As long as they both were there, he would make it a point to monopolize her attention.

The colorful, hand-painted posters advertising the third annual Ladies Library Association supper and dance promised the event would be superior to its predecessors, and those two had been well-organized, beautifully orchestrated affairs. "Come dressed in your best finery," the posters encouraged, "and assist the Association in its efforts to establish a permanent reading room and library necessary to the comforts and cultural benefit of our residents."

Prairie's meeting with King Clarkston threw her into such a turmoil that by the time Saturday evening arrived she didn't care if she went to the dance or not. As a member of the Association, she knew her presence was expected; as the foster daughter of the event's host and hostess, she had no choice. But attending out of a sense of duty rather than a desire to kick up her heels and have a good time put a damper on her naturally high spirits.

A part of her desperately wished Sam Blackman had asked to take her, but in all likelihood he wouldn't even be at the dance. According to Michael and Doc, Sam was working his crew night and day in an effort to remove the remainder of the sand from the hole. Besides, she reminded herself, she'd run from him—made an absolute ninny of herself trying to take his surrey. Whatever interest he'd had in her she'd managed quite successfully to destroy.

Yet . . . he might be there. It was possible. Any- thing was possible, Prairie assured herself as she ad- justed her white sateen, straight-front corset over a camisole that barely covered her breasts. The off-shoulder style of the new gown she'd had made expressly for this dance required such a camisole. A moment's scrutiny in front of her cheval glass proved the camisole tightly tucked but revealed a bunched petticoat at her waistline. Prairie jerked on the white taffeta, then turned her profile to the mirror to inspect herself from behind.

Anything was possible. If she didn't believe that, she wouldn't have put so much time and effort into finding her family. How long would it take, she wondered, for Mrs. Albert Byers to receive her letter and return a reply? It had been two weeks since the woman's letter had arrived, ten days or so since Prairie had mailed her own reply, via David. Any day now . . .

Satisfied at last that the undergarments would lie flat beneath her gown, she stepped into the dress, a peach and cream foulard with a full, unadorned skirt. Mrs. Simmons, the dressmaker, had begged Prairie to let her add a fashionable ruffle or two to the bottom, but she had refused. Later, second thoughts had plagued her, but as she stood in front of the mirror and surveyed the results, Prairie knew she'd been right. Ruffles around the hemline would most definitely have detracted from the wide, creamy lace ruffle that spilled over her breasts and upper arms, following the margin of cream-colored satin which bound the wide neckline.

It was this ruffle, she'd insisted to Mrs. Simmons, which should dominate the gown. And it did. Quite charmingly.

In compliance with this principle, the sleeves, which had been cut from matching lace, were long and tight, ending in a point over the backs of her hands. They were so tight, in fact, that the seams threatened to give as she twisted her left arm behind her back and reached with her right arm over her shoulder to attach a train—made of the same fabric as the gown—beneath the lace ruffle and then again at the waistline.

A final check with a hand mirror assured her that the train was straight, and her poufed hair unaffected. Her fingers sought the edge of the comb to which a froth of the cream-colored lace had been attached, and this she pushed more securely into the thick roll of dark brown hair she'd pinned behind her head.

Yes, any day now, she affirmed with a quick nod of her head, *the mail should bring an answer from Mrs. Byers. Any day now* . . . Mrs. Byers was bound to be related to her, one way or another. The thought sent a wave of hope through her and she smiled for the first time since she'd started to dress.

Just as she was putting on her ivory kid pumps, a knock resounded through her small house. That would be Winkle, come to collect her in the Donovans' carriage. She gave her hair a final pat, pinched her cheeks until they bloomed pink, then dipped her forefinger into a tiny pot and smoothed the clear, jelly-like substance over her lips.

The knock resounded again.

"I'm coming!" she called, surprised at the normally placid Winkle's impatience. Hastily she wiped her finger on a linen towel, grabbed the reticule Mrs. Simmons had made to match the gown, and extinguished the lamps in her bedroom.

No one could have been caught off guard more than Prairie Jernigan when she opened the door and saw Sam Blackman standing there.

He watched her glistening lips form themselves into an O, watched her spice-colored eyes widen in astonishment, and suddenly felt extremely warm, though comfortably so.

"Hello."

The word hung in the air, hovering in the space between them, its tone so melodious Sam couldn't believe he had uttered it. He twisted his head around to see if it had come from someone standing behind him, then felt foolish when both the steps and graveled path proved empty.

"I . . . wasn't expecting you."

Sam looked back at her, noticed for the first time the formality of her attire, and locked his gaze on the swell of her bosom above a wide flounce of creamy lace. Obviously, she was expecting *someone,* someone for whom she had chosen to bare her shoulders and a good portion of her chest. Too much of her chest, to his way of thinking. His throat constricted and a wave of some emotion so foreign to him he couldn't name it swept through him. Whatever this feeling was, he knew he didn't like it. It made him feel like someone had punched him in the stomach, then taken off with his wallet.

"Who were you expecting?" he choked out, appalled at his sudden lack of control over his voice.

"Uh, Winkle—you know, he works for Wynn and Michael. Takes care of their yard and their horses, that sort of thing. He's supposed to drive me over to their house."

Prairie clamped her mouth shut to stop herself from babbling, but the firm line of her lips quickly disappeared, to be replaced by a broad smile. She'd wanted him to come, and there he was, at her door, looking a bit uncomfortable and not dressed quite elegantly enough for the occasion, though she supposed his crisp white shirt, black string tie, and dark blue trousers would do.

"You are, uhm, going to the Donovans' for supper?" he asked, running a forefinger around the inside edge of his collar.

"Yes," she said, beginning to wonder if, perhaps, he'd missed seeing the Library Association's advertisements.

He'd thought to take her to supper himself, maybe to Louella's. Sam looked at Prairie again, taking in every aspect of her appearance from head to toe. He found it hard to believe she'd wear such a formal gown for a mere family meal. "They're . . . having other guests?"

"Yes." So! He had missed seeing the posters.

"Well, I won't detain you, then." He turned away and started down the steps.

Dadburn it! He'd left the rig at a time he had no business leaving, driven all the way into town, then spent two hours at the barber shop getting a shave, a haircut, and a bath—and all that for nothing! A nagging voice said, *You knew you should have asked her first. You knew she might have other plans. You can't blame her for being so confounded pretty.*

But he did. If she weren't, he reasoned, he'd still be out at the rig, where he ought to be, not here in town on a Saturday night with nothing to do—now.

"Sam!"

Her use of his first name stopped him dead in his tracks. He loved the way she said it, almost in two syllables: *Sa-uhm,* her sweet voice singing the vowels. He heard the absence of the sound of gravel crackling beneath his feet, heard the birds twittering in the trees, heard his heart pounding in his chest. He felt the freshness of a cool breeze on his cheek, a breeze that carried the acrid smell of resin from the recently milled pine being used in the new construction going up everywhere, a smell not wholly unpleasant. Suddenly, his whole body seemed acutely sensitized.

"Sam!" she called again. "Aren't you going to the dance?"

97

Dance? There'd been talk of a dance in the barber shop, but Sam hadn't paid much attention. He turned around, shaking his head. "I wasn't invited."

"Well, I'm inviting you," Prairie said, "although a personal invitation isn't necessary. This is the annual fund-raiser for the Ladies Library Association — a supper and dance at my parents' house. If you don't have a ticket, you can buy one at the door."

"And that's where you're going?"

She nodded.

"And this is a formal affair?"

"Sort of."

He laughed. "Then I suppose I'd best go back to Miss Bidwell's and change into something" — he waved a hand down his torso — "more formal."

Prairie watched him walk — no, she amended, he was almost sprinting — down the walk and climb into his red surrey. He lifted a hand and waved, smiling broadly, then slapped the reins against the mare's white back. The horse bolted, her hooves kicking up little explosions of dust, her pace setting the gold fringe in motion.

A surge of delight set Prairie's pulse aflutter. Maybe the evening would prove enjoyable after all.

Every horse-drawn vehicle in town must have been put to use that night, Sam decided as he parked the surrey several blocks away from the Donovan house. Music and laughter drifted on the breeze, the commingling sounds promising a night of gaiety. He stepped down from the surrey, tied Dolly's reins to a fence rail, then retrieved his top hat and cane from the back seat.

He'd thought he'd have to wear his black serge suit, the one he saved for church and important business meetings. But he'd walked into his room at the boardinghouse to find his tuxedo jacket and

98

matching trousers laid out on his bed, along with a white tucked shirt, wide white cummerbund, white spats, black stockings, black bow tie, black top hat, and silver-tipped black cane. His black dress shoes sat on the floor.

For a moment, he'd wondered how it all had gotten there — not just on the bed, but in Jennings, period. He knew he'd left these things in Beaumont, never thinking to need anything so decorous in Jennings. Indeed, he'd never have purchased such fancy clothes in the first place had Captain Lucas not thrown a formal dinner party in his and Wayne's honor following the gusher at Spindletop.

But there they all were, down to the white spats.

"Sorry it took me so long to get back with these," Wayne announced, coming in through the door Sam had left open. He was already dressed in similar finery.

"But — how? When?" Sam sputtered.

"I wired J.C. Everything arrived terribly wrinkled, of course, and what with the big to-do tonight, the laundry was swamped. I'd thought to get back before you left, but I had to wait while they finished the pressing."

"That's not what I mean," Sam said. "How did you know I'd come back to town today? I hadn't planned to."

Wayne's eyes, blue but a grayer shade than Sam's, twinkled merrily. "Never mind. I knew. I also knew you'd want to go to the dance, once you found out about it. Where have you been, anyway?"

Sam got the distinct impression Wayne didn't need an answer to his question, so he asked one of his own. "You going by yourself?"

"Naw. I'm taking Miss Bidwell."

It was, apparently, Sam's night for surprises. "Miss Bidwell?"

Wayne shrugged. "Why not?"

"Because she's—" Sam hesitated, not knowing how to finish the sentence tactfully.

"She's not that old," Wayne defended, "and she's not that fat. Besides, she cooks my favorite meals and washes my shirts and socks. And she's good company, Sam."

"Do you even know her first name?"

"Sure I do. It's Lily. Who are you taking?"

"No one," Sam said quickly, pulling on a string of his tie and nodding toward the hallway. "Do you mind closing the door?"

Wayne hesitated for the briefest of moments, his expression that of disbelief. "I was on my way downstairs anyway. I'll see you there."

Sam supposed Wayne and Miss Bidwell—Lily—had already arrived, as had everyone else in town, from all appearances. This must be some wingding. The strains of a waltz filtered through partially open windows festooned with sprays of delicate white flowers and big bows of burgundy satin ribbon. White Japanese lanterns emblazoned the brick walk and front porch, where several small groups of men congregated. Sam recognized a few of them: Joe Corley, Johnny Perkins, Dub Jackson, Reverend Milhouse, and Enoch Nolan. They nodded to him as he walked across the porch. Enoch detached himself from one of the groups and joined Sam at the front door.

"Didn't expect to see you here, young man," he said, grinning mischievously. "I don't reckon certain other folks expected to see you, either, but I'm glad you made it."

They walked in together, stopping at a small table in the hall where Sam paid the required sum to a lady he knew he'd met but couldn't quite place. She flashed him a smile so wide it cracked the powder on her full cheeks, then said, "We're glad you could be here, Mr. Blackman. Do enjoy yourself."

Doc took Sam's elbow and led him toward the dining room. "It's hard for a body to recognize Hazel all dressed up like that. Always throws me. I want to tell her to go back home and put on that silly-looking sailor hat she wears every day so I'll know who she is."

Of course! Sam thought. *The postmistress.*

"There's food aplenty laid out in here. Just serve yourself. Dancin's across the hall in the front parlor, if you're interested. If you're not, you're welcome to join us menfolk out on the porch."

"Thanks, Enoch," Sam said, food and male company the last thing on his mind. He got his fill of both on a daily basis. No, tonight he wanted to feel the softness of a certain woman in his arms, to smell the sweet fragrance of her essence, to dance with her until his feet hurt.

He turned away from the impressive buffet in the dining room and headed across the hall, his gaze searching the crowd for cream-colored lace.

She'd been watching for him, jumping every time the screen door creaked open. When Wayne and Miss Bidwell arrived, Prairie was at the buffet with King Clarkston. The two moved into the dining room and she waited, breathless, for Sam to follow them. When he didn't, she insisted on sitting on the staircase to eat, a position which gave her a bird's-eye view of the front door.

As she'd expected, King seemed bent on dominating her time. He kept up a constant chatter, to which Prairie only half-listened while she nibbled on food she didn't taste.

"What's got into you tonight?" King asked, taking her plate and assisting her to her feet.

101

"Nothing. Nothing at all."

"Something has," he insisted. "You're as jumpy as a bullfrog on a pond full of rotten lily pads." He deposited their dishes on a tray Zoey carried and whisked Prairie into the parlor.

They were in the middle of a waltz, King holding her closer than she liked, when she spied Sam, standing in the dining room doorway, talking to Doc. She caught but a glimpse of him, auburn streaks gleaming through his shock of brown hair, his tall frame resplendent in a black cutaway jacket with a split tail that hung almost to his knees. When he said formal, he meant it.

Another couple moved into her line of vision and she craned her neck, trying to see around them. King's arm stiffened at her back, pulling her even closer as he maneuvered them away from the front hall, deeper into the throng of dancers, across the room to French doors thrown open to the dim paper-lantern glow from the front side of the wraparound porch and the pleasant chill of the night air.

Before Prairie realized what he was up to, King waltzed her right through the open doors and onto the porch. She could hear men's voices around the corner, but this portion of the porch was empty and dark. In one swift motion, King let go of her left hand and moved his right arm around her rib cage. His head dipped perilously close to hers.

"What are you doing?" she gasped, struggling to extract herself from his arms, a part of her wanting to scream. But she foresaw no reason to create a scene over something so minor. This wasn't the first time King Clarkston had toyed with her. She'd always managed to control the situation before; she would now.

"Trying to kiss you."

"I don't want you to kiss me, King!" she hissed. "Let go of me!"

"No."

In the dim light of the paper lanterns, King's black eyes glistened with determination. They were the eyes of a serpent, heavy-lidded, deceptively dangerous. She'd never realized before how closely he resembled a snake, a king snake, and she was his chosen victim. His grasp constricted, the strength of his hold combined with the tightness of her corset threatening to suffocate her. She tried to take a deep breath, tried to draw in enough air to scream, knowing now that she should have screamed loud and long when she'd had the chance.

But she couldn't do it, not with his hold so tight. Her lungs were beginning to burn. Her throat and lips felt parched. From the corner of her eye, she could see the light of a lantern hanging at the front corner of the porch. The light shimmered and spun, round and round, its radiance searing into her brain.

King's wet mouth, sealed over hers, made breathing even more difficult. His exploring tongue repulsed her. She pushed against him, marginally aware of the feebleness of the gesture yet determined to force him to release her. It would never work. She was too weak. But she had to try.

Then, quite suddenly, his arms loosened their hold and he spun away from her. Without his support, she crumpled to her knees, coughing, gagging on the rush of air into her lungs, reluctant to expel it in the fear it would be snatched from her again.

As she struggled to regain her equilibrium, she heard a familiar masculine voice command King to leave, heard the report of a fist connecting with bone, heard the music cease and the parlor erupt with ear-splitting applause for the string quartet.

A hand, warm and tender, closed around her elbow and gently pulled her to her feet.

She looked up into a face black with anger, chiseled lips drawn back in a snarl, dark, straight eyebrows low and menacing, a face totally incongruous with the tender touch. In the shadowy light, she watched, fascinated, as the facial muscles shifted, the lips first covering the gleam of white teeth and then the brow relaxing. He blinked twice, then bestowed upon her a gaze as tender as the touch of his hand upon her arm.

"Are you all right, Miss Jernigan?"

She nodded, not trusting her voice box to operate properly quite yet.

"Do you want to go back inside now?"

"No," she whispered, inclining her head toward the porch swing, praying that she wasn't borrowing more trouble with Sam Blackman.

Sam's arm encircled her narrow waist and he pulled her against his side, guiding her deeper into the shadows.

Chapter Seven

After a while, the paper lantern stopped spinning and Prairie's pulse stopped racing and her flesh stopped shivering. In the aftermath, she felt a warm glow envelop her. The source of that glow sat beside her on the porch swing, his arm around her tuxedo-wrapped shoulders, his length pressed close to her side.

The absence of fear brought awareness. With each deep, cleansing breath she inhaled his essence, the fragrance of soap and hair tonic underlaid with a clean, masculine musk. With each relaxing nerve she felt his strength, firm bone and hard muscle covering a solid wall of confidence beneath his comforting embrace. With each sigh she snuggled a bit deeper into that embrace until Sam's discreet "Ahem!" wrenched her into full alertness.

Intending to scoot over, Prairie jerked away from him, but Sam gently pulled her back, settling her head into his shoulder once more. She didn't know when she'd felt so utterly content, so secure, so safe . . .

She twisted her head around and looked up at Sam. The pale light from the paper lantern limned the planes of his face—the firm jaw, wide brow, and long nose—and turned the unruly curls wisping over his crown and behind his ears into a luminous halo.

"Do you feel better now?" he asked, his voice soft and slightly raspy.

She nodded against the crook in his arm. "Uhm-hm. What happened to King?"

Sam smiled down at her, his blue eyes glistening in the lantern light. "After he went over the rail and into the bushes?"

Prairie laughed. "Did he really?"

"Yes. And I honestly don't know what he did after that. He may still be in the bushes. Do you want to go see?"

"No."

"Did he hurt you?"

She lowered her head and snuggled closer. "Not really. He scared me, though. I thought I could handle him, but . . . I'm very glad you came along when you did."

His arm tightened around her shoulders for a moment, then relaxed. Through the fabric of his jacket, she felt the tips of his fingers trail up and down her upper arm, their tingle at once soothing and titillating.

"Eventually, someone's bound to miss the two of us—the three of us," he amended. "What do you want me to say about the other fellow? What did you call him?"

"King. King Clarkston. And we don't know where he went, do we?"

Sam squeezed her against him. "No," he said, laughter in his voice. "We certainly don't. He's probably off somewhere nursing a sore jaw and picking twigs out of his backside."

"Thorns, more than likely. The bushes on this side of the house are ornamental hollies."

They both laughed at that, their laughter that of conspiratorial compatriots.

She'd turned her face up to him again. His head cast a shadow over her eyes, but Sam suspected they

106

shimmered with her mirth. Thank goodness for that, he thought, the memory of her earlier devastation making him shudder inside. He didn't believe the Clarkston fellow would actually have physically harmed her, not within such close proximity of the crowd and of her family. But the man had certainly frightened Prairie half out of her wits. Sam found himself wanting to be her protector, and not merely for the course of the evening. He lowered his head to hers, aiming to sip from the sweet nectar of her lips once again.

"We'd best go back inside," she said.

Her words brought him back to reality. He shook his head, trying to dislodge the spell she had cast over him. Whatever had he been thinking? Kissing her was one thing; wanting to set himself up as her permanent champion was something else entirely.

"Yes," he whispered through the catch in his throat. "I suppose we'd better." He rose from the swing, pulling her up with him.

She stepped aside, suddenly awkward with him. Something was different, and though she couldn't say exactly what, she wasn't the least bit certain it was bad. She slid his coat off her shoulders and held it out to him. When he had slipped his arms into the sleeves, untangled the tails, and straightened the lapels, he picked up the end of her train and placed it in her left hand.

"May I have this dance?" he asked, his mouth so close to her ear his warm breath tickled her neck, raising the fine hairs there and eliciting gooseflesh on her arms. Without waiting for an answer, he guided her into the steps of the waltz and thus through the open French doors and back into the parlor.

Although she had other dance partners throughout the evening, Prairie found herself in Sam's arms more often than not. He was an excellent dancer, light on his feet and skilled at guiding. When she waltzed with him, she felt as though she floated.

The more she danced with Sam, the more the memory of King Clarkston's amorous advances faded into obscurity. The night would have been perfect had Michael not claimed her for the next to the last dance.

At first she thought nothing of it. Indeed, she'd fully expected her foster father to dance with her at least once. But the waltz had barely begun when he said, "I thought telling Sam Blackman to stay away from you was enough. I see now that it wasn't. Since he refuses to pay heed to my wishes, you'll have to assume responsibility, Prairie. Stay away from him."

He couldn't have surprised her more. "Why?" she asked, surprise and confusion written on her face.

"He's . . . dangerous."

"Dangerous? Sam?"

"Yes, Prairie. Perhaps reckless is a better word, but for men, the two are synonymous. You can't trust him."

Prairie could hear the smack of bare knuckles against solid jawbone, could feel Sam's comforting arm around her shoulders, could hear his soft voice in her ear. Sam Blackman might be a lot of things, maybe even reckless. But dangerous? Surely not to her. He'd saved her from danger.

She hesitated to tell Michael about what had happened on the porch. He'd always thought so highly of King Clarkston. She couldn't help wondering if he'd believe her—and knew that if he did, he'd go after King with a vengeance. Prairie didn't think King would cause her any more trouble, nor could she see any good coming out of more violence, and yet she couldn't allow Michael to think so negatively of Sam.

In the midst of her hesitation, Michael said, "Good. I'm glad that's settled."

She stopped moving, pulling back in Michael's

arms and pinning him with a determined stare. "Nothing's settled, Michael," she said. "Sam and I are both adults. If trusting him is a mistake, I'll find out on my own."

"Prairie—" he warned.

"I mean it, Michael. Thanks for caring, but please trust me to manage this. And if I'm hurt in the end, I'll survive."

She spoke firmly, with conviction, but when the piece ended and she found herself in Sam's arms once more, she didn't feel quite so confident. There was something about being with Sam Blackman that made her feel paradoxically weak and strong at the same time.

As he whirled her around the floor, she lost herself in the tranquilizing rhythm of "The Merry Widow," one of her favorites. Too quickly, the string quartet finished, ending both the dance and the evening. Prairie waited breathlessly for Sam to release her, knowing that when he did she would lose not only his physical support but the warmth of his nearness as well. She steeled herself for the moment.

But he didn't release her. Instead, he steered her toward the front hall.

"May I escort you home, Miss Jernigan?" he asked.

Michael's warning sliced through her, but Prairie shoved it away. Whatever bad blood might exist between her foster father and Sam didn't concern her.

"Yes, thank you," she said.

"Are you sure it's permitted?"

"Oh, I'm quite sure it's not, but I'm feeling a bit reckless tonight."

Still, doubts plagued her while she was collecting her wrap and finding Winkle. After all, she had never imagined King Clarkston hurting her. No, that wasn't exactly true, she mentally corrected. Somehow, she'd known there was something disturbing about King. And Michael said Sam was dangerous. There was still time, she reminded herself, to change her mind. Winkle could drive her home.

But even as she considered that possibility, she heard herself tell the handyman otherwise and hurried back to the front hall, where she found Sam talking to Wynn.

"Good night, then," he said, turning slightly to take Prairie's elbow.

"Do you need me to help clean up?" Prairie offered, the wisdom of her decision stinging her again.

"No, thanks," Wynn said, smiling and pulling Prairie against her chest for a brief hug. "Zoey and Marmie will make short work of the dishes, and we'll move all the furniture back later. Good night, dear."

And then they were out on the front porch, out into the clear, crisp night, out onto the brick walk with the stars twinkling above them and the beaming face of a full moon lighting their way. They walked in silence, each acutely aware of the other, neither knowing what to say nor caring whether words passed between them.

Other couples moved along with them, chatting pleasantly among themselves, but Prairie didn't see them, didn't hear them. For her, no one else existed at that moment except Sam. They continued down the street until they reached Sam's surrey. He helped her up onto the front seat, took his own place, then clicked his tongue to Dolly. The mare stepped forward, her initial tug on the surrey so slight Prairie barely felt it begin to move.

"So that's how you start her!" Prairie exclaimed.

Sam's full-bodied laughter erupted beside her. "Always—unless, of course, you want her to bolt. Then, you slap the reins against her back."

"Why?"

"Why would you want her to bolt?"

"No. Why does she? Why would you train her to do that?" Prairie asked.

"I didn't. Her previous owner abused her, beat her with a whip."

"Oh, how awful! I can't imagine why — she's such a beautiful animal. And she seems quite docile when treated properly."

Prairie watched the silver glow of moonlight reflect off Sam's front teeth, which his wide grin exposed. "You should have seen yourself the day you tried to take off in my surrey. It was a sight to behold!"

"Humph! I'm glad you think it was so funny. My knees are still bruised," she grumbled good-naturedly, rubbing her bent legs through her gown. Then she laughed, too. "I can see why it would have its amusing side — for someone watching."

She paused, worrying her bottom lip with her teeth, trying to think of a diplomatic way to ask him something, posing the question in her mind from several angles, and finally blurting out, "Why do you own a red surrey?"

Sam leaned back in the seat and howled, his sides shaking with mirth. "There's not a shy bone in your body, is there, Miss Jernigan?" He didn't wait for her answer, but plunged right into his own. "For many reasons, I suppose."

He transferred the reins to his left hand, lifted his right into a fist, then opened his fingers one at the time as he ticked off the reasons. "One, it never gets lost in a crowd of black buggies. Two, it's sort of like my signature — you know, uniquely me. When people see it, they know Sam Blackman's in town. Three, there's ample room for my brothers and our baggage. We travel a lot. And four" — his hand snaked out and touched her lower arm, slowly, sensuously stroking — "it reminds me of a woman, sleek and elegant, all decked out in her best finery and raring to go somewhere to show herself off."

His touch changed from a delicious tingle to a stinging burn. Prairie lifted his hand from her arm

111

and put it down on the seat next to his thigh. "I'm not sure I appreciate that last remark, Mr. Blackman."

"What? About a woman wanting to show herself off?"

"Yes, that one!" she snapped, trying to hold on to her composure.

"You don't think—oh, you do think—" He pulled back on the reins, halting Dolly in front of Prairie's house.

"And what do I think, Mr. Blackman?"

"That I think you got all decked out in your best finery and went to the dance to show yourself off."

"Well, don't you?"

"No, I don't." The words were spoken leisurely, separately, each one bringing him inches closer to Prairie. "You tried your best to make me think you were that shallow last week when you drove out to the rig, but it was all an act, wasn't it, Miss Jernigan?"

A combination of shame and frustration washed over her, and she focused her gaze on the folded hands within her lap. Sam took her face between his palms and gently turned her head toward him, forcing her to meet his gaze. "Wasn't it, Prairie?"

She nodded, as taken aback by his use of her first name as she was with his question.

"For the life of me, I can't figure out why . . ."

He paused, allowing her time to respond. When she didn't he said, "We started something that day, something that's going to take a lot of practice if we ever want to get it just right."

His face was but a hairbreadth from hers, so close his speech tickled her lips.

"And what was that?" she whispered, knowing full well what he meant.

"This," he said, touching her tingling lips with his own, very lightly, then drawing back and repeating the caress. Calling what he was doing kissing barely fit the definition, but never had anything affected her

112

so. She felt as though a fire smoldered deep inside her and his touch was a breath from a bellows, brightening the glow, promising a full complement of the element necessary to stir it into roaring flame.

Her eyelids fell shut and her body tensed with longing. He kissed her again, as faintly as before, then withdrew his hands from her face.

"End of lesson one," he said, his voice husky.

Her eyes flew open and she looked at him as though she were a child allowed to lick a peppermint stick for the first time — and he the adult who'd offered it, then pulled it away and said, "It may taste good, but it's bad for your teeth."

In amazement, she watched him scoot over on the seat and alight from the surrey. She was still sitting there staring when he took her hand in his and helped her to the ground. She wanted to lash out at him, to demand that he proceed with lesson two, but to do so would appear wanton — and could very well lead to a part of the subject she wasn't quite prepared to explore.

She bit her tongue and fought back the frustration of piqued but unfulfilled passion until Sam had seen her safely inside and left without anything more than a simple "good night." Then she removed her gown, corset, and petticoat, curled up on her bed, and gave him the tongue-lashing he so richly deserved. It was a shame, she thought when she'd finished, that he'd missed it.

But she went to sleep dreaming about the form and content of Sam's next lesson in the art of kissing.

The next morning, Sam put on his work clothes, left the boardinghouse, collected Dolly and the surrey at the livery, and was headed east before the sun cleared the horizon. He followed the route that had been laid out for the pipeline instead of taking the road, checking the progress along the way. At the rate

113

the crew was going, he decided, they might finish the pipeline before the well had been cleared of sand.

At the field, he found the well crew hard at work. He poured stale coffee into a tin cup and pulled Jake Daniels, the driller, off to the side.

"Glad you showed up today," Jake said in a chipper voice that belied the lines of fatigue around his eyes and mouth. "I think we're about ready to bring this baby in again."

"I haven't been gone twenty-four hours, Jake," Sam argued, "and we still had a long way to go yesterday. Are you sure?"

Jake shrugged his massive shoulders. "Who can ever be sure in this business? But if my calculations are correct, we're almost to the bottom."

Sam hastily drank the coffee and took his place on the derrick, working with the crew throughout the day and much of the night, finally falling into a tent just before three in the morning. At daybreak, he was up again and back at work, standing in the pit mixing thin mud with a hoe, checking the two Smithvale pumps and the forty-horse boiler to ensure their continued reliability, watching the mud coming out of the hole. The pumps pushed the thin mud from the pit into the drill pipe, and the mud's pressure combined with the pumps' to push sand-filled mud back out through the casing.

Jake might be right, Sam decided, about being close, but they weren't there yet. The mud coming out of the hole was still full of sand.

Sam awoke Tuesday morning to the sound of lumbering wagons. He pulled on his boots, splashed clean water on his face, smoothed back his hair with the flats of his hands, and dashed out of the tent to see what was going on.

To the northwest, some distance from the well yet within plain sight of it, several heavy wagons were being pulled into a semicircle.

"What's going on?" Jake asked.

"I don't know, but I'm going to find out," Sam replied.

"Do you want me to go with you?"

"It probably wouldn't hurt." Sam scratched his head, frowning at the wagons. "Let's have a cup of coffee first and just watch for a few minutes. Can you see what they're hauling?"

Jake squinted his eyes and whistled. "At least one wagon's full of timber and two more are carrying some kind of heavy equipment. You don't suppose Donovan's decided to start another well on his own?"

"Looks like somebody's going to," Sam agreed, "and just outside the boundary of my forty-acre plot."

When he spied King Clarkston among the crowd of men—which was easy since the man was wearing a three-piece suit and just standing around watching the lumber and equipment being unloaded—Sam's fist tightened up against his thigh and his jaw clenched.

"Easy, now," Jake warned in a whisper. "Let's find out what's going on before we get too riled up."

As much as Sam wanted to hit Clarkston again, he knew Jake was right. He relaxed his hand and jaw.

"Ho, there, Mr. Blackman!" King sneered. "Come to see how an oil well ought to be drilled?"

The hand formed itself into a fist again, the bruised knuckles itching for further abuse. Sam couldn't help it. Nor could he stop himself from grinning at the dark blue circle on Clarkston's jaw and the way the man favored the left side of his mouth when he talked.

"What are you doing out here, Clarkston?" Sam asked.

"I just told you, Blackman. I'm going to drill a well." Clarkston paused, folding his fingers into his palm and studying the tips of the manicured nails for a moment. "Yesterday Nolan and Donovan sold me the lease on these six acres. I'm going to drill here, and I'm going to bring in this well, so you just go on back over there to Blackman Number One and play with washing the sand out of yours. We have work to do."

Sam's grin disappeared and his fist flew up, but Jake caught it in midair.

"Come on, Sam," the driller said. "Let's leave Mr. Clarkston to his playacting. We have *real* work waiting for us."

From that moment on, Sam was more determined than ever to bring in his well. Though it took a mighty will, he concentrated on his own work and tried not to look too often at the goings-on to the northwest.

On Wednesday morning, just before noon, the mud ran clear. It was time to remove the drill pipe.

The operation progressed smoothly for a couple of hours. Then, as they were removing one of the pieces of pipe, the well came in, flowing between the four-inch casing and the two-inch drill pipe.

Those who were smoking quickly dropped their cigarettes and crushed them beneath their booted toes.

"Hurry, men!" Sam called. "Get that drill pipe out!"

Muscles strained and nerves stretched to the breaking point. A tense silence reigned, broken only by an occasional oath or a command from Sam. Before the drill pipe could be removed, however, the well sanded up again, firmly sticking a piece of pipe.

For the remainder of that day and most of the rest, Sam and his crew attempted to fish out the drill pipe. Finally, on Thursday afternoon, Sam halted operations and called a meeting of the crew.

"I'm not a quitter," he said, holding up a restraining hand to stall the sudden grumbling. "I know you all want to see this well come in, probably almost as much as I do. But it isn't going to happen. Not with this well."

He bummed a cigarette from Jake and took an inordinate amount of time lighting it. "I'm not a smoker, either," he continued, coughing a bit from the harshness of the unaccustomed smoke, "but times like this call for a detour from the ordinary. Times like this are what turn a man to drink — and worse!"

The men laughed. Sam smiled. They'd needed to loosen up a bit.

"We may have to abandon this well, but we're not quitting. I'm not giving up. I knew there was oil here, and this well proved I was right."

"What are you going to do now?" one of the men asked.

"For now, we're all going to take a well-deserved break. When I sent Cook into town this morning for supplies, I told him to bring back some steaks and a keg of beer. We're going to have ourselves a barbecue tonight, and tomorrow we're going to start drilling another well."

Sam pointed due east. "In the morning, you're going to take down this derrick and move it right over there and start all over again. Jake will be here to supervise. In the meantime, I'm going back to town. I'm going to hole up in my room at the boardinghouse and try to figure out a way to control this sand — 'cause if we can't control the sand, fellows, we'll end up the same way all over again."

And so will King Clarkston, Sam thought. But he found no real pleasure in contemplating Clarkston's failure.

Chapter Eight

While Sam, Jake, and the crew out at Blackman Number One were eating steak, drinking beer, and talking about moving the rig, the members of the Jennings local of the Women's Christian Temperance Union were nibbling on finger sandwiches, sipping lemonade, and planning a way to foil Sam Blackman.

The purpose of the meeting shocked Prairie to her toes. She'd expected a typical agenda for this regularly scheduled W.C.T.U. gathering at the parsonage of the First Congregational Church. But Agnes Milhouse, the president, skipped right over greetings, roll call, and rallying song, choosing instead to rally the members with her impassioned speech.

"The drilling must be stopped!" the minister's wife shouted, her puffy face mottled with indignation. "I find no fault with new families moving into Jennings. I find no fault with prosperity. But we cannot afford to sacrifice all we hold dear. We cannot afford to compromise our principles for the sake of wealth. The coming of oil is destroying our peaceful town. Undesirable men are pouring in by the droves. Saloons and brothels are springing up everywhere, catering to their vulgar tastes. We must make every effort to maintain the moral fiber of this community."

Agnes continued speaking for some time, expounding on the evils of liquor and tobacco and quoting statistics which would have been staggering had the members not heard them repeatedly: "Annually in this country, eleven million dollars is paid out for Christian missions while six hundred thirty million is spent on tobacco and an astounding one billion two hundred million on liquor."

At long last, the minister's rotund wife concluded her diatribe with a truly astonishing statement. "We can put a stop to this offensive influence," she said, emphasizing each phrase with a pound of her fist upon the speaker's stand, "by forcing the departure of those who are perpetrating it."

Ruth Nolan stood and was recognized. "The drilling was not accidental, Agnes. You're forgetting that my husband started it."

"And mine," Wynn added, foregoing formal recognition. "You'd better think twice, Agnes, about trying to run Doc and Michael out of town. You may find yourself tending bar in Beaumont."

A loud snicker arose from the group. Everyone knew, either firsthand or through the perpetual grapevine, about the Congregationalist minister's original attempt to run Wynn Donovan out of town back in '85, before she married Michael. Instead, the homesteaders put the Reverend Vanderhoeven on the train, and the last anyone heard of him, the man was tending bar in Beaumont.

"You misunderstand me, Wynn," Agnes said, the fan she employed with exaggerated vigor not hiding the obvious fluster on her face. "I'm suggesting we run Sam Blackman out of town, not Doc and Michael."

"Are you going to run King Clarkston out of town, too?" Lily Bidwell asked.

"King doesn't know anything about drilling for oil," Agnes argued.

"Besides which, he's one of the largest contributors to the church," Wynn whispered to Prairie.

"Chances are good he won't be successful," Agnes continued, glaring at Wynn. "It's Sam Blackman who concerns me. He's the expert, not King."

"But what if King is successful? What if others decide to drill? We can't stop everybody, Agnes," Lily countered.

"That's why we need to do something *now*. If we nip this problem in the bud, we will be effectively preventing future drilling."

"I don't know, Agnes. The possibility of there being oil around here has already boosted business in Jennings."

While Lily Bidwell cited her own accounting of increased commerce, Prairie watched her foster mother chew her bottom lip. She knew this discussion held many facets for Wynn, most of them quite personal. On the one hand, Wynn had to consider Michael's initial involvement in the oil business, and Prairie knew Wynn would do whatever was necessary to protect Michael from public scorn. On the other, if the W.C.T.U. did manage to halt drilling and dispense with Sam Blackman, the old hotel would revert to Wynn, and she could finally have her hospital.

"We managed just fine before," Hazel Kinnaird pointed out. "Jennings has shown continual growth in the past seventeen years. Why, we grew by over three hundred percent in the last decade, and settlers are still coming in. We're as big as Abbeville and almost half the size of Lafayette. We don't need oil. I say Agnes is right. Let's get rid of Mr. Blackman."

As opinions flew and the discussion became steadily more heated, Prairie paid less and less attention. Good Lord! she thought. If these women had their way, Sam Blackman would soon be heading back to Beaumont. She wasn't the least bit sure she liked that idea.

With him would go as well most of the new families who'd moved into town in the past few weeks. She'd seen the light of hope in the eyes of children who'd never enjoyed such simple pleasures as three square meals a day or more than one change of clothes, much less a new wagon or store-bought doll. Those hopes would be dashed without oil—without Sam Blackman.

Yes, Sam had brought hope to Jennings. Hope and excitement and a spirit of adventure. And these women wanted to take all that away. She'd called them self-righteous to David, and that's what some of them were, too. A bunch of self-righteous fuddy-duddies! Prairie solidified her assessment with a firm nod.

She had her own personal reasons for not wanting Sam to leave, but they were less concrete. She knew only that her heart had never felt so full, her soul so invigorated as when she was with Sam. If he should leave, she would manage, just as Hazel had said. But since she'd met Sam, Prairie had left part of her life behind—a part marked by a peculiar loneliness. She had no desire to return to it.

Whether or not Sam brought in his well would make little difference for her, she supposed. Regardless of what happened, he would leave eventually, and then the loneliness would return. The thought saddened her.

A tug on her sleeve interrupted her preoccupation.

"Let me take your plate and glass, dear," Wynn said.

"Oh! Of course," Prairie said, coming out of her reverie and noting that the meeting was breaking up. What had been resolved? she wondered. What had they decided to do about Sam Blackman? Why hadn't she paid more attention? She felt as though she would burst without knowing, but she dared not ask right there in the Milhouse parlor and expose her lack of attention to the entire membership of the W.C.T.U.

"Wynn," she hissed to her foster mother's back, "may I walk you home?"

"Certainly. Just give me a few minutes to help Ruth in the kitchen."

Prairie collected their shawls from the back of the dark green velvet settee where they had sat, then moved quickly into the front hall to await Wynn. As the women filed out, some of them took her hand and patted it and murmured enigmatic phrases she could make no sense of: "Good luck, Prairie," and "God go with you, child." She smiled and said "Thank you" without having a clue as to what was going on.

Her mind was racing with possibilities when Wynn slipped her shawl from the crook of Prairie's arm, then replaced it with her hand.

"You haven't signed the petition, Wynn," Agnes said, her voice accusatory, her bulk blocking the door. She held out a sheet of paper and inclined her head toward the hall table, upon which rested a fountain pen and inkwell.

"I want to think about it, Agnes. So does Ruth. We have a few days, you know."

Agnes wagged a thick finger. "Not long, Wynn. We want this matter resolved before the Sunday train comes through. You'll see to it on Saturday, won't you, Prairie?"

Prairie blinked inanely and muttered, "Ma'am?" But as the paper was thrust into her hands, the score of possibilities she'd been chasing around in her head coalesced into one obvious truth. Somehow, she'd managed to agree to deliver the petition. "Oh, yes, ma'am," she said then, pasting a smile on her face and scurrying past the formidable Mrs. Milhouse.

The minute they closed the picket fence gate, Wynn laughed softly. "The scrapes you get yourself into, Prairie!" she teased.

"How did this happen? What does this petition say?"

"It asks Sam Blackman to abandon the well, to pull out and leave Jennings."

Prairie stopped walking and turned to face Wynn. "He isn't going to do that! Why, he'll laugh in my face!"

Wynn chuckled. "Probably."

"Well, pardon me if I don't see any humor in it!" Prairie snapped. "And I never agreed to deliver this—" she shook the paper, making it rattle "—this ridiculous document. I'm taking it back right now."

"Yes, you did and no, you're not." Wynn moved forward again, pulling Prairie along with her. "Come along, dear," she coaxed. "This night air isn't doing my leg any good."

"No, I didn't. I wasn't even listening, Wynn. How could I have said I'd do this?"

"You didn't actually *say* you would. Agnes asked you and you nodded."

Prairie gave that revelation a bit of thought, then said, "That must have been about the time I was calling her a self-righteous fuddy-duddy."

"You didn't!" Wynn sounded more amused than annoyed.

"Not out loud, of course. You taught me better than that, Wynn."

"Well, I like the sound of it. I may just call her a self-righteous fuddy-duddy to her face."

"Be my guest. But that won't solve my problem.

123

What am I going to do about this petition?"

"You're going to deliver it, dear, and without my signature on it. I'd like nothing better than to have the old hotel building back for my hospital, but I won't be a party to expulsion." Wynn shivered. "A self-righteous fuddy-duddy tried that on me once, and I'll carry the memory of my anguish to the grave."

"I don't want to sign this thing either," Prairie said.

"Then don't. Just put it in Sam Blackman's hands. Winkle can drive you out to the well on Saturday. Do you want to come in for a few minutes?"

Prairie looked around and wondered how long they'd been standing on Wynn's brick walk. "No, thanks. Before you go in, though, please tell me why I was the one chosen for this abominable task. Surely someone else—"

"You are the perfect candidate—a lovely young woman who those fuddy-duddies think can charm Sam Blackman into anything. Personally, I think you're perfect for another, entirely different reason."

"And that is?"

"It will give you a legitimate reason to see him again. Sam's sweet on you, Prairie. Didn't you know that?"

Prairie shrugged. "He seems to like me—sort of. And I like him. I can't do this!" she protested.

"Yes, you can. Think about it, Prairie. If you care about Sam Blackman at all, think about it. Men can be such idiots sometimes. Sam has spent a small fortune trying to draw oil out of this ground, and he will bankrupt himself continuing to try—unless someone persuades him to quit. That petition won't do it, but you might be able to. Beaumont isn't that far," she added. "If Sam wants to court you, he'll be back."

"You wouldn't mind if he did court me, would you, Wynn?"

"No."

"Why does Michael dislike him so much?" Prairie's voice caught in her throat.

Wynn hugged Prairie against her chest and said in a tone of confidentiality, "It's not that Michael doesn't like him. Michael's afraid of Sam Blackman."

Prairie gasped in astonishment. She couldn't imagine Michael being afraid of anyone. "Why?"

"Sam reminds him of everything he was twenty years ago — reckless, daring, impulsive, sometimes imprudent. That frightens him. He's worried that you'll fall in love with Sam."

"And what would be so bad about that?"

"Sam isn't the kind of man who commits to a relationship. He isn't the marrying kind."

Prairie thought about that for a moment, then asked, "And Michael was like that?"

Wynn laughed. "Yes, dear, he was. Which is why I'm not worried at all."

Prairie shifted her weight from one foot to the other and glanced again into the hall at the narrow staircase. She didn't know why she kept looking. The steps creaked so loud she'd be able to hear him coming downstairs.

Lily Bidwell kept a neat but homey parlor, replete with comfortable seating, fresh-cut flowers, and a neatly folded copy of the latest *Times* on the dark mahogany coffee table. The sight of the newspaper made Prairie cringe. She wondered if Sam had seen this issue yet and knew in the depths of her soul that he had.

If Jonas Richardson had just bided his time . . . If Sam had just stayed out at the rig like everyone expected him to, her task would have been much easier.

But Sam had returned to the boardinghouse yesterday and Jonas had published an editorial this morning about the W.C.T.U. petition. There was no way Jonas could have seen the actual document, since Prairie had kept it under lock and key, but he knew what was in it, almost to the letter. More than likely, Agnes had been the one to fill him in. Agnes Milhouse suffered from a severe case of indiscretion.

The editorial destroyed any element of surprise. Sam was bound to know about the petition; he just didn't know when he would get it or who would bring it to him.

She was willing to bet he knew now, or at least had a pretty good idea. Prairie wished for the nine hundredth time that she wasn't that person. All day long she'd moved from one activity to another — cleaning house, hand-washing undergarments, mending stockings — anything that would postpone the inevitable meeting with Sam. While the chores occupied her hands, they didn't require much mental energy. That left a lot of room for contemplation.

About mid-afternoon, she admitted defeat and drew water for a bath. This activity she managed to drag out for almost two hours by washing her hair, applying a mud mask to her face, manicuring her hands and pedicuring her feet, then brushing her hair out in long strokes until it dried. She spent another hour dressing her hair and selecting a gown, hat, gloves, and parasol. Finally, seeing no further alternative, she set out for Miss Bidwell's boardinghouse.

She'd been standing in Lily's homey parlor for almost ten minutes, waiting for Sam Blackman to come downstairs. The longer she waited, the more fidgety she became. But Wynn was right, she'd decided. Someone needed to save the wildcatter from himself. And perhaps she was the person to do it.

Whether Sam would appreciate her effort she couldn't know. She knew she couldn't imagine him giving in to the whims of a group of self-righteous fuddy-duddies. That thought brought a wisp of a smile to her face and a flutter to her heart.

Sam paused in his descent three steps down from the landing and stood staring at Prairie Jernigan's back. Slanted rays from the late afternoon sun streamed through the parlor windows, gilding the light blue and black striped taffeta of her gown and the poufs of blue chiffon, black lace, and large yellow roses adorning her hat. The tall concoction added several inches to her stature, but Sam had realized weeks before that what Prairie lacked in height, she made up for in grace and poise.

As though she felt his scrutiny, her back stiffened and she turned, slowly, hesitantly, toward him. The hat cast her face in shadow but it could not hide the quick intake of breath or the sudden tightening of her gloved fist upon the black lace parasol hanging at her side. So! She felt guilty. And rightly so.

"Where are you hiding it?" he asked, his gaze perusing her figure as he resumed his descent.

"Pardon?"

"Not inside that close-fitting jacket, though perhaps under its lapels." He paused for a moment, pursing his lips as he considered the notion, then shaking his head and taking another step. "Not inside that hip-hugging skirt, though perhaps under the wide flounce at the bottom."

"Whatever are you babbling about?" she demanded.

Unperturbed, he continued his discourse and his

descent. "My guess is it's concealed somewhere within that cobweb of blue chiffon on your head. Or—"

His foot hit the floor and he quickly closed the distance between them. "Or, you've stuck it down inside this parasol."

Before she could stop him, Sam snatched the parasol out of her hand and opened it.

Prairie giggled.

Sam's good humor evaporated and his voice became sharp. "What's so funny?"

"You are! Standing here in Lily's parlor with a lady's parasol over your head!" she tittered.

He tried to close the black lace contraption but couldn't make it work. In frustration, he shoved it back at her and proceeded to flip back the white lapels, which were embroidered with black French knots.

"Don't even consider it," she said, snapping the parasol closed.

"Don't consider what?"

"Looking under my skirt. If you try it, I'll wallop you with this parasol."

He smiled despite himself. "I know you brought it, Prairie. Where is it?"

"Where is what?"

"Don't stand there simpering and pretend you don't know, young lady."

She planted her hands on her hips and gave him stare for stare. "I don't simper!"

"The hell you don't! You're playing games with me again, Prairie Jernigan."

From the vicinity of the hall, a cough resounded. Sam ignored it, but Prairie cut her eyes toward the sound. "People are coming downstairs," she hissed.

"Yes. It's suppertime."

He narrowed his eyes at her; she followed suit. He

clenched his jaw; she clenched hers. In unmasked irritation, he grasped her elbow and steered her unceremoniously toward the door.

"Where are we going?"

"For a walk."

"I don't feel like walking!"

"Then we'll sit in Lily's garden for a spell. Or don't you feel like sitting either?"

"You don't have to be so contrary!"

"And you don't have to be so sneaky." He couldn't help grinning at her gasp and then the way her pouty mouth snapped shut.

The screen door banged closed behind them. He led her down the steps, around the house to the lovely cottage garden in the rear, and over to a wrought-iron bench set among mounds of yellow, lavender, and white chrysanthemums.

Prairie sneezed.

"Do you have a hanky?" he asked, pulling a large one from his pocket.

"Yes," she managed, taking his and sneezing violently into it. "It's the mums," she said, sneezing again.

"The mums?" he asked in genuine bewilderment.

"They make me sne—hahchoo!"

"Do pansies make you sneeze?" he asked.

"I—hahchoo! I don't think so."

"Let's find out."

Moments later, they were seated on another bench in the far corner of the garden, well away from the chrysanthemums. Sam allowed her time to wipe her watery eyes with her own clean handkerchief before he recommenced with the grilling.

"Are you or are you not a member of the Women's Certified Teetotalers Union?"

Prairie laughed. "Yes and no."

"It's one or the other, Prairie, not both."

"If you're referring to the Women's *Christian Temperance* Union, then the answer is yes, I'm a member."

Sam shrugged. "They're one and the same."

"Maybe." She wiped her eyes again, but Sam suspected this time the tears resulted from mirth rather than a sensitivity to mums.

"I've never heard anyone call us 'Certified Teetotalers' before," she continued, "but I suppose that's what we are. At least that's what Agnes Milhouse and Hazel Kinnaird and most of the others are. I can't honestly say that I share their zeal."

"Then why do you belong?"

"It's expected of me, as a teacher—and as the daughter of the mayor. Ruth and I co-chair the Jennings Public School Anti-Tobacco League."

There! She'd said it, said she was Michael's daughter. It gave him the opening he'd been waiting for and he took it. "I wish you'd explain something to me," he said.

"What?"

"Why your name is Jernigan."

"Because the Donovans aren't my natural parents. I'm surprised someone hasn't already told you the story," she said. "It's common knowledge. I must have been about four when I came here with my father. I was sick and he left me with Wynn. They found him later by the river, a victim of diphtheria. There was an epidemic. No one knew if I had any relatives or where they might be, so Wynn and Michael became my legal guardians."

"And that's it?"

Prairie twirled the tassel on the end of her parasol, not meeting his probing gaze. "Basically."

Sam was sure she wasn't telling him everything. "Haven't you ever wondered if you have relatives somewhere?"

"Of course."

"But you've never tried to find them?"

"Where would I look?"

"Well, you could always . . . or you could . . ." His voice trailed off as he pondered the situation. She had to remember something else. He was certain she did, but it was really none of his business. So he said, "You're right. Where would you look?"

"Wynn and Michael have been good to me," she said. "I couldn't have asked for better foster parents."

"Why do you call them by their first names?"

"At first, I called them Dr. Wynn and Mr. Donovan. That was before they got married. Since I knew they weren't my real parents, I didn't feel comfortable calling them Mother and Daddy, or Mama and Papa, or whatever. Michael insisted I call him Mr. Michael, and later, when I was much older, they asked me to drop the titles altogether. So I did."

Neither said anything else for awhile and Sam felt the tension building between them. Prairie had the W.C.T.U. petition. He knew she did. And he'd told her he knew she had it. He supposed the next move ought to be hers.

"There's something I need to discuss with you," Prairie said finally.

"Yes?" he prompted.

"You've read the paper?"

"Yep."

"So you know the 'Certified Teetotalers' are blaming you for the influx of what they consider undesirable elements into Jennings society."

"Do you blame me, Prairie?" he asked, his voice whisper soft.

"No, Sam. But I am worried about you — worried about your investment. People are saying you can't

131

control the sand, that you're wasting time and money even trying to. And now, they say, King Clarkston has fallen into your trap. If he fails, Sam, they'll blame you for that, too. King is one of their own. They could become vicious. Perhaps you should give up. No one would think less of you if you called it quits."

"I would. And it's me I have to live with for the rest of my life, Prairie, not the gossips in Jennings. I don't care what they think."

"But what about the sand?" she asked. Is it true that the well came in again, then sanded right back up like before?"

Sam planted his elbows on his knees and leaned forward, resting his chin on an upturned palm. "Yes, it's true. But I'm working on that. There has to be a way to make it work. That's why I came back to town, where I could be by myself and think about it."

"Have you come up with any ideas yet?"

"Not really. But I will." He sat back and looked at her, long and hard. "Has life ever challenged you, Prairie? Demanded that you beat it at its own game?"

A cloud fell over her features and he watched her focus on the bed of pansies, their vivid colors as muted in the gray light as her expression. "Yes," she whispered.

"And did you meet its challenge? Did you win?"

"Not yet." She shuddered, then lifted her head and met his probing gaze. Her voice was firm, her tone full of conviction. "But I will, Sam. God help me, I will!"

Sam couldn't avoid wondering about her particular challenge, but she offered no explanation. She was quiet for a moment, her hands occupied with opening her reticule and removing a piece of paper that

132

had been folded over and over itself until it was a small, thick square.

"This was not my idea, Sam," she said, handing him the square. "You won't even find my signature on it. I want to see you succeed. Truly, I do. I didn't know how much I wanted you to succeed until just now."

He shoved the folded square into the inside pocket of his jacket, then lifted her right hand and began to remove the black kid glove, one finger at a time.

"What are you doing?" she gasped.

"Lesson number two," he said. "Hush and enjoy it."

Chapter Nine

Slowly, methodically, he removed the glove, his fingertips caressing the back of her hand and the lengths of her fingers with light, sensuous strokes. When her hand was finally free of its covering, he traced her lifeline with his forefinger.

Prairie shivered as waves of pleasure rippled through her. A small voice bade her protest this sinful, wicked feeling, but it was only a small voice, and one easily silenced.

He captured the other hand and began to remove its glove in a similar manner. When both hands were bare, he lifted them, kissed the back of first one and then the other, lingering over each one. He turned her hands over and planted his lips on the sensitive flesh of her palm. A nest of warmth curled deep inside her, its embers spiraling outward with each flick of his tongue upon her skin. The fire grew hotter when he moved his mouth to her other palm.

Her breath was coming in short pants and a thin film of perspiration broke out on her brow and upper lip. Her eyelids grew heavy and slid shut while her mouth fell open and her tongue flicked out to moisten lips suddenly gone dry. The fire he'd started leapt to her heart, consuming her, and at the same time, making her feel curiously empty.

When his mouth left her palm and he folded her

hands into his, she waited breathlessly for the taste of his lips upon hers.

"Are you hungry?" he asked, his mouth close to hers, his breath sweet, his voice soft.

"Famished," she breathed, waiting.

"Me, too. Let's go eat."

She didn't believe she'd heard him correctly. "What?" she gasped, her eyes flying open in astonishment. But already he was pulling her to her feet.

"Lily serves fried chicken for Saturday supper—with big, flaky biscuits and rice and lots of gravy. And there's peach cobbler for dessert."

"But, Sam!" she protested, pulling against his tow. "That was—"

"Lesson two," he finished for her, his voice blatantly casual. "Did you learn anything?"

"Yes, but—" *Did you feel anything?* she wanted to ask, but her instincts warned against linking emotion to his lessons, against putting her heart into his hands.

"Be careful where you step. These bricks aren't level."

Her infuriation at his casual attitude overrode instinct. "Sam Blackman!" she railed, tugging him to a halt. "You are the most exasperating man I've ever met!"

"Good, because you're the most exasperating woman I've ever met. I believe that makes us even."

Prairie tried a different tack. "Just how many women have you schooled in the art of kissing before?"

"None. You're the first."

"So these lessons . . . you're making them up as you go along?"

"Yep. Improvisation, pure and simple. That's what I'm good at. That's why I know I can devise something that will keep the wells around here from sanding up."

"Oil is never far from your thoughts, is it?"

135

"Never. It's my life."

He opened the back door and held it for Prairie to enter ahead of him. She stepped over the threshold, then turned around, blocking his entrance. "What will you do, Sam, after you bring the well in?"

"Do?" He shrugged. "Find another challenge, I suppose."

"And that means leaving Jennings?" Never, when she'd posed the question mentally, had it hurt as this verbalization did.

"Probably. But don't worry," he said, grinning, the light spilling down from the front hall catching the twinkle in his blue eyes. He tucked a crooked finger beneath her chin, leaned forward, and brushed her lips with his. "I'll be around long enough to finish our lessons."

His indifference stabbed at her heart. "This is all a game to you, isn't it?" she cried. "And I'm nothing more than a pawn for you to pick up and twirl in your fingers while you plan your strategy."

Sam let go of her chin, trailing his finger down her neck and over the brooch attached to the high collar of her shirtwaist. As though stung, he snatched his finger away, tucked his hands into his trouser pockets, and looked off down the hall.

"I don't mean to toy with you, Prairie. I like you, honestly I do." He frowned then, and his shoulders sagged into a slump. "Why must women expect a commitment from every man who gives them a second look? Why can't women and men be friends?"

She swallowed hard and fought back the wave of disappointment that threatened to steal her composure. "Is that all you want from me? Friendship?"

"For the time being. Who knows what either of us will want a few months down the road?" He wrapped an arm around her shoulder and hugged her against his side. "But for now, I need you, Prairie. You're the only friend I have in this town, and everyone needs a

136

friend. Please don't try to turn our relationship into anything more."

Prairie tucked her head into Sam's shoulder, effectively hiding, she hoped, the rush of tears pricking at her eyes. Wynn had told her about men like Sam—but she'd also said Michael had been like him once. Prairie didn't know another man as committed to marriage, as committed to his wife and family as Michael Donovan was. And Sam's question about the future gave her hope.

She reminded herself that she could easily be married if she wanted to be. But marriage in itself wasn't enough. She'd refused both David and King for two reasons: neither stirred her blood, and she herself wasn't ready to commit to a relationship. Not until she uncovered her roots. Just being with Sam Blackman excited her, but she didn't suppose she was ready for a commitment any more than he was.

Nevertheless, she wanted more from him than friendship. She didn't want the same sort of relationship with Sam that she had with David, but she decided she'd take whatever she could get. And she wouldn't let him know how much it hurt her to settle for so much less than she wanted.

Though it would be difficult, answering him was necessary. "All right, Sam. I'll be your friend. That's what I want, too."

His voice was as husky as hers. "Are you sure?"

Prairie willed a firmness into her voice she didn't feel. "Yes, Sam, I'm sure. Now, let's go eat some of that fried chicken you promised me."

Later that night, alone in his room, Sam unfolded the piece of paper Prairie had given him and read the demands issued by the W.C.T.U.

"Whereas," the petition began.

"Whereas?" he muttered to himself. *Whereas?* Did

they think they were writing a law or something? A cursory glance revealed more whereases and a number of wherefores with a few wherebys thrown in for good measure. But it all boiled down to one simple fact: The women who had signed the petition blamed him for the sudden increase in liquor and tobacco sales and the presence of the painted hussies who operated out of Madame Angelique's striped tent. In essence, they thought if he packed up and left town, so would the bartenders and the hussies.

Why, the very idea was ludicrous! He hadn't invited those people to Jennings. No one had. They had come of their own free will. They stayed because the law allowed them to.

But he, Sam Blackman, *had* been invited—by two of the town's most prominent citizens, one of whom was the mayor. Sam wondered what Nolan and Donovan thought about the petition. He scanned the list and noted the absence of both Ruth's and Wynn's signatures. At least their wives weren't against him. Nor, did it seem, was Prairie.

He'd left the rig and come to town in search of peace and quiet—and run right into a hornet's nest. But he had his own ideas about how to clear up some of the problems.

He put the petition in the top drawer of the bureau, undressed down to his undershirt and drawers, and hung his suit over the valet. On the table by his bed lay a copy of Pampas J. Rose's latest dime novel, *Sacramento Sam, or A Sawbones Redeems Himself.* The vendor had saved this copy for Wayne, who swore it was Rose's best one yet.

Sam hoped it was. He needed to lose himself in someone else's troubles. He stretched out on top of the quilt, piled both pillows at his back, and picked up the thin paperback. For a long time, he stared at the name on the cover. *Pampas J. Rose.*

Why did that name seem so familiar to him? he

wondered anew. Never in his life had he known anyone named Pampas. It was such an unusual name, almost feminine-sounding. Pampas. He'd heard the
word before, but as a word, not a name. He was sure
of that. But what did it mean? What was a pampas?

Sam made a mental note to look it up in the first
dictionary he came across, but he refused to let it
bother him anymore that night. He might not know
what a pampas was, but he'd been to Sacramento. It
would be interesting to see if Mr. Rose had ever been
there, too.

When Sybil James left the dry goods store in Welsh
at ten that evening, she had every intention of going
straight home. But she had no intention of walking
the three miles out to the family farm, not if she could
help it — not after standing on her feet all day. More
than likely, she wouldn't have to. Someone almost always offered her a lift.

She paused outside the store, looking up the street
one direction, then down it the other. Although there
were a few farm wagons and buckboards and a number of saddled horses lining the street, none of them
were moving. Oh, well, she thought, setting off toward home, someone would come along eventually.

Sybil didn't mind working at the dry goods store.
The job gave her an excuse to be in town every day,
away from the drudgery of the farm, and an opportunity to meet eligible bachelors. Her family needed the
money she made to purchase things like shoes and
food the farm didn't provide, but she wished sometimes her parents would let her keep just a little bit of
her wages for things like handkerchiefs and parasols.

If she didn't catch a ride, though, she did mind the
long walk home every night, especially on Saturday
when the store was open late. She couldn't understand
why her daddy wouldn't let her ride one of the horses

139

or send Nick, the oldest of the three boys, to get her. At sixteen, he was plenty old enough. Why, she was only eighteen herself and she'd been working at the store for nigh on to three years now.

But there was no accounting for her father's reasoning on the matter. He either refused to listen to her pleas or slapped her for questioning his wisdom.

At the outskirts of town, Sybil paused long enough to remove her shoes and stockings, then recommenced walking, enjoying the feel of the squishy sand between her toes. A lopsided moon rose high overhead, so bright it was hard to see the stars, and the night air smelled crisp and clean.

When she heard the low thrum of an engine approaching from behind, she jumped off the road, half terrified. What in the world was it? she wondered, staring into the darkness and seeing a single bright light coming toward her.

The driver, who was dressed all in black, braked to a halt, dropping one booted foot to the ground to brace the two-wheeled vehicle with the sputtering engine. Silvery moonlight ricocheted off the shiny black surface of the vehicle and glistened in the driver's black eyes.

"Well, hello there, young lady," he said, his voice as smooth and slick as his black leather jacket. "Where you heading?"

"Home," she croaked, her nervousness pitching her voice high.

"And where's home?" he asked.

Sybil swallowed and raised a pointing finger. "A few miles down the road."

"You want a lift?"

Her eyes bugged and she turned the pointing finger to the contraption he straddled. "On *that* thing?"

He hiked one shoulder. "Haven't you ever seen a motorcycle before?"

"No."

"Well, hop on behind me," he invited with a grin, "and I'll show you what this baby can do."

Sybil hesitated the briefest of moments. After all, it was a lift. "Just let me put my shoes back on."

No matter how hard she willed them to stop, Prairie's hands wouldn't quit tingling. She'd washed them thoroughly, soaked them in warm water, and massaged them with milkweed cream, but none of those measures made a smidgen of difference. Twice she climbed into bed, hoping sleep would eradicate the tingle—or at least make her oblivious to it, but she discovered the tingle prevented rest.

Around midnight, she gave up the fight, lit the lamps in her study next to the bedrom, and sat down at her desk. It was time to start another story, and she supposed a sleepless night was as good a time as any to begin one. Besides, she reasoned, writing provided for her a better escape than any other activity. And tonight she needed to escape from the memory of Sam's touch and her discontentment over his request for her friendship alone.

When she'd first started writing, Prairie couldn't finish one book before another cast of characters began parading themselves through her brain, a forgivable annoyance. Such had not been the case recently, however. She'd been desperate for an idea when she'd met Sam. And now, almost two weeks since she'd put Prospector Pete's story to rest, Prairie didn't have a single idea for another dime novel.

She rolled a sheet of paper into the old Remington, placed her tingling fingers upon the worn keys, and sat staring at the blank page until she thought she would go stark raving mad. After awhile, she got up, made herself a cup of tea, and sat down in the dark kitchen, trying to summon the muse as she sipped the hot, sweet beverage. But all she could think about was

141

Sam Blackman—and the petition from the W.C.T.U.

That was a story in itself, she realized—and one worth telling, if she could disguise it well enough. Her protagonist would be a white woman, she decided, raised by Indians, struggling to regain her heritage and establish a sense of self in a small Texas town full of narrow-minded people who, in the end, discovered her to be their liberator rather than their nemesis.

Would Sam prove to be Jennings's liberator? she wondered, wishing she could shape events for him as easily as she could for her fictional characters.

She rinsed out the teacup and returned to her desk, where she spent most of the night filling page after page with the story of Cherokee Sally and her half-breed son, Wolf's Leg. Where had that name come from? Prairie wondered, somehow convinced she'd heard the strange, almost nonsensical name before.

Sam put the book on the table, turned out the lamp, and stretched out in the bed, propping the soles of his feet against the footboard. He folded his arms, laid one palm inside the other, rested his head on his hands—and smiled.

Rose was a good writer. Sam couldn't deny that. The man had a knack for dialect, seemed to understand human nature, and could spin a tale almost as well as Mark Twain. But Pampas J. Rose had never been to Sacramento—probably hadn't visited most of the places he wrote about. For some reason Sam couldn't put a mental finger on, knowing that about Rose pleased him.

"I wish you'd quit that infernal pacing and sit down," Michael Donovan said irritably, waving his hand at the empty chair in front of his desk.

Sam ignored him. "You have to do something to appease these women—and quick!"

Seemingly unperturbed by Sam's fervor, the mayor leaned back in his chair, steepled his fingers, and rested his chin on his fingertips. "I wouldn't put much stock in that petition, if I were you."

"It's not the petition," Sam declared, stopping in front of Donovan and laying his palms flat upon the top of the desk. "It's those women! Since they learned I was back at the boardinghouse, they haven't given me a moment's peace. They come and go, all day long and well into the evening, every day. Poor Lily's wearing her legs out trotting up and down the stairs."

"Tell her to ignore them."

Sam threw up his hands and commenced pacing again. "I did tell her that! I told her to tell them I wasn't in, but they just march right up the stairs and pound on my door anyway."

"Why not leave during the day?" Michael suggested. "I know you have an office in town. I own the building, remember?"

"Yeah, I remember, and so do those women! Don't you think I tried that?" Sam stopped in front of the desk again. "Look, Donovan, you have to do something. I came to town for some peace and quiet so I could figure out a way to hold the sand back. I know you and Enoch don't have much financial interest in the well anymore, not since you sold out to Clarkston, but can't you see what oil would mean to this town? We're talking jobs, Donovan, scores and scores of jobs, and money pouring in as fast as the oil flows out. But there won't be any jobs and there won't be any money, because there won't be any oil if I can't keep the wells from sanding up. You have to get those women off my back!"

"They're not doing anything illegal, Blackman. I can't have them arrested, so what do you suggest I do?"

143

"Have the Board of Commissioners pass an ordinance prohibiting saloons and brothels within the city limits. If we can move them out of town, the Certified Teetotalers won't have anything else to complain about."

Michael snorted good-naturedly. "Oh, they'll find something to complain about, Blackman. Believe me, they will. But you may have an idea there. I'm not so sure about the saloons—we've had them in town for years, though certainly not so many, and never any with gambling rooms before. The problem with moving the saloons is that the married men can hang out there without causing too much of a stink at home. But the brothels—now, that's a different story. The men would probably appreciate a more discreet location for them."

"So you'll try it?" Sam asked hopefully.

Michael nodded. "I'll draft a resolution and present it to the Board of Commissioners when they meet next week. I don't believe we'll have any opposition at all to moving the brothels."

Sam offered Michael his hand and was rewarded by a firm shake. "Thanks, Donovan. I owe you one."

"You don't owe me anything, Blackman. If you can make the oil flow, I'll owe you one. You're a better man than I'd pegged you for."

Sam grinned. "Does that mean I have your blessings where courting Prairie is concerned?"

A menacing frown cut a deep ridge into Michael's forehead, emphasizing his hawk's nose. "You need to understand something about teachers, Blackman, or rather about school boards. Most of them enforce strict rules concerning courting, especially by female teachers. The fact that we don't have an official school board here doesn't give you the right to free rein with her. Her conduct must always be beyond reproof. And if you hurt her, Sam, you'll have to contend with me. Do you understand?"

"Yes, Michael," Sam said, his expression serious. "I understand completely. I wouldn't expect less of you."

Prairie's heart skipped a beat when she opened her mailbox and saw the envelope from David. Was it possible? she wondered, tucking the letter down inside her parasol before she moved over to the counter to purchase a stamp from Hazel.

She needn't have bothered to hide it.

"I see you got your letter from your gentleman friend in Lafayette," Hazel observed, winking conspiratorially at Prairie.

"Yes, ma'am," Prairie murmured in a voice as polite as she could manage, hoping Hazel would drop the subject. "Could I have a two-cent stamp, please?"

"Of course, my dear." The postmistress took an inordinate amount of time folding and tearing the stamp from the sheet. "I guess you delivered the petition?"

"Yes, ma'am," Prairie murmured again, groaning inwardly. Why, oh, why couldn't there be another customer waiting behind her? Hazel would never question her with another customer present.

"How did Mr. Blackman take it?" Hazel asked, returning the sheet to her drawer and then pushing the stamp across the counter.

Prairie decided she'd had just about enough of this interrogation. She winked back at Hazel and grinned wickedly. "He took it in his hands, of course. And then he shoved it into a place where the sun doesn't shine."

Hazel's face turned the identical shade of red as the pompon on her silly-looking sailor hat. "You are — well, you're impertinent, that's what you are, Prairie Jernigan. I told Agnes she shouldn't have asked you." She took Prairie's nickel and practically threw it into the drawer, then she thrust her fingers into the penny section and drew out three coppers. "Here's your change."

"Thanks." Prairie sailed toward the door, her smile growing broader with each step. At the door, she turned and waved. "Have a nice day!"

She laughed most of the way home, the letter in her parasol momentarily forgotten. But as soon as she opened her door and reached to hang the parasol's loop over one of the brass hooks on her hall tree, she remembered it.

Her fingers trembled when she broke the seal. Her hands shook as she removed the smaller envelope nestled inside. Her gaze flew to the postmark: Texarkana, Texas, and then to the return address: Mrs. Albert Byers.

Prairie took a deep breath and then another, but her heart refused to return to its normal, steady beat. Tears collected in her eyes, blurring her vision, and her knees sagged. She plopped down into the nearest chair, a platform rocker that popped with the sudden burden, then tilted back crazily, teetered precariously, and threatened to spill her onto the floor. In reaction, her feet sailed up and her arms went wide.

When the chair settled back onto its platform, her feet hit the floor with a resounding thump and her heart stopped lurching. In reaction, Prairie pressed the letter against her breast and burst into laughter.

From behind the chair, a voice said, "Mind if I join in the mirth?"

The voice startled her into immediate silence and she jumped up. "Sam!" she gasped. "Where did you come from?"

He motioned toward the open front door. "I knocked, but I guess you didn't hear me, which is not surprising, considering the noise you were making in here. That letter must be awfully funny."

Prairie looked down at the envelope she clutched against her bodice, the envelope that was addressed to

146

Pampas J. Rose. Her eyes popped wide open and she felt the color drain from her face.

"No," she said quickly, sidestepping across the room to a low chest and pulling out a drawer. "I hadn't read it yet. It's just a letter from my aunt." She dropped the letter into the drawer.

"Your aunt?" he asked, obviously puzzled. "I thought you said you didn't have any relatives—none that you knew about."

"Uh, not *my* aunt," she spluttered. "Wynn's aunt . . . Martha. From Illinois."

"Oh."

She was handling it badly. He didn't look the least bit convinced. She had to do something, say something, and fast. She chose the obvious route. "What brings you here today?"

It worked—she thought. At least his expression softened considerably. "You."

The single word caught her off guard. "Me?"

"Yes, you. I got a hankering to see you again. Plus, I had to get out of that boardinghouse before another one of your Certified Teetotalers showed up to ask me if I was leaving town." He took a step toward her.

With her hands behind her, she leaned back against the chest and pushed the drawer closed. "Well, are you?" she asked.

"What a leading question! Of course not! Did you expect me to?"

She shook her head. "No."

Sam glanced around the room. "Aren't you going to ask me to sit down?"

"Why don't we go for a walk?" she suggested. "The weather is lovely."

"Fine," he said. "Are you in the mood for a soda? We can walk down to the drugstore and order big, tall chocolate sodas with lots of foam on top."

"Sure. Why not?"

Relieved, Prairie collected her parasol and reticule,

and locked the door behind them.

"What were you laughing so hard about?" Sam asked.

Prairie laughed lightly, stalling while she scrambled for an explanation that would not require mentioning the letter, which was easy enough. "Hazel Kinnaird. Actually, it was something I said to her about you. Something you may not find so humorous."

On the way to the drugstore, she related the conversation. Sam did think it was funny. He laughed so hard people on the street stopped and stared at him.

"She had one thing right," he said through his laughter.

"What was that?"

"You *are* impertinent! I'm surprised they let you teach school."

Prairie drew her chest up and pinned him with a wounded look. "I'll have you know, Sam Blackman, that I'm a good teacher. I would never be impertinent with my students."

"No—just with defenseless little old ladies!"

"A few minutes ago, you were calling her a Certified Teetotaler. That doesn't sound so defenseless to me. Besides, she's a nosy old biddy. She deserved it."

He laughed. "I suppose she did."

They strolled into the drugstore and sat down on two of the stools in front of the soda fountain counter. Today, Prairie thought, she felt the friendship between them, but that didn't erase the deeper feelings Sam's mere presence stirred in her. Perhaps, with time, those feelings would dissipate. Until then, she supposed she'd have to learn to tolerate them. But at the moment, sitting next to him and knowing she had to maintain an air of platonic friendship was sheer agony.

She grasped for a subject, any subject. Something to take her mind off his chiseled lips and clear blue eyes. "Tell me how your project's going," she said.

"I have a couple of ideas, but the only way I can be sure they'll work is by actually trying them out."

"Which means?"

"Which means I'll have to set a device in place before the well comes in. If it doesn't work, the hole will just sand up again, and we'll be right back where we started. We'd have to drill another well to try a different device. That's expensive and time-consuming. I want to be sure in my mind that my device will work before I try it."

Sam paid for the sodas, then took a long swallow from his straw while Prairie absently swished her straw around in the semi-thick chocolate.

"There's no way to test it first?" she asked.

"None that I know about."

"What about King's well?"

"What about it?"

"If he brings his in first—without your device, it will more than likely sand up, too, won't it? Like Blackman Number One did?"

"Yep. Are you going to drink your soda, or just stir it all day?" he teased.

Prairie obliged him with a sip. "This is good. Thanks." She took another sip, her mind on King's predicament, a predicament she doubted King, being inexperienced in the oil field, fully appreciated. "Are you going to help him?"

"I don't know," Sam said. "Maybe. If he'll even let me."

That seemed to exhaust that particular subject and Prairie could think of no other, not with Sam so near—and not with the letter sitting in her drawer, waiting to be read. She drank her soda quickly, but Sam now seemed bent on lingering over his. The longer he dawdled, the more anxious she became.

Sam noticed it. "You're awfully jittery all of a sudden," he observed. "Am I holding you up from a date or something?" He grinned. "Is there a meeting of the

Certified Teetotalers tonight?"

"No." She chuckled. "It's not that. It's . . . well, I have some papers to grade and lessons to prepare. I really need to be getting back home. But finish your soda first, Sam," she added. "I'm not in that much of a hurry."

But she was. She was in a desperate hurry to read the letter from Mrs. Albert Byers.

Chapter Ten

Although she'd felt certain that she had, at last, found a relative, Prairie had answered the original letter from Mrs. Byers as Pampas J. Rose, routing her reply back through David and Beadle and Adams. Before she exposed herself as the successful dime novelist to anyone, including the elderly lady from Texarkana, Prairie had to know beyond a shadow of a doubt that the woman was, indeed, her aunt.

She had often wondered what direction her life would take at that point. Would she continue to teach school? To write anonymously as Pampas J. Rose? Would she disclose her true identity to her relatives and then request their confidentiality? Or would she go public and to heck with the consequences? Would she remain in Jennings, or move closer to her relatives? Could she make a living from her writing alone? Would Beadle and Adams continue to publish her works if they knew Pampas J. Rose was a woman?

Before, those questions had not required immediate answers. Should the letter she held in her hand provide the long-awaited evidence of her heritage, however, she would be forced to examine her alternatives.

Until recently, Prairie had not considered a romantic relationship to be among those alternatives, for marriage would surely be the death of her dual career. And then Sam Blackman had come along, a man who epitomized her idea of a hero, the only man she'd ever met who might be worth the sacrifice. But Sam had made it crystal clear that he wanted nothing more than friendship from her.

And he was right, she affirmed with a shaky nod of her chin. They both had their own personal challenges to face, their own personal byways to travel. At the moment, they stood at a crossroads of their perpendicular paths, waiting for a signal from life before continuing their individual journeys. Sam waited for the oil to flow, and she had only to open the letter to discover if her own waiting had finally reached its end.

Suddenly she didn't want to know, not if it meant embarking on a path that would take her away from Jennings, away from Wynn and Michael and the boys, away from Ruth and Doc and school — away from Sam. She should be eager to find out, she mentally berated herself, eager to read Mrs. Byers's response to her inquiries, eager to leave the crossroads and begin the next leg of her life's journey. But she wasn't.

Prairie wiped at the tears puddling in her eyes and ripped open the envelope.

"Dear Mr. Rose," the missive began, "I am writing this letter for my grandmother, who has taken to her bed with a bout of influenza. She wishes me to tell you she is much flattered that you think she may, perhaps, be your aunt, but she can offer little information to substantiate your claim. In fact, she is certain you are mistaken.

"She has no recollection of ever living near a town called Big Spring, nor can she remember any family member ever mentioning this place. Neither has she knowledge nor memory of a dragonfly brooch, nor of anyone named Martha or Susie.

"Her sister Annie, whom she mentioned in her previous letter to you, was born near St. Louis, Missouri, in the spring of 1839. Thus, if she still lives, Annie turned 62 this year. My grandmother has neither seen nor heard from her since 1855."

Anna had been young when she died, perhaps no

older than twenty-two, which would have placed her birth year at 1862 or later. Prairie was certain of that. She remembered Anna's smooth, unlined face and coal black hair too well.

Prairie let the letter fall to the table top and swiped at a tear that seemed determined to drip off her cheek and spoil the ink. She took a fortifying swallow of coffee, then another sip for good measure, and returned to the letter.

"As for toodlum gravy, my grandmother says she has no clue, other than she's never heard anyone use the term except her sister. It is, admittedly, an odd expression, but probably one with more widespread usage than we are aware.

"Since she is infirm, I read to her daily, and often from your work. You have moved her to laughter and tears, stirring memories and emotions in a most beneficial way, and for that we are both grateful. She bids me thank you for instructing Beadle and Adams to send her a collection of your novels, and to extend to you an invitation to visit us, should you ever travel to this area. We both wish you godspeed."

The letter was signed "Keith Murphy for Mrs. Lucy Byers."

So! Her name was Lucy.

Prairie racked her brain, trying to recall Anna's use of the name, but if her mother ever had, the memory evaded her. Despite the lack of such memory — even coupled with the elderly lady's belief that no relationship between them existed, Prairie was not convinced.

She picked up a pencil and scratched some dates onto the back of Lucy's envelope. Annie would have been sixteen when she left home — a marriageable age. She could have run off with a man, could have settled in Big Spring, could have had a daughter of her own she named Anna.

It was a fabrication, she knew, but not one without possibility of fact. Annie was old enough to be her grandmother, and Lucy had no idea what had happened to her. Prairie had always believed her mother had made up the word "toodlum," but now she wondered if perhaps Anna had learned it from her own mother. And if the fabrication were true, she had a grandmother named Annie somewhere. Big Spring, perhaps?

She carefully folded the letter, slipped it back into the envelope, and carried it to her room, where she put it in the stationery box with Lucy's other letter and the one from Aunt Martha.

Hope flowed again from the deep wellspring within her. Certain she was right, Prairie intended to plant these new clues, clues which might garner a letter from another possible relative, another link to her past. With an eagerness she hadn't felt for several days, Prairie returned to the story of Cherokee Sally.

He was waiting for her when she got off work—not out in front of the store where someone might see him and tell her daddy, but at the spot just out of town where she'd first met him the week before. Right where he told her he'd meet her again.

Sybil James grinned shyly at him, then looked away, her gaze skittering around. "Where's your motorcycle?"

He inclined his head toward a copse of trees. "Over there. Out of sight. I brought a quilt this time."

She followed him into the grove, thinking how strange it was that he never held her hand or touched her in any other way that could be considered affectionate. But what did she know about affection? she asked herself. What little knowledge she possessed was based on observation rather than experience. No one, including her parents, have ever even hugged her before, let alone held her hand or patted her on the shoulder.

Maybe it wouldn't hurt so much this time. But if it did, she would endure it. Pain was no stranger to her, and in the end, it would all be worth it. After all, he'd promised to marry her and take her away to live in a great big house with lots of servants. He said he would buy her anything her heart desired, and she could eat chocolate everyday if she wanted to.

From somewhere close by, an owl hooted, while overhead a breeze rustled the dry leaves still hanging on the trees. Sybil shivered and fell back a step. Then, reminding herself of the promise of servants and chocolate, she moved forward into the shadows, into the steel trap of his embrace.

Despite the trouble Sam had encountered with the oil sand, people continued to move into Jennings.

There were no ordinances on the books governing either building codes or restrictions. Pine shacks were going up everywhere, with no consideration as to beauty or stability, but rather how fast four walls and a roof could be put together.

Some of the shacks were houses, but most of them were intended for commercial use. The increased population required more stores, more hotels, more restaurants, more professional offices. And, catering to the pleasures of the men, opportunists provided saloons with gambling facilities and houses of prostitution. Scoffing at rumors that prostitution would soon be outlawed within the town proper, Madame Angelique had a brothel under construction, as did Cora Jones, another madam who had recently come to Jennings.

While many of the new residents were single men, families were moving in, too — families with school-age children.

"If this keeps up we'll have to add onto the school," Ruth observed to Prairie one afternoon as the students filed out to go home. "We're running out of room."

"No, Ruth, we *are* out of room," Prairie corrected. "I couldn't squeeze in one more child if I had to, and I doubt you could either."

They had run out of desks and chairs with the first wave of new settlers, forcing many students to sit on benches behind makeshift tables hastily constructed of planks nailed to sawhorses. Maintaining discipline in the overcrowded classrooms was becoming increasingly difficult.

"We're also going to need another teacher. Maybe two more," Ruth added. "Do you know what Michael's planning to do about it?"

"No. Why don't we go talk to him?"

Michael Donovan quickly set their worries to rest. "The Commissioners meet tonight," he reminded them, "and this issue is on the agenda. I foresee no opposition to expanding the schoolhouse and hiring additional teachers. Hopefully, we can begin construction within the next few weeks. What I can't promise you, though, is that the initial measures will be adequate. In fact, they may not even be necessary."

"But they are!" Ruth contended.

Michael agreed, in part. "At the moment, perhaps, and most assuredly in the future. I have no doubt Jennings will continue to grow at a steady rate even without oil, at least for the next decade or so. But this surge is totally dependent on Sam Blackman's ability to control the sand. Without the flow of oil, the boom will be short-lived. And heaven help us if he figures out how to do it."

"What do you mean?" Prairie asked.

"That what we've seen this past month will be nothing compared to what may be in store."

What actually lay in store for Jennings that autumn of 1901 fell beyond the realm of reasonable conjecture.

A cold front blew in the last week of October, its icy breath dislodging the last leaves from the trees and hurling them earthward. "Nature's way of cleaning house," Ruth called it.

Keeping the schoolyard clean was one of Prairie's least favorite aspects of teaching. "Cleaning, my eye!" she argued, venting her wrath on the crackling brown leaves. "More like nature's way of causing me to spend my Saturday raking leaves instead of curled up in front of the fire with a good book."

"Raking's good for you," Ruth insisted, "and so is the cold air. Keeps the blood pumping, stimulates the humors, that sort of thing."

"My humors will surely not suffer today from lack of stimulation, then," Prairie grumbled, frowning at the thick carpet of sycamore leaves.

"You ought to be happy we have some trees now, Prairie," Ruth admonished. "Don't you remember how barren this place was when we first came here? The only trees for miles around were those oaks down by the depot."

"I remember when the only tree in your yard, which was Wynn's then, was a scrubby little fig bush in the back," Prairie said wistfully. "And, despite my aversion to raking, I *am* glad we have trees now."

"Well," Ruth said, "here comes a diversion for your aversion."

Prairie laughed at the silly rhyme and turned her attention to the street.

"Need some help?" Sam called.

Prairie leaned on her rake and watched him secure Dolly's reins. "Did you bring a rake?" she asked, her voice suddenly bright, the sight of him altering her entire mood.

He ambled toward her. "Don't own one."

"You mean you don't have one with you," Prairie said.

"No. I honestly don't own one. People who don't have yards don't need a rake," he explained.

Prairie had never stopped to think about where Sam lived. Oh, she knew he stayed at the boardinghouse when he was in town and slept in a tent when he was out at the rig. But she'd never considered where and how Sam lived in Beaumont. "You don't have a house?" she asked, somewhat incredulously.

"Nope." He took her idle rake and went to work. "Never stayed anywhere long enough to want one."

Prairie couldn't quite imagine not having a house to go home to, yet his comment dredged up a vague recollection of wandering from place to place, sleeping on the ground or under a shelter of canvas, and later being in awe of the trappings of a home she had since come to take for granted. Things like hearth rugs and cast-iron cookstoves and feather mattresses.

Sam, on the other hand, had brothers—three of them, and possibly his parents were still living, though he never mentioned them. Surely the family had a home, somewhere.

"Where do your brothers live?" she asked.

"On the family farm near Beaumont."

"So, you do have a house," she argued, glad Sam hadn't missed having the stability of a home as she had before she came to Jennings.

"Sort of," he said. "I never think of it as mine."

"Since we're short a rake, why don't you go make us some coffee, Prairie?" Ruth suggested.

"Gladly," she agreed, happy to escape into the warmth of her little house. While the coffee dripped, Prairie straightened her kitchen and made some cinnamon toast. When she went to collect Ruth and Sam, she couldn't believe the progress they had made.

"Wow! You two work fast!" she called to them.

"We make a great team," Sam said, winking at Ruth, then turning his attention back to Prairie. "Actually," he admitted a bit sheepishly, "I have an ulterior motive in wanting to finish up here. I'm going out to the rig and I thought you might like to ride along."

"Thank you. I'd like that," she said, thrilled with the opportunity to spend a day with Sam—and to witness the drilling operation again. She still wanted to know about the pumps. "But," she added, turning to Ruth, "I don't know if it would be considered proper."

"Oh, go on!" Ruth declared. "If anyone asks, say it was W.C.T.U. business. Just behave yourself," she warned.

Sam and Ruth propped their rakes against a tree and

158

surveyed the neat piles of leaves. "It ought to take about an hour to burn these," Sam said, "and then we can be on our way."

What warming effect the coffee and bonfire didn't accomplish, the sun did. By the time Prairie and Sam headed out of town, the air had lost its nippy sting and the earth fairly glowed from the golden light of the noonday sun. Prairie coaxed Sam into talking about his brothers and growing up on a farm, and before she knew it, they were pulling up in the rice field.

Prairie's amazement at the short task Sam had made of the leaves didn't compare to his amazement at the fast work Jake Daniels and the crew had accomplished at the rig.

"How far have you drilled?" he asked Jake in a voice that mirrored an expression of pure astonishment.

Jake readjusted the chaw in his cheek, aimed a stream of tobacco juice at an empty lard bucket, hit it dead center, and lifted his massive shoulders in a gesture of nonchalance. "Oh, about five hundred feet, I s'pose."

"And that's a lot?" Prairie asked.

"Given soft ground like this," Sam explained, "five hundred feet in two weeks is about average if you're running two shifts, working around the clock. But not when that two weeks includes disassembling, moving, and reassembling the derrick, and then having to spud in the hole. How did you do it, Jake?"

The driller grinned, exposing teeth as big and strong as his body, and angled his head toward King Clarkston's rig. "We, uh, we sorta got in a contest with those fellers over there. We started out almost a week behind, but we've narrowed the gap by a day already."

"That's amazing!" Sam said, still in awe.

"Shore is. These men want to see this well come in; that's a fact, but I don't think we're gonna be able to catch up with Clarkston. He got too big a jump on us. It'll be close, though," Jake claimed.

Prairie was only half listening. Her mind had

clamped down on an oil field term she hadn't heard before. Even though it was too late to do anything about its omission from Prospector Pete's story, she wanted to know. "What does 'spud in' mean?" she asked.

"It comes from the name the English gave a tool they used for digging way back a long time ago," Sam said. "The spud was a cross between a spade and a chisel. After awhile, they started calling the digging itself spudding. Now it's oil field talk for that first chip we punch out of the ground when we start drilling. We call it spudding in."

"That's interesting," Prairie said.

Sam noted the sincerity in her voice and was at once both impressed by what appeared to be genuine interest in the rig and reminded of her coquettish attitude on one particular visit — the day he'd kissed her for the first time. She'd wanted something that day — and it wasn't a kiss. He'd bet on it.

But he sure was glad he'd kissed her. And damn if he didn't want to kiss her again! Something happened between them, something special, when he kissed her. That something had nothing to do with friendship. A part of him wished he'd left their relationship alone. He wondered where it might have led, wondered if maybe he didn't want to find out. But Prairie had said all she wanted was friendship, too, so perhaps he'd better leave well enough alone.

"We got some fresh coffee in the mess tent," Jake said, "and some cold ham and beans and cornbread, if ya'll are hungry. Fact is, I ain't had my dinner yet."

"Then let's go eat," Sam said.

The mealtime conversation centered around the rig and the trouble with the sand, a topic which couldn't have pleased Prairie more, although the two men apologized from time to time for leaving her out of the conversation.

"Have you come up with any ideas for controlling the sand?" Jake asked.

Sam shook his head sadly. "I thought about using a

piece of leather as a sort of boot on the end of the pipe, but I don't think it would hold up under the pressure. What do you think?"

"The same thing," Jake agreed. "But there's gotta be a way, Sam. And if anyone can figure it out, you can. Just keep thinking about it. Who knows? It may come to you in the middle of the night."

"Well, it better come fast. At the rate you guys are going, I don't have long to come up with something." Sam ate his meal in silence for awhile, then said, "Do we have a spy at Clarkston's rig?"

"No. Why?"

"I wonder if they've realized they're going to have the same problem, Jake. They're fools if they think they aren't. Who's Clarkston got drilling for him?"

"Raymond Guidry."

"That's right. I'd forgotten."

"Ray's a good enough driller," Jake allowed, "but he ain't much when it comes to working out problems out of the ordinary anymore than I am. He ain't thought of nothing. He probably ain't even worried about it. But if you want me to, I'll mosey over there late tonight and talk to him about it."

"I'd appreciate that, Jake."

Sam and Prairie left soon after they finished the meal. Most of the way home, Sam was pensive, his eyes on the rice fields they passed, but Prairie didn't think he was actually looking at them. He seemed to be far away.

When they reached the outskirts of town, Prairie broke the silence. "This thing about the sand really has you worried, doesn't it, Sam?" she ventured.

Sam blinked a couple of times and turned toward her, looking as though he'd just remembered she was there. "Yes," he said, his voice low, his tone solemn.

"Maybe you're thinking about it too hard. Sometimes it's better to forget about something and just let it stew in the back of your mind for a spell."

"You don't understand, Prairie. I'm running out of time."

"I do understand, Sam. I've had problems of my own from time to time. You'll come up with a solution. And you'll do it in time. I know you will."

The corners of his chiseled lips lifted in a wan smile that didn't reach his eyes. "Thanks, Prairie. I hope you're right."

It was almost dark when Sam pulled the surrey up in front of Prairie's house. A few embers burned brightly among a mound of ashes, testimony to the morning's work. The evening air was redolent with the pungent fragrance of charred leaves.

"Thank you for helping with the raking," Prairie said, wanting desperately to break through the barrier of politeness but not knowing quite how.

"I'm going to bank those embers good before I leave," he said. "We don't want to start a fire."

Prairie could think of nothing she'd like better than starting a fire with Sam, though not the same sort he referred to. "Would you like to come in?" she asked, her tone hopeful. "I could make us some hot cocoa, or coffee if you'd rather."

Sam ran his fingers through his hair, suddenly looking very uncomfortable. "Wayne will be expecting me back at the boardinghouse. He'll want to know how things are going out at the rig. I—I'll see you again soon."

Prairie tried not to sound too disappointed. "All right, Sam. I enjoyed myself today."

"Yeah, I did too," he said, but his voice lacked conviction. He had that faraway look in his eyes again.

I'm going to break through that barrier of yours, Sam, Prairie silently promised. *Somehow, some way, I'm going to break through it.*

In the wee hours of the morning, a crystal clear voice startled Sam from a deep sleep, filling him with excitement. He sat straight up in bed, his spine tingling, his muscles tense, his ears straining to hear the voice again.

But the only sound in the room was the steady ticking of the wind-up clock by his bed.

For a long time he sat there, his back against the tall headboard, his eyes searching the deep shadows for the darker figure of a woman.

"Prairie, are you there?" he whispered.

No one answered.

Feeling a bit foolish, Sam lit the lamp on the bedside table. Its soft glow assured him he was alone, that he had only imagined the voice.

Imagined or otherwise, it had been Prairie's voice. He was sure of it. But what had she said? What could she have said to make him feel so much excitement — and relief? The only thing that could make him feel those things, he thought, was a solution to controlling the sand.

He racked his brain, willing the dream to return, and heard her imagined voice say, "You're thinking about it too hard. The solution is simple. Remember the rice fields."

The rice fields? Whatever did rice fields have to do with controlling sand in an oil well? And what would Prairie Jernigan know about either one?

He turned off the lamp and slipped back into the warmth of the bed, pulling the quilt up against the chill that permeated the room.

Sleep evaded him. For the remaining hours of darkness, Sam tossed and turned upon his bed, scoffing at the dream and yet knowing in the depths of his soul that the answer to his sand problem lay somewhere in the rice fields.

Sundays for Prairie generally began with sleeping as late as she dared, which was eight o'clock, then waking up slowly, letting the luxury of an unhurried schedule wash languidly through her. She lingered over coffee, nibbling on a piece of toast and reading the *Times* from cover to cover before dressing for church. Following services, she had dinner with the Donovans.

Her Sunday afternoon schedule varied, depending on the social calendar, the weather, and her mood. The first Sunday afternoon in November, Prairie succumbed to pleas from the two youngest Donovan boys to play a game of croquet with them. The leisurely game, which required more skill than strength, lasted well into the afternoon, with Mickey emerging as the winner.

Wynn and Michael watched from the rear terrace, and Prairie joined them there while Patrick and Mickey pulled up the wickets and packed them, along with the mallets and balls, back into their box.

"Whew!" Prairie said, plopping into a lawn chair and gratefully accepting a tall glass of iced tea from Wynn. "This has been my weekend for fresh air and exercise." She pushed back a loose tendril of sweat-dampened hair and took a long swallow of the mint-flavored tea.

"What did you do yesterday?" Wynn asked.

"Raked leaves with Ruth and rode out to the well with Sam."

The frown that flitted across Michael's forehead was so slight Prairie wondered if she had imagined it. She didn't imagine the sudden tapping of his forefinger on his tea glass, though. "How are things going out there?" he asked.

"Quite well, actually," Prairie responded with enthusiasm, warming to the subject. She gave them an update on the drilling and told them about the contest between the two crews. "But Sam says it doesn't matter who brings in the next well. It will sand up just like his first one did if he can't figure out a way to stop it."

Michael shook his head and the corners of his mouth drooped. "When Doc and I first decided to pursue this oil business, I felt like a kid again, but now . . . now I wonder if we didn't make a big mistake."

Wynn laid her palm on Michael's knee. "You haven't lost any money, Michael. King's buying you out saved you there."

"This isn't about money. It's about hopes and dreams, growth and progress. It's about farmers struggling to get by who stand to make a killing off their land. And it's about a surge of gamblers and prospectors, men out to make a quick buck and ladies of easy virtue threatening to destroy everything we've worked so hard to build here."

"But, Michael—" Wynn protested.

"I know. Those activities we can control. And the 'get-rich-quick' schemers will leave fast enough without the income from oil to finance them. I can't help but wonder, though, if we've opened Pandora's box."

"You didn't open it, Michael," Wynn said soothingly. "You merely pointed out that it was there. You can't open it, because you don't have the key. Sam Blackman does."

Chapter Eleven

Sam Blackman did, indeed, hold the key, and thanks to his early morning dream, spawned by a combination of Prairie's admonition to quit worrying and their ride through the rice fields, he thought he'd found it.

Never had he considered that the time he'd killed talking to Jude Langley would pay off. When Sam first came to the Louisiana prairie, several weeks passed while he negotiated with Jude, Michael, and Enoch, and then waited for all his equipment to arrive. Not one to sit still for long, Sam followed Jude around his fields, and the two kept a steady stream of conversation going.

Sam's natural inclination toward engineering prompted a slew of questions about Jude's irrigation system. One thing he'd learned was that the water wells used to irrigate rice were equipped with a screen to hold back grit and gravel. Why wouldn't a similar screen hold back the sand and let the oil come through?

The more he thought about it on Sunday, the more confident he felt about the idea. He spent most of the day making notes and sketching designs, trying to figure out the best way to devise the screen with enough strength to take care of the pressure from the gas, oil, and rocks.

Sam wanted to hightail it over to Prairie's house

and kiss her silly, but he didn't. For one thing, he reckoned she'd think he was nuts if he told her how he'd heard her voice in the middle of the night telling him what to do. For another, Sam thought it was probably best not to tell anyone of his idea for the present. There was no point in fostering false hopes in people who were holding their collective breaths waiting to see if the sand could be controlled. There would be ample time later to talk to Prairie—and to thank her properly.

He did decide, however, to discuss his idea with Wayne.

"You're thinking right," Wayne agreed. "Let's keep this a secret for now. Send away for whatever you need, but use the mail, not the telegraph."

"We're going to have to find someone who can make the screen, too," Sam added.

"You get the materials," Wayne said, "and then we'll go to Lake Charles together and find someone. If we have to, we'll go to Beaumont or Houston."

Sam wrote an order for some inserted pipe and sixty-mesh copper wire gauze, which Wayne took down to the depot to post on the Sunday train. Sam then set to work drawing detailed plans. Several times, he caught himself whistling and realized how tense and preoccupied he'd been since that night in September when the well had come in and then sanded up a few hours later.

For the first time in weeks, he felt free and unencumbered with worrisome details. It was a heady feeling.

Shortly after dark that night, a cruel north wind roared into Jennings, sending folks scurrying indoors to huddle before fires or to take themselves to bed earlier than usual. The wind whistled around eaves and battered shingles, howling like a banshee.

167

It was almost ten when Jonas Richardson finished running the Monday morning edition of the *Times* and locked up to go home. Main Street was deserted. Jonas turned north, into the wind, bending his head low against the force of the wind and jerking the collar of his coat over the back of his neck. A few blocks from the newspaper office, a wooden shingle soared past his shoulder, missing him by inches and then clattering on the boardwalk behind him.

Fearing more hurtling shingles, Jonas ducked under the shelter of a covered doorway, intending to stand there only long enough to discern the source of the flying shingles. But what he saw across the street sent him running for help.

The closest occupied building was Michael Donovan's hotel. Jonas dashed inside, found the lobby empty, and sprinted down the hall to the clerk's room, which bore a "Private" sign on the door.

"Johnny!" he hollered, pounding on the door with a tight fist. "Open up!"

The paneled door swung inward and Johnny Perkins appeared in the doorway, his own fists shoved into his eyes and his mouth open in a wide yawn. He was wearing a faded blue union suit.

"Get dressed, Johnny!" Jonas barked. "Rally every man in the hotel and send them for every bucket they can find. The roof of Dudley's Restaurant is on fire."

Johnny Perkins removed his fists from his eyes and stared stupidly at the newspaper editor. "What?"

"Fire, Johnny—in this wind. If we don't hurry, the whole town will burn to the ground." Jonas turned to leave.

"Where you going?" Johnny asked.

"To wake some more people up. Hurry!"

When Sam's adrenaline stopped flowing, the long-denied fatigue kicked in. Utterly content and at peace

168

with himself, Sam put his drawings and notes away and went to bed without ever going downstairs to eat supper.

He felt as though he'd just fallen asleep when a light in his face, a severe shaking of his shoulders, and an insistent voice awoke him. He swiped at the rude hands and growled irritably.

"It's me — Wayne," the voice said. "Wake up. We have to get out of here."

Sam's mind was fuzzy with sleep. "Why?"

"There's a fire. A bad one. Get up, Sam."

Immediately alert, Sam threw the covers back, jumped out of bed, and headed for the door.

"Aren't you going to get dressed?" Wayne asked.

Sam hesitated, his hand on the door knob. "Is there time?"

Wayne was pulling a pair of jeans and a flannel shirt out of a bureau drawer. "It's not the boarding-house, Sam. It's the business district on Main Street. We're needed to fight the flames. Here. Put these on. I'll wait for you."

"No, you go on. I'm going to check on Prairie first."

Sam's sole experience with fire had been in the oil field, where monstrous flames leapt skyward and dense clouds of black smoke obliterated the sky. He expected a comparable situation, but all he encountered when he left the boardinghouse was a strong northerly wind that carried the smell of smoke. To the north, a red glow lit the night sky, the only visual indication of danger.

But the real danger stemmed from the wind and the dry conditions, as volatile a fuel as the natural gas that fed an oil field fire. The flames might not pose an imminent danger for Prairie, but the potential was frightening.

He headed southwest, toward the schoolhouse, his

long legs sprinting down the wide dirt paths that served as streets. The wind buffeted his back and lobbed limbs, shingles, and debris from the street at him, but Sam felt nothing more than the pounding of his heart and an inner voice urging him to hurry, hurry.

Clamoring shards of noise battered her ears, striving to disrupt her sleep. Prairie buried her head under her pillow and willed the crashing to cease. Despite her efforts, the noise continued, seeming to surround her little house.

It was the loud banging upon the window glass that finally penetrated Prairie's consciousness—that and a voice that doggedly called her name. Still half asleep, she dragged herself from the warm comfort of her bed to the window. She pushed the heavy drape aside and tugged on the bottom of the shade, then jumped when the roller jerked the shade all the way to the top of the window.

Someone stood outside, banging on the glass with his fist. Her blood surged in immediate fear, slowed when she recognized Sam, then surged again as partial understanding pierced her hazy logic. Something was wrong, else Sam would not have come.

Prairie pulled on a dressing robe and hurried to the back door, which was closer to her bedroom than the front. A gust of wind hit her full in the face and ripped the door from her grasp. The panel banged against the wall and she leaned against it to hold it steady.

"Sam!" she called, the wind tossing her voice hither and yon. "I'm around here."

Within seconds, he was in her arms, hugging her close and kissing the top of her head. She detected an urgency in his embrace that had nothing to do with passion.

"What's wrong?" she croaked, her heart in her throat, making speech difficult.

"Fire. On Main Street. It's above you right now, but who knows how far it will spread?"

"Fire? In this wind? Oh, my God!"

He pulled away from her, holding her upper arms in a tight grip. Though both his voice and his touch carried his concern, she wished she could see his face better. She could feel his eyes upon her, straining in the darkness to see her better, too.

"Do you keep any clothes at the Donovans' house?" he asked.

"Yes."

"Good. Are you wearing shoes?"

"No."

"Then put some on. Some good, sturdy ones. And hurry. I'll wait here for you."

A few minutes later, Prairie returned to the kitchen, carrying a lamp in one hand and a tapestry bag in the other. Sam took the lamp from her, set it on the table, and extinguished its light.

She held her breath, waiting for him to fuss at her for taking the time to pack a bag, waiting for him to open it and see the stack of typed papers she'd thrown inside—her Cherokee Sally manuscript. If she had to explain to him, then so be it, but she wasn't about to lose her work. Instead, he grasped its handle in one hand, her elbow in the other, and together they fought the force of the wind.

Sam joined Wayne in a line of men stretched from the flames to a pump. Similar lines radiated out to other pumps nearby. Since the town had no water system and no fire department, the only way to fight the fire was by bucket brigade. Water was drawn by working pump levers, a time-consuming task in the midst of a roaring conflagration.

Sometimes the wind-scattered embers landed on one of the men, setting clothes on fire or singeing hair before they were doused with water from one of the buckets. Luckily, no one was seriously injured.

From the time they started, Sam knew it was hopeless. Nevertheless, the men filled buckets, passed them along the lines, and hurled the water onto flames fanned by the brisk wind. They could see their efforts were futile, but they didn't stop trying.

The norther blew the blaze from one frame building to another, making short work of igniting the dry tinder. Soon, the whole west side of Main Street, from the restaurant where the fire had started south to Market Street, was ablaze.

Suddenly the wind changed course. Flames and sparks ignited wooden buildings across Market Street where Main made a turn toward the depot. The Citizens Bank went up in flames, as did several doctors' offices and a print shop.

Those who weren't part of the bucket brigades were busy evacuating hotels, saloons, boardinghouses, and residences along both Main and Market, and moving records, furniture, merchandise, and machinery out of buildings which lay in the path of the flames.

The wind changed course again, this time throwing red embers onto roofs of buildings on the east side of Main Street. Donovan's old hotel building—the one Wayne had leased for Blackman Brothers, Well Contractors—was on the east side.

Sam and Wayne unlocked the front door and left it standing open to take advantage of the light from the fire. They snatched up files containing important contracts, invoices, and leases. These they threw into a corrugated box, which Wayne volunteered to take back to Lily's boardinghouse for temporary safekeeping.

"You'll find my notes and drawings in the top drawer of my bureau," Sam said. "Put them in

172

there, too, just in case one of us has to grab that box and run with it."

"I'll be back as soon as I can," Wayne promised. He looked around briefly, shaking his head. "I don't think there's much hope for this building."

"There isn't much hope for the whole town, Wayne," Sam said dryly. "We can only hope to save a few things we'd play hell replacing, like those papers."

At the door, Wayne hesitated. "There are six box-cars full of freight down on the tracks and no engine to move them, Sam. If this fire is as devastating as we think it's going to be, this town's going to need that freight."

"I'll go talk to Slim," Sam said. "And, Wayne, be careful."

"Yeah. You too."

One fork of the fire was headed straight toward the Southern Pacific station. Sam burst into the door of the depot and hollered for Slim.

"In here," Slim hollered back from the vicinity of the telegraph room. As Sam neared the room, he could hear the syncopated clicking of the message Slim was sending and then the return clicks.

"You wired for help?" Sam asked when the clicking ended.

"Had to," Slim said. "There's no way we can physically move those cars. Good thing the train was late today. As soon as it arrives in Welsh, they'll uncouple the engine and send it back. I hope it gets here in time."

"What about other help?"

"I'm fixing to send a telegram to Lake Charles. Maybe they can send us some equipment to fight this fire with."

"You'd better hurry," Sam urged. "The fire is almost to the telegraph lines."

Slim sent the cable, then he and Sam stood tensely, waiting for the reply. Though only a few minutes passed, it seemed like a lifetime to Sam. Outside, the fire roared ever closer to the depot and the boxcars. The heat it generated turned the station house into an oven. Sam backhanded his forehead, smearing soot and ashes into his hair.

Slim handed him a wet towel, which Sam held gratefully against his face until he heard the sweet singing on the telegraph line: "Hook-and-ladder wagon and hose cart en route."

Slim hollered, "Whoopee! That's a relief."

Sam didn't want to dampen the stationmaster's enthusiasm, so he kept his doubts to himself. "Are you going to be all right here, Slim? Do you need me for anything?"

"Naw. I'm going back outside myself to keep an eye on that fire."

"Me, too. I'll spread the word about the equipment," Sam said. "Those men need a shot of hope."

There were few victories over the unrelenting flames that night. The SP engine, pushed to a sixty-mile-per-hour run, arrived in the nick of time, thus saving the six cars and their precious freight. But the hose cart, sent by flatcar from Lake Charles, was useless in a town that had no mechanical water pumps and no pressure.

Rain was the only real prospect of salvation, but the heavens refused to cooperate. From time to time, a roll of distant thunder or a flash of lightning to the northwest would raise hopes, but the lack of fruition soon dashed them again. Although the wind was cold, few felt its icy blast through the heat of the blaze.

The fire had almost spent itself when, close to dawn, the blessed rain started, a heavy downpour that doused the remaining embers. The men who had so valiantly fought the flames, and were themselves nearly spent, grabbed each other and frolicked in the streets, much in the same way those who had been present the night Sam's well came in had celebrated.

Prairie and Wynn heard the whoops and hollering from the front veranda, where they had sat with the restless and talkative boys throughout the night.

"It's all over," Wynn said, tears streaming down her face. "Thank God, it's over."

Prairie squeezed Wynn's hand. "They'll be back soon, now," she assured her foster mother, knowing Wynn understood the reference to Sam, Jason, and Michael.

Wynn nodded. "And they'll be tired and hungry and in need of a bath. Mickey, go tell Marmie and Zoey to make the necessary preparations."

"Can we go see now, Mama?" Patrick asked. "Please, let us go see."

"I'll take you later," Prairie said, "after it stops raining."

"You've been telling me later all night!" the youngest Donovan whined.

"And I meant it. Later isn't here yet, so stop pestering me. Besides, your daddy will be home soon, and you don't want to miss him. He'll tell you all about it."

But another hour passed before Michael and Jason appeared. Michael's shoulders were drooping and his feet dragging as he came up the walk in the pouring rain. Their faces, hands, and clothes were covered in soot, and their eyes were bloodshot. Prairie ran to get some blankets.

She returned to find Michael sitting in a rocker surrounded by his sons, the two younger ones both asking him questions at once. Prairie had a few of her own.

"Was anyone hurt?" she asked, tucking a blanket around him.

"No one I know of—outside of some cuts and minor burns. But they're still going through the wreckage. So many new folks in town, it's hard to know who

175

might be missing . . ."

"Is Sam all right?" she asked, her voice a thin thread.

Michael nodded. "I spoke to him and his brother as I was leaving. Doc's all right, too. The old coot! He had no business trying to fight a fire at his age, but he took his place in one of the bucket lines and refused to budge."

Prairie breathed a sigh of relief and pulled an empty chair up close to the group.

"Do they need me, Michael?" Wynn asked.

"I don't think so. Doc Petersen and Doc Wilkinson were there. Right now, Wynn, I need you here with me, but I'm going back in a little while. You can go with me, if you want to. Mickey, put on your oldest clothes. We have a mess to clean up."

"I'll go, too," Prairie offered, and Patrick said he wanted to go, but Michael had other plans for the two of them.

"The fire didn't reach the school. I want you and Ruth to hold classes today for the younger children—to keep them out of the way. That includes you, Patrick. The older kids can help downtown."

Marmie brought the coffeepot and a plate of biscuits out onto the porch, and she and Zoey and Winkle joined the family.

"It's bad," Michael said, defeat evident in both his bitter voice and his slumped posture. "This house is the only building we own that's still standing. The fire didn't get everything. The Travelers Home Hotel and the livery were saved, and that line of pine shacks south of the new Calcasieu Marine National Bank. Otherwise, the entire business district is in ashes."

"Humph!" Wynn snorted. "It could have taken those pine shacks with my blessings."

"Mine, too," Michael agreed, "but the bank is brick. It stopped the fire."

"The old hotel?" Wynn asked, her voice cracking.

"A pile of charred timbers," Michael said. "But don't worry about it, darling. I'm going to build you a hospital. Out of brick and with a slate roof! No more frame buildings and wood shingles for me. Not after tonight."

Was everyone else as cold and hungry and bone tired as he was? Sam wondered. He hadn't stopped long enough to notice, but a quick assessment of sooty faces and drooping bodies validated his reflection.

He'd never seen such a mess — nor so many people band together in concerted effort. They weren't letting either their obvious fatigue or the pouring rain slow them down.

A few people rushed from one group to another, seeking loved ones they'd been separated from. For the most part, families were reunited in short order, but one particular woman became frantic when she couldn't locate her husband. They were new in town, she explained unnecessarily. Her husband was the tall, slender man L.W. Dalby had hired to deliver groceries. His name was Ethan — Ethan McCormack.

Folks shook their heads sadly. No one had seen him.

After Mrs. McCormack spoke to Slim, he hollered to the folks around him, "Hey, ya'll! Listen up. I just thought about that feller who came in on the train yesterday. The merchant. Anybody seen him either?"

"I don't know," Otis Hill, who was sober for once, said. "I helped him haul a wagon load of stuff from the depot over here to one of Donovan's old buildings, the one that stood rye-chonder." He pointed a crooked finger at a pile of charred rubbish. "He paid me in sour mash. It's a crying shame the rest of it burned up."

"Maybe there's some left," Orville Mason suggested. "Why don't you go see?"

"But what happened to the merchant?" Slim persisted. "I don't recollect seeing him this morning. You don't reckon he stayed in that building, do you?"

Sam joined the small group to investigate, but several hours of digging through the rubble and sifting through ashes produced no bone fragments or other indication that the merchant had died in the blaze. To Otis's dismay, there was not one unbroken whiskey bottle to be found.

As the morning wore on, the rain diminished, then finally stopped altogether around eleven. Conversely, indignation increased with each passing hour, until by early afternoon the crowd's grumble had become a low drone.

Everyone had an opinion, but they were all in agreement on two items: It was high time Jennings had both a fire department and a water system.

Michael called an emergency town meeting for seven that evening. The residents turned out en masse, lending their full support to whatever measures were required to implement the two systems immediately. Key committees were formed and chairmen appointed. Folks went home that night with wan smiles on their dirty faces.

While there were many conjectures, no one honestly knew how the fire had started. Nor, they decided, did the exact cause matter. They were alive—almost every last one of them. Around mid-afternoon, they'd found Ethan McCormack's body among the ruins. With the exception of the merchant, who they decided must have run off, no one else was missing; nor had anyone who survived been seriously injured. That was something to be thankful for, indeed.

Perhaps, they reasoned, the fire had done the town a service. They'd talked about organizing a fire department and putting in a water system before, but no one had ever really worried about the lack of

178

either. Now, they knew they had no choice. The fire had destroyed a number of buildings that had been true eyesores. They pledged to rebuild with care and pride.

Though no one actually voiced it, everyone wondered how they would afford to replace everything that had been lost, how the town would afford to build the new water system and finance a fire department. Now, more than ever, Jennings needed a miracle.

Would that miracle be oil, they wondered, or was that prospect nothing more than a pipe dream?

The proof lay with one man—Sam Blackman.

The night before, they'd been at the mercy of two elements, wind and fire, and they'd prayed for another element—rain. Now they were at the mercy of the earth, the one remaining element. That night, they prayed Sam was smart enough to control the heaving sand that threatened to deprive them of their miracle.

"You can tear up that petition," Agnes Milhouse told Sam after the meeting. "The W.C.T.U. will not stand in your way. But we will continue to fight the demons liquor, tobacco, and vice!"

Sam got the distinct impression that admitting defeat where he was concerned was the last thing Agnes wanted to do, but the fire had removed any choice in the matter. He smiled into her surly face and said, "I wouldn't expect anything else from you, ma'am."

Chapter Twelve

"How do you like teaching the younger children?" Sam asked, turning from the blackboard to watch Prairie, who was busy cleaning the top of her desk. Since most of her students were involved in the massive clean-up effort, she'd taken some of Ruth's to teach, an arrangement which temporarily eased the overcrowding problem at the school.

"It's wonderful!" she said without looking up, her concentration centered on a recalcitrant spot of ink, but he couldn't miss the wide smile that creased her cheeks. "They're so eager to learn. And they're always so happy."

I would be, too, Sam thought, *if I could look at you all day.*

Prairie looked up at him and burst into laughter. Sam glanced over his shoulder, but there was no one behind him. Nor did there seem to be anything humorous on the slate — unless one counted a half-clean blackboard as humorous.

"What's so funny?" he asked.

A smile perked up the corners of her mouth and she strolled toward him, carrying her cleaning rag. When she spoke, her voice was light and airy. "You are." She wiped at the end of his nose with a corner of her rag. "You have chalk dust all over you."

"You'd think by now I'd be able to clean this thing

without making such a mess," he said, his smile taking the sting out of his words.

"Don't despair," she said, flicking at his clothes with her rag. "You've only been at it for a week. I've been cleaning that blackboard every day for five years, and I still make a mess." She stopped swiping and asked, "How's the work going downtown?"

"Pretty good. Lots of folks come every day, whether they lost property or not. Otis is one of them. Can you believe he's been sober since the fire?"

"Really?"

Her wide-open eyes sparkled like ginger-colored crystals, evoking Sam's ardor. He knew he had no business coming to see her everyday. Just looking at Prairie Jernigan made him forget everything he'd ever planned for his life. He cleared his throat and turned back to scrubbing the blackboard.

"Really," he said. "He says he was well on his way to oblivion that night, and Jonas saved his life when he found him in the alley. I think the reality of his close call didn't actually hit him until we were sifting through those ashes looking for the merchant who disappeared."

"No one's heard from that man?"

"Nope."

"That's strange. I wonder what happened to him. You're sure he didn't die in the fire?"

"There would have been bone fragments, Prairie."

"He couldn't have been in one of the other buildings?"

Sam shrugged. "It's possible, but not very likely. We'll know by the time we finish clearing out all the debris. But even if we find his remains, we don't know who he was or where he came from."

Prairie put her rag away and started sweeping the floor. For awhile, the only sounds in the room were

181

the swish of the broom upon the floor and the water dripping out of Sam's rag when he squeezed it into the bucket. Sam pondered her sudden silence for a moment, then he could have kicked himself when he realized what he'd said.

No one had known anything about her father, either. Within a few hours, the merchant had appeared in Jennings and then disappeared—just as her father had seventeen years before. The similarities in the two incidents was uncanny.

He'd opened his mouth to apologize when she spoke, her voice unnaturally bright. "Well, I'm about through here. How about you?"

"Almost."

"If the drugstore hadn't burned, I'd let you buy me a soda," she said.

"Since it did, I'll let you make me a cup of coffee," he countered. "Why don't I finish up here?"

Despite his resolve to leave his attraction to her out of their relationship, her smile tore at his heartstrings. "Fine," she said. "I'll be next door."

Although two weeks had passed since he'd conceived the idea, Sam had yet to breathe a word to Prairie about using a screen to hold the sand back. He wanted to tell her, desperately, but his promise to Wayne held him back. In fact, they'd gotten into a big argument over the issue.

"She's the reason I had the idea in the first place," Sam had argued.

"No, she's not," Wayne countered. "You heard her voice in your sleep because you were dreaming about her. Prairie Jernigan wouldn't have the least idea about how to control the sand."

"But if she hadn't told me to quit worrying about it, I might never have thought of using a screen," Sam reasoned.

"Look, Sam," Wayne said, "we swore a pact to

182

keep this thing a secret. I shouldn't have to remind you that the success of our number two well—and of our company—depends on secrecy right now. If King Clarkston gets wind of this—"

"What can he do?"

"Have one made, just like we're doing."

"And then?"

Wayne threw up his hands. "Don't you even care if you get credit for it?"

Sam tried a different approach. "Prairie won't tell Clarkston anything. She's not talking to him at all and probably won't ever talk to him again."

"But she might tell that other teacher, or the Donovans, and then it would get back to King. You can't tell her, Sam. It would be disloyal, to me and J.C. and Myron—and to yourself. You can't do it."

Although Sam finally agreed to silence, he knew the change in his outlook must be obvious to Prairie, must give her some notion that he'd worked out his problem. Every day, he expected her to mention it, but thus far she'd come no closer than skewering him with a "there's something you're not telling me" look.

Maybe it was the deviation from his own natural straightforwardness that made him suspicious of Prairie, but Sam couldn't help thinking there was something she wasn't telling him, too.

"You figured it out, didn't you?"

He had to have expected it, Prairie reasoned, yet her question seemed to stun him. He blew on his steaming coffee, taking an inordinate amount of time cooling it off. His squinted eyes, which were focused on the slick surface of the liquid, provided no clue to his thoughts, but she couldn't miss the obvious hesitation, or his tightened grip on the cup han-

183

dle, or the sudden tensing of his jaw and neck muscles. Yet, when he raised his head and looked at her, his expression was one of pure bewilderment.

"Figured what out?" he asked.

"How to control the sand," she replied, certain he faked the confusion.

If he did, he refused to let go of the charade. "Why do you think I have?"

"Because you're different—more at ease with yourself. You almost never frown anymore, and when you do, there's an obvious reason."

He eased his guard a bit and gave her a half smile. "I took your advice and stopped worrying."

"Did it work?" she pressed.

"Apparently. You just said I was more relaxed."

"You didn't answer my question, Sam!" she accused good-naturedly.

His smile widened, lighting his blue eyes. "Yes, I did."

"No, you didn't." She took a deep breath, rolled her eyes, and tried again. "Did you or did you *not* solve your problem?"

Sam laughed. "I'm not sure."

"Which means you aren't going to tell me. All right, you win. No more questions—except one. When will I know?"

"When I test it and it works."

"So, you do have something in mind?" she prodded.

"I didn't say that."

"Oo-oo-oo!" she wailed in exasperation. "Sam Blackman, you are impossible."

"I know," he said, too complacently, his attention drawn to the mending basket Prairie had left on the floor by her chair the night before—the chair Sam occupied now. Prairie gaped in horror as he set his cup and saucer on the table, reached into the open basket, and slipped a copy of *Prospector Pete* from beneath a torn tablecloth, which had only partially covered the paperback.

Why, oh why, hadn't she moved it? she mentally scolded herself. But it was too late. He was regarding the cover with intense interest.

His momentary preoccupation with the novel gave her only seconds to recompose herself. Quickly, Prairie clamped her mouth shut and bade her heart to stop beating so fast. Whatever she did, she couldn't let him see how nervous she was. She made herself breathe slowly and deeply, hiding behind the raised cup from which she dared not sip, lest she choke on the coffee.

"Where did you get this?" Sam asked, glancing up.

She supposed his question was innocent enough, yet there was something about the way he looked at her that sent spider legs running down the back of her neck.

"In the mail," she said.

"How did you get it in the mail? I thought you had to buy these from the vendor at the depot."

She could play Sam's game and avoid answering his questions, but she had no desire to raise his suspicions, as his reluctance to talk about the device for the well had raised hers. No, she decided, it was best to be as direct and honest as she possibly could. Although the copy he held was one of the five author's copies Beadle and Adams had sent directly to David and he had then forwarded to her, she couldn't tell him that. So she chose a half truth. "I have a subscription."

Which she did, but the subscription copy hadn't arrived yet, and probably wouldn't for another couple of weeks.

His eyebrows shot to mid-forehead, but his voice

suggested surprise rather than disbelief. "You can get a subscription to these?"

"Certainly. See," she pointed, "right there beneath the logotype."

"The *what?*"

Prairie set her cup and saucer down, moved to stand beside him, and placed her forefinger on the cover. "This wide band across the top that says *Dime Library*. See how it says *Beadle's* here, and beneath it is a picture of a dime, then here, under the word dime, it says *New York*. That's the logotype. It's exactly the same on every one of their dime novels."

He shot her a look fraught with curiosity. "How did you know that?"

She couldn't say, *Because I'm one of their writers,* so Prairie used the first reason that came to mind. "I'm a teacher. Remember?"

She hoped her answer didn't sound as idiotic to him as it did to her. She certainly hadn't learned about such things as logotypes at Normal, but Sam probably didn't know what they taught at a teachers' college.

"See—right there," she continued, "under the logotype it says *Price Ten Cents, $5.00 a Year*. They publish one of these every week. With a subscription, you don't have to fight the crowds at the depot, or be disappointed if the vendor is out of the latest title. You can order a subscription to their half-dime library, too. It's two-fifty a year."

"And you read these?" Sam asked.

"Yes," she admitted without hesitation, her defense ready should he choose to malign the genre. Prairie cringed every time she heard someone refer to her writing as "pulp," but only those who didn't read dime novels called them that. She tried to imagine Sam reading a dime novel and failed. It wasn't his style. Still, it wouldn't hurt to ask.

"Do you?"

His answer caught her totally off guard. "Only those written by Pampas J. Rose. He's good."

"Do you really think so?" she asked eagerly, so full of pride she didn't stop to think about the essence of his declaration.

"I sure do, and so does my brother Wayne. He was the one who got me started on these. But Wayne hasn't bought this one yet. Do you mind if we borrow it?"

Oh, no! she thought, glad she stood behind him, glad he couldn't see the brief wave of anxiety that washed through her. She could make an excuse, tell him she hadn't read it yet or something, but she couldn't stop him from buying a copy. He was bound to read it eventually.

"We'll take care of it," he promised.

"Of course, you may borrow it," she said—nonchalantly, she hoped.

"Thanks," he said, tucking the slim book into his coat pocket and twisting his head around to look at her. "Did you finish your coffee?"

"No, but it's cold now." His interest in Pampas J. Rose made her terribly uncomfortable, but she felt compelled to ask him if he wanted more coffee.

"I think I *will* have another cup," he said, rising. "I'll get it."

"The pot's on the reservoir," she said, mentally scrambling for a change of conversation topic—something definitely safer than dime novels, but she couldn't think of anything they hadn't already discussed.

It didn't matter. Sam didn't give her a chance to say anything. He'd barely resettled himself in the chair before he said, "This Pampas J. Rose fellow is truly amazing."

Prairie watched him sip his hot coffee and waited

187

for him to explain. When he didn't, she said, "Really? In what way?"

"Haven't you noticed? No two of his stories are alike; his heroes bear little or no resemblance to each other; and he paints such vivid pictures of his settings you'd think he knew about everyone of them personally. But he doesn't."

"How do you know?"

"Have you read his Sacramento Sam story?"

She nodded.

"Have you ever been to Sacramento?"

Prairie's heart skipped a beat. "No."

"Well, neither has Pampas J. Rose. It'll be interesting to see how much he knows about drilling for oil."

"But what makes him amazing?"

"I'm sorry. I got off track. Maybe amazing is the wrong word, but I can't think of a better one. Anyway, here you have this master storyteller who never tells the same story twice, yet he uses the same trivial details in every book. Such repetition must be intentional, don't you think?"

She took a long swallow of her cool coffee, so intent on stalling she didn't notice how cold it was. There had to be a way to steer him away from this subject, but at the moment he awaited her response.

"I, uhm, I suppose," she hedged, her fingers moving to her high collar and restlessly caressing the filigree wings of her dragonfly brooch pinned there.

"Surely you've noticed," he continued. "There's the aversion to brown gravy, ridiculously referred to as toodlum gravy. Then there's the recurrence of certain female names, and there's always a town named Big Spring thrown in somewhere. And *then* . . ."

This was too much. The tension was eating her alive. She had to ease it—before she became defensive and said something she wished she hadn't. And she had to end Sam's tirade before she screamed from biting her tongue. The best way to do that, she figured, was to throw him a curve. Prairie burst into a giggling fit.

"This is the second time today you've laughed at me," Sam grumbled, rubbing the pad of his thumb on the end of his nose and turning red. "What is it this time? Coffee?"

"No. It's the berry stain on your cheeks."

He rubbed his cheeks and then examined his palms. "I haven't been eating berries," he said.

"Of course, you haven't. Never mind. Let me take your cup." She whisked it from the table and sailed down the hall to the kitchen. When she returned to the parlor, Sam was standing at the door, his trilby in his hand.

"I'll see you tomorrow, I suppose," he said, twisting the brim of the hat and looking at her as though she'd sprouted horns.

Prairie grinned, lifted herself on tiptoe, and kissed his cheek. "Tomorrow," she agreed, praying he would forever drop the subject of Pampas J. Rose.

When Sam didn't come the next day, which was Thursday, nor the one after, Prairie feared her worst-case scenario had finally come true. Someone had finally put it all together. *Sam* had put it all together. He knew she was Pampas J. Rose.

That had to be it, she decided. She shouldn't have made Prospector Pete's story so similar to Sam's. She wouldn't have if she'd had any idea he'd ever read it.

Prairie had always known someone would figure it out eventually, but she'd expected it to be someone who'd known her for years, someone who knew about her Aunt Martha and Big Spring and toodlum gravy. But not Sam. Yet, she'd given him ample clues: pampa being a synonym for prairie, the drag-onfly brooch she wore almost daily, her aversion to brown gravy—and for Prairie, it wasn't just a dis-like, it was an aversion.

Maybe Sam hadn't picked up on that particular aspect of her personality, but she'd bet he had. The night she'd had supper with him at the boarding-house, she'd almost gagged when Sam ladled brown gravy over his rice and biscuits, and she had staunchly refused any of the stuff for herself, even when he pressed her to try it.

He might think the name, the brooch, and the gravy were all coincidental; perhaps he hadn't even thought of all three things at once. But the addition of Prospector Pete's story had been a dead giveaway.

She knew it had. She knew that was why he hadn't come back. And now, he would tell people that she was Pampas J. Rose, and her hopes, her dreams of locating her relatives would be shattered beyond repair.

Friday night, Prairie slept fitfully, nightmares ruining what little bit of rest she might have gotten. Saturday morning, she was up and dressed before sunrise, her mind made up.

There was no way around it. She had to confront him. She had to explain why she'd written all those books as Pampas J. Rose. She had to ask him not to give her away. Not yet. Not when she had come so close to finding a link to her past. She had to hope he would understand.

Fortified with a pot of coffee and a bowl of cinna-mon-laced oatmeal, determined to see Sam before he had a chance to leave the boardinghouse, Prairie set out at six-thirty.

The November air was brisk and clean-smelling and wonderfully bracing. Prairie filled her lungs with great gulps of it and breathed it out in wispy puffs of vapor that were barely visible in the thin, pre-dawn light.

A boy on a bicycle skittered past her, the folded newspaper he held aloft brushing her shoulder before he raised his arm higher and flipped the paper onto a front porch.

"Sorry about that, Miss Jernigan!" he called, and she recognized his voice as that of Kevin McCormack. He was taking his father's death in the fire far easier than she'd expected, pitching right in to help his mother by taking a paper route. When she had casually mentioned this to Wynn and Michael earlier that week, she'd been totally unprepared for the pain that washed over Michael's features.

He explained that he'd lost his own father at the same age as Kevin. "It makes a little boy grow up fast," he told her. "Suddenly, he's the man of the family. All his protective instincts take over. That child is hurting, Prairie, but he'll never let it show."

For a moment, Prairie stopped walking and turned around, watching Kevin until he turned a corner and disappeared. She wished there was something she could do for him, something to ease his pain.

Frank Bardell's ice wagon lumbered down the dirt street, its springs screeching as the big, iron-bound wheels bounced down the rough, hole-ridden lane. His two big draft horses wore bells on their harness, and these jingled incessantly, alerting homemakers of his approach. Close behind him came Bert Caston, a bell in his hand and a load of big cans of milk in the back of his wagon.

Prairie paid little heed to the jangling bells or the voices of the men hawking their wares, her attention on the matter at hand. As she walked, she mentally practiced her speech, pitting first one approach against another. She had no intention of being anything other than completely honest with Sam. She'd tried playacting with him once—and failed miserably. Yes, honesty was required, but that didn't mean she had to be tactless or abrupt. Whatever happened, the last thing she wanted to do was evoke his pity.

Despite the ten-minute exercise of both body and mind, she arrived at the boardinghouse not the least bit satisfied that she could handle the situation well. Prairie hesitated at the door, suddenly dubious and definitely frightened.

What if he refused to listen? What if he'd already blabbed the whole story—or rather the part of it he'd pieced together—to everyone at the boardinghouse? What would she do then?

Before she fully collected herself, Lily Bidwell opened the door. "Why, good morning, Prairie," she said, startled. "What brings you here so early?"

Prairie hesitated for an instant, then blurted, "I need to see Mr. Blackman."

"Which one?" Lily asked, her voice sharp.

Prairie had forgotten about Wayne. "Sam."

Lily's frown disappeared. She sidled around her and picked up the newspaper from the porch floor. "He isn't here, dear. He left early Thursday morning. Said he was going out to the rig, but he didn't say when he'd be back."

Prairie worried her bottom lip. The trip couldn't have been planned; Sam had told her he'd see her Thursday. Had something gone wrong with the well?

"And Wayne left Wednesday on the train," Lily said. "He didn't say where he was going or when he'd be back, either."

Prairie laughed. "You sound just a little put out, Miss Lily. You're not sweet on Wayne, are you?"

Though she denied any such attraction, the spinster blushed a deep shade of pink. "It's the money. If

192

I knew for sure how long those two were going to be gone when they left here, I'd rent out their rooms for the duration. Did you know folks are paying three dollars a night for a cot in one of those tents down on South Main? I'm getting four here—from everyone except the Blackman brothers. That Wayne Blackman, now he's a smart one."

Lily smiled and shook her head, her voice no longer fretful. "Right after that well came in, he paid up for six months in advance—at a dollar a day. I was happy enough to get the money at the time. Now, there's no telling how much I'll lose all together."

"Yes, ma'am," Prairie said, impatient to be on her way.

Lily opened the screen door, then turned back to Prairie, "Would you like to come in for a cup of coffee?"

"No, thank you."

"Do you want me to tell Sam and Wayne you called?" Lily asked.

Prairie shook her head and started down the steps. "It wasn't that important. Good day, Miss Lily."

She retraced her steps, feeling much better despite not having seen Sam. She was sure now that he hadn't gossiped about her, at least not to the boardinghouse crowd. Otherwise, Lily Bidwell would never have treated her so courteously. In fact, she wasn't so certain anymore that he'd linked her to Pampas J. Rose. She couldn't help but wonder, though, why he hadn't told her Wednesday afternoon that he was leaving town the next morning. Maybe something had come up unexpectedly . . .

Prairie turned onto her walkway and ran straight into Jim Thompson, Slim's delivery boy.

"My ah . . . apologies, Miss Jernigan," the young

193

man said, backing quickly away and stammering in his embarrassment.

"Mine, too, Jim," Prairie said, wondering what he was doing at her house. "I don't suppose either one of us expected to encounter the other on this walk."

"No, ma'am. I mean, yes, ma'am. I mean . . . well" — he thrust an envelope at her — "I have this here tellygram for you, Miss Jernigan. Would you mind signing 'for it, please?"

Prairie's head spun so fast she thought she would surely faint before she could make it into the house. Who would send her a telegram? Someone who knew her parents, perhaps? Lucy Byers, or her grandson? Maybe Lucy had remembered something else. Keith had said she was ill. Had she died?

There wasn't enough light in the house to read by, but the telegram wouldn't wait long enough to light a lamp. Prairie took it to a window, tearing open the envelope on the way.

She scanned the handwritten note, looking for the name of the sender.

David Hamilton.

Prairie closed her eyes and took a deep breath. Knowing the message was from David carried a degree of comfort, but he wouldn't cable her unless there was a problem — a serious problem.

She focused on the telegram again and read:

ED B ADAMS COMING FROM NEW ORLEANS STOP TO ARRIVE SUNDAY TRAIN STOP NEED ROSES IMMEDIATELY END

Ed B. Adams? Who was he?

Frowning, Prairie went to the kitchen and put her teakettle on the stove.

And what did David mean about needing roses?

Only someone with a hothouse would have any this late in the year. Even if she found some, how was she supposed to get them to Lafayette by tomorrow?

She lit a lamp, measured coffee into the drip pot, poured in the water, then sat down at the table and looked at the telegram again. Suddenly, David's message became quite clear.

Ed B. Adams was not the name of the man. It was his title — editor, Beadle and Adams. And roses didn't apply to flowers. David meant her.

Unconsciously a hand flew up and clutched her throat, as though it could stop the sudden constriction there. She stared unseeingly at the telegram again and knew beyond a shadow of a doubt that she was right.

An editor from her publishing house was in New Orleans today, but tomorrow he'd be on the train to Lafayette. And when he got there, he expected to meet Pampas J. Rose.

Chapter Thirteen

Once she got over the initial shock, Prairie sat in her kitchen and laughed until tears gathered in her eyes and her ribs felt bruised.

What a delightfully clever message! She wondered how long it had taken David to compose it. He'd had to recover from his own shock first and what a shock hearing from the editor must have been. She supposed she would experience a degree of panic once reality sank in, but in the meantime, she couldn't help finding the situation hilarious.

Poor David! She had no right to take enjoyment from his misery, and she was quite certain he was miserable. Probably to the point of pulling his hair out, waiting to receive a reply from her.

Oh! she gasped. She hadn't thought of that. She hoped he realized she couldn't afford the risk of sending a return cable. The minute she walked in the depot door, Slim would bombard her with questions, and he would never let her get away with a message as cryptic as David's. Slim Moreland had been a friend of her foster parents too long. He'd consider it his duty to ferret out the truth. She was surprised Slim hadn't taken it upon himself to deliver David's telegram and demand an explanation.

No, there could be no reply. David would know she was coming. He'd know she wouldn't leave him to handle this alone. Hadn't she assured him from the beginning that all he would have to do was accept her mail? When she'd asked him to pretend to be her, that hadn't meant leaving him alone to deal with an editor from New York who happened to be traveling across South Louisiana.

But how was she going to get to Lafayette? And once she did, how was she ever going to convince this editor that she was a man?

She'd really gotten herself into a scrape this time — a scrape that was becoming less humorous by the minute.

"You do understand what I want?" Sam asked Henry Boudreaux. Sam suspected the machinist understood him far better than he understood the stumpy Cajun.

Well known for his skill, Boudreaux had come highly recommended. The man rocked his entire body forward and back while he talked. "But of course. You want I should put some holes in this pipe and then you want I should solder that copper wire gauze onto it. And then you want I should wrap it wit' galvanized wire lack a water well screen, no?"

Sam grinned. "You make it sound so simple I wonder why it took me so long to figure it out. The holes must be three-eighths of an inch and the galvanized wire needs to measure sixty mesh. You don't mind if I hang around while you do it?"

Boudreaux managed to convey a shrug with his lips and jaw. "There's a stool right over there. Jus' pull it up, but not too close."

"If this works, I'm going to need a lot more of them. You think you can remember what to do?"

The machinist smiled. *"Oui.* I remember."

There were a couple of able machinists in Beaumont who could have made the screen for Sam, and probably several more in Lake Charles, but he'd decided against going to either place, for a variety of reasons, none of which made sense to Wayne.

"I'm going to Beaumont anyway," Wayne had pointed out earlier in the week. "Why don't you go with me and have it done there?"

"You're not going to Beaumont this week, Wayne. J.C. and Myron can handle business over there until you get back."

"So where *am* I going?"

"To New Orleans," Sam announced, thoroughly confusing his brother.

"Why New Orleans?"

"Because we're fixing to build a refinery in Jennings."

"Hold on a minute, Sam," Wayne protested. "You're way ahead of me. We don't even have a producing well yet. And what does New Orleans have to do with a refinery? They don't have any there."

"No, but they have banks. Big banks. And wealthy investors by the score."

"So does Houston."

"But Houston is in Texas, and to folks around here, Texas is another country, not another state," Sam said. "You know how people treat us — almost as though we were foreigners. This is going to be a big field, maybe as big as Spindletop. We weren't ready for Spindletop, but we're going to be ready for Jennings. And we're going to do business with Louisiana folks — as much as we can, anyway. It's their state that will reap the financial rewards. They ought to be a lot more eager to help us than Texas folks."

"But I don't know anybody in New Orleans," Wayne argued.

"Precisely."

"Pardon?"

"That's the point, Wayne. If we go back to Texas, everyone who hears about our deal will jump on this opportunity. There are too many Texas oil companies far bigger than Blackman Brothers. Right now, they're watching and waiting, but the minute word gets out that the sand can be controlled, Jennings is going to boom—big time. We're liable to lose our only chance to be the major company to develop the field."

Wayne nodded then. "It's finally sinking in. You're thinking that since no one in New Orleans really understands an oil boom, they won't take it seriously."

"Right."

"Then how am I going to convince them to lend us the money?"

"With all the persuasive powers and solid business sense you have. Convince them they stand to make a fortune. Ask them for the loan contingent on my ability to bring in the well, so what will they have to lose? And, *insist* they sign a confidentiality clause. Tell them that if word leaks out, the deal is off. Right now, just lay the groundwork—open an account, sign the necessary papers, that sort of thing—so that when the well comes in, all we have to do is cable the bank with the news."

"But a refinery? Are you sure that's a sound investment?" Wayne asked, not completely convinced.

"Not if all we're going to refine is coal oil, not when a dime's worth lasts an average family for a week. But the future is gasoline. There may not be many automobiles on the roads now, but there will be in a few years. Most people can't see that, but I know it's coming. Someone, probably Henry Ford, will make them affordable. The first thing I want you to do when you get to New Orleans is go to the library, dig up as much information as you can, and then put together a projection of consumption for all petroleum products currently on the market."

They spent the better part of Tuesday night putting together the skeleton of Wayne's proposal. The only question Wayne had concerned the maker of the screen.

"I'm not going to Texas," Sam said, "for the same reasons you're not. Nor am I going to Lake Charles. It's too close to Jennings."

"So where are you going?" Wayne asked.

"East, to Lafayette. I can get there from the rig without anyone knowing about it. I'll wait for you at the depot there on Sunday."

"And if I haven't completed negotiations by then?"

"Stay in New Orleans until you do. And don't send me any telegrams," Sam warned. "If you're on the train, you're only going to get off to stretch your legs while it's stopped in Lafayette. That ought to be long enough to fill me in, then you'll get back on the train and wait for me here. I don't want anyone in Jennings to know I've gone any farther east than the rig, so be careful how you answer any questions."

Sam didn't like the clandestine atmosphere he and Wayne had created for themselves, but he understood the need for secrecy. He hoped Prairie understood why it had to be this way. Sam hated telling her he'd see her on Thursday when he knew he couldn't, but the tiny lie prevented questions from her he couldn't asnwer.

He hoped the people in Jennings would understand when this was all over. Although he had no intention of staying there for the rest of his life, he planned to conduct business in Jennings for years to come. He wanted to see an end to the tension and rivalry that had surrounded his transactions thus far.

Overnight, he'd rocketed from lunatic status to that of hero in the eyes of the Jennings population. When the cavity he created failed to control the sand, his hero status had slipped. Now, Sam wasn't sure where they put him on the scale, but he figured it came closer to lunatic again with each passing day. He felt like a greased steel ball on one of those contraptions carnival hawkers made a fortune with — just waiting for a strong man to come along and hit the lever hard enough to send him all the way to the bell on top.

Whether or not he rang that bell depended on the screen Henry Boudreaux was making. Sam hoped it worked. He hoped, too, that Jake Daniels and the crew at Blackman Number Two, presently at almost a thousand feet, could catch up with the progress at Clarkston Number One, where the depth was well over twelve hundred. He wanted to use the screen on his own well first.

Sybil had begun to dread Saturday nights. In desperation, she'd asked her father again that morning to allow her to take a horse to town or send Nick to get her at ten. Her left cheek still stung from his reply.

All day long, she prayed that someone would come along and offer her a ride home before she reached the place where the dark man on the motorcycle awaited her, the man who'd told her to call him King since she was his queen. Only he didn't treat her like a queen. Far from it.

Last week, when she'd told him she didn't want to meet him anymore, he'd slapped her around pretty good, leaving bruises on her naked body she didn't dare show to her parents. King's abuse was bad enough, but if her father found out, he'd beat her half to death. Grasping for a valid excuse, she'd told

201

him her father *did* know about their secret meetings and that he'd threatened to come after King—would have already if she'd known where he lived. The dark man had laughed at her.

There had to be a way to put a stop to it all, but Sybil couldn't figure out how—outside of being offered a ride before she left town. She didn't dare spend the night in town. Even if she did, she suspected King would be waiting for her on Sunday morning, so she prayed for divine intervention.

Not long after dark, Isaac Fontenot, a Calcasieu Parish sheriff's deputy, came into the dry goods store and asked for her. Sybil's heart pounded out of control. *Oh, my God!* she thought. *What have I done to be arrested for?*

The deputy whispered something to Mr. Glass, the proprietor, who then whispered something in response and nodded toward the back of the store. His expression unreadable, Fontenot took her arm and escorted her into the storeroom. Once inside, he pulled out two crates and directed her to sit on one of them.

"I don't know any other way to tell you this except straight out," he said. "Your parents and your brothers are dead."

For a moment, Sybil's vision blurred and her heart stopped beating. She must have fainted, because the next thing she knew, the deputy had his arms around her and he was gently slapping her cheeks.

"How?" she squeaked.

"Murdered. Someone shot 'em and then took an axe to 'em. One of your brothers—the oldest—managed to crawl to the ditch before he died. I found his body on my way into town. He'd been dead for some time."

Sybil's gorge rose in her throat. "Oh, my God!"

she whispered.

"You can't go back out there," Fontenot said. "I've arranged for you to stay with Mr. and Mrs. Glass for the time being. I have to ask you, Miss James, if you have any idea who might have done this."

Although she thought immediately of the dark man, Sybil shook her head. Why would he want to kill her folks? It didn't make sense.

"Did your father employ a hired hand?"

She moistened her dry lips with her tongue and swallowed hard. "Watson," she said. "He just started working for us last week. Is he dead, too?"

"No, ma'am. He wasn't anywhere around. Do you know where he might be?"

"Lake Charles. Daddy said he was going to send him to Lake Charles today to buy a pair of mules. But I don't think Watson—"

"Let us do the thinking, Miss James," Fontenot interrupted. "Are you going to be all right now?"

Sybil nodded weakly, thinking, *Lord, this wasn't what I meant to happen.*

"I wish you'd quit fidgeting!" Prairie fussed quietly. "You're making me nervous."

"Well, I am nervous and I don't mind saying so!" David declared.

"Sh-h-h!" she warned.

He lowered his voice. "What if we can't pull this off?"

"We won't pull if off if you don't stop twisting that wedding band. Anybody watching you would know you're not used to wearing it. And quit paying so much attention to this crowd. Most of them are here to watch the train come in, not to observe us, and the others are meeting somebody."

"But what if someone I know sees me with you?"

You and your what-ifs, she mentally grumbled. Prairie had one of her own. "What if they do? Are you embarrassed to be seen with me?"

"No, but how will I explain it? The wedding bands, I mean."

"If it happens, just follow my lead," she said, putting more confidence into the words than she felt.

"But—"

"I got here, didn't I?" she whispered. "And I thought of this scheme. Trust me to make it work. Just don't say anything more than you have to. Now, put your arm around my shoulders and smile down at me from time to time. Act as though we're married."

What in the world was Prairie Jernigan doing at the Southern Pacific depot in Lafayette?

At first, Sam didn't believe it was her. He kept telling himself it wasn't possible. Some other woman was her height. Some other woman had hair the color of molasses. Some other woman had a big black hat with poufs of blue chiffon and yellow silk roses on it. Some other woman owned a dress made of blue and black striped taffeta. Some other woman was standing there next to a tall, handsome man, wearing his arm on her shoulder with such ease and smiling up at him so warmly.

But it wasn't another woman. It was Prairie.

The realization knifed through his belly, startling him with its intensity. What in blazes, he asked himself again, was she doing there? And who was the man she was with?

Sam inched his way forward to get a better look at her until he stood less than ten feet away. All she had to do to see him was glance over her right shoulder. He turned around and walked back, well away from the tracks, and located a spot on a crowded outside stairway where he could see her. Should she look his direction, all he had to do was duck behind the man beside him.

He wasn't spying, he told himself. Could he help it if she and her beau stood directly in his line of vision? He'd have to move farther away—he couldn't afford for her to see him and ask later why he was there. He wasn't supposed to be in Lafayette any more than she was.

But at least he was there on business. The way she was looking at the fellow next to her, the way she let him embrace her in public, led to only one conclusion. The man was her lover.

Sam couldn't believe that either. Not of Prairie Jernigan. But what other explanation could there be? He was still pondering that question when the train whistle blared and the steam engine roared into sight.

From his spot on the stairs, Sam watched the passengers disembark. They flowed around the tall man and Prairie until all but one of them had found their waiting parties and moved away from the tracks. Prairie and the tall man walked toward the lone remaining passenger, a short fellow wearing a homburg and a brown tweed suit. They spoke briefly to him. He nodded his head, and the three walked toward the station house.

He wasn't surprised when Wayne didn't get off the train; he honestly hadn't expected him to conclude his business in New Orleans so quickly. Until he'd spotted Prairie, he'd hoped Wayne would be on the train. Now Sam was glad he hadn't been. Prairie would surely have recognized Wayne when he got off, and then would most probably have seen him, too.

Sam walked to the street, hailed a hansom cab,

gave the driver the name of his hotel, and breathed a sigh of relief when the carriage pulled away from the station. He'd escaped detection, and in the morning he'd be gone. In the meantime, he'd have a hearty supper at the hotel, then retire early to his room, and no one from Jennings would ever know he'd gone to Lafayette.

One would not have described the Evangeline Hotel on Jefferson Street as imposing, but with four stories, fifty rooms, and a restaurant, the Evangeline was the largest and finest hotel in Lafayette. Constructed of red brick, it was a boxy building reminiscent of eighteenth century Georgian architecture, sitting stark and plain on its corner amid a sea of Victorian turrets, porches, and gingerbread trim. No dormers decorated its low mansard roof, and neither pediment nor portico graced its paneled front door. The dark green shutters flanking its windows provided the building's sole adornment, and they were there for protection against tropical storms, not decoration.

David turned the corner and drove the buggy under a porte cochere at the back. A black valet shuffled around the buggy to take the reins from David, while a doorman assisted both Prairie and Theodore Stephenson, the editor from Beadle and Adams, to the ground on the passenger side.

"Will you be staying overnight, sir?" the doorman asked, inclining his head toward the small bag on the buggy seat.

"Yes, I will," Stephenson said. "If you would, please take my bag to the desk and inform the clerk I'll be checking in later, after dinner. I'd like a corner room, away from the street, with a private bath, if you have it."

"Yes, sir. I'll take care of it for you, sir," the doorman said politely. If he noted the man's Yankee accent, he didn't allow it to show on his face. "And you, ma'am?"

"My husband and I are here for dinner only," Prairie replied, amazed at the glibness with which her tongue told the lie.

"This hotel is certainly not as elegant as you're probably accustomed to," Prairie said to the editor, "but you should be comfortable here."

Theodore Stephenson took Prairie's elbow and smiled warmly at her, deep dimples piercing his round cheeks. Behind his wire-framed spectacles, his hazel eyes twinkled. "You're a most charming lady, Mrs. Hamilton," he said, his compliment eliciting a similar smile from her. "I'm certain I shall be quite comfortable. Perhaps I shall decide to stay in Lafayette for a few days."

The smile froze on Prairie's face. That would never do at all. She couldn't afford to stay in Lafayette much longer, and David would never be able to handle the editor alone. While she scrambled for a polite way to send him back to New Orleans post haste, David said bluntly, "There's really nothing to do here, sir, and you wouldn't want to miss your boat."

David walked around them, leading the way through the door and down a wide hall to the restaurant, which was on the front side of the Evangeline Hotel.

"You're right, of course," Stephenson said on a sigh. "I've wanted to meet my favorite writer for a long time. Now that I have, it seems such a shame to have only this one night to spend with you."

Thank goodness that's all you have, Prairie thought, so wrapped up in worry she didn't note the implication that *she* was his favorite writer. Instead, she was hoping she could maintain her equilibrium until she and David could make their departure. The earliness of the present hour guaranteed a lengthy evening in the company of Mr. Stephenson. At least the restaurant wasn't crowded. Indeed, only two other couples occupied tables there.

"Where would you prefer to sit?" the maître d' asked, waving his arm to indicate the many available tables before accepting the men's proffered hats. David selected a table in the corner farthest from the door and windows, then ordered coffee.

"Tell us about your trip," Prairie said the moment they were seated, knowing that the more she could get the editor to talk about himself, the fewer questions she and David would be required to answer.

Stephenson's reply disappointed her. "There isn't much to tell," he said. "The train ride from New York to New Orleans was long, tiring, and uneventful. I suppose I should be grateful for the latter. I apologize for not writing to you before I left, to alert you of my visit, but I honestly thought everyone in Louisiana lived within a few miles of New Orleans. Strange how one misconceives a place one has never visited."

His observation reminded Prairie of Sam's remark about Pampas J. Rose never having visited Sacramento. She wondered how many more places she'd written about from a foundation of misconceptions.

"Since I had planned a week's stay in New Orleans, I was certain we could easily arrange a convenient time to meet," the editor continued. "As it turned out, I was hard-pressed to make arrangements to get here and back, but the concierge at the Cosmopolitan was most helpful." On the way, he had told them he would be returning to New Orleans the following morning via hired coach, a three-day trip.

His ship left on Thursday.

"Have you ever been to Barbados before?" David asked.

Stephenson said he hadn't, then launched into a lengthy discussion of his itinerary. He spoke passionately of the tiny Caribbean island and his lifelong desire to visit it.

"Perhaps you'd be interested in setting a story in Barbados," the editor suggested. "I'd be happy to collect some material for you."

David's eyebrows rose in the barest hint of movement. Prairie's chin dipped slightly as she sipped her coffee.

"Thank you," David said, "I'd appreciate that. Are you ready to order?"

Prairie felt better with each passing minute. They'd been in the editor's company for a little over an hour, and thus far he'd been perfectly happy with small talk, though most of it she'd found quite boring. Better to be bored, she decided, than exposed.

While the editor studied the menu, David described many of the local dishes and elaborated on Cajun cuisine. Stephenson settled on a bowl of gumbo and shrimp etouffée, which David assured him would be served with crusty French bread and fresh creamery butter.

When the waiter had taken their orders, the editor leaned back in his chair and said, "Well, tell me about yourself, David."

"What exactly would you like to know?" David asked.

Stephenson stroked his clean-shaven jaw for a minute. "First," he said, "I think I'd like to know where your pen name came from. Unusual name, Pampas."

David visibly stiffened. Prairie reached beneath the table cloth and laid a comforting hand on his knee. Expecting such questions, she had drilled David repeatedly during the few hours they'd had between her arrival and Stephenson's. She breathed a bit easier as she felt him relax, but she left her hand on his knee for good measure.

"Yes, sir," David agreed. "I wanted a simple but unusual name, one people would remember. Actually, it was my wife who came up with it."

Prairie had cautioned David to toss the conversation her way as much as he possibly could. "Pretend it's a hot potato," she'd said. "You toss it up a time or two, then get rid of it before it burns your hands." So far, so good, she thought. Before offering an explanation, she measured Stephenson's reaction, which was nothing more than a simple nod of understanding.

Theodore Stephenson pursed his thin lips and regarded Prairie for a long moment. "Now I see," he said. "You chose a name synonymous with your wife's. Prairie is a very unusual name. I don't think I've ever known anyone else named Prairie before."

"Nor I," she said, then attempted to change the subject. "How do you like Louisiana coffee?"

"Very full-bodied, but the flavor is quite peculiar."

"That's the chicory," she explained. "The Creoles learned to add it years ago when coffee was scarce."

"Yes, I know," the editor said. "You wrote about that in *Fiery Flora*." At her look of surprise, he corrected himself. "I mean, your husband wrote about it."

He watched them closely, too closely, Prairie thought, as though he were gauging their reactions much as she had measured his moments before. "While I was in New Orleans, I visited some of the places you wrote about—the opera house, Jackson Square, the cathedral, the French market. But I couldn't find the old cemetery, the one with the oven

210

vaults. Could you please tell me how to get there? I'd like to see it before I leave."

David's hand covered Prairie's then, silently asking for help. She'd visited New Orleans on a number of occasions with the Donovans, who loved roaming the Vieux Carré and pointing out sites of historic interest. David, on the other hand, had never even been to New Orleans.

A surreptitious glance at his face confirmed her worst fear. David's composure was quickly crumbling.

"It's, uh, let me think how to tell you . . ." he stumbled.

Prairie schooled her voice into a light, airy tone. "You remember, dear. It's on the outskirts of the quarter, away from the river. Is it Rampart Street?" She turned to Stephenson. "Ask the concierge at the Cosmopolitan. He can direct you there."

Her suggestion hit her hard in the gut. *The concierge at the Cosmopolitan was most helpful,* Stephenson had said. The editor probably knew the exact location of the cemetery. He was testing them. But why—unless he was suspicious?

"You know, David," Stephenson continued, "I've had the privilege of editing most of your stories, a pleasant task, I can assure you. Most of our writers do not share your command of the English language. Nor do they spell and punctuate as well as you do."

"Thank you, sir, but I doubt many of your other writers are teachers."

Stephenson shrugged. "I wouldn't know. We don't require résumés. I would be surprised, however, if they were. I wonder how you manage it."

"Pardon?"

"Oh, not merely juggling two careers. I expect the real problem comes from sneaking your identity past the board of education. I can't imagine they'd approve."

"I'm certain they wouldn't," David agreed. "That's why I use a pseudonym."

"Oh, yes, the pseudonym. You didn't tell me about the rest of it. Is Rose, perhaps, your wife's middle name?"

"Yes, it is," David replied.

Prairie pinched his thigh, but it was too late.

Stephenson nodded again and his hazel eyes glistened with the spark of complete understanding. His bespectacled gaze darted back and forth between Prairie and David, making her feel like a goldfish in a crystal bowl. Her heart pounded in her chest and her hand tightened on David's knee.

If Sam had been surprised to see Prairie at the Lafayette depot, he was flabbergasted to find her sitting in the restaurant at the Evangeline Hotel — and with her hand on the tall, slender man's knee.

In public! his mind railed. Her show of affection was bad enough at the depot — but it was nothing compared to this! This was too much. He started toward her, intending to confront her right then and there, but reason intervened before he'd taken three steps. Fortunately, her back faced the door, thus preventing her from seeing him.

Nevertheless, Sam dared not tempt fate any further. There were other restaurants in Lafayette — and other hotels. Should he move to one of them? he wondered. After all, he couldn't be certain Prairie was staying at the Evangeline. More than likely, she was staying with the tall man, wherever that was.

No, he decided. The best strategy was to have supper delivered to his room and stay there until morning. He didn't know how Prairie planned to get

212

back to Jennings that night, but her presence was required at school the following morning, which should make his leaving then safe. Thank goodness, he thought, he'd brought a wagon instead of his red surrey, which was too easily identifiable for a man on a clandestine mission.

What he had to do at the moment was get out of the restaurant before she happened to turn around and see him. Unable to take his eyes off her, Sam backed toward the doorway. Just as he reached the hall, she raised her left hand, the one that had been resting on the man's knee, and used it to tuck a stray lock of hair back under her hat.

Sam's stomach knotted up and he swallowed hard before a tide of anger surged through him. All this time, he'd known she was keeping something secret. He'd known it! Now, he knew what it was.

No wonder she let the man embrace her in public. No wonder she rested her hand on his knee and smiled at him so sweetly. She was married to him. The thin gold band on her left hand proved it.

Chapter Fourteen

The gumbo arrived in the nick of time — or so Prairie thought. The last thing she wanted this conversation to lead to was a confession, but if they weren't extremely careful, that was exactly where it would end.

Theodore Stephenson removed his glasses to eat. Without them, he seemed far less formidable, far less intimidating. But his mind, Prairie discovered, worked like a steel trap. Midway through the course, he slipped the spectacles back on his face and pinned her with a steady scrutiny.

"And you, Mrs. Hamilton, what do you do while your husband is at work?" the editor asked.

This was a question she and David had prepared themselves for. They wouldn't say she was a teacher, too. Although a teacher's salary alone would not support a family, the additional income from writing would provide ample supplement. Nor were married women allowed to teach in most places, including Lafayette. Therefore, to avoid further explanation, they created a plausible lie that wasn't too far from the truth and hoped they didn't stumble over their contrivances.

"I work at home, Mr. Stephenson," Prairie replied, smiling.

"Forgive me, Mrs. Hamilton, if this sounds offensive, but I cannot imagine a woman of your obvious

214

intelligence spending her days cleaning, cooking, and mending." The editor paused to take a sip of water, but his eyes never left her face.

"No offense taken, sir," she said. "I find it most pleasant to converse with a man who understands the mediocrity of housework. I do some private tutoring in the afternoons, and I type all my husband's stories. He composes them in longhand, you see."

Stephenson's round chin bobbed. "Yes," he said slowly, "I think I do see."

He finished his gumbo without further comment, possibly because David embarked on a discourse concerning the differences in Creole and Cajun gumbos. Prairie silently blessed David for purchasing them some time.

A waiter refilled their water glasses and whisked away the bowls. Her limbs tense and her chest tight, Prairie awaited the editor's next question, for she harbored no doubts there would be more interrogation from the little man. She didn't have to wait long.

Stephenson wiped his mouth with his napkin, then rested his elbows on the table and steepled his fingers. "One thing that's always amazed me," he said, "about the Pampas J. Rose stories is the author's sensitivity. We don't often see that, not in the dime novel trade. In fact, I personally think it's that sensitivity that has made Rose so popular, though the majority of our male readers would never admit it."

Prairie prayed that David could see the question that was forthcoming. Stephenson merely waited for David's comment, like a coiled snake poised for the strike.

"No, I don't suppose men would admit such a thing," David said.

"Do you admit it, Mr. Hamilton?"

David's eyebrows rose to mid-forehead. "Pardon?"

"Are you supplying the sensitivity? Or is it, perhaps, your wife?"

Prairie didn't think she'd ever seen anyone look quite so stricken as David Hamilton did at that moment. She hastened to his rescue. "I do hope you aren't implying that a sensitive nature diminishes a man's masculinity."

She was rewarded by Stephenson's spluttering.

"Oh, well, of course not. I only meant . . ." He stopped, seemingly at a loss for words. Prairie wasn't about to let him off the hook so easily.

"What exactly did you mean, then, Mr. Stephenson?"

"When you said you typed the stories, I couldn't help but wonder if, perhaps, you made some changes, Mrs. Hamilton. It would be a natural thing to do."

"I offer some suggestions from time to time," Prairie replied, "but the stories are David's. I would never change anything without discussing it with him first."

The waiter appeared with the entrées, thus stalling the editor's grilling for the moment. Stephenson commented on the delicate flavor of the etouffée as opposed to the spiciness of the gumbo, creating an opening for David to expound further on the many aspects of Cajun cuisine.

"You seem to be quite an authority on the subject," the editor commented. "I'm surprised you haven't written a Cajun story yet."

"He did," Prairie said, quickly, before David had an opportunity to deny it. David shot her a *please help me!* look. "You know, dear," she continued, "the one about the Cajun trapper. Dugas was his name, if I remember correctly."

David nodded, somewhat nervously. "Oh, yes. That one."

Prairie didn't like the way Stephenson was looking at the two of them again. Behind his spectacles, his hazel eyes resembled two iridescent beads. "I don't recall that one myself. Someone else must have edited it. Do, please, Mr. Hamilton, tell me about Dugas, the trapper," Stephenson said.

He made a point of addressing his question to David, almost daring Prairie to answer it. Though she desperately wanted to, she knew she had to allow David a chance. As far as she knew, he had read all her books, either in manuscript form or after publication. She hoped he recalled the Cajun story.

David frowned in concentration. "Let me think," he said, quite casually. Prairie sighed inwardly, but she didn't let down her guard. "That one was some time back. When you've written as many stories as I have, Mr. Stephenson, it's hard to sort them out after awhile."

Prairie seized the opportunity he'd left open to her. "Wasn't Dugas the one who killed alligators for their hides?"

David grinned. "Oh, yes! And their meat, too. Have you ever eaten alligator, Mr. Stephenson? No? You should try it sometime. It's considered a delicacy among us city folk, but to the Cajuns who live along the bayous, eating alligator is commonplace."

Prairie relaxed while David submitted another lecture on Cajun food. She'd had no idea until that night how knowledgeable David was on the subject. He expanded his colloquy to include a history of the Cajuns, which took them through the end of the main course and into coffee and dessert.

But the minute he exhausted the topic, Stephenson posed another question. Prairie had watched him closely, had seen him open his mouth each time David paused for breath, and knew he itched to quiz David about his writing again. She hoped this would be his final query.

"There's something else I must know," the editor said, "and that is why you choose to repeat certain trivial details in each of your stories."

A look of genuine bewilderment overcame David's normally placid features. This was another question they'd practiced answering. Prairie silently applauded her friend's acting ability. "Details?" David asked. "Which ones?"

As Stephenson listed them, Prairie ticked them off in her head. He mentioned every one.

If possible, David looked even more puzzled. "Do I do that? Honestly?"

Prairie didn't like the editor's condescending tone. "You must know you do, son. I can't believe it wouldn't be intentional. For the life of me, though, I can't fathom a reason for it."

"Nor I," David said with a careless shrug. "It must not bother my readers. They continue to buy my books. I'd like to ask some questions of my own now, Mr. Stephenson."

The abruptness of David's change of subject startled the editor, which tickled Prairie. She nudged David's knee with her own, urging him to continue before Stephenson had a chance to recover. She wasn't disappointed.

"First of all, I'd appreciate your telling me all about production. Who decides which scene will be depicted on the cover? Who sets the release date? How many copies of my books does Beadle and Adams print? How many subscribers do you have? That sort of thing."

David's questions kept Stephenson too busy to ask any more of his own. Prairie found herself so wrapped up in listening to the editor discuss the dime novel publishing business that she was surprised when the waiter quietly informed them the restaurant was closing.

They said their goodbyes at the desk, then she and David made good their escape. But they held back their exultation until they were more than a block away from the Evangeline Hotel.

"We did it!" Prairie exclaimed, planting a kiss on David's cheek. "Or rather, you did. I'm so proud of

218

you, David."

In the glow of the street lamp, she could see the haughty thrust of his chest and the arrogant tilt of his chin. "I'm rather proud of myself, too," he said smugly. "I may run off to New York and audition for the stage. I've always wanted to play Hamlet." His mien grew serious then. "But there were a couple of times when I almost lost my composure, Prairie. Thanks for pulling me back."

"I should be thanking you! You didn't have to do this for me. I do appreciate it—and everything else."

He slipped his arm around her shoulder and pulled her against him. "When you started this," he said, his voice suddenly tender, "I thought you were crazy, but that letter from Mrs. Byers made me see that this whole notion might just be crazy enough to work. If it does, it will have all been worth it."

Prairie snuggled against him, glad she could call David Hamilton her friend.

When the buggy turned the corner and disappeared from sight, Sam let the drapery fall over the second-floor window, collapsed into a chair, and plunged both hands into his hair.

He'd been such a fool! Such a fool to let her under his skin. And that's what he'd done, he realized. The day before, he would have staunchly denied any such thing. But seeing Prairie with that man, seeing the wedding band on her finger and her hand on his knee, seeing her kiss him . . . Witnessing those things had wrenched at his gut in a way he would never have believed possible.

Sam wished he didn't have to go back to Jennings. He wished he never had to set eyes on Prairie Jernigan again as long as he lived. He'd known she was holding back on him, keeping something a secret. And now that he knew what it was, he almost wished he didn't.

You ought to be thanking your lucky stars, man, he told himself. *This little trip saved you a passel of potential trouble.*

He had the well to think about. Nothing—not even Prairie Jernigan—was as important.

That's what he told himself most of the night, before exhaustion finally overcame him.

Less than an hour after Sam finally succumbed to sleep, Prairie was on the road back to Jennings.

The fact that she'd managed the trip at all amazed her. She could never have accomplished it without assistance from Doc and Ruth. Securing their help had required telling them everything, but if there were two people she could trust, they were the Nolans.

She'd avoided going to Wynn and Michael, who were too close to her to be objective. They might have been supportive, but Michael would have insisted on accompanying her to Lafayette and then sticking to her like glue. That kind of help she could do without.

Going straight to the livery was out of the question. Within an hour, everyone in Jennings would know she'd rented a buggy and left town. Someone, probably Michael, would follow.

But the real problem was school on Monday. There was no way she could make it back in time, and only Ruth could cover for her.

"The biggest problem will be getting you out of town and then back in again without arousing suspicion," Doc had said. "You have no business going alone, Prairie, but I can't see any way around it. Not if you're determined to keep this trip secret."

He pulled on his ear for a minute, thinking. "Ruth, take our buggy north, then turn east when you're well out of town. Prairie, you hide under a quilt in the back. I'll rent a rig from the livery. I can tell them old Dobbin is lame. Ya'll wait for me at the Evangeline fork."

They got there without incident. Doc handed Prairie his pistol. "Don't hesitate to use it," he admonished. "Stop and water the horses regularly and let them cool off." He looked at the sun and whistled. "Damn, girl, it's already near ten o'clock. You'll never get there today. Lay over at the way station in Duson and go on to Lafayette in the morning. If the horses can't make it back in one day, spend Monday night on the road, too. We'll cover for you here. And, by all means, be careful!"

She promised him she would. Ruth got in the rig with Doc, and Prairie took their buggy to Lafayette. When she arrived Sunday morning, she went straight to David's boardinghouse, where she rented a room for the night by claiming to be his sister. By the time he got home from church, she had bathed and changed into her blue and black striped taffeta dress. After dinner, they prepared themselves for the editor's visit, which, thankfully, was history now.

Thus far, the weather had behaved beautifully, even if it was rather cold. But better cold than wet, she thought. The clear sky—sullied by only a few big, puffy clouds—promised continued cooperation. In fact, she acknowledged with a firm nod, everything had gone as well or better than she could possibly have hoped.

Her primary concern at the moment lay with Wynn, who was certain to check on her the minute Patrick got home and told her Prairie had missed school because she was sick. Ruth promised to stay at school for as long as she could that afternoon in order to waylay Wynn when she showed up. Ruth would tell her that Doc had examined Prairie, who was supposedly sleeping, and ascertained a mild case of catarrhal fever. They could only hope Wynn would trust Doc's

221

diagnosis and decide to allow Prairie her rest.

Since determining her time of arrival in Jennings was virtually impossible, Doc and Ruth would not be able to sneak her back in the same way they'd sneaked her out. She would have to wait for the cover of absolute darkness, the later the better.

As Prairie followed the Old Spanish Trail, a decent enough road and one well-traveled, she checked her watch against landmarks, attempting to time her progress between stations. Fortunately, these were placed every eight to ten miles. In between each one, she stopped to rest the horses for a spell.

Although she kept the pistol tucked under her lap robe, Prairie met no unsavory-looking travelers. On Saturday, the road had been packed with farm families on their way to or from the nearest town. Despite her fear that someone would recognize her, Prairie found comfort in their presence. But today, she was practically alone on the road. The few people she passed looked at her oddly but continued on their way without comment.

The long ride allowed much time for contemplation. Two and a half years earlier, when she'd started writing dime novels, she had put David at minimal risk. The visit from Theodore Stephenson, however, had changed all that. She shuddered to think what might have happened to David had they run into one of his colleagues at the depot or the hotel. Explaining the wedding bands would have been difficult.

She did have them with her, didn't she? She had put them in her reticule, she was sure of it. Nevertheless, Prairie transferred the reins to her left hand and used her right to open the drawstring on her handbag. Once it was open, she plunged her hand inside and explored the meager contents until she felt the coolness of two metal rings against her fingertips. Only then did she expel the breath she'd been holding.

The rings belonged to Doc and Ruth, and though

they'd exchanged them for wider, more ornate bands years before, Prairie knew how significant these originals were to them. Ruth had offered them willingly, but her eyes had misted when she handed them to Prairie.

By enlisting their help, she had placed Doc and Ruth in some jeopardy. Should her foster parents ever learn of this particular deception, they would be furious with the Nolans. Nor would the townspeople understand, especially the self-righteous members of the W.C.T.U.

It had to stop somewhere. Uncovering her roots was not as important as the reputations of those she loved. When she had told David she couldn't do anything about society's narrow-mindedness, she was thinking only of herself. Now, her quest seemed terribly selfish.

She'd been given the prime opportunity to reveal her identity to an editor from Beadle and Adams, and what had she done? Taken the coward's way out. When she sent the Cherokee Sally manuscript, she would enclose a letter to Mr. Stephenson, tell him everything, and let the pieces fall where they may. If forty published stories over a thirty-month period hadn't accomplished her goal, there was no sense in continuing. Especially when the longer she maintained her pretense, the more precarious it became.

Prairie was so preoccupied with her deliberations that she didn't see the skunk dart out onto the road until it was too late. The horses whinnied and reared. Caught off guard, Prairie jerked on the reins. The team bucked and snorted, backing away from the skunk, pushing one of the back wheels off the road and into the ditch. She felt the buggy pitch sideways and fought with the reins, calling to the horses, begging them to be still.

For a moment, the buggy balanced precariously on two wheels. Prairie held on to the reins as tightly as she could, but when the horses suddenly bolted, the reins slipped through her palms and she pitched into the air. Her scream pierced the air. Then all was silent.

Sam wished he'd brought the surrey. He could have made much better time in it, and suddenly he was in a hurry.

It was funny how things worked out, he thought as the wagon springs creaked and popped. He'd spent an entire evening tossing and turning over nothing. Well, almost nothing, he corrected. There were still a hell of a lot of questions Prairie Jernigan was going to answer for him, whether she liked it or not. And he'd rather ask his questions on neutral ground. If he could catch up with her, he'd be able to.

Drained from a lack of rest, Sam figured he would have slept until noon had the hawkers on the street not awakened him shortly after dawn. While he was reviving himself with several cups of strong coffee in the hotel restaurant, the short man he'd seen at the depot with Prairie came in and ordered breakfast. Sam was sitting close enough to hear the man's accent, which was decidedly that of a New Yorker.

What had Prairie been doing with a Yankee? Sam wondered. It didn't make sense. He sat and watched the man until he couldn't stand it anymore. He had to know. And, by dinghies, he was going to ask!

On his way to the door, he stopped at the man's table. "Pardon me, sir," he said, tipping his hat and waiting for a response.

"Yes?"

"I saw you yesterday at the depot with a lady I think I recognized. I didn't know she was living in Lafayette now, or that she had married. I'm here on business and I'd like to look her up while I'm in town. I wonder if you could tell me where I might find her."

That sounded plausible. Didn't it? Sam hoped so.

The man didn't crack quite so easily. "And what, pray tell, is your friend's name?"

"Her maiden name was Jernigan. Prairie Jernigan."

The man nodded then. "Must be the same lady, then. There can't be that many women named Prairie. Her married name is Hamilton, Mrs. David Hamilton." He removed a small black notebook from his inside coat pocket, opened it, and showed Sam an address. "Do you need to write it down?"

"No, sir. I can find it. Thanks!" Sam gushed, not believing his luck.

Sam did find the address—a boardinghouse not too far from the hotel. He asked the proprietor if Mrs. Hamilton was at home.

"Mrs. Hamilton?" the middle-aged woman asked in some confusion. "The only boarder I have named Hamilton is David."

"That's the one. Is his wife here?"

The woman narrowed her eyes at him. "You must not know Mr. Hamilton. He isn't married."

"But I saw him yesterday with his wife," Sam insisted.

"That was his sister from Crowley. She left early this morning. Wouldn't even stay for breakfast, but I insisted she take a couple of biscuits with her. Her room is vacant, if you need a place to stay."

Sam frowned, confused himself. "His sister?" Suddenly he understood. "Oh! His sister Prairie. I'd forgotten he had a sister."

The woman smiled then. "Yes. That's the one. Shall I tell Mr. Hamilton you called?"

Sam was already on his way to the door. "No, thank you. I'll try to see him next time I'm in town," he called over his shoulder, knowing it wouldn't matter if the woman did tell David a man had come by looking for his nonexistent wife. Hamilton wouldn't have a clue as to his identity.

What was Prairie up to, though, with this Hamilton character? She'd taken quite a risk leaving Jennings by herself and missing a day of school, which meant someone in Jennings had aided and abetted her trip.

The Donovans? Not likely. Not the way Michael overprotected her. And certainly not any of Prairie's W.C.T.U. cohorts. King Clarkston? Sam didn't think Prairie would ask him for the time of day, not since the library association dance, anyway. The Nolans! It had to be them. Prairie would have had to tell Ruth she wouldn't be at school today. Otherwise, Ruth Nolan would have the town in an uproar looking for Prairie.

That explained how she'd managed the trip, but Sam had no clue as to why she'd gone to Lafayette—except that the New Yorker was somehow involved.

He'd had such capital luck playing detective that morning, he decided to try again at the way station in Rayne.

"Yes, sirree," the stationmaster said. "That little lady stopped here not two hours ago. I 'member her well. Cute little thing. Not big as a minute. Ate some stew while her team ate and rested up a bit. I told her she didn't have no biness traveling alone. Course, I told her that same thing Saturday when she stopped here on her way east, and she ignored me then, too."

By his calculations, Sam had gained a little over an hour on her. He traded his team at the Rayne station, which he reckoned should buy him at least another thirty-minute advantage. He pushed the fresh horses hard and traded them again in Crowley, where he learned Prairie was only a little over an hour ahead of him. By Estherwood, he'd gained another half-hour.

The blazing afternoon sun dipped lower and lower until the road appeared to run straight into the burning ball of fire. With one hand, Sam shaded his eyes against the blinding light, and with the other, he slapped the reins against the backs of the horses, urging the team on at breakneck speed toward the golden horizon.

A few miles out of Estherwood, the horses whickered and shook their heads as their hooves stirred up the putrid odor left in the dirt by a skunk. Sam snatched his handkerchief out of his pocket and held it over his mouth and nose until the wagon had cleared the nauseating smell.

Behind him, Prairie groaned and rolled over in the ditch.

Chapter Fifteen

"What the hell!" Sam hollered, squinting against the brilliant sunlight and pulling hard on the reins to avoid running the team over the buggy sitting dead center in the middle of the road. "Whoa, there!" he called, tugging harder against the tow.

The pair pranced to the left and the wagon skittered around the buggy. The back wheel on the right side of the wagon hit the buggy, knocking the smaller vehicle sideways. Sam heard a loud crunch and the groan of springs before his team came to a halt several yards down the road. Quickly, he secured the reins, jumped off the wagon, and sprinted back to the buggy, his tongue aching to administer the lashing he planned to give its driver.

But there was no driver. The seat was empty.

Certain his wagon had thrown the driver out when it hit the buggy, Sam darted around the vehicle and scanned the shallow ditch. It was empty.

"You didn't get here by yourself," he muttered, then choked on the fetid stench permeating the air.

It was the odor of skunk.

Until then, he hadn't noticed the lathered flanks of the horses or heard their labored breathing. The team looked awfully familiar. A second, harder look at the buggy convinced him it was Enoch Nolan's. It was possible the elderly doctor had been driving it himself, but Sam was willing to make bet it had been Prairie.

He'd also be willing to make bet that she — or Enoch, if he was wrong — was in the ditch back down the road, probably at the spot where he'd smelled skunk the first time.

If there had been any water around or mud in the ditch, the horses wouldn't be standing in the road. And as soon as they caught their second wind, they'd be off again, sniffing for water to wash the smell of skunk off their legs. Sam tied their reins to the back of his wagon, then turned around and headed back, slowly this time. He wouldn't be able to smell the skunk odor in the road again, not with it wafting off the horses the way it did, so he tied his handkerchief over his mouth and nose and let his gaze volley from one ditch to the other.

Having the blinding sun behind him helped. Sam hoped he'd find Prairie soon, before the sun completely disappeared, but if he had to, he'd look all night. He had a lantern and ample coal oil in the wagon.

The deep lavender of dusk set in, bringing with it a cold wind. Sam figured he'd traveled close to a mile since he'd turned around. Surely, he thought, he should have found her by then. He racked his brain, trying to recall a landmark near the place where he'd first smelled the skunk — a farmhouse or tree, something. But it was all a blur in his mind.

Purple shadows rendered the ditches far darker than the road, making visibility almost nil. Sam stopped the team, pulled the lantern out of the back of the wagon and lit it, then climbed down to the road. Walking with the horses would be even slower, but he didn't dare leave them, not with Enoch's team wanting to bolt for the nearest water hole.

He couldn't be certain which ditch she would be in, but the one on his left would be the most likely. It would have been on her right since she had been heading west and the closer one, assuming she'd been driving on the right side of the road. Of course, he realized, that wouldn't hold true if the team had pulled the buggy a piece before spilling her out. He had to start somewhere, though.

Dusk gave way to darkness, but Sam plodded along, holding the lantern out as far over the ditch as he could. The wind had picked up. It blew in gusts, buffeting him from one side and then another, stirring up dust on the road and hurling it into his eyes, making it increasingly harder to see.

He had decided he might as well turn around and try the opposite ditch when the wind changed direction again, blowing from the east, blowing the smell of skunk directly at him. He spotted her then, lying in a crumpled heap of brown skirts, the lantern light flashing off the edge of her white petticoat.

At the sight of her lifeless form, a sharp pain knifed through his chest. Without giving the horses a second thought, he dropped the reins and set the lantern down on the road, then clambered down into the ditch and scooped her into his arms. She sagged limply against him and moaned. Sam's heart soared at the sound.

Gently, he laid her on the wagon seat, then retrieved the lantern and the reins and remounted. By his reckoning, they couldn't be far from the Estherwood station. Sam didn't know if Estherwood had a doctor, but he knew he had to get Prairie out of the wind and into a warm bed, and the sooner the better.

He set the lantern into a mounting on the front of the wagon, then pushed the horses as hard as he dared at night, his gaze bouncing between the lantern-lit road and the darkness ahead, seeking the lights from the way station. They appeared as no more than tiny pinpoints at first, earthbound stars twinkling on the eastern horizon, but growing larger, clearer, with each *ker-thunk* of the horses' hooves upon the hard-packed road.

* * *

Something was different, though Prairie wasn't sure exactly what at first. She didn't know how long she'd faded in and out of semi-awareness, oblivious to everything except the extreme soreness in her head when she was conscious. She reached upward with a tentative hand and pressed her fingers against the dried blood on her temple. Her body bounced, the unexpected movement dislodging her hand and sending barbed tentacles of pain through the right side of her head.

In pain and fear, she cried out. Her hands flew up, groping for something to hold on to, anything to keep from falling again. She encountered an arm, felt a hand close tenderly over her fingers, heard a voice, low and soothing, assuring her that all would be well. Sam! The whinny of horses further comforted her, as did the realization that the gentle bouncing originated from the springs of a sturdy wagon.

Not far ahead, the warm glow of lights beckoned, promising shelter from the wind. Thunder rumbled in the distance, faint and pulsating at first, increasing in volume and reverberating with a terrible violence as they neared the lights.

The tender voice called "Whoa!" and the bouncing ceased just as the first drops of rain pelted against her bare cheek. Seconds later, strong arms lifted her from the seat and strong legs ran with her toward the light. Prairie sighed, buried her head against Sam's shoulder, and faded again into the dark, obscure world that seemed wont to claim her.

"What happened to *her?*"

The stationmaster's ruddy face indicated far more concern than his brusque tone allowed.

Sam inclined his head toward a door set in a side wall. "Is that room for rent?"

The stationmaster bobbed his nearly bald head, snatched up a lamp, and scurried to open the door. He followed Sam into the room.

"That the woman you was lookin' fer?" the man asked.

"Yes. She was thrown from her buggy," Sam said, laying Prairie on the bed. "I need warm water, clean cloths, bandages, and a hot water bottle. Is there a doctor anywhere around here?"

The man set the lamp on an unfinished pine table by the bed. "Naw. Closest one's in Jennings."

When the man hovered near the bed, Sam prodded him. "Could you get those things for me, Mister—?"

"Webb. Jackson Webb. Yes, sir. I'll be right back."

"Someone needs to take care of the horses, too, Mr. Webb," Sam added. "I hope you have some tomato juice; one team's got skunk all over them. And I'll need the bags out of both the wagon and the buggy."

The man's round head bobbed again as he pulled the door closed behind him.

Immediately, Sam went to work removing Prairie's shoes and stockings. When these had been cast aside, he took off her hat and pulled the pins out of her hair, finger combing her thick, dark locks and settling them about her shoulders. Then he unbuttoned her jacket, but the left sleeve stuck over her hand and refused to budge. Sam pulled the sleeve back up her arm and found the culprit to be the drawstring bag hanging from her wrist.

He paid no attention to the bag until it clanked against the bedside table. Sam knew he had no business looking in her purse. He told himself that even as his fingers worked the drawstring loose. Perhaps, he argued, attempting to justify the action, there was a pillbox inside. And perhaps she had some aspirin in the pillbox. He turned the bag upside down and shook its contents onto the bed.

Out came a leather coin purse with a metal clasp

top, the silver dragonfly brooch he'd often seen her wear—and two gold wedding bands.

He didn't know why he did it. He didn't think about it at all. He just did it. He slipped the rings onto their fingers.

Hers was too big and his was too small. Sam didn't know how much too small until he couldn't get it off. He tugged at the band but it wouldn't move past his knuckle.

That was a problem he would deal with later. He put the brooch and coin purse back in the bag, set the bag back on the table, and returned to the task of removing her jacket.

Jackson Webb bustled in with a large enamel pan, a stack of folded cotton cloths, and a kettle of water. Sam made room on the table for the pan and Webb poured the water. Sam wet a cloth, squeezed it out, and began to wash Prairie's face. When she jerked, he winced, but he knew he had to clean the wound. He also knew she needed a doctor. She might prefer Wynn Donovan, but Sam had a sneaky suspicion Prairie hadn't told her foster mother where she was going.

That would mean they'd both left town under pretense. The last thing he wanted to do was expose either one of them, but he couldn't see any way around it. If anyone in Jennings knew what Prairie had been up to in Lafayette, it was Enoch Nolan.

The stationmaster came back with bandages and the hot water bottle Sam had requested.

"Can you send a telegram?" Sam asked.

"Yes, sir."

"Then send a wire to Dr. Enoch Nolan in Jennings."

Webb stood in the doorway, scratching his bald pate. "Who do I say wants him?"

"Rose." There was no sense in alerting the whole town, and if he understood the situation correctly, Enoch would know who Rose was. Sam turned back to bathing Prairie's face, summarily dismissing the stationmaster. He listened for the telltale click, smiled when he heard the "message received" reply. That meant Slim was still at the depot and would, most likely, see that the telegram was delivered without delay.

Sam had his doubts, however, that Enoch would attempt the trip to Estherwood in the storm. From the sound of the crashing thunder and the frequency of the lightning flashes, it was a bad one.

With the dried and caked blood washed away, Sam could see that the gash on Prairie's temple was not nearly as bad as he'd first thought. Her lassitude indicated a serious blow to her head, however, and she had begun to shiver.

His first priority was to get her into bed, but he didn't want Webb barging in about the time he got her clothes off. He checked the public room, but Webb wasn't there. Sam opened the door, found both the wagon and buggy gone, and assumed Webb had taken them to the barn.

Though the stationmaster ought to be awhile taking care of the horses, Sam locked the door to the private chamber. Under other circumstances, he would have enjoyed removing Prairie's clothes, would have teased her, kissed her, caressed her as he leisurely untied a ribbon bow or slipped a button through a hole. But these circumstances were dire and a certain haste was required.

Still, his fingers trembled and his heart pounded as he removed her skirt and shirtwaist. The corset came off next. Sam marveled at her ability to breathe with the garment laced so tightly around her rib cage. He himself breathed easier when he laid it aside.

What did she sleep in? he wondered, thinking a pair of his longhandles would be best — if they weren't a mile too big for her. She looked so tiny on the big bed. He remembered thinking of her as a child-woman the first time he saw her, out at the well with Enoch and Ruth. Her curves had convinced him that day she was no longer a child. Some women, he'd been told, padded their breasts and hips to create curves nature hadn't given them. The evidence that Prairie's curves were entirely hers lay before him.

Now was not the time, he reminded himself, to feast his eyes upon the swell of her breasts above the lace of her camisole. In an effort to warm herself, she had rolled onto her side and pulled her knees into her chest.

Sam glanced around the room, looking for their bags. They weren't there. Forget the longhandles, he thought, or the nightgown he felt certain she'd packed, at least for the moment. The camisole and petticoat would have to suffice. He put the hot water bottle on her feet and eased the thin cover over her. A pine box at the foot of the bed yielded a heavy quilt. He lamented the lack of fuel for the fireplace, but dared not leave her side. Webb should be back soon. He'd ask him.

Thinking about the stationmaster reminded Sam that he'd locked the door. He slipped open the bolt, peeked outside, then returned to sit by the bed and wait for Jackson Webb to come back from the barn.

Prairie snuggled deeper into the bed. She hugged herself, wrapping her arms around her rib cage and tucking her hands under her arms. It felt so good to be warm.

The inside of her right elbow encountered a ring, a plain, overlarge band that slipped up and down when she rubbed her hand against her arm. She smiled without knowing why and floated back into oblivion.

"Sorry your bags got wet," Jackson Webb said

sheepishly, setting the soaked luggage on the floor near the fireplace. "I plumb forgot about 'em. Let me git you a fire goin' in here and I'll rustle up a clothes rack so's you can dry these things out. I know I got one, somewheres."

"Thank you," Sam said. "I'd appreciate that."

Webb brought some firewood in, laid on some kindling, and struck a match. "That ought to warm ya'll up," he said, standing up and rubbing his work-roughened hands near the flame. "I got some stew on the stove. You want some? And maybe some coffee?"

"Yes, thank you, Mr. Webb."

The stationmaster turned around and frowned at Sam. "You know, mister, it'd be a sight easier talkin' to you if'n I knew your name."

"Sam."

"Just Sam?"

"That'll do for the time being."

Webb eyed the bed, stared hard at Sam's left hand, opened his mouth, closed it, and scratched his head. "Well, let me go git the stew and then I'll find that rack."

A short time later, Sam assured the stationmaster that he had everything he needed, bade the man good night, then set about unpacking the bags and hanging the damp clothes over the rack. He'd forgotten he packed Prairie's copy of *Prospector Pete* until he pulled it out of his bag.

Fortunately, the book had suffered little damage, no more than a few water spots on the cover. Sam laid it on the foot of the bed. He hadn't read it yet, hadn't actually thought about it since he'd borrowed it. If it was anything like the other Rose novels he'd read, it would keep him awake better than two pots of coffee would, and he needed to stay awake.

Sam didn't know much about medicine, but he'd heard that people who get hit on the head need to be watched closely and awakened every hour or so. No one could prevent him from watching Prairie, and he didn't see how waking her every once in awhile could hurt anything.

He jostled her shoulder, his voice a loud whisper. "Hey, Prairie. Wake up."

Her eyelids fluttered and she mumbled something, but her voice was so low he couldn't understand what she said. He tried again, jostling a bit harder, talking a bit louder. That time, she opened her eyes and looked at him. "Sam?" she said, almost disbelievingly.

"Yes, it's me."

"Good," she said on a sigh, then used her tongue to moisten her lips.

"Are you thirsty?"

"Uhmhm."

Sam took that to mean yes. He poured a glass of water from the pitcher Webb had brought, then held her head while she took a few sips.

When she was sleeping soundly again, he pulled the only chair in the room — a plain straight chair with a slatted seat — next to the bed, pulled another quilt out of the box, and collected the book from the bed. Within minutes, he had adjusted the lamp, wrapped himself in the quilt, propped his feet on the bed, and become engrossed in the story of Prospector Pete.

Amid boisterous claps of thunder and brazen streaks of lightning, strong gusts of wind hurled sheets of rain against the way station. Throughout the cacophony, Prairie slept, stirring only when Sam woke her, and then only long enough to take a few sips of water. Sam stirred himself only long enough to minister to her needs and tend the fire. Otherwise, he sat in the chair, reading.

From time to time, he lifted his head from the book and stared at Prairie's tranquil face. *What a little liar you are,* he thought. But when he replayed their conversations in his head, he could not pinpoint one actual prevarication. *Schemer, then,* he amended. That's what she was. A schemer.

After all, she hadn't written the Pampas J. Rose books. That tall fellow she was with in Lafayette, David Hamilton, had. Sam was certain of that. But Hamilton couldn't have written the Prospector Pete story without the information Prairie had supplied him. Had she honestly thought Sam wouldn't recognize his own story?

How many of the other Rose books had Prairie contributed to? he wondered. And what would the Certified Teetotalers think if they knew? Michael Donovan could provide only so much protection and defense. Why would she take such a risk?

Sam knew why. Prairie took risks for the same reason he did. For the sheer thrill of it. He hadn't realized until that moment how very much alike they were.

But that didn't excuse her. Neither she nor David Hamilton had the right to capitalize on the story of his life. Dadburnit! It was *his* life — and he didn't like thinking that people all over the country would soon be privy to all the intimate details.

What he really didn't like thinking about was Prairie and this David Hamilton fellow. She had pretended to be his wife, at least while in the company of the brown-suited man from New York. That still didn't make any sense.

Unless she was married to the man.

Hell, that didn't make good sense either.

A violent shiver awoke her. The room was dark, the orange glow of low-burning flames the only source of illumination. The wood frame building creaked and groaned under the barrage of pelting rain and gusting wind.

Where was she? Prairie wondered, trying to recall

the events of the evening. She'd been on her way home from Lafayette and something had spooked the horses. She frowned in concentration, then winced at the pain that shot from her right temple straight into the middle of her head.

A skunk. A dadblasted polecat was responsible for this misery!

She remembered coming off the buggy seat. It had felt so strange, not having anything solid beneath her. She had floated, suspended in midair, knowing gravity was working against her, knowing that it pulled at her weight, knowing she was falling, yet denying it with every bit of willpower she possessed.

That was all she remembered. Where had she landed? On the road? In the ditch? Her head had hit something hard, probably a rock, but she didn't remember. Couldn't remember.

Someone had carried her to a wagon and brought her here, wherever here was. Someone in whose arms she felt safe and secure . . .

Sam.

Where had he gone?

In tiny increments, Prairie rolled onto her back and turned her head toward the opposite wall. Every movement hurt, no matter how tiny. She thought how odd it was that all the pain appeared to be centered in her right temple. Surely, if she had fallen, her body would be bruised and sore. By rights, she ought to have a broken bone or two. But nowhere else did it hurt.

The pain radiated out from her temple, searing in its intensity, blurring her vision. She blinked and tried to focus, then closed her eyes, resting them for a moment. Gradually, the pain eased somewhat. She looked again and saw shadows and shapes, but none that could belong to Sam Blackman.

Had he left her there, in a strange place? She couldn't believe Sam would desert her. Maybe he had

239

made himself a pallet on the floor. She inched over to the edge of the bed, far enough so she could see the floor. He wasn't there, either.

A tear leaked out of one eye, trickled across her nose, and plopped onto the floor.

The door creaked open then, and Sam came in. She could see him out of the corner of her eye, could see that his arms were loaded with a stack of firewood. In her joy over his return, Prairie turned her head too quickly. Sharp daggers of pain exploded behind her right eye and she screamed in agony.

Sam's anger over her deception vanished with her heartrending cry. He dropped the firewood and rushed to the bed, gathering her in his arms, holding her head against the hollow of his shoulder. His voice was low and soothing.

"I know it hurts, baby. You must try to be still."

"I—I can't move my head, Sam!" she sobbed.

Instinctively, he wanted to rock her, but he was afraid to try, afraid the motion would cause her additional pain. For a long time, he held her close, smoothing the hair on the back of her head, careful not to bring his hand too close to her temple. Her sobs subsided to sniffles, but still he held her.

When she had been quiet for some time, he whispered, "Prairie? Are you awake?"

The tears had left her voice raspy. "Yes."

"Do you want to lie back down now?"

"I think so."

"I'll be gentle," he promised. Very slowly, he lowered her to the bed, his arms still holding her against him until her head touched the pillow. Sam slid his arms out of the way and propped his weight on his palms. The golden light from the lantern he'd left on the counter in the public room spilled through the open doorway, onto her face.

"How do you feel now?" he asked, gazing down into tortured eyes.

Her attempt at a smile twisted his heart. "Better."

"Be very still," he murmured. "Don't try to move. I need to tend the fire and fix your hot water bottle, but I'll be right back."

She blinked, in acquiescence, Sam presumed. He hated to leave her side, even for the few minutes his duties required. He eased himself off the bed, mindful of the slightest movement, then hurried to complete his tasks. Moments later, he was back, sliding the hot water bottle under the covers.

"I'm c-c-cold, Sam," she said, her teeth chattering.

"I'll get another quilt."

"No. You can keep me warm better than a quilt."

He swallowed hard, a combination of concern and awe and something akin to apprehension all knotting up together in his chest. "Are you sure?"

"Yes, Sam. Please, make me warm."

That was exactly what Sam was afraid he'd do.

Chapter Sixteen

Prairie might have been cold, but Sam wasn't. He pulled off his boots, stripped down to his union suit, and climbed into the bed, thinking the whole time how risky it was to get this close, physically, to Prairie.

Perhaps if he merely lay with his back against her side, it would be enough.

It wasn't.

"Sam," she implored in a tone he couldn't ignore, a tone that quivered from the chill that beset her. "Please, hold me."

He turned toward her then, folding an arm across her rib cage and snuggling against her. She felt so soft, so feminine, so warm despite her shivers. *This is dangerous, man. Be careful,* an inner voice warned. Sam closed his eyes and trembled.

"Are you cold, too?" she asked.

"No—yes. Let's try to get some sleep, Prairie." Sam figured there was no way he was going to sleep, not lying so close to her, but Prairie would go back to sleep as soon as she got warm. Then, he'd get up and go back to his chair.

"I need to go home, Sam. Will you take me?"

"Yes, but not until Enoch says you can travel."

"Doc?" she asked, bewilderment in her voice. "What does Doc have to do with it?"

"I had the stationmaster send him a wire. If the

242

weather wasn't so bad, he'd probably be here by now."

"Why did you do that?"

The panic in her voice made Sam wonder if he'd come to the wrong conclusions. "Isn't that Enoch's buggy you were in?" he asked.

"Yes."

"Did you borrow it without permission?"

"No, but you needn't have concerned yourself about the buggy. Doc can manage without it for awhile."

Concerned about Doc's buggy! Was she crazy? Did she think he was that insensitive?

Sam wanted to take her cheeks in his hands and make her turn her face to his, even if he couldn't see her very well. He didn't like talking to the side of her head—and he wanted her to *see* his exasperation, not just hear it. But he couldn't force her to look at him. Not with a concussion.

"I'm not worried about the damned buggy, Prairie. That's not why I sent for Enoch. You need a doctor."

"No, I don't," she argued. "You forget I grew up with one."

"I didn't forget! That doesn't make you an authority on medicine. You still need to be examined by a physician."

She sounded about as put out with him as he was with her. "Look, Sam. I fell. I hit my head. Now I have a concussion. The treatment for concussion is a few days' rest in a dark room. There's nothing Doc can do for me that you haven't already done."

"I want him to look at you, Prairie. Besides, it's too late now. No one's at the depot to receive a telegram. If Enoch knows you have his buggy, what difference does it make if he comes over here?"

"Where are we, anyway?"

243

"At the Estherwood station. It's a good thing I came along when I did." Sam bit his tongue, but it was too late.

"Where were you going, Sam?"

He supposed he could ask her the same thing, see what she'd say, but they could continue this question and answer session all night. So instead, he said, "There will be plenty of time tomorrow to talk about why we were *both* traveling today. For now, you need to rest."

He heard her sharp intake of breath, felt her heart beat faster against his chest, and knew he'd rattled her. The last thing she wanted to talk about, he reckoned, was her reason for being on the road.

"All right. You win," she said irritably. "I'll go to sleep."

He smiled to himself, oddly content.

Despite her promise, Prairie lay awake listening to the rain, trying not to think about Sam lying there beside her. It was a long time before her pulse slowed and her body relaxed. By then, Sam had been asleep for some time.

While Prairie and Sam slept, the rain slowed to a drizzle, and though it eventually stopped, it left in its wake a thick mist that clung to the window glass with damp tenacity, blocking much of the thin light sifting through the heavy clouds. The gray morning combined with the light, rhythmic dripping of moisture off the eaves was conducive to sleep.

Prairie awoke to the sound of voices raised in argument, her brain as foggy as the clinging mist.

"I didn't know they weren't married. Honest, mister. What was I s'pposed to think? They're both wearin' weddin' rings."

Though she didn't recognize the country twang as

244

belonging to anyone she knew, the booming timbre directly following it stirred a spark of memory.

"What? That's not possible."

"I'm not blind," the twang said.

Prairie wished they'd carry their argument somewhere else — anywhere, so long as it was away from her door. She pulled the quilt over her head, muffling their quarrel but not obliterating it. She huddled deeper into the quilt . . . and closer to Sam.

"Hmm," he murmured, burying his nose in her hair. His hand slid up from her waistline, coming to rest on her breast.

"Where —" she heard the vaguely familiar voice say, then a door banged against a wall and the heavy fall of booted feet marched across the floor, the thunderous cadence vibrating the bed.

Without warning, the cover — sheet, blanket, and quilt — came off and was snatched clear to her bare feet. Before she could recover, a large hand closed over her right forearm and jerked her away from Sam.

Needles of excruciating pain shot through the right side of her head, blinding in intensity. Prairie screamed in protest of both her treatment and the agony it wreaked.

All hell broke loose around her. Even through the haze of her pain, she could put names to voices — all except the twanging one.

"What do you think you're doing?" *Sam.*

"What do I think *I'm* doing? What do you think *you're* doing?" *Michael.*

"Both of you! Hush! Can't you see she's hurt?" *Doc.*

"I tried to tell you, mister." *Twang.*

Gentle hands, horny with age, touched her cheek, the rough fingertips scrubbing away her tears. "Calm down, missy," Doc said. It had been years since he'd used the endearment. "I just want to get a closer look at this cut."

Prairie winced when his fingers pressed against the tender skin. "I'm sorry," Doc said. "I know that hurts. This is only antiseptic I'm putting on it. It's going to sting a little bit."

She wished Doc would hush so she could hear what Sam and Michael were saying, but while Doc droned on, their voices moved farther and farther away.

Sam Blackman had been in pickles before. But never like this one. No, never like this one.

He let Michael rant and rave for a bit while he examined his options. The way he figured it, he didn't have many: he could tell the truth or lie through his teeth. Either way spelled trouble with a capital T.

The problem with the truth was that it was going to sound like a lie, but if Prairie backed him up, then maybe Donovan would believe it. *If* Prairie backed him up. *If* she didn't fabricate a story.

Sam wished with all his heart that he'd answered her last question, and then made her tell him exactly what she'd been doing in Lafayette and how she'd managed to leave Jennings for three days without Michael Donovan calling out a search party. He couldn't help wondering if Donovan hadn't known all along that Prairie was gone and what she was doing.

Of course, Sam reminded himself, if he'd never gone to sleep, he wouldn't be in this pickle.

Donovan's bark brought Sam abruptly back to the present.

"You *will* answer my question, Blackman!"

He should be angry, too. He had every right to be angry. Dammit, he *was* angry! But he didn't expect anger to get him very far. Sam molded his voice into the most humble tone he could imagine, humbleness being a foreign virtue to him.

"I'm sorry, sir. What was your question?"

"We're not playing games here, Blackman. This is serious business."

Michael looked mad enough to hit him. Sam reckoned he wanted to real bad. The thought was comforting. That meant Michael Donovan was not in control, and control was the key to victory.

"I appreciate the seriousness of the matter, Mr. Donovan. Prairie's injuries are quite serious."

The older man's face flamed beet red. "We're not talking about Prairie!" he railed.

Sam frowned. "We're not?"

"You know damned well we're not—I mean, we are, but we're not—" Donovan stopped sputtering, raked his fingers through his damp hair, and looked down at his feet for a moment. When he spoke again, he was much calmer—and, Sam thought, much deadlier. "It's you we're talking about, Blackman. Where have you been the last few days?"

"What does my whereabouts have to do with anything?"

"Just answer the question!" Donovan barked.

"Out at the rig."

"Not since Friday morning."

Sam's heart skipped a beat. "Why would you think that?"

"I don't think it. I know. Folks from town do go out there pretty often, you know. Word gets around. Now, I want to know where you've been and why."

"That's my business, Donovan."

Michael took a step toward Sam, his face blazing with anger. "I'm making it mine."

Sam hiked a shoulder. "I had business in Lafayette."

"Can you prove you were there?"

"Why the third degree?"

Michael's fists clenched at his sides.

"Okay," Sam said. "Yes, I can prove I was there. What's going on?"

"You better be able to prove it, Blackman. Saturday night, an entire family was murdered near Welsh. Somebody shot them, then took an axe to them."

Sam gaped in horror. When he could speak again, he said, "You don't think I did it, do you?"

Michael raked his fingers through his damp hair. "I don't want to think you'd do something like that, but I never thought I'd catch you in bed with my daughter, either. Tell me the truth. Are you two married?"

"The truth? No, we're not."

"Just what I thought!" Donovan flared, grabbing Sam by the front of his union suit and hauling his face right up to his. "You've ruined my daughter's reputation. I want to know what you're planning to do about it."

"I wanna know what he's plannin' to do 'bout standin' ou' cheer in his drawers," Jackson Webb, who had just come in carrying a load of stove wood, said on a snigger. "Folks'll be arrivin' terrectly, and I don't think they'll take too kindly to seein' a man ain't fully dressed. I got my own reputation to uphold, you see."

Michael let go of the undershirt and Sam started for the door, wondering how much the stationmaster had heard. He supposed it didn't really matter. Even a moron could see what was transpiring, and Webb was certainly smarter than a moron.

"Wait!" Donovan called. "I'll get your clothes. You stay out there." To Webb, he said, "Don't let him go anywhere."

248

Just where did Michael think he was going in his union suit? Sam wondered. He caught a glimpse of Prairie when Michael opened the door and again when he came back out. He wanted to go back in and talk to her—alone, but he knew he'd have to fight both Enoch and Michael to do it.

Donovan didn't even allow Sam time to finish putting his clothes on before he started grilling him again. "If you aren't married, then what's all this foolishness about the two of you wearing wedding bands?"

Sam had forgotten all about the rings. At that moment, his left hand was inside the sleeve, somewhere between the shoulder and the cuff of his shirt. He wished he could leave it there.

While he buttoned his shirt, he watched Jackson Webb slowly load the wood, one stick at a time, into the stove. Sam looked pointedly toward the front door. "You think there might be some place a little more private where we could go to discuss this?" he asked.

"This discussion isn't going to last long enough to bother carrying it somewhere else," Donovan snapped, but he glared disapprovingly at the stationmaster. "Mr. Webb, isn't there something else you need to be doing right now?"

Webb slammed the stove door closed and his round head bobbed. "Oh, yes, sir, Mr. Donovan. I'll just go feed them horses. There's some fresh coffee here on the stove, if'n ya'll want some."

"I do," Sam said. He poured out a cup and took an inordinate amount of time blowing on it and then taking a sip. Sam knew he was stalling, but it was his only strategy at the moment.

"Well, Blackman, I'm waiting."

Sam took a deep breath. "Look, Donovan, things aren't always as they appear. Prairie had an accident. I found her and brought her here."

"What was she doing way out here by herself?"

"I don't know. You'll have to ask her. All I know is she needed someone to take care of her, and it was either me or Webb. I could have hightailed it out of here after I sent the wire to Enoch, but I didn't."

"That brings up an interesting point," Donovan said. "Why did you call her Rose? And how did Doc know Rose referred to Prairie?"

"He didn't tell you?"

Donovan frowned. "He *refused* to tell me."

"It's a long story," Sam said. "Prairie will have to tell you. I was trying to protect her."

"From what?"

"You know damned well what!" Sam closed his eyes and told himself to calm down, then managed in a cooler tone, "From gossip, that's what."

"Why didn't you wire Wynn? Or did you forget she's a doctor?"

"You know what the weather was like last night, Donovan. Besides, Prairie was in Enoch's buggy. It just seemed natural to send for him."

Donovan frowned. "What did you say?"

"That it seemed natural to send for Enoch."

"No, before that."

"I said she was in Enoch's buggy."

While Michael pondered that revelation, Sam wondered for the first time why Prairie's foster father had come with Enoch. Sam asked him.

"Doc and I were playing cards when the telegram was delivered. Doc's an old man, Blackman. I didn't think he needed to be out in that weather by himself—or alone on the road, period, after what happened to that family the other night, so I offered to come along. We brought my carriage, and he didn't tell me Prairie was here until we arrived. You still haven't told me why you were in bed with her."

Sam didn't like the accusative tone in Michael's voice. "She had a chill and I got in bed with her to keep her warm. I didn't intend to go to sleep, but I did. If we'd been naked or something, I could understand—"

"You don't understand. That's the problem."

"Then why don't you explain it to me?"

Michael poured himself a cup of coffee and went to stand at the window. For several minutes, he stared into the gray mist. His face looked old and haggard. Sam couldn't recall ever thinking Michael Donovan was old before.

Without turning around, Donovan said quietly, "Do you think we can keep this a secret, Blackman? In a few days, everyone in the southwest corner of this state will know Prairie's character has been sullied. Even if what you say is the truth, no one will believe it."

The bedroom door opened and Doc came out shaking his head. "What that girl needs is a good lickin' with one of her own hickory switches, but I ain't gonna be the one to give it to her."

Michael turned from the window, puzzlement defining his features. "What do you mean, Doc?"

Doc snorted. "I mean she's got too much spunk for her own good. She'll be just fine in a few days— if she'll lie still and stay quiet."

"Oh, she'll behave," Michael said. "Wynn will make sure of it. Is she ready to go?"

"Prairie ain't goin' nowhere, boy," Doc said. "Not with a head injury. She'll have to stay here for now."

Sam thought Michael would argue with Doc, but he didn't.

"She wants to see Sam," Doc continued. "Alone."

"Now, see here—" Michael protested.

"She's in pain, boy, not in heat," Doc said. Sam marveled at the old man's bluntness.

251

"She can talk to him later. Right now, she's going to talk to me," Michael declared. His glower dared Sam or Doc to argue with him.

They didn't.

While Donovan was talking to Prairie, Sam and Doc drank coffee in silence. Sam wanted to ask Enoch about the buggy, about why Prairie had been in Lafayette, but Doc clamped his mouth shut and stared at a cobweb in the corner. It was just as well Doc was so reticent, Sam thought. He needed to hear the explanation directly from Prairie. After what seemed like forever to Sam, Donovan came out.

"I'll be right here," Michael warned. "If you try anything—"

Sam left the threat hanging and went to see Prairie.

She'd always known it would come to this, but she'd hoped she would have located a relative by then. Prairie didn't know how Sam was going to take her confession, but she owed him an explanation. Huh! she thought. She owed everybody an explanation.

Doc didn't agree. Bless his heart, he told her to keep her trap shut and he'd take full responsibility for her escapade. That ought to buy her a little more time, he said. Prairie refused to allow it.

Since she'd already confessed to Doc and Ruth, she expected the repetition of her story to be easier. It wasn't.

Although Michael seemed to understand her motives, he made it clear he didn't approve of her methods. What was done, was done, he said, but her relief at his philosophical attitude was short-lived, for he launched directly into his plan to "fix" her problem. Prairie wasn't the least bit sure she liked it—and she was almost positive Sam wouldn't like it at all.

"How are you feeling?" Sam asked, sitting in the slat-seated chair.

"I'm fine, so long as I don't turn my head," she said, her voice far brighter than she felt. She reached over her shoulder and thumped the stack of pillows at her back. "Sitting up like this helps."

"I, uh, I'm sorry about the trouble I caused you with your—with Donovan," Sam said.

"You didn't cause it, Sam. I did."

"He doesn't see it that way."

"He will," she said firmly, "eventually. At the moment, he's trying to reconcile his conception of what he thought I was with the realization of what I am." Prairie realized how that sounded and blushed. From the stunned expression on Sam's face, he was thinking the absolute worst.

"It's not—I'm not—" she stuttered.

"I didn't think you were *that*," Sam said, blushing himself.

"What I am," she said, "or rather *who* I am, is Pampas J. Rose."

Sam didn't say anything. He just sat and stared, dumbfounded, frowning one second, blinking the next, and then shaking his head in disbelief, but not saying anything.

Prairie wanted him to say *something*, though she wasn't sure exactly what. Maybe that he was impressed. Maybe that he was glad. Anything except what he did say—finally.

"No," he denied. "Not you. I know better. David Hamilton is Pampas J. Rose."

It was Prairie's turn to be stunned, but she wasn't speechless. "How do you know about David?"

"Because I saw you with him in Lafayette."

253

"You saw me? But how do you know David?"

"I don't," Sam said. He told her about talking to the man with the Yankee accent, learning David's name, and going to the boardinghouse to see *Mrs. Hamilton*. "I didn't figure it all out, though, until last night. While you were asleep, I read the Prospector Pete story. That's when I knew you'd been feeding plots to your friend Hamilton."

In his concern over Prairie's injury followed by the turmoil of the morning, Sam had forgotten all about how mad that story had made him. His mentioning it brought the anger roiling back, and he lashed out at her.

"What made you think you could take something as personal as the story of a man's life — a real flesh and blood man, not someone you made up — and put it in a book for everyone in the world to read?"

Prairie was taken aback. "What are you talking about?"

"Prospector Pete, that's what!" he yelled at her. "Prospector Pete! Ugh! Whose idea was it to use that name anyway, yours or Hamilton's?"

"Mine," she defended, thrusting her pointed chin out defiantly. "I told you *I* am Pampas J. Rose."

"In a pig's eye!" he spat.

"And just why don't you believe me?"

"Because no woman could have written those books."

"Why not?"

"Because women don't understand men that well. Women don't know how it feels to sleep out under the stars and like it. They've got to have a mattress beneath them and a roof over their heads. They scream when they hear a coyote howl and faint when they see a snake. They want homes and children, a wardrobe full of clothes they'll never wear and little do-dads all over the house so they'll have something

254

to dust. Women write stories about heartaches—
things like children dying or their husbands being
out of work, or they write poetry. They don't know
squat about fencing and fist fighting and defending
honor, so how can they write about it?"

"Are you quite finished?" Prairie asked through
clenched teeth.

Suddenly, Sam looked a mite sheepish. "I suppose."

"Then please get it through your thick skull, Sam
Blackman. *I am Pampas J. Rose.* I have been since the
beginning. Not David Hamilton, nor anyone else.
Only me. I've written every single one of those
books by myself, and it wasn't always easy. I've
missed a lot of meals and a lot of sleep over the past
few years. I've sweated every time I sent in a manuscript, certain it would be the one Beadle and Adams sent back with a note saying they didn't want it.
And I've sweated, too, over someone who knows me
putting two and two together and telling the world
that Pampas J. Rose is really Prairie Rose Jernigan."

Sam took a moment to digest the implications of
her avowal. "I knew I was supposed to know what a
pampa was. I kept thinking of pampas as a singular
thing, and that's what threw me. I meant to look it
up. And Rose is your middle name. No wonder the
name Pampas J. Rose sounded sissy to me."

"So you believe me?"

"I—well, I suppose it's possible. I never thought of
you as crazy, but what you just described to me
sounds almost insane. Why did you do it?"

"To find out who I am."

That didn't make a lick of sense to Sam. Maybe,
he thought, he'd been a little hasty about the insan-
ity part. "You don't know who you are?" he asked
incredulously.

"I told you I was an orphan, Sam," she reminded

him, her voice sharper than she meant for it to be. "I don't know anything about my ancestors. I wrote those books hoping someone somewhere would recognize me. You caught on to what I was doing, you just didn't know why."

Sam frowned. "Caught on? What are you talking about?"

"Dragonflies and toodlum gravy."

"Oh. Yeah. The brooch you wear—"

"Was my mother's. Her name was Anna, she was from Big Spring, and she called brown gravy toodlum gravy."

"Who are Martha and Susie?"

"My father's sister and my doll."

"And no one ever wrote to you?"

Prairie told him about Lucy Byers and her theory that Lucy might be her great aunt.

"What are you going to do now?" Sam asked.

She lifted her shoulders in the tiniest of shrugs. "I don't know. Stop writing, I suppose."

"You can't do that, Prairie!" he protested vehemently. "You're too good!"

She smiled. "Thanks. Am I forgiven, then?"

"For what?"

"Prospector Pete."

Learning that she was the author, and not David Hamilton, eased his anger. In fact, her perception of him as hero material swelled his head just a mite. "Aw, no one will know but me and you and my brothers and maybe a few hundred other people I know."

"I'm sorry, Sam. I shouldn't have written that one, but I honestly didn't stop to think about how closely it resembled your own life story. I wrote it so fast— and I was so caught up in not understanding what the pumps do that, well, I just didn't stop to think about it."

He put his hand on her arm. His touch sent shivers dancing down her spine. "It's all right. Really. Now that I know what you were trying to do. But why didn't you just ask me about the pumps? I would have been happy to explain."

"I was afraid it would make you suspicious."

"Just like the folks in Jennings are going to be when they hear about Enoch and Michael walking in on us this morning. What are you going to do about that?"

Prairie looked down at her hands for a moment, gathering her strength. Sam wasn't going to like what she had to say, but she'd rather he heard it from her than from Michael. When she was ready to speak, she looked him straight in the eye and stiffened her back to brace herself for his yelling. He was certain to scream and holler and curse.

"Michael says we have to be married. Today, if he can get a preacher here. Tomorrow at the latest."

Chapter Seventeen

He didn't scream and holler and curse, though he wanted to. Instead, he sat pensively, chewing his bottom lip.

Sam knew he should have been prepared for it, but he wasn't. Somehow, he'd thought they could work this out without invoking the bonds of matrimony. He supposed he could refuse to marry her. After all, he was innocent of any wrongdoing. And he'd always imagined *he* would do the proposing, should he ever decide to join himself to a woman. He didn't take too kindly to anyone else telling him what he was going to do with his life.

On the other hand, Michael Donovan wielded a hell of a lot of power. With a mere whisper in a judge's ear, Donovan could ruin him, ruin his chances of bringing in the well. And Sam figured that was what would happen if he refused to go along with Donovan's scheme. He'd end up in jail, charged with rape, or maybe even murder.

In light of the alternatives, marriage to Prairie might not be too bad, he thought. But before he had time to fully digest the implications of marrying her, she started talking again—all in a rush, as though she was afraid if she didn't say it all at once, she'd lose her nerve.

"I don't want this anymore than you do, Sam. Honest, I don't. And I want you to know how much

I appreciate what you did for me. I'm sorry I got you into all this trouble. But Michael is insistent. When he makes up his mind about something, there's no changing it. But the marriage can be in name only. Just until I find another position. Then you can get an annulment."

She'd said so much at once that Sam didn't know which item to respond to first. The part about her not wanting him wounded his pride. Sam wasn't so sure he didn't want the marriage, but he wasn't about to give her the opportunity to tell him again that she didn't want him.

He started with her job. "You don't have to work, Prairie."

"I know, Sam. I could always move back home, but I'd never live down the shame of a failed marriage. Not in Jennings. It would be better if I went somewhere else—a long way off, where I could take back my maiden name and no one would ever be the wiser."

In exasperation, he drove his fingers into his wavy, uncombed hair. There'd been no time that morning for grooming. "That's not what I mean. I can support you." He smiled then, remembering the screen he'd had Henry Boudreaux make, the screen that was in his bag over in the corner. "I'm about to become the richest man in this part of the state, Prairie. I can afford to keep you very well. You needn't worry about earning a living."

Prairie moved her head in negation, then winced at the pain the movement caused. "I couldn't let you do that, Sam. I won't be a kept woman."

"I'm not asking you to be a kept woman!" he argued, but the hardness of her features convinced him to change course. "Look, I hadn't planned to get married, not any time soon, but since it looks as though I'm about to take a wife, I'd at least like to

259

have the opportunity to invest some time in the relationship, to try to make it work. This marriage doesn't have to fail before it ever gets started."

Sam smiled at his ingenuity. He'd stated his position without offering her his heart to cut into little pieces.

Prairie's eyes bugged at his audacity. How dare he make it sound like a business proposition! She didn't intend to bear his seed, and then raise the child without the benefit of a stable home, without the benefit of a father.

"Not on your life!" she snapped, taking Sam aback, making him forget his determination to leave his heart out of this discussion.

"Is the prospect of living with me so repulsive?" he asked.

"No. It's the prospect of ending up pregnant that sickens me."

She might as well have slapped his face. Not only did she not want him; she didn't want his children, either. "All right, Prairie," he said, his voice sharp, "you can have your marriage in name only. I was planning to stay out at the rig anyway." He stood up and ran the flats of his hands down his thighs. "I'll go tell Donovan."

Prairie tried to look at the humorous side of the simple ceremony.

The preacher, a tall, bony man with sparse black hair and a pencil-thin mustache, stood at the foot of the bed, using the iron railing as a rest for his prayer book. While his position might be comical, his appearance was not. He looked more like an undertaker than a man of the cloth, she thought, with his gaunt cheeks, heavy eyebrows, and beady black eyes. There was certainly nothing warm or friendly about him. Even his name sounded cold: Osterman.

She would have preferred Reverend Milhouse, but Michael refused to allow it. He wanted it to appear as though she and Sam had eloped. To accomplish this illusion, he sent Webb for Osterman, who was the minister of Estherwood's only church, and removed himself to the barn for the interim.

Jackson Webb promised to keep quiet. "They're doin' the right thing," he said, his round head bobbing. "No sense startin' 'em off on the wrong foot by spreadin' rumors. No, sirree. You can count on me, Mr. Donovan. I won't never say nothin'."

Michael figured the goodly sum he'd paid him for stabling the horses and renting Prairie the room ought to keep the man's mouth sealed.

The stationmaster had been pleased to stand with Doc as a witness. Now, there was a comical pair—both short, paunchy, and nearly bald, both grinning from ear to ear. They stood behind and to the side of Osterman, whose dry voice droned on incessantly.

Sam stood beside her. Neither of them had packed clothes appropriate for a wedding, but Prairie thought he looked marvelously handsome in his dark suit and pin-striped shirt. She wore a simple white shirtwaist over her camisole with her dragonfly brooch pinned at the throat. Both her blouse and his shirt could have used a good pressing.

She'd tried to talk Doc into letting her get out of bed long enough to repeat her vows, but he staunchly refused. Webb turned up a white candlewick spread, which Doc draped over the thick pile of quilts. The cover rode her waistline, forming a "skirt" for her shirtwaist.

It took some doing—scads of soapy water and a lot of pulling, but Sam finally managed to remove Doc's old wedding ring. Although Webb greased the worn gold band well, Sam said the last thing he wanted to do was put it back on. Prairie couldn't help wondering if his reluctance had nothing to do with the size of the ring.

It didn't matter, she supposed. In a few minutes, he could slip the ring off and head back to his precious drilling rig. By the first of the year, she hoped, she would have found another teaching position. Then he could dissolve the business he'd conducted this day and forget he'd ever made this alliance.

Could she forget? she wondered. Would she ever forget Sam Blackman?

The thought brought the sting of tears to her eyes. She wished with all her heart things didn't have to be this way. If they had just had a little more time . . .

Osterman cleared his throat, claiming her attention. "Do you, Prairie Rose Jernigan," he repeated, "take this man . . ."

Though it caused her both physical and emotional pain, she turned her head toward Sam and pinned her gaze on his tan cheek.

". . . to have and to hold from this day forward, for better or for worse . . ."

A nervous tick pulsed at Sam's temple and his Adam's apple bobbed in his throat. His clear blue eyes stared at Osterman, but Prairie suspected Sam didn't see the man at all.

". . . till death do you part?"

"I do." The lie caught in her throat, for that was what it was—a lie. She was borrowing Sam's name for a spell, to wear as a badge for propriety's sake. Yet, the words didn't feel temporary. Now that she'd said them, they felt rather permanent.

Sam clenched his jaw tight and endured the ceremony.

Prairie deserved better than this, he thought. She should be in a church filled with flowers, wearing an ivory gown and a veil, holding a bouquet and surrounded by her family and friends. She should have attendants and a ring that fit her properly. This should be one of the happiest days of her life.

But she was miserable. She didn't want to marry him; that much was clear. He'd thought maybe she would change her mind about him, but her tear-washed eyes persuaded him otherwise.

Well, he didn't want this, either, he told himself, then repeated the silent declaration in an attempt to convince himself that it was true. He had a well to bring in, a company to save, a dynasty to found. There was no room in his life for a wife and family. He was doing the only honorable thing, and when it was over, he'd vamoose right out of Prairie's life for good.

". . . in sickness and in health . . ."

Where would she find another teaching position? he wondered. She'd said she wanted to go far away. Would he ever see her again?

The absence of Osterman's voice snagged Sam's attention. "I do," he said, and meant it. He wished Prairie believed him.

Two days later, Doc took Prairie home to Jennings, but to the Donovans' house, not to Prairie's. "I don't want you by yourself right now," he explained.

"I would rest better at home," she argued.

"You might, but I wouldn't. Not with a murderer running loose."

"I thought you said they arrested the hired hand."

"They did," Doc said, "Watson. But he was in Lake Charles, and there are multiple witnesses to back him up. I think they've got the wrong man."

"Who else would have killed those people?"

Doc hiked his shoulders. "No one knows. The Jameses didn't have any close neighbors, so no one saw or heard anything. But people don't kill without a reason, Prairie. As far as the sheriff knows, Watson had no motive."

"The whole family is dead?"

"Both parents and all three boys. Everyone except the daughter."

"How did she survive?" Prairie asked.

"She was at work at a dry goods store in Welch when it happened."

"And she has no idea who might have wanted to kill her folks?"

"Nope."

The possibility that there was an axe murderer running loose made Prairie sick at her stomach. Her only comfort was Doc's statement that people don't kill without a motive, and she knew of no reason anyone would want to kill her.

"I know you'll move back home next week," Doc said. "Do you still have my pistol?"

"No—at least, I don't think so," she said, worrying her bottom lip. "I forgot all about your gun, Doc. It was on my lap, so it must be in the ditch somewhere."

"Then it's probably long gone now."

Prairie apologized for losing it.

"No problem. I know where I can buy another one, but I think you'd be better off without a gun in the house, Prairie. At least until someone teaches you how to use one."

When they stopped by her little house, which she'd lovingly filled with overstuffed furniture and far too many knickknacks, it seemed so empty. No, she realized, it wasn't the house that was empty. It was her heart.

She missed Sam, missed already the future they might have had together, missed the children she might have borne him. But Sam had left the Estherwood station almost immediately after the ceremony, and she nurtured little hope of seeing him again soon.

"I have to go," he'd said, taking both of her hands between his palms and leaning down to kiss her on her forehead. For the briefest of moments, his blue eyes searched her face; then he looked away, settling his trilby on his head and busying himself with creasing the crown. His face still close to hers, he said, "I have to go back to the rig. The sand won't wait for me, Prairie."

She remembered the ecstatic sparkle in his eyes the previous week when he'd mentioned the sand. He had the same look in his eyes now. "You've done it, haven't you?" she asked.

"Done what?"

"Figured out how to control the sand."

Sam smiled and kissed the corner of her mouth. "I can't tell you anything right now," he whispered.

Prairie understood—at least, she thought she did. "Too many ears?" she murmured, glancing toward the doorway, where Doc and Michael stood talking.

"Something like that," he said. "Take care of yourself, Prairie."

And then, he was gone. Gone from the room. Gone from the station. But not gone from her heart.

Prairie dreaded the next few days, which Doc said she must spend resting. Although she would complete her recuperation at the Donovans', she suspected she would be equally as lonely, whether she was alone or surrounded by people. And though she suspected there was little chance Sam would come to town, she wanted to be at home—just in case. She supposed he would know where to find her.

But if he came, what would she do? She was his wife now. Would he honor her refusal to consummate the marriage? Would she be able to stand her ground, to resist his kisses when the very memory of his touch sent shivers dancing down her spine and made her feel all warm and golden inside?

Wynn told her she was making a mistake by pushing Sam away.

"He doesn't want me!" Prairie declared.

"Yes, he does," Wynn said, smiling. "He just doesn't know it yet. Or maybe," she added, pursing her lips as she gave brief consideration to the idea, ". . . he knows it but he hasn't told you yet."

Prairie frowned. "I don't understand."

"If you want him, Prairie, you have to tell him, and not with words alone."

Prairie thought it was Wynn who didn't understand, and if she was to hold up her end of the bargain, she knew she'd better write some letters of application and get them in the mail. The first of the year was only a little over a month away.

Sam didn't think he'd ever been quite so eager to complete a project, but for him, Blackman Number Two couldn't come in fast enough.

"All in good time," Jake said, his sides shaking with good-natured laughter. "You might as well calm down, Sam. You're gonna wear yourself to a frazzle out here. Save some of that energy for your new wife."

Jake was right on target, but Sam let the comment fly. He knew he ought to be far angrier about being forced into marriage than he was. He'd told no one about the extenuating circumstances, nor did he intend to—not even Wayne. That way, if word ever got out, he'd know he hadn't been the tattler.

But the bare truth was that he wanted to see Prairie far more than he wanted to be out at the rig. The sooner the well came in, the sooner he could see her.

They had drilled to twelve hundred feet and Clarkston Number One was at almost fourteen hundred. "There's always the chance we'll catch 'em," Jake allowed, "but I have my doubts."

"So do I," Sam agreed.

"If we don't, what're you gonna do about the screen?"

Sam shook his head. "I don't know. I'm still thinking about it."

He didn't tell Jake, but Sam knew his decision would be based on Wayne's success in New Orleans. If the bank offered the refinery financing contingent on the success of the field, he'd be crazy not to offer Clarkston the screen, otherwise Clarkston's failure might kill the deal. *Oh, hell,* he thought. He'd probably offer it to him regardless. He just hoped the screen would work.

From the time he got back to the rig on Wednesday until Sunday morning, Sam toyed with the idea of going into Jennings to meet the westbound train. He wanted to see Wayne, who ought to be on it, at the earliest possible moment.

If he went to Jennings, though, he'd have to see Prairie. He didn't figure he'd be able to stop himself, and even if he could, his presence in town would require a visit to his bride. Tongues were probably wagging anyway; he wouldn't feed the rumormongers additional fodder by pointedly ignoring Prairie.

So Sam stayed out at the rig and waited, as patiently as he could manage, for Wayne to show up on Monday.

* * *

As excited about Prairie's escapade as they'd been about the fire, the children bombarded her with questions when she went back to school on Monday.

"What do we call you now, Miss Jernigan?" they asked.

Hearing them call her Mrs. Blackman was going to take some getting used to.

"How does it feel to have one of them con . . . con — them head injuries like you had?"

"One of *those concussions,*" she corrected. "It hurts."

"Are you going to stop being our teacher now?" Rebekah Milhouse asked.

"Not immediately," Prairie said. "Why would I?"

"Because my mama says what you did was scan — scand'lous. She says teachers don't get away with stuff like that."

Prairie grinned, thinking, *The self-righteous fuddy-duddy strikes another blow to perceived immorality!* "I'm sure my behavior would appear scandalous to your mother. Please tell her I'll be more than happy to discuss it with her personally."

The class snickered and Rebekah's face turned red. Prairie felt a twinge of guilt. She hadn't intended to embarrass the child, even if she was a miniature replica of her mother.

"We missed you," Kevin McCormack said, his voice scratchy. "Some of us was afraid you wouldn't come back."

His consternation filled her heart with warmth even as it clogged her throat. "Thank you, Kevin. I missed you all, too. I'm glad to be back."

And she was. She was glad to have something to do away from her house, something to keep her mind off Sam.

268

* * *

The more Sam thought about it, the less he wanted to talk to Wayne out at the rig. He wasn't the least bit sure who he could trust anymore, especially within such close proximity of Clarkston's rig. He expected King Clarkston would pay dearly to know what the Blackman Brothers were up to. Sam didn't want Clarkston's men to even see Wayne.

After breakfast on Monday, Sam borrowed a horse from one of the crew members and rode the sorrel about halfway to town to wait for Wayne. Lately he'd begun to think owning a red surrey wasn't such a great idea. It was too damned conspicuous. But no one would give much heed to a lone man on horseback.

He stopped at a stand of pine saplings, tied the horse, and took the saddle off. He might have to wait for some time, and he didn't intend to stand there for hours or sit on the damp, cold ground. The saddle didn't make the most comfortable chair, but it was better than nothing. Sam positioned his seat so he could get a clear view of the trail to the west and settled down to wait.

Fortunately, it wasn't long at all before Wayne, also on horseback, came tearing down the trail. Sam's shrill whistle and flagging arms claimed his brother's attention.

"We got it!" Wayne hollered, throwing his right leg over the horse and bounding to the ground.

"Whoopee!" Sam yelled, feeling like a kid with a new bicycle. "I want to hear all about it."

Wayne grinned. "Of course you do. Why do you think I got up at the crack of dawn to ride out here?"

It hadn't been easy, but Wayne said he'd found a man in New Orleans eager to help him put together a deal. "I can't wait for you to meet him," Wayne said. "He's a character and a half, but quite an intelligent man. I almost let his name put me off meeting him. He's German, you see, and I was afraid I'd say his name wrong and ruin everything."

"What *is* his name?"

"Let me fix my tongue just right or I'll say it wrong," Wayne teased, working his jaw and wallowing his tongue around in his partially open mouth. "Waldemar Paxton Wolfeschlegelsteinhausenberger."

"Whew! That's a mouth and a half full," Sam agreed, laughing. "How did you meet this Wolf's Leg fellow?"

Wayne did a double-take. "Do you know the man?"

"No. Why?"

"Because people in New Orleans call him Wolf's Leg behind his back. Seems to me, if a body wanted to shorten it, he'd say Wolf *Shleg*."

Sam chuckled at Wayne's lack of imagination. "What do they call him to his face?"

"*Sir.* Anyway, a man at one bank sent me to a man at another, and so forth, until someone finally sent me to Wolfeschlegelsteinhausenberger."

"His name sounds like it belongs to a law firm: Wolfe, Schlegel, Stein, House, and Berger." Sam ticked the names off on his fingers. "That would make him five people. I'll call him Wolf's Leg, thank you. So, what did he offer us?"

"A hundred percent financing on the refinery, so long as we don't want more than half a million, contingent on a producing field."

Sam's eyes grew wider and wider and he swallowed several times. When he could speak, he said, "I don't know if I want to be in debt for half a million, Wayne. That's a hell of a lot of money."

Wayne grinned. "We're going to make a hell of a lot of money, Sam. Mr. Wolfeschlegelsteinhausenberger says you're right about Henry Ford and the future of the automobile. Besides coal oil, we'll make Russian white oil for medicinal purposes, and in a few years, when motorized vehicles are affordable, we'll switch to gasoline. I think we need to go with it."

"Yeah, you're probably right. Why don't you wire J.C. and Myron? Tell them to come over here as soon as they can, but don't tell them why. Wolf's Leg did promise to keep this on the Q.T.?"

"Yep."

"Good. But I want to clear this with J.C. and Myron. If we aren't unanimous, it's no go."

"Now that we got that settled," Wayne said, grinning, "you can tell me about the shenanigan you pulled."

"What shenanigan?"

"I should've known better than to leave you to your own devices, baby brother."

"Baby?" Sam balled up his fist and gave Wayne a soft punch on his upper arm. "Who're you calling a baby?"

"Do you have one started yet? Am I going to be an uncle soon? What are you doing hiding out here in the country when you have a new bride in town?"

How had he ever thought he could lie to Wayne? Sam wondered. "Oh, hell," he said disgustedly. "I might as well tell you everything or you'll never shut up about it."

When Sam finished his tale, Wayne slapped his thigh and howled. "The fact that one of us finally got hitched is amazing in itself, brother. But you went and married Pampas J. Rose! I can't believe my favorite author is a woman—and that I've known her for several months. Or that my brother married her! Do you know how long I've wanted to meet Pampas J. Rose? And now you tell me I can't even

271

let on that I know who she is. That's gonna be real tough."

"Which is exactly why I didn't want to tell you — why I probably shouldn't have told you. You're going to have to keep quiet about this, Wayne. I mean it. Prairie's in enough trouble without one of us making it worse. But there is something you can do for me."

"What's that?"

"Keep an eye on her."

"You afraid she'll cheat on you?" Wayne teased.

"No," Sam said disgustedly. Sometimes Wayne didn't know when to hush. "Because of the axe murderer."

Prairie knew she'd given the fuddy-duddies something new to gossip about, but she had no idea what a furor she had created among the Certified Teetotalers until they marched into her room that afternoon.

The six days of almost complete lying-in left her far weaker than she'd imagined. She'd swept only half the floor and not even started on the blackboard when Ruth stuck her head in the door and told her a contingency of women, led by Agnes Milhouse, was coming across the schoolyard.

"Why don't I meet them and tell them you're busy?" she suggested. "Then I'll come back and help you finish up in here."

Prairie shook her head. "I might as well go ahead and get this over with."

"Well, I'm staying. I have a right. I'm your supervisor. And I was your co-conspirator."

"Please, Ruth. Let me do the talking."

"All right," she reluctantly agreed. "But I'm staying."

The front door creaked open and half a dozen women bustled into Prairie's classroom. Prairie wondered how Hazel Kinnaird had managed to leave the post office so early.

"Afternoon, Ruth," Agnes said, snapping her chin and setting the long purple feather on her hat aquiver. "We want to talk to Prairie—*alone*."

Ruth drew up her flat chest and thrust her freckled chin out. "I'm the senior teacher at this school, Agnes. That gives me the right to be here. As a matter of fact, all parents are supposed to schedule conferences through me. I don't recall that you requested one."

Prairie hid her grin behind her hand. She should have known Ruth couldn't be quiet. Before Agnes could collect herself, Ruth turned to the postmistress. "And you, *Miss* Kinnaird. When did you become a mother?"

Hazel's chin shot up so fast her red pompon practically jumped off her navy blue sailor hat. "Why, of all the nerve—"

"You have it," Ruth finished for her. "And you, Susan Kennedy. Your children have all outgrown this school. Aren't they attending the academy now? What about you, Margaret Stanley? If I remember correctly, your only child is what, three years old now? And since I teach your children, Inez Winters, I can't imagine why you'd want to talk to Prairie. That leaves Agnes and Emily. If the two of you want to stay, you're welcome, but you'll have to wait in my room until we finish cleaning up in here."

"Well!" Agnes huffed. "We'll just take our complaints elsewhere!"

"Go right ahead," Ruth offered. "I believe the person you need to see is Michael Donovan. Of course, he's going to send you right back to me. The best thing for you to do is go wait in my room like I told

273

you. You and Emily. The rest of you can go back home, or to work"—this she directed at Hazel—"where you belong."

"That's all right," Agnes said, deflated. "It wasn't that important." Then she rallied long enough to hurl, "But what this town needs is an official Board of Education!"

When the door closed behind them, Prairie let go of the giggle she'd been choking on.

"You aren't mad at me?" Ruth asked. "I did promise to stay out of it."

"No!" Prairie gasped. "You were wonderful. I'm far too woozy-headed to handle Agnes Milhouse, and I could never be so eloquently blunt, no matter how well I felt."

"Yes, you could," Ruth assured her. "It just takes a little practice. I've had thirty-five years of it. Don't worry about Agnes. She's a pussy without her cronies to back her up. She won't be back. Now, you go on home and go to bed and leave this cleaning to me."

Chapter Eighteen

J.C. and Myron came in on the Wednesday night train.

Prairie heard about it from Ruth first thing Thursday morning. It didn't take much figuring to know they were in town to talk to Sam and Wayne. The question was, would the three Blackman brothers go to Sam or would he come to them?

All day long, Prairie tried to keep her spirits on an even keel, which was a difficult task. She wanted Sam to come to town, and then she didn't. If he came in and avoided seeing her, she would be crushed. But could she maintain a nonchalant attitude with him? she wondered.

Sam didn't make her wait. The minute school was out, he sauntered into her classroom, just as he had all those times before—just as though nothing had changed between them.

"Hi, Prairie," he said, his voice betraying a certain awkwardness that was at odds with his casual demeanor. "How are you feeling?"

She relaxed her guard a mite and gave him a thin smile. "The headaches are gone. And I can turn my head now." She showed him.

"That's good." He took her bucket and went outside. She listened to the pump handle creak while she finished straightening her desk. Her eyes misted and she sniffled. Quickly, before he came back in

275

and caught her, she located her handkerchief and blew her nose.

What had she expected? Hugs and kisses? Declarations of undying affection? She wasn't in love with him or he with her! Why was she acting like such a ninny?

Prairie was pushing the broom with a vengeance when Sam came back in.

"You must be feeling better," he observed with a twist of an eyebrow. "I've never seen you sweep quite so energetically before."

They completed their tasks in short order. The second she dumped the dust into the wastebasket, Prairie wished she'd taken the job at a more leisurely pace. Her head was throbbing and her heart was pounding, as much from anticipation, she surmised, as from exertion.

"Are we all finished?" he asked.

Prairie gave the room a thorough scrutiny before answering. "Yes, I think so." *What happens now?* She said the first thing that came to mind. "Would you like a cup of coffee?"

Sam grinned. "I thought you'd never ask."

They walked next door, Sam hanging back just a bit. Prairie craved his touch, even if it was nothing more than his hand on her elbow, yet she knew all he had to do was touch her and she would be lost to him forever. The too-large wedding band she wore on her left hand afforded her that privilege, but she dared not risk having his child.

Prairie was amazed at how strongly she felt about that. She had always wanted to have children one day, had always thought she'd make a decent mother. And now an overwhelming desire to have Sam's children burned within her breast. But some vague memory she couldn't quite capture fluttered at the edge of her consciousness, whispering on gossamer

276

wings, "Don't make the same mistake I did, Prairie."

Sam was no more certain than Prairie that his seeing her was a good idea. He found himself desperately wanting to touch her, and more. This was what he'd been afraid of. He'd wanted to hold the powwow out at the rig, but Wayne insisted they meet in town.

"You know you want to see her again, Sam. This will provide you with a darned good excuse."

"But she doesn't want to see me," Sam argued.

"You said she wants to keep up a pretense, at least for the time being. People are gonna get real suspicious if you never go into town."

Sam did want to see Prairie. He needed to be assured she had recovered from her concussion and was taking proper care of herself. But there was more to his desire to see her than reassurance and he knew it.

He followed her into her little house, down the hall to the kitchen, and made himself comfortable at the table while she pumped water and set about making coffee.

"My brothers are in town," he said.

Prairie was bent over the wood box. "Yes, I know. I assume you four have something important to discuss."

He noted the economy of her movements as she poked stove wood into the firebox and felt a stir of pride in this woman who was his wife. "We *had* several important matters actually, and now that we've discussed them, I'm free to tell you all about my little sand-control device."

Prairie turned from the stove and beamed at him. Her smile warmed his heart. "I *knew* you could do it! What did you come up with?"

"Actually, it wasn't my idea at all, Prairie. It was yours."

She couldn't have been more surprised. "But, Sam," she denied, "I didn't give you any ideas. I don't know anything about drilling for oil."

Sam snorted good-naturedly. "Tell that to Prospector Pete."

"All right, so I know a little," she allowed, wiping her hands on her apron and coming to sit across from him at the table. "But only what you taught me. Not enough to design a sand-control device."

"This is going to sound crazy, so bear with me. Remember the day we went out to the well together? The Saturday before the fire?"

She nodded. "You were very quiet on the way home."

"I was thinking about thinking too hard." He chuckled. "That night, your voice awakened me from a deep sleep. It was so real, I lit the lamp so I could see you, but of course you weren't there. I couldn't remember what you were saying when I woke up, but I knew it was significant. Finally, I heard it again; heard you say, 'You're thinking about it too hard. The solution is simple. Remember the rice fields.'"

The kettle whistled, summoning Prairie to pour the hot water into the coffeepot. "I did say you were thinking about it too hard, but I never said anything about the rice fields. How did they solve your problem?"

"It's not the fields themselves, it's the screens they use in the water wells that feed the irrigation lines." He described the screen he'd had Henry Boudreaux make and explained how he planned to use it—once they drilled into the oil sand. "Now we play a waiting game."

"Why have you been so secretive about all this?" she asked.

"Because I didn't want someone else to steal my

278

idea. I didn't want anyone to rob me of the prestige of being the first oilman to try it—and now I'm going to give it away and probably lose the credit."

Prairie poured up two cups of coffee. "Why? Who are you giving it to?"

"Clarkston—if he'll take it."

"If anyone around here would claim credit he didn't deserve, King would. But I don't understand why you're giving it to him now, or why you couldn't tell me about it before."

Sam winced inwardly at the hint of wounded pride in her voice. How could he explain to her about his close-mouthed brothers, who were insisting now that he not tell her about the refinery? He ached to tell her about Wolf's Leg.

"I know you wouldn't have told anyone, not intentionally, but Wayne was afraid you might let something slip." He grinned. "We didn't know at the time what a marvelous keeper of secrets you are."

At least *he* knew how well she could keep a secret, but he hadn't managed to convince his brothers.

She tucked her bottom lip under her top teeth for a moment. "The screen—that's why your brothers are here?"

"One of the reasons." Sam sipped his coffee. "I didn't want to offer the screen to Clarkston without their approval. We aren't just brothers. We're all business partners, too."

"Why don't you take the screen over to Jonas Richardson at the *Times* office?" Prairie asked, resting her lower arms on the table and leaning toward him. "Show it to him and explain how it's supposed to work. Then King couldn't take the credit."

Sam shrugged. "I suppose I could, but the credit isn't that important to me anymore, Prairie. Bringing in this field is. I've never thought much about

279

what a woman's term would be like, but I imagine I'm feeling the same sort of anxiety as an expectant mother in her eighth month. It's been almost that long for me, and I'm ready for this baby to be born."

His analogy brought a rush of pain to Prairie's heart. Why did she suddenly want to have his baby? All along, he'd made it clear that oil ran through his veins. His commitment was to his work, not to her, not to a family. When his hand closed over hers, she jerked as though it were a hot poker.

Although Sam felt her recoil, he didn't let go. Instead, he stood up, took a long step around the end of the table, and tugged on her hand, pulling her up, out of her chair. His hands moved to her upper arms and his clear blue eyes demanded her attention. "Do you find my touch so repugnant?"

She looked away. "No—"

He took her chin between his thumb and forefinger and tilted it up. "Look at me, Prairie." He waited until she complied. "I can remember a time not so long ago when my touch made you shiver in delight. What happened? Why don't you like me anymore?"

"It's not that. I . . . I'm afraid."

His thumb rubbed at the tear on her cheek. "I would never harm you, Prairie."

"I know."

"Then what do you fear?"

Her tears flowed freely. Sam wanted desperately to pull her against his chest, to take the pins out of her hair and comb his fingers through its thick, molasses-colored length, to hold her and comfort her and assure her everything would work out. But he couldn't do that. Not with her fear between them.

"What do you fear, Prairie?" he asked again.

"Having a child," she said.

He held her then, close against his chest, her head in the hollow of his shoulder. One hand caressed her back while the other held her head until her sobs subsided.

"Do you want to talk about it?" he asked, and was rewarded by the up and down movement of her chin against his chest. Sam guided her across the hall and into her bedroom.

"We shouldn't be in here, Sam," she said, sniffling.

"Yes, we should. I'm your husband now, remember?"

They sat on the edge of the bed, with Sam's arm around her and her head against his shoulder. Prairie wiped her eyes with the skirt of her apron and trembled. Sam held her tighter.

"It's been so long since I remembered anything," she began.

"About your childhood?" he prompted.

"Wynn never believed that the man who brought me here was my father."

"Jernigan?"

"Yes."

"And you've remembered something about him?"

Prairie sniffled again. "Not about him as much as about my mother. Wynn was right. He wasn't my father."

"How do you know?"

"My mother told me so."

"Did she tell you anything about your father? His name? What happened to him?"

"No. Not that I remember." But she did recall something else. Anna had said he was married to money, not to her. She had told Prairie not to make the same mistake, and she had. She'd married a man far more interested in the pursuit of a fortune than in her. Sam had told her he would soon be filthy rich, that he could keep her in style for the rest of her life. She'd married a man just like her father.

But she couldn't tell him that. She couldn't listen to his denials, couldn't allow him to persuade her with his gentle touch and tender kisses that he was different. She knew better.

She could tell him about Wolf's Leg, she supposed, but she couldn't see how that would help. The name couldn't mean anything more to him than it did to her, and she had no evidence to tie this particular recollection to her father.

Prairie took a deep breath and pulled away from his embrace. "I'm all right, Sam. I think you'd better go now."

"Go? I just got here."

She stood up, willed her legs to stop shaking, and walked to the window, where she clutched the curtain in a tight fist. "We have no future together, Sam. You know that. Please don't try to make this marriage something it isn't."

Sam didn't move. He sat on the bed, staring at her back, wondering what demons she fought. He'd bet she remembered something else about her father, something she wasn't telling him for a reason he couldn't fathom.

"Could we at least have supper together, Prairie?"

Her back stiffened and the lace of her curtain bit into her palm. "I don't think that would be a good idea."

He rose and went to stand behind her. His hands massaged her shoulders until he felt her relax a bit. "It'll be dark soon," he said, his mouth close to her ear. "I can't go back to the rig until morning. Besides, I promised you another lesson."

She was weakening. *Lord, help me!* she prayed, even as she sighed and let her hand drop to her side. She closed her eyes and wondered if this was

282

how her mother had felt with her father, if his touch had stirred the same feeling of helplessness in Anna that Sam's stirred in her. His mouth dropped to her neck, just below her ear, and she shivered.

"Sam, please don't do this!" she begged.

His lips nibbled the sensitive skin near her hairline. "Don't do what?" he asked.

Sam knew exactly what he was doing to her—and he didn't intend to stop. Not when she smelled so delightfully feminine. Not when her skin was so warm and soft beneath his trailing lips. Not when standing so close to her, holding her, kissing her sent delicious little quivers rippling through him. Not when he'd waited so long . . .

He turned her toward him, his mouth never leaving her neck, his lips working their way across her jawline and up her tilted chin until they reached her lips. Their tremble fueled his ardor; her sighing breath fed his passion; her hands, sliding up his arms and coming to rest on his shoulders, kindled flames of desire deep within his belly.

An inner voice warned him to move slowly with her. Though it was difficult, he ignored her partially open mouth, concentrating on its corners, on the depression above her upper lip, on the fullness of her bottom lip, plucking, nibbling, teasing, tormenting himself along with her.

She had to stop him. Heaven, help her! She had to stop him before he destroyed all her willpower, before the languor seeping into her limbs and the heat burning in the nether regions of her being completely overwhelmed her. How could she feel so weak and so strong at the same time? she wondered. So helpless and so powerful?

It wasn't a matter of stopping Sam, she realized. It was a matter of stopping herself, and that she wasn't the least bit certain she wanted to do. At the moment, she was nowhere close to losing her virginity. Perhaps allowing the lesson to continue a bit longer wouldn't hurt . . .

She moved her hands from his shoulders to the back of his neck and slid her fingers into the wispy curls at his nape. His hair was coarse and springy, its texture a delightful contrast to the stiff fabric of his collar. She pulled his head closer to hers and pressed her lips against his, hungry for more than his nibbles bestowed.

When Sam felt the willing, eager press of her lips, he lost all reason. His tongue took its natural course, tasting, flicking, plunging into the warm depths of her mouth, while his hands plundered her torso, coming to rest on the proud thrust of her breasts. Beneath his roving thumbs, her nipples grew firmer and ripened, their rigidity evident even through the multiple layers of camisole and shirtwaist. Suddenly, he wanted to feel their hardness, touch the throbbing buds without the stricture of fabric.

Prairie gasped when his fingers parted the opening in her shirtwaist and his hand slipped inside. When had her buttons come loose? When had she allowed the heat of passion to replace rational thought? She garnered her fortitude and pulled her mouth from his.

"Sam!" she rasped. "This has to end—now."

"No, it doesn't," he averred, kissing the tip of her nose.

"Yes, it does." She pushed herself away from him and stumbled as her blood rushed to her head.

Sam caught her shoulders and pulled her against him, resting his chin on the top of her head. "I'm sorry," he said. "I thought you wanted this as much as I do."

"I don't want your baby, Sam. And I don't know

284

how I can have this without the possibility of acquiring one."

There it was again, her insistence that she didn't want his child. He didn't know whether he wanted a child either, for that matter. There were ways to get around conception, ways he was certain she had no knowledge of. But her words cut like a knife into his heart. By rejecting his seed, she was effectively rejecting him.

Sam stepped sideways to avoid touching her again and left the room.

Prairie's heart leapt into her throat. Somehow, she felt as though she'd just thrown away her only hope of enduring happiness. She rushed after him.

He was standing at her front door, one hand on the knob, the other settling his trilby on his head.

"Where are you going?" she asked, wincing at the sharp, fishwife tone of her voice.

He glanced over his shoulder, his eyes smoldering blue crystals. "Back to the boardinghouse for the night. Back to the rig in the morning."

"When will I see you again?"

He opened the door, then turned halfway around. "Does it really matter, Prairie?"

The slamming door jarred her from head to toe, but she felt only the wreath of sadness closing slowly around her heart.

Waldemar Paxton Wolfeschlegersteinhausenberger closed the folder, tapped his forefinger against the cover, and sat staring off into space, his vision unfocused, his mind dredging up a memory twenty-three years old.

Anna Rose O'Malley was, without doubt, the most beautiful woman he'd ever seen. Against the screen of his memory, he could still see her face, after all these years. The image was so real he felt as though he could reach forth a hand and feel the softness of her cheek against his palm or lower his mouth to hers and taste the honeyed sweetness of her pouty lips.

He'd met her in Kansas City at the drugstore where she worked as a clerk. It was her hair, he recalled, that had first caught his attention—dark and rich and thick as molasses. But it was her smile that had stolen his heart, a smile that made her face glow like a lantern.

Laughter often followed her smile. Lord, how Anna O'Malley loved to laugh. And how he loved to watch her laugh, loved to watch her little pointed chin jiggle and her eyes crinkle up into slits so narrow they barely let the amber light of her irises shine through.

The day he walked into the drugstore had marked the first of many long treks by horseback from his ranch into town to see Anna. He'd bought the Big Spring, as he called his spread, at a sheriff's sale; he was on his way to making his first million.

Even then, folks called him Wolf's Leg behind his back, since few could remember his name, and even fewer could vocalize it without stepping all over their tongues. Those who hadn't met him always gaped in some surprise at his blond hair and blue eyes. Though they never said so, he knew they expected to meet a half-breed. Who else would have a name like Wolf's Leg? Certainly not a big, brawny German with a name that sounded as long as he was tall.

But Anna could say Wolfeschlegersteinhausenberger without blinking an eye, and she could write it on his charge slip without a single hesitation of the pen.

"Call me Val," he told her.

286

"Oh, that wouldn't be proper!" she said, aghast.

"It would be if you were my wife," he answered.

She was barely sixteen, she argued. Old enough, he insisted. Her family had neither wealth nor social status, she pointed out. Neither did his, he said. He didn't want a pampered, spoiled miss for his wife. He wanted a sturdy woman from the working class, one who understood what back-breaking labor and long hours at little pay were all about.

Not that he expected his wife to labor from sun-up to sundown. There were servants for that. But he didn't want her to forget what it felt like. Not knowing where next month's rent was coming from strengthened character, and Val wanted a woman of strong character.

He couldn't have been happier. Nor, did he think, could Anna have been. Under her expert supervision, his big, rambling house became a home — a home he found himself frequenting less and less as his expanding business interests took him farther and farther from Kansas City for longer and longer periods of time.

Anna wanted to travel with him, but he insisted she stay home, where she would be safe. She said she was miserable at the Big Spring, isolated as it was, with only the servants and ranch hands to talk to. He said she needed a baby to occupy her time and energy. He'd been so pleased to learn she was pregnant, he didn't notice her disinterest.

He should have known better, he told himself countless times later. He'd snatched a girl from the hustle and bustle of city life, plucked her from a bevy of friends, removed her from a family she loved, then dumped her out in the middle of nowhere and expected her to be happy. He should have known she'd leave at the first chance she got.

But he didn't stop to think about all those things

then. He left her on the Big Spring. Left her for three long months while he chased an elusive deal without so much as a letter telling her he missed her. The servants said she ran off with a drifter, a gaunt, lean fellow just passing through who'd stopped for a hot meal at the ranch house. They didn't even know his name.

For the better part of twenty-three years, he had looked for her, had searched, too, for the child she had carried last he saw her. His child. A tear escaped the inner corner of his eye and coursed, unchecked, down his cheek.

Anna could not have vanished into thin air, but she had effectively eluded him. He'd employed every resource, every contact at his disposal, to no avail. But he'd never given up. One day, he was convinced, he would find Anna. And when he found her, he would also find his child.

There were so few clues, so little information for his hired detectives to go on. He provided each of them with a photograph of Anna and a description of the one piece of jewelry he'd given her that was missing from her jewelry box: a silver filigree dragonfly brooch with garnet eyes.

Certain she would eventually contact her mother, he'd stayed in close contact with Annie O'Malley and her family and made certain they had his current address each time he moved. He'd been in New Orleans for almost a decade. If any of the O'Malleys had ever heard from her, they had kept her whereabouts a secret.

Although he never lost hope, he had begun to think that when he did locate Anna and his child, they would be in a cemetery somewhere—until six months ago, when one of the detectives in his employ had brought him a stack of dime novels written by a certain Pampas J. Rose.

288

"I know it's a long shot, sir," Stephenson had said, "but I think this author may know your wife."

As Val read the books, he became convinced Theodore Stephenson was on to something. What concerned him, however, was that the author might *be* his wife. If that were the case, he dare not alert her to his discovery, lest she run again.

He and Stephenson launched an elaborate plan, which required the detective to become an employee of Beadle and Adams long enough to unearth an address for Pampas J. Rose. Stephenson's employment would also provide enough insight into the publishing business to allow him to pose as an editor, should such deception become necessary.

Staying in New Orleans when he wanted to go straight to Lafayette to meet this David Hamilton fellow took every drop of Val Wolfeschlegersteinhausenberger's self-control. He couldn't believe the author lived in Louisiana, less than a day's train ride away. "Find out everything you can about him and everyone he knows," Val instructed Stephenson. "Follow up on every detail, no matter how trivial it may seem."

Stephenson had called him from Lafayette. "We were wrong," the detective said. "David Hamilton cannot possibly be your son, but I think I've found your daughter. Her name is Prairie and she's the spitting image of your wife. And listen to this: she was wearing the dragonfly brooch. She told Hamilton's landlady that she lives in Crowley. I'm convinced Hamilton isn't Pampas J. Rose; Prairie is. I think she wrote those books hoping you would find her."

"Go easy, in the event you're wrong," Val cautioned. "I don't want to come this close just to scare her off."

Val sent him to Crowley, which turned into a dead

end. But Stephenson was an excellent detective. From the desk clerk at the Evangeline Hotel, he'd learned the identity of the young man who had inquired about the Hamiltons. Even a novice investigator could uncover mounds of information on the famous oilman, Sam Blackman. Since Stephenson had met Blackman, Val called him home and sent another man to Jennings. With all the prospectors and gamblers pouring into the booming town, what was one more stranger?

Then, right on the tail of hearing about one Blackman brother, another one showed up at Val's office. Convinced the Blackmans were acquainted with Prairie, he'd readily agreed to Wayne's proposal. Even if he was wrong, he reasoned, it was a damned good business deal.

But he wasn't wrong. He could smell it. Wolf's Nose would have been a more appropriate nickname. He hadn't become one of the richest men in the country by making mistakes.

As he collected the stack of folders and moved to his wall safe, Val Wolfeschlegersteinhausenberger smiled to himself. Almost effortlessly, the pieces of the puzzle were finally coming together, and within another week or two, he would be able to see the entire picture. The only thing left, then, would be finally meeting this daughter of his.

Chapter Nineteen

Prairie ached for Sam. She ached for his touch. She ached to know him, physically. But most of all, she ached for his companionship. His departure left her feeling woefully incomplete.

Throughout her life, she'd never felt whole. The uncertainty of who she was had always loomed like a black, gaping hole, a void waiting to be populated by a host of ancestors. She'd thought wholeness and happiness lay in uncovering her roots.

Now she didn't feel nearly as confident. She began to wonder if her pursuit of family would ever lead to anything more than a mere satisfaction of curiosity.

No! she mentally argued. She wasn't about to throw away her life's dream. Not for a man like Sam Blackman. Not for a man whose primary interests in life revolved around accumulating wealth.

"I won't make the same mistake you did, Mother," she murmured aloud.

But even as she said it, she wondered if perhaps the mistake hadn't already been made.

"I told you going to see her would be a mistake!" Sam railed as he paced his room, which he and Wayne were sharing while J.C. and Myron were in town. Between the oil boom and the fire, there were no available rooms anywhere in Jennings.

There were a few beds—cots actually, inside large tents; at three dollars per cot per night, the tent owners were making a killing. There was no point in sending Myron and J.C. to such communal "hotels" when the brothers could double up for a couple of nights. Nevertheless, having to share a bed with Wayne rubbed Sam the wrong way. By rights, he should be sleeping with Prairie.

"Didn't you make any progress at all?" Wayne asked, the corners of his mouth twitching in barely suppressed amusement. "Do you need us to tell you how to woo a woman?"

"I don't know why you take so much pleasure in my misery," Sam complained.

"That's what you get for being the youngest," J.C. said.

"And the best looking one of the bunch," Myron added.

"Well, I didn't ask for either. Nor did I ask to marry Prairie Jernigan. It just . . . happened."

"What did we tell you the first time you fell off a horse?" J.C. asked.

Sam frowned. "To get back on him. But what does that have to do with—oh, no. I'm through with Prairie. She's made it very clear she doesn't want anything to do with me."

J.C. grinned. "Did you quit when I told you Patillo Higgins and Captain Lucas were fools?"

"Did you quit when the people in this town called you 'that lunatic with a red surrey who's drilling for oil in a rice field'?" Myron asked.

"Did you quit when the well sanded up and the pipe got stuck?" Wayne put in.

Sam stopped pacing and looked hard at each of his brothers individually, then addressed the three of them. "You guys are all against me!" he accused.

"No, we aren't," Wayne defended. "We're trying to help you see what you're doing—to yourself, to Prairie, to any future you two might have together. You're not a quitter, Sam."

"Well, I'm about to become one," Sam said firmly, but in the back of his mind, he knew he wouldn't quit. His brothers were right. He didn't have it in him to give up.

Sam had planned to go back to the rig the next morning, but his brothers talked him into staying in town through the weekend. There was no way, they reasoned, that Clarkston Number One could hit the oil sand before the end of the next week, and Blackman Number Two was still several days behind. Since they had decided to offer Clarkston the screen, Sam ordered another one from Henry Boudreaux.

"Besides," Wayne added, "we're gonna need another office building. Let's buy a lot and build our own, and while we're looking for a lot, we can scout out some prospects for some land to put the refinery on. You know, use the lot as a sort of smoke screen."

Sam was amazed at the progress the town had made in the two weeks he'd been away. All the debris left by the fire had been cleared away and foundations laid for many of the buildings that had burned to the ground. Most of the replacements would be brick.

The fire had destroyed the two brothels that were under construction. Saloons were going up in their places. True to his word, Michael Donovan had sponsored an ordinance prohibiting houses of prostitution within the confines of Jennings. Sam and his brothers heard all about it while they were getting their hair cut in Dub Jackson's barber shop.

Though they'd grumbled aplenty, Cora Jones and Madame Angelique moved their establishments to the outskirts of town, just beyond the official limits. Cora's was on the road to Hathaway, north of town, and Madame Angelique's was on the eastern route to

Crowley. Word was that two other madams were taking the south and west roads. Pretty soon, folks said, no one could come in or leave without passing a brothel. Sam wondered what the Certified Teetotalers thought about that.

They heard a story in the barber shop that kept them in stitches for awhile. Many of the men who were frequenting the brothels found it convenient to rent livery stable horses to make their treks to see the "girls," and the horses were quickly becoming accustomed to stopping at the brothels.

"You should aheard Mort Salley talkin' 'bout takin' his girl for a ride in the country last Sunday," Dub Jackson told them. "Mort rented a horse and buggy from the livery and they drove north. When they got to Cora's place, the horse turned right up her driveway. Mort said no matter how hard he jerked on the bridle, that dadblamed horse wouldn't budge. He had a time tryin' to explain it to Sally Morrison. Course, I told him she didn't have no biness hitchin' up with him anyways. If she did, her name'd be Sally Salley."

There was talk, too, about the new water system and the telephone and electrical lines that were being installed. It was hard to believe that a town the size of Jennings would be electrified within the next few months.

"There don't appear to be too many lots left to buy in this town," Wayne commented when he, Sam, J.C., and Myron left the barber shop. "No commercial ones of any size."

"Except that triangle where Main and Market meet," Sam observed.

Wayne snorted. "Who'd be foolish enough to put a building there?"

"We would," Sam said. "It's perfect—right in the hub of town."

"But it's such a narrow lot!" Wayne argued. "And the shape is awful." J.C. and Myron agreed.

"Two more reasons why it's perfect," Sam argued. Like you said, no one else would want it."

Wayne held on tenaciously. "It will take a man of uncommon vision to see any potential in that piece of property."

Sam grinned. "Exactly. Let's go look at it and I'll explain what I have in mind."

Before the day was out, the Blackman brothers had signed a contract to purchase the triangular lot downtown and to lease, with an option to buy, several acres between Jennings and Evangeline—between town and the oil field. Everyone expected them to build an office building and no one thought twice about the acreage. Sam and Wayne had been leasing land since they'd first come to Jennings.

Now they were set. Though they were still skeptical about the lot, J.C. and Myron promised to find an architect in Beaumont or Houston who could design a building to fit into the long, narrow triangle. And they couldn't have chosen a better spot for the refinery—right along the pipeline and not so very far from town.

They had the financing. They had the land. All they needed was a producing field, and Sam felt confident they'd have one within a few weeks.

Somehow, Sam didn't believe he would be satisfied, even with all that.

By early Saturday afternoon, Prairie gave up trying to forget Sam was in town and decided to take Wynn's advice and do something about it.

Her first inclination was to march right over to Lily's boardinghouse and apologize for sending him away. But that would alert Lily and her boarders to their problems. Prairie didn't think she was quite ready to air her personal difficulties to the entire town.

But she had to see Sam — and she didn't think he would come back to her house without an invitation. She took pen and paper and wrote him a note, sealed it in an envelope, then tucked it in her apron pocket. As much as she detested yard work, she collected her rake from the shed and busied herself cleaning her front yard.

A while later, Kevin McCormack rode by on his bicycle. "Hi, there, Miss Jernigan — I mean, Miz Blackman," he called, braking to a halt. "You need some help with them leaves?"

As she walked toward Kevin, Prairie bit her tongue to keep from correcting him. "Not with the leaves, Kevin, but I could use some help. I wonder if you might deliver a letter for me."

"Sure, Miz Blackman. Long as it's in town. I promised my maw I wouldn't be gone too long."

Prairie removed the envelope from her pocket and handed it to the boy. "It's a message for my husband. His brothers are in town and they're all over at Miss Bidwell's discussing a business deal. Do you know where her boardinghouse is?"

"Yes'm. I'll be happy to take it over there for you."

"And I'll be happy to give you a glass of milk and some cookies when you get back."

Kevin grinned. "Oh, thank you, Miz Blackman. I won't be long."

True to his word, Kevin came right back. "He wasn't there," he said, panting. "Miss Bidwell said they hadn't come back from having dinner downtown. She said she'd make sure he got the letter as soon as he got back."

Prairie bit her lip, wondering what to do next. While Kevin was eating his cookies, she asked him if he had time to deliver a list to the grocer for her.

"Sure, Miz Blackman. That's on my way home."

She wrote the list, then gave it to him with a dime.

"Gee, thanks, Miz Blackman!" he said, rubbing the

296

shiny coin between his thumb and forefinger. "You didn't have to pay me. Them cookies was real good, too."

"Thank you, Kevin. Now, you run along before you get in trouble with your mother."

Prairie didn't know what she expected Sam to do, but whatever it was, it didn't include leaving her dangling all afternoon. She tried to avoid thinking about him by staying busy. She finished cleaning the yard, then took a long look at her parlor. Though it suited her needs well, she found the room sadly lacking intimacy.

She scooped up her mending basket from the floor and a stack of books from a table. Back and forth she went, from parlor to bedroom or kitchen, finding places to stow away the clutter. In its stead, she put out every candlestick she could find. She fluffed pillows, moved furniture around, arranged long stems of pussy willow in a porcelain urn.

As soon as Mr. Dalby's grocery boy brought the box of food, she set to work preparing supper—roast chicken with cornbread dressing, candied sweet potatoes, and green peas. Since she was using the oven for the chicken, she decided to prepare a cooked custard for dessert.

Outside, the weather was pleasantly cool, but inside Prairie's kitchen, it was hot. As she stirred the custard, sweat trickled down her chest and puddled between her breasts. From time to time, she parked the long-handled wooden spoon long enough to wipe her face with the skirt of her apron. Locks of hair came loose from the bun she'd pinned on top of her head and hung in damp strands down her neck and across her forehead. When she finished the custard, she decided, she'd take a bath.

"Dadburn custard," she seethed. "Thicken up!"

When it refused to cooperate, she slid the pan off onto the reservoir and went to open the window. In her haste to return to the custard before it lumped up, she pushed one side of the window harder than the other and got it hopelessly stuck.

Well, she thought, there was always the door. She opened it wide, then swiped her left foot against the brick she used as a stop, stubbing her big toe in the process.

"Yipes!" she hollered as pain shot through the toe. Prairie hobbled over to a chair, sat down, and removed her shoe. The toe was fiery red and swelling fast.

Forgetting all about the custard, she used a pick to chip off a piece of ice from the block in her icebox, then sat down again and held the ice against the throbbing toe. Gradually, the pain began to ease, but she wasn't the least bit certain she'd be able to stand on her left foot long enough to finish cooking supper.

Sam had a difficult time maintaining a straight face.

She was a sight to behold, sitting at the kitchen table, her left ankle atop her right knee, her foot bare. A large, dark circle stained her teal blue shirtwaist between her shoulder blades; more sweat plastered wayward strands of hair to her cheeks. Amid the damp strands glistened streaks of something buff-colored, something that appeared to be terribly sticky.

He'd never thought of her before as domestic; nor did she appear very comfortable in the role. But Sam didn't think he'd ever felt so attracted to her as he did then. He cleared his throat and stepped into the room.

Prairie spun around on her seat, her face aghast. "What are you doing here? I mean, where did you come from?"

Sam smiled. "What? You sent for me. Where? Through the front door and down the hall." He stepped closer to her and saw the size of her big toe for the first time. "Is it broken?"

Her shoulders slumped. "I don't know." She hurled the piece of ice at the dishpan. It careened off the lip, fell to the floor, and shattered.

"Let me see," he said, falling to one knee and pressing on the toe gingerly with his fingers. "Have you tried wiggling it?"

She shook her head. "I was afraid to."

"So am I," Sam admitted sheepishly. "Do you want me to get Doc or Wynn?"

She chuckled, but Sam could see the pain in her spicy eyes. "I don't think it's that serious. If we had electricity in Jennings, Wynn could take a picture of it with her new X-ray machine."

"You're the doctor's daughter. What do you think we should do?"

"We need something to stabilize it. Let me think what we could use . . ."

"How about a shoehorn?" Sam asked.

Prairie grinned. "That might just work. You're amazingly ingenious."

Sam laughed. "You were thinking about it too hard. Where will I find one?"

"In the bottom drawer of my bureau, on the right side. It may be under something."

"I'll find it. You sit right there."

It was under something—under the saddlebags that must have belonged to Jernigan, the man who'd brought her to Jennings but who wasn't her father. She had spunk, he thought, writing all those dime novels, planting her few clues. He wondered if her efforts would ever pay off.

"Here it is," he announced, coming back into the kitchen. "How shall I attach it?"

A few minutes later, when Sam took Prairie's hand to help her stand on the bandage-wrapped foot, his fingers grazed the wedding band she wore.

299

"Sometimes, I almost forget we're married," he said, verbalizing what he'd intended to be a thought.

"Perhaps that's best," Prairie murmured.

Sam ignored her, his eyes on the thin gold band that was at least a size too large. "I'll buy you another one," he said. "One that fits."

"That really isn't necessary."

"Yes, it is. You're going to lose that one. And I can't wear mine—it's far too small. Besides which, Ruth and Enoch would probably appreciate getting theirs back." He grasped her hand more firmly and pulled her up. "Try putting your weight on it. Does it hurt?"

"No," she said in astonishment. "Padding it with soft cloth was a good idea. Thanks."

"My pleasure." Sam smiled broadly at her, then sniffed. "What's cooking?"

Prairie clasped a hand over her mouth. "Supper! I completely forgot about it."

Sam pulled one of the chairs around to the end of the table. "You sit down and prop your foot up," he gently ordered, "and let me worry about supper. You can tell me what to do."

She had him baste the chicken and check on the candied sweet potatoes. "There's a fresh loaf of bread in the safe," she said, "and I thought I'd open a jar of peas when I put the dressing in the oven. And for dessert—oh, no!"

Thinking her exclamation was related to her toe, Sam rushed to her side. "What's wrong?"

"The custard! I forgot it. It's probably one solid lump by now."

Though he found her distress amusing, Sam stifled the chuckle rising in his throat. "Don't worry about it, Prairie. We can manage without dessert."

"But I wanted everything to be perfect," she said dejectedly.

On his way through the parlor, Sam had noted the

300

way she'd turned the room into a cozy retreat. Had she done that for him? he wondered. What else besides supper had she planned for the evening? Without stopping to think about what he was doing, Sam squatted down beside her chair, took her hands in his, and said, "As long as you're here, it will be."

"Oh, Sam!" she groaned. "It's not just the custard. Look at me."

"I *am* looking."

She wrinkled her nose. "Are you smelling, too? I'm all sweaty."

"Yeah, you are. And now I know what that is in your hair."

She pulled one of her hands from his clasp and felt along the top of her head. "Ew! Custard! How did it get up there?"

"I don't know, but it's all over the front of your apron, too. Don't fret. We can easily remedy the situation. Where's your bathtub?"

"Oh, no!" she protested. "I'm not taking a bath while you're here."

"And why not? I am your husband."

"But—"

"But nothing. Where's your bathtub?"

Prairie sighed and pointed over her shoulder. "Behind that screen."

Sam raised his eyebrows. "You live by yourself and you keep the bathtub behind a screen?"

"I don't like looking at it."

"Whatever," he allowed, moving to the sink and pumping water into the kettle.

"There's warm water in the reservoir," she reminded him.

"I know, but it's not enough. Besides, I want some coffee. How about you?"

As Prairie watched him grind the beans, she wondered what sort of trouble she'd plunged into by inviting Sam to her house. Somehow, she couldn't quite imagine his succumbing to the tranquil evening she had planned.

He set the prepared coffeepot aside, picked up the pot she'd left on the reservoir, lifted the wooden spoon. The custard dripped in a thin stream back into the pot. "It's not the blob you feared. Tell me what to do to finish it."

"It's not lumpy?"

"No."

"Well, it should be. Bring it here." Frowning, Prairie stirred the custard, then tasted it. "No wonder it wouldn't get thick!" She laughed. "I forgot to put the flour in it."

"Can it be remedied?"

"I doubt it."

Sam moved the pot out of the way and sat down in the chair in front of Prairie, putting her foot in his lap. "Can we be remedied, Prairie?"

She plucked at the skirt of her apron. "I don't know, Sam."

"Would you like to try?" he asked.

Prairie lifted her head and met his gaze. "Would you?"

He pinned her with an assessing gaze but found it impossible to discern her thoughts. If she wasn't willing to put forth a little effort—and her question made him think she wasn't, then he wasn't about to waste his time or energy on a relationship that was headed nowhere.

Prairie cringed inside, but she was careful to wear a poker face. Had he forgotten that she had invited him to supper? Couldn't he see she wanted to try? That she *was* trying?

"Men can be so pig-headed sometimes," she said.

Sam smiled and stood up. "I'm going to take that to mean you're willing. And, yes, I'd like to try, too." He lifted the kettle and headed for the corner. "Are you ready for your bath?"

"Are you going to stay on this side of the screen?" she asked, then laughed at the way he jiggled his eyebrows up and down. But when she narrowed her eyes at him, he threw up his hands.

"All right. I'll just . . . sit here and drink my coffee."

While he hauled water to the tub, Prairie laid out a towel and bath cloth, then hobbled to her room to collect fresh clothes. She hadn't given much thought to what she would wear, but it should be something feminine, she decided. This night was important, perhaps the most important night of her life.

She flipped through the garments hanging in her wardrobe, discounting first one and then another until she came to a pink silk moire dress she seldom wore. She gave it quick scrutiny, then pulled it out of the wardrobe and hung it on a wall hook.

Prairie peeked out her bedroom door to make sure Sam was preoccupied with preparing her bath, which he was. She locked the door, then stripped down to her panties and camisole and pulled on a heavy chenille robe.

She wondered if she could do this, suddenly understanding what having cold feet meant. Could she open the door, walk across the hall and into her kitchen — where Sam waited — in nothing but her underwear and robe? Could she take a bath behind the screen while he sat at the table drinking coffee?

Most importantly, could she prevent intimacy with Sam? She'd stopped him before. Did she honestly want to stop him tonight?

Sam Blackman and her father were two different men, weren't they? She'd never known her father. Perhaps her mother had been wrong about him. Perhaps, if Anna had given him a chance, if she hadn't left him, their lives would have been different.

Anna had left her father.

The acknowledgment jolted her. All this time, she'd

shied away from Sam because she was afraid he'd desert her. But her father hadn't left her mother. It had been the other way around. Anna had left him.

Sam hadn't even put up a fuss when she told him they had to get married. She couldn't believe he would have taken it so well had he not wanted to marry her. Yet, not once had he mentioned the word love.

"Hey, Prairie!" he called. "Are you all right in there? You need some help?"

It's now or never, she thought. *You've been taking risks for years.*

But none that involved another life. She wouldn't risk doing to another child what her parents had done to her.

Thus resolved, she turned the key and opened the door.

Sam sensed her reserve immediately. They needed to talk. More than anything else, Sam wanted to spend the entire night with Prairie. He wanted to touch her and hold her and kiss her again. He wanted to make love to her, too, but he knew she might not be ready for that. In time, she would be, and Sam was a patient man. He could wait.

He swished his fingers around in the water. "I added some bath salts," he said. "I hope you don't mind."

"No, not at all," she said, pulling nervously at the lapels of her robe.

"Well, I'll just—" he waved an arm toward the table. "I'll just go sit over there." He looked down at her bandaged foot. "Can you manage with that foot?"

"Yes, I think so."

He moved away from the tub, pondering her sudden shyness. Funny, he'd never thought of her as shy. And that's what it was, too. She wasn't being coy. He'd bet his interest in the well on it.

Listening to her soft hum and the splash of water became torturous before she finally emerged from behind the screen, dressed in her robe again, the custard washed clean from her hair. Shimmering in burnished splendor, the dark, wet skein fell in a tangled mass over one shoulder, spilling over her breast. Sam felt his blood quicken. He cleared his throat and looked away.

Prairie stared at the back of Sam's head. Funny, she'd never thought of him as shy, but he was certainly acting that way. She smiled to herself, then retrieved her hairbrush from her dresser and pulled a chair in front of the stove.

Sam sipped his coffee and listened to the crackling noises the brush made as she pulled it through her hair until he thought he would go stark raving mad. Finally, he gave up trying to ignore her and turned around.

Watching her, he realized too late, was even worse. But he couldn't stop himself. She sat with her head bent low, her hair falling forward almost to the floor as she made long, even strokes with the brush. His breath caught in his throat when she flipped her hair back. The unruly mass billowed in a dark cloud around her head, a fitting frame for her ivory skin and ginger-colored eyes.

His gaze left her face, seeking safer territory, and ran straight into imminent danger. The robe fell open almost to her waist, exposing a good portion of her breasts above the low-cut camisole she wore. Sam's throat went dry.

"There," she said, apparently unaware of the effect she was having on him. "It's almost dry. Have you put the dressing in the oven yet?"

He shook his head, unable to speak.

Prairie put the chair back, opened the ice box, and removed a large bowl. "I've already stuffed the bird. If you don't mind, put this in the roasting pan with the chicken and open this jar of peas. Can you season them?"

Sam swallowed. "I think so."

"Good. By the time I finish getting dressed, supper should be ready. I don't know about you, but I'm hungry."

"Me, too," Sam said. But he didn't mean for food.

Chapter Twenty

It was a night for surprises, Sam thought as he accepted a filled plate from Prairie. He'd learned she could be both domestic and shy. And now, looking at her in the pink gown with her hair piled on top of her head, he tossed out his conception of her as being merely pretty and acknowledged that she was one of the most beautiful women he'd ever laid eyes on.

No, he mentally corrected, she *was* the most beautiful woman he'd ever seen, and she was his *wife*. Sam's chest filled with pride, marred only by the fact that the marriage had yet to be consummated. That was something he intended to change. Tonight, if possible.

If it had been up to Sam, they would have skipped the main course and gone straight to dessert — and he wasn't thinking about the soupy custard. But Prairie had obviously worked hard to prepare the meal, which was actually much better than he expected, even if the chicken was a bit overdone and the dressing on the bland side.

"I never imagined you could cook," he admitted, casting around for a safe subject — something to take his mind off dessert.

Prairie smiled. "Does that mean I can or I can't?"

"It means you can," he answered, exhausting that topic. "Did I tell you we bought a lot for a new office building?"

"No. There aren't many available. Which one did you take?"

Discussing the odd shape of the lot and his ideas for a building to fit it consumed several minutes, and then, there he was again, fishing for something to talk about. He wanted to tell her about Wolf's Leg and the refinery, but it would have to wait, he supposed, until the well came in and the deal was finalized. Sam hated not being able to confide in her. Prairie's reluctance to trust him completely, however, made him skittish about trusting her.

"Do you want some more?" Prairie asked, drawing him back to the present.

"No. No, thanks. But it was very good," he hastily added, rising with Prairie and carrying his plate to the sink. "Let me help you with the dishes."

When the last pan was dried and put away, they stood facing each other in the warm kitchen. Sam wondered if he looked as tense as Prairie did. He knew he felt plenty tense. An unspoken question — What do we do now? — hung between them.

She untied her apron, a white, ruffly thing, looped its shoulder straps over a wall hook, and folded her hands together in front of her, a picture of composure, except for her eyes. They looked like they ought to belong to a scared rabbit. "Would, uh, would you like to sit in the parlor?" she finally asked.

At his nod, she took some matches out of a metal wall holder with a rose decal on the front and headed toward the hall. Sam followed.

When she lit the first lamp, he wasn't surprised. After all, the parlor was dark and the lamp provided ample light to see the wicks of the candles. But when she started to light the second lamp, Sam took the matches from her. "Allow me," he said.

The candlelight cast a soft, intimate glow, conducive, Sam hoped, to relaxation. He suspected that was why Prairie put all the candles out in the first place. If he was right, then she must want to settle things between them as much as he did. Maybe she'd just been afraid to take

308

he initiative. Sam sat down beside her on the narrow sofa.

She had clasped her hands together again. Sam took them from her lap, separated them, and folded his fingers over her palms. He intended to do nothing more than talk to her, but the minute he took her hands, the minute he touched her, Sam forgot all about talking.

Prairie watched him lean toward her, knew he meant to kiss her, knew that was what she wanted him to do. When his lips grazed hers, a peace unlike any she'd ever known filled her soul. His kiss was tentative at first, touching, tasting, teasing, a lingering of lips upon lips that tantalized and tingled and begged her to respond.

Terrified that kissing her was a mistake, Sam held his breath, waiting for her to pull away. Instead, her lips softened beneath his and her hands clutched his tighter. Fire ripped through him. He moaned, fighting the need to pull her hard against his chest and plunder her sweet mouth with his tongue.

Never had Sam wanted anything quite so much as he wanted Prairie. Never had he moved so cautiously, so slowly, so carefully. Never had he worried so about having the object of his desire snatched away from him.

Never until that moment had Prairie felt she belonged to someone, but she belonged to Sam. He told her so with every nuance of his touch. No one, she thought, who loved her that much would leave her with a child to raise on her own.

And she belonged to him. She told him so by raising his hands to her shoulders and then sliding her arms around his rib cage. When the tip of his tongue explored the seam of her mouth, she opened her lips to him and succumbed to the warmth radiating upward from her belly.

Sam had known a few women in his day, but not one of them had touched his heart. Not the way Prairie did—so much that he thought his heart would burst from loving her.

Ever so slowly, he plied her mouth with his. Ever so slowly, he caressed her face, her neck, her shoulders with his hands. Ever so slowly, he broke down their mutual hesitation and Prairie's inhibitions. When he released her and rose from the sofa, he felt as though a part of him had been physically severed.

For the briefest of moments, Prairie closed her eyes and fought back the sting of tears. So this was what it was like to love someone, she thought. This was why people said love hurt. It did. She'd never felt such pain, such excruciating longing for the feel of a man's arms around her. And now that man was leaving her to deal with the torturous ache alone.

When Sam scooped her into his arms, she thought at first she'd wanted it so much, she'd surely imagined it. But she knew she wasn't imagining his lips upon her eyelids or the whispery sigh of his voice.

"If you don't want me, say so now—before it's too late."

She opened her eyes and searched his face, seeing there a reflection of her own pain. "I do want you, Sam," she said, lifting her head to seal her vow with a kiss. For a moment, he didn't move. When he started toward the hall, she reached out and grasped a candlestick to light their way.

With an amazing tenderness, he laid her upon the bed, taking the candlestick from her hand and placing it on her dresser in front of the mirror. Prairie waited, breathlessly, for Sam to join her.

He sat down on the end of the bed and took her right foot in his hand. Slowly, methodically, he removed her shoe, then massaged her foot through the silk stocking. With the bandage on her left foot, she wore only the one. She trembled when his hands moved up her leg until his fingers encountered the garter. Down came his hands, bringing the garter and the stocking with them.

Off went his shoes and then his socks. When he

eached for the string tie at his neck, Prairie stopped
im. "Come here."

Hearing the intensity of her own yearning sent a
hudder through him. He scooted toward her, leaned
nto her, kissed her all the while her fingers worked loose
he tie and then the buttons on his shirt.

"Sam!" she gasped when his chest was bare. "Oh,
5am!" She ran her palms across his shoulders, down his
)ectoral muscles, over his nipples, and drove her fingers
nto the crisp, curling hair on his chest.

All his determination to go slow and easy vanished
vith her eagerness. He pulled her to her feet and began
o unfasten the hooks running down the back of her
lress.

Minutes later, their clothes scattered everywhere
about the room, they fell onto the bed. The golden
gleam of the single candle flame bounced off the mirror,
shimmering and dancing, glistening off the thin film of
perspiration on Sam's forehead and setting Prairie's
dark curls ablaze.

She marveled at the smooth texture of his skin, the
bulge of his muscles, and the thick dusting of brown
hair on his chest.

He marveled at the firm globes of her breasts, the
dark rosy color of her areolas, the tiny circle of her
waistline.

They caressed each other with their eyes, their hands,
and their mouths, exploring, learning, astonishing
themselves and each other with the depth of emotion
their lovemaking stirred.

"I don't mean to hurt you," Sam whispered when it
was time. "Maybe it won't last long."

He clamped his mouth over hers, absorbing the
shock, taking her pain into his very being. When her
shudder of agony subsided, he lifted his head, his gaze
searching hers. The lamplight twinkled in a single tear
beneath Prairie's eye. Sam kissed it away. "I'm sorry," he
murmured.

311

"I'm happy," she said.

"There's more," he promised.

She smiled and pulled his head back to hers. "Show me," she whispered.

And he did.

She floated on an enchanted plane, somewhere above the earth, as light and airy as a cloud, never falling into a deep sleep and yet feeling more rested than she had in years.

Twice more before morning Sam awoke her ardor with his kisses and caresses. Twice more she gave herself to him, wholly, completely, taking him fully, accepting his seed without qualm. Twice more he guided her to a height of ecstasy she hadn't imagined possible.

She discovered, however, that the physical gratification paled in comparison with the emotional intoxication she experienced when they made love. Surely, she reasoned, lying in his arms, the pink glow of early morning sifting around the window shades, only love could pack such a powerful punch.

"Good morning, beautiful," he said, trailing a finger down the length of her nose. "How do you feel?"

"Wonderful. And you?"

He smiled and kissed her forehead. "The best I've ever felt, I think. You're incredible."

"You're not so shabby yourself."

He jiggled his eyebrows at her. "Not so shabby? Come on, Prairie. Is that the best you can do?"

She grinned. "Well, definitely above average."

"Average implies a basis of comparison, and I happen to know for a fact you have no basis, wife."

She propped herself up on an elbow and pinned him with a look of sheer disbelief. "I'll have you know, husband, that I have three — count them, *three* experiences on which to base a comparison."

"And how, pray tell, would you evaluate those three experiences?"

Prairie put on her best schoolmarm face. "Each one was better than the last, which leads me to believe we have yet to reach our full potential."

"Then I suggest a full regimen of drill and practice, Mrs. Blackman."

She nodded. "That's exactly what I had in mind."

An hour later, Sam rose and pulled on his trousers.

"Where are you going?" Prairie asked, knowing that he would leave her, hoping they'd have a little more time together first.

"To build a fire and make some coffee," he said, putting a hand on each side of her head and leaning down to press a kiss on the tip of her nose. "Stay here and I'll bring you a cup."

She smiled and snuggled deeper into the bed, drawing the warm glow of her happiness around her. Within minutes, it seemed, he was back with the coffee. She sat up, propping her back against a mound of pillows, and accepted the steaming cup.

Sam sat down on the side of the bed and gave her a look fraught with mischief. "I suppose this means I can't get an annulment."

Though Sam didn't seem the least perturbed about the change in their relationship, his comment drove home the harsh reality of what they'd done.

Her voice was small and weak. "No, I don't suppose you can."

He smoothed back a wayward strand of hair, his palm lingering on her forehead. "The annulment was never my idea, Prairie."

He picked up his cup from the bedside table and took a long swallow of coffee, his gaze never leaving her face. "Would you like to go to church?" he asked.

"I usually do, but we don't have to, Sam."

"I think I'd like to go. I want everyone in this town to see us together as man and wife."

His male pride stung her, but she knew he had a valid point. The gossips would tire soon enough of wagging

313

their tongues, but a display of model behavior would silence them faster. Prairie supposed she owed her students that much.

"All right," she said. "We'll go." She sipped her coffee, studying the planes and angles of his face, memorizing every detail. There would come a time—sooner than she'd like—when Sam would have to return to the rig. The practical side of her demanded that she ask.

"I ought to go today," he said, staring at a window, "but it can wait until tomorrow, I suppose."

The reality of it was that he didn't want to go at all. Sam couldn't believe he'd actually rather stay with Prairie. But there was nothing for him to do in town while she taught school, and he wasn't a man who could handle idleness. There were always the weekends.

He looked around the room, absorbing it for the first time. It was obviously a woman's bedroom, yet it lacked blatant femininity. The massive black walnut furniture, reminiscent of a bygone era, would serve a man equally as well. Would serve a *couple* equally as well, he amended. He didn't think he'd mind sharing it at all. And that was exactly what he intended to do. He'd made Prairie his wife in every sense of the word—and he wasn't about to let go.

What the room didn't have that he expected to see was a desk.

"Where do you write?" he asked.

With her cup in her hand, Prairie gestured toward a closed door set into the wall opposite the bed, splashing coffee onto the quilt in the process. "Oh, bother! What a mess."

Sam got a wet rag and scrubbed at the spreading stain.

"I'm sorry," she said. "I'm not used to drinking coffee in bed."

"Well, you'd better get used to it—and a lot of other things, too."

Prairie couldn't help wondering what "other things" he meant.

"I want to keep writing," she said. She'd intended to make it a firm statement, but it came out sounding as though she were asking for his permission.

Sam shrugged. "I don't know why you can't, at least for now."

A warning bell sounded in her head. "Why couldn't I later?"

"I suppose you could, so long as it doesn't interfere with our marriage—or your motherhood."

"And what about your work, Sam?"

"What about it?"

"Will you let it interfere with our marriage—or your fatherhood?"

He stood up and walked away from the bed, shoving his hands into his trouser pockets. "That's different, Prairie."

"Why?"

He turned around. "Because it is. A man has to work."

"Not to the exclusion of his family," she argued.

"I didn't say that. But there will be times when I can't be here. You know I don't spend every day in an office."

"And I don't intend to spend every day shackled to housework—or sitting here wondering when you're going to decide to come home."

"Nobody said you had to." He came back to the bed and sat down again. "Look, I'll do my best to schedule short trips and let you know when I'll be back. That's all I can promise. And if I make the money I think I'm going to make, we'll hire a housekeeper and a cook, if you want to. You won't have to work at all."

Prairie could see no point in pursuing the argument further, but she certainly intended to at a later time. "I need to get up and take a bath if I'm going to church," she said.

Sam's eyes twinkled. "That sounds like a good idea. I think I'll join you."

Prairie needn't have worried about the gossipmongers. Cora Jones and her girls provided enough material to last the fuddy-duddies for a week.

A hush fell over the congregation when Cora walked into church, her girls trailing like an entourage behind her. They marched right up front and sat down on the third pew. Prairie wondered if the scarlet ladies wouldn't have taken the first or the second had either been empty. Surprisingly, for prostitutes they were modestly dressed.

Prairie watched Agnes Milhouse, who was seated on the aisle side of the second pew, directly in front of Cora and her girls. When she heard the shuffle behind her, Agnes turned around and the smile froze on her face. Her eyes bugged and her face blanched. Cora reached up and patted Agnes's shoulder.

"Don't you wish you could hear what Cora's saying?" Sam whispered in Prairie's ear.

Prairie suppressed a giggle. "Do I ever!"

Patrick, who was sitting on the other side of Prairie, elbowed her. "Who are those ladies?"

"Ask your father—after church," she said. "Be quiet now. The choir's coming in."

When the service was over, Wynn and Michael invited them to dinner. Prairie hesitated. With Sam leaving the next morning, she knew she'd rather go back to her house. Suddenly, food seemed terribly unimportant. But Sam might think it was a good idea. More model behavior.

"We appreciate it," Sam said for both of them. "Maybe next time."

Wynn winked at Prairie, then whisked Michael and the boys away.

"I hope you don't mind," Sam said, taking Prairie's elbow and steering her toward home.

316

"Not at all. But what are we going to do for lunch? Aren't you hungry?"

Sam grinned. "Yes, ma'am, I sure am. Best I recall, we've got enough food left from supper to see us through the day." He stopped short then and frowned at her. "You don't normally have a passel of company on Sunday afternoons, do you?"

"No, not normally."

He let out his breath on a long whistle and hurried her down the street. "Good, 'cause I don't intend to share you with anyone today."

The next morning, Sam rose well before daylight and went outside to get some more wood for the stove. During the night, the temperature had dropped considerably and a thick bank of clouds had rolled in. He shivered in the pre-dawn chill, as much from the prospect of leaving Prairie as from the nippy air.

There wasn't anything he could do about leaving, however. His future, and Prairie's too, depended on bringing in the well. He dared not delay another day, lest Clarkston's well come in without the benefit of the screen to block the sand. He hoped Prairie would understand.

Sam was having difficulty understanding her possessiveness. Part of what had attracted him to her in the first place was her fierce independence, and she had made it clear she wanted to continue her life much as she had lived it before. Why, then, was she so worried about his being home every night?

He could understand her attitude if Michael Donovan had seldom been at home while Prairie was growing up. But she'd had a father—

That was it, he realized as he closed the firebox door. Prairie hadn't had a father. She'd never really thought of Michael as a parent. Now, she remembered that Jernigan hadn't been her real father. Well, Sam thought, he wasn't her father, either, nor was he about to let her

317

think of him that way.

Although both his parents had died when he was a kid, Sam knew it wasn't the same thing. At least he'd known them, and he had his older brothers. He had blood kin, whereas Prairie didn't—none that she knew of anyway. Hers were a special set of needs. While he couldn't substitute for a parent, he could shower her with all the love and affection she could handle. That he wouldn't mind doing at all.

Just thinking about it got his blood to pumping. He found her sleeping soundly, her legs curled up, her arms hugging a pillow, her hair a dark cloud against the stark white bed linen. Sam turned the lamp down low, shucked his clothes, and slipped into bed beside her.

Despite the chill pervading the room, Prairie awoke to a heat building in her loins. She stretched her torso and pulled the source of the heat closer, reveling in the feel of Sam's hot mouth on her breast. She breathed in the essence of him, a combination of wood smoke and her lemon verbena bath salts.

He nuzzled his way up to her chin. "Good morning, sleepyhead," he teased. "Sorry I woke you up."

"I'm not," she said emphatically, molding her length against his. They fit so perfectly, as though their bodies had been created one for the other. She rolled into him, pushing him over on his back and propping herself on her elbows. "I love you," she said.

While she awaited his response, Prairie's heart pounded in her chest. Why had she said it? Why had she bared her soul to him? Why had she left herself so vulnerable?

He laid a palm on each cheek and pulled her head down to meet his. "Show me," he whispered.

Though neither of them mentioned Sam's imminent departure, it tempered their lovemaking, turning it into a frenzied drama of groping hands, clutching arms, and intertwined legs. It left Prairie feeling physically sated and emotionally drained.

In the aftermath, Sam combed her hair through his long fingers and rained kisses upon her eyelids and temples.

"I'm going to miss you," he said. "Promise me you'll take care of yourself."

"I'll miss you, too," she murmured in a voice as husky as his.

"What will you do while I'm gone?"

"Write, I suppose. I started another story before I — before *we* went to Lafayette."

Sam rubbed her back. "What's this one about?"

"A Texas woman named Cherokee Sally." She smiled. "And, yes, you inspired this one, too."

"Me?" he asked, his raised eyebrows crinkling his forehead. "How?"

"You'll see when you read it."

"Aw, shucks!" he teased. "I thought half the beauty of being married to the famous Pampas J. Rose would be hearing the stories directly from you and not having to wait until they're published."

She shook her head. "No way. At least not this time. Besides, if I told you the story now, I'd be late for school."

Prairie trembled at the reminder and Sam hugged her against him. Life would go on, she supposed. Somehow, she'd make it until the well came in and Sam came home.

And then? Where would he go and what would he do? Where would his obsession with amassing a fortune lead him? And where would it leave them — and the child she might be carrying in her womb?

The pain she'd felt Saturday night when she thought Sam was leaving returned. This time, she didn't expect it to go away.

Chapter Twenty-one

"You'd be a fool not to try it, Clarkston!"

Sam wanted to wallop some sense into the man. Instead, he shoved his hands into his jeans pockets and gritted his teeth. Behind him, the boiler at Clarkston Number One sang and the pumps hummed. Their music had once sounded sweeter to Sam than all the waltzes in the world. Suddenly, however, he heard nothing more than squeaks and groans and hisses from the equipment.

"I don't trust you, Blackman," King said. "Why would you want to help me?"

Sam took a couple of steps toward the fool and leaned forward at the waist, putting his face almost in Clarkston's. "Don't you get it? I don't trust you, either. And I honestly don't want to help you."

"Then why are you insisting I use this screen thing you keep talking about? What does it look like, anyway?"

Sam threw his hands up. "What difference does it make what it looks like? The point is your well is bound to sand up just like my number one well did—unless you do something to prevent it before it happens."

"And you can guarantee this screen will work?"

"No, I can't. No one's ever tried it before."

"So you want to use my well as a laboratory, is that it?" King sneered. "Try it out on Clarkston Number One. If there's a problem, then you have time to fix it before your number two well comes in. I don't like the odds, Blackman."

"You don't like the odds? Let me tell you what the odds are, Clarkston. Don't use the screen and you fail for sure. Use the screen, and you have at least a fifty-fifty chance of success. What in the bloody hell do you have to lose?"

King Clarkston waved an elegant hand at a chair and lifted a bottle of whiskey. "Why don't you have a seat, Blackman, and let me pour you a drink."

"Pour yourself one, if you like," Sam said. "I never touch the stuff."

Clarkston's eyes widened in disbelief. "I never pegged you for a sissy."

Sam wanted to tell him that getting drunk had nothing to do with being a man, but he didn't. He'd just make Clarkston mad, and that was the last thing he wanted to do. So instead, he said, "Are you going to use my screen or not?"

Clarkston pursed his lips. "I don't know. You said you don't want to help me, so why are you giving it to me?"

Sam tried to erase the irritation from his voice, which was difficult. The man definitely stretched his patience. "Because I want to see this field come in. Can't you understand that?"

"I think there's something else," King said, pouring out some of the whiskey into a fat tumbler. "Something you're not telling me, though for the life of me, I can't figure out what."

"Will you take the screen, Clarkston? Just tell me yes or no. I need to get back to my own rig."

Clarkston took a long time thinking about it, alternately sipping his drink and rubbing his chin. Sam figured King did it to aggravate him, that he knew all along he would take the screen. Finally, Clarkston said, "I want to think about it. I'll let you know."

"Don't take too long. You're running out of time."

Staying away from Prairie was driving Sam nuts.

Why couldn't he be excited about two things at once? he asked himself. Why had he never seen the monotony in drilling for oil?

And that's exactly what it was, too. Monotonous.

For the next several days, Sam tried to break the monotony by dividing his waking hours between his rig and Clarkston's. He talked to Ray Guidry about the screen, hoping the driller could persuade King to use it.

"I'm good enough at my job, I suppose," Guidry said, "but there isn't a man in the oil business who's as well respected as you are, Sam. If you say this screen will control the sand, I believe you. I'll do my best with Clarkston, but the man's awful stubborn."

Together, they watched the mud, examined the cuttings, and swapped oil field tales. "If you ever decide you want to work for me, just say so," Sam told him.

"Oh, working for Clarkston's not so bad. Or, it hasn't been, I guess I should say. The man's never around."

That much was true. Since King refused to spend the cold nights in a tent, he went back to town late every afternoon and seldom arrived at his rig before noon every day. Some days he didn't show up at all.

Sam got in the habit of taking occasional short naps instead of sleeping all night. By napping in the afternoons, he managed to avoid Clarkston almost completely.

Then, bright and early Friday morning while Sam and Guidry were sitting at a makeshift table drinking coffee, King rode up on his motorcycle.

"You're out awfully early," Sam observed, his voice dry.

"Fine way to greet a fellow," Clarkston said, pouring himself a cup of coffee and smiling rather smugly.

"Don't tell me you're concerned about this well."

"This isn't your well, Blackman. It would be to your

322

advantage to remember that." King sat down on one of the camp stools and reached for a metal can that held sugar. "In fact," he added, stirring several heaping spoonfuls of sugar into his coffee, "you would do well to concern yourself a bit more with your own interests."

"What's that supposed to mean?"

Clarkston hiked his shoulders. "Nothing, really. But if I were you, I'd make it a point to get back to town every once in a while and check on that little wife of yours. You know, see what she's been up to while you've been away."

Sam's heart skipped a beat. "Is Prairie all right? Did something happen to her?"

"Oh, she's hale and hearty enough, if that's all you're worried about. I've never seen her look so good. Yes, sir. She is one lovely woman. It's a shame her man ain't around, though. It's hard to tell what a woman like that'll do when she gets tired of being lonely."

Sam shot off the stool so fast it fell over. Without rational thought, he propelled the upper half of his body over the table and grabbed a fistful of King's shirt. "I don't like the implication of that remark, Clarkston."

Though King's dark eyes widened and his tongue skimmed his lips, he kept his voice even and low. "Just a friendly warning, man. That's all it was."

Sam gave Clarkston a little shove, then let go of his shirt. "That better be all it was. Stay away from my wife, do you hear me?" He waited for King's acknowledgment, then he looked at Guidry and said, "I'll be seeing you. Let me know when you hit the oil sand."

"Sure thing," the driller replied. "We oughtta be gettin' close."

Damn Clarkston and his insinuations! Sam thought as he walked back to his rig. He couldn't believe Prairie would give the man a second look, not since the dance, but he didn't trust King Clarkston as far as he could throw him. The snake-eyed rascal was just cocky enough to try something with Prairie while Sam was

323

out at the rig, and she was certainly no physical match for him. Sam realized he didn't know whether she owned a gun or even if she knew how to use one, but he intended to find out.

For the remainder of the morning, Sam made a point of keeping an eye on the trail back to town, waiting for Clarkston to leave. Call it pride, Sam thought, but he didn't want Clarkston to think he'd scared him. Besides, Prairie would be in school until mid-afternoon.

Finally, while Sam was eating his noon meal, he spied Clarkston leaving on his Indian motorcycle. Sam didn't bother to finish his hash but immediately began hitching up Dolly to the surrey.

"Where you goin'?" Jake Daniels asked him.

"Back to town."

Jake almost swallowed his wad of tobacco. When he quit choking and sputtering, he said, "But I thought you wasn't goin' back till this well come in."

Sam adjusted the harness. "Changed my mind."

"When you comin' back?"

"There's no need to panic, Jake. I'll be back tomorrow. We've got a couple hundred more feet to go. Besides, you can handle it."

"What about Clarkston's well? It's liable to come in while you're gone."

Sam mounted the surrey and took up the reins. "Not likely. They haven't hit the sand yet."

"What if they do? Did you give them the screen?"

"Guidry's got it and I told him what to do if Clarkston gives him the go-ahead."

"But—"

Sam smiled. "You aren't a greenhorn, Jake. You'll be fine."

Jake grinned sheepishly. "Guess I just got used to having you around, Sam. You're good company. Don't worry about comin' back tomorrow. Spend a couple of days with your wife and don't worry about a thing."

Sam hoped he didn't have anything to worry about. He supposed he'd find out soon enough.

It was the longest day at the end of the longest week of her life.

Prairie stood at the door and surveyed the empty school room. The blackboard and the floor could wait. Spending every moment possible with Sam couldn't.

"He may not come," Ruth said gently.

"He will. I know he will," Prairie insisted.

"Promise me you won't spend the weekend crying if he doesn't."

"You know me better than that, Ruth."

Despite her assertion, Prairie knew she was setting herself up for a major disappointment if Sam didn't come home. She could always rent or borrow a buggy and drive out to Jude's rice field, but since her accident, she was reluctant to travel alone. Add to that fact the lack of both comfort and privacy at the rig—and Doc's continued insistence that Watson, the hired hand, wasn't the axe murderer, and she knew she might as well stay put and wait for Sam.

In an effort to ward off her loneliness, Prairie spent her leisure time that week planning the weekend. Although Sam hadn't seemed to mind her scraggly hair and the soupy custard, she didn't intend for him to catch her so ill-prepared again. Her ice box contained a pot of chicken and dumplings, cooked the night before and only needing to be heated, and two steaks she'd had the butcher cut for her early that morning. From the baker's wagon, which she'd caught during the noon hour, she selected apple turnovers, fresh bread, and a Boston cream pie. Sam would certainly not go hungry.

It was too cold to leave her front door standing open, but Prairie left it unlocked as she scurried about her little house, lighting fires on the two hearths, setting a kettle of water on the stove, straightening pillows on the sofa and pictures on the walls. As she worked, she hummed one of her favorite tunes, "A Bicycle Built for Two."

She was in the kitchen, grinding coffee beans, when a deep male voice picked up the words, substituting her name for Daisy's. *Sam!* She'd never heard him sing, but it had to be him.

Her face alight with joy, she wiped her hands on her apron and dashed into the hall, her arms open for Sam's embrace. The sight of King Clarkston coming toward her stopped her cold.

"King!" she gasped. "What are you doing here?"

"Don't you have a kind word for an old friend?" he asked, his mouth twisted into a leering grin.

"You have no business here. Please leave."

He ignored her and kept walking. "You know the old saying, Prairie. 'When the cat's away, the mice will play.' Well, the cat's out in the rice field playing with his bits and pumps and screens, and here we are. We might as well make the best of it."

She backed into the doorway. "Sam's coming home, King. I'm expecting him any minute."

Clarkston shook his head. "No, he isn't. He isn't leaving the well until it starts producing, and that could take another week or two. You married a man who is far more interested in poking holes in the ground than he is in keeping his pretty little wife happy. But that's where I come in. I can make you very happy, Prairie."

Her heart was going lickety-split and she felt faint, but through sheer determination Prairie maintained her hold on reality. She had to get rid of him, somehow . . .

"Get out of here, King, or I'll — I'll — "

He had backed her into the kitchen. "Or you'll do what?"

She glanced over her shoulder to get her bearings, then immediately regained eye contact with King. "I'll scream."

King took another step toward her. "No, you won't."

Prairie took another step backward, subtly shifting her course toward the stove and bending her right elbow. Though it took a great deal of mental effort, she sustained an unswerving stare into King's glistening black eyes.

The hot stove stood directly in her path. The second she felt its heat upon her back, she extended her hand up and out, reaching blindly for the kettle. In one swift movement, she found the kettle, snatched it off the stove, and swung it at King.

What happened then Prairie would never recall as anything more than a blur. He screamed and fell to the floor, writhing and hurling obscenities. Prairie ran to the back door and jerked on the knob. The door refused to budge. She jerked again, then remembered it was locked.

Watching King out of the corner of her eye, she groped along the top of the ice box for the key, found it, and shoved it into the hole in the metal plate beneath the knob. All the while, her pulse raced, making her head spin. No matter how hard she twisted the key, it refused to spin the tumbler.

King was getting up. She didn't need to see his face to know he was more than angry. Prairie jiggled the key while she pushed with her shoulder against the door.

"Bitch!" he roared.

He was on his feet, his left arm dangling at his side, his face mottled with rage.

The key caught and then clicked as she turned it, but before she could open the door fully, he was upon her, his right arm stretching out, his hand slamming the door shut.

"I'll get you for this," he hissed, pinning her against the door and sticking a fist in her face. A feral sneer bared his teeth and his eyes were narrow slits.

The knob bit into the small of her back and her head hit the solid wood hard as he crushed her against the door, but she felt no pain. Her only thought was, *God, help me! He's going to kill me.*

She squeezed her eyes tight and stiffened her frame, waiting for the first blow. He backed off, for leverage she supposed, but it was the break she needed. In a flash, Prairie slithered to the floor, removing her head from the path of his fist, thinking to crawl away before King realized where she'd gone. She heard a crash and a yelp and felt a surge of victory.

Her triumph was short-lived. Strong arms encircled her rib cage, pulling her upright. Prairie fought like a wildcat, kicking, flailing her arms, twisting around and tearing at the man's legs with her fingernails, ignoring his pleas. She'd give him no mercy. He might eventually kill her, but she would leave her mark on him first. She opened her mouth wide, filled her mouth with soft denim, and bit down hard into his kneecap.

His ear-splitting cry fueled her struggle. She raised her head and bit again, this time into the inside of his thigh. She was rewarded with another yelp.

Feeling more confident with each bellow of pain, she positioned her teeth for another bite, but his screech delayed her chomp. "Prairie! Stop it! It's me — Sam!"

He didn't sound like Sam. She cut her eyes upward but could see nothing more than his crotch. Certain it was a ploy, she refused to let go. She clamped her teeth into the fabric of his pants and looked down at the skinned toes of his dusty boots.

She recognized them as Sam's. So were the jeans she held between her teeth. King never wore work clothes.

Waves of relief washed through her, eroding her strength. She relaxed both her jaw and her limbs and clutched her arms around his legs, needing their support in her sudden trembling weakness.

"Oh, Sam!" she sobbed.

"It's all right, Prairie," he soothed, tugging at her arms until she let go. He pulled her into his arms and

328

held her close. "I'm here now. If that bastard hurt you—"

"No. Not really." She twisted her head around until she could see King, who was lying face-down on her kitchen floor, not moving at all.

Prairie shivered. "Did you kill him?"

Sam snorted. "Not hardly. But he'll have a sore head for a couple of days. I guess we ought to get him over to the Nolans' and let Enoch look at that burn you gave him."

"Is it serious?"

"I don't think so, but I honestly haven't looked at him that closely. You're the one I'm worried about."

She snuggled deeper into his embrace. "What's wrong with him, Sam? Why does he want to hurt me?"

"I don't know, but this time we're telling Michael."

"I wish you'd told me about the other incident," Michael said, pinning first Sam and then Prairie with an accusative glare. "Especially you, Prairie. You've known King Clarkston for years. You know what he's like."

"But I had no idea he was capable of such violence!" she protested. "He's acting as though he has some sort of vendetta against me."

Michael ran his fingers through his hair and sighed. "He probably does."

Prairie frowned. "I don't understand."

"Just think about it for a minute. King's father spoiled him rotten. In Rupert Clarkston's eyes, King could do no wrong. He pampered and petted and protected King to the point of obsession. As a result, King has no idea what it means to be held accountable for his actions, nor does he know what it's like to do without or to have to work for anything. Rupert always gave him everything he wanted, then left him a fortune. King could probably buy half the state and still have money left over."

"So, what you're implying," Sam said, "is that King Clarkston thinks he should get whatever he wants, and that includes Prairie."

Michael nodded. "Something like that."

"And whether or not she wants him is relatively unimportant?"

"I'm afraid so. Apparently, he doesn't intend to allow your marriage to get in his way, either."

"What are you planning to do about it?" Sam asked, his voice clearly carrying his doubt that anything Michael could do would prove effective.

Michael rubbed his chin. "I'm going to have a little chat with him, and when I'm through, he'll understand implicitly that if this happens again, he'll go to jail. I think Prairie should move back in with us until the well comes in."

"No!"

Both men looked askance at Prairie, who realized with a start that she had voiced the protest. Before she could formulate an argument, Sam said, "It will only be for a couple of weeks, Prairie, and we can stay at your house when I'm in town."

Because she honestly had no reason to disagree, Prairie relented. Later, when they were alone, Sam asked her why she didn't want to stay with the Donovans.

"It's hard to explain," she said. "Part of it, I suppose, stems from living alone for several years. Although I enjoyed staying with the boys while Wynn and Michael were in Buffalo, I couldn't wait to move back home, to my own peace and quiet — and my own schedule."

"But mostly it's because you're so damned independent," he offered. "You can't stand the thought of not being able to take care of yourself."

His disapproval, which was evident in both his tone and his expression, surprised and wounded her. "What's wrong with independence?" she snapped.

Sam clamped his mouth into a tight line and pierced her with a look akin to stupefaction. Prairie didn't believe for one minute her question had struck him dumb, but in the interest of harmony, she dropped the subject. Nevertheless, their minor, unresolved skirmish cast a pall over the evening.

Early the next morning, Sam threw the covers back and dragged Prairie out of bed. "What are you doing?" she moaned, rubbing fists into her eyes. "I don't want to get up yet."

"I need to get back," he explained, "and I'm not leaving you here by yourself. Hurry up and pack a bag so I can take you to the Donovans' house. I've already hitched Dolly to the surrey."

"I'm not a child!" she protested. "I can take myself later."

"I just told you I'm not leaving you here. Not with both King Clarkston and an axe murderer on the loose. Now, hurry up!"

Prairie shot him a sullen look and vowed to take as much time getting ready as she could squeeze out. Seething, she put on her robe and went to the kitchen to pour herself a cup of coffee.

There was none. The stove was cold and the kettle was empty.

"You can have coffee and breakfast at the Donovans'," Sam said from behind her.

Humph! she thought. Forcing her to get up so early on such a cold morning was bad enough, but to deny her her coffee was grounds for mutiny. Prairie stuffed short chunks of wood into the firebox and took the kettle to the sink. On the third pump, Sam's hand closed over her arm.

"How dare you ignore me!" he snapped.

"How dare you order me around!" she countered.

He elbowed his way into the spot where she'd stood and finished pumping water into the kettle. "How can you treat this situation so casually? Clarkston could have seriously harmed you yesterday."

"Don't you think I know that?"

"You don't act like it!"

Prairie dumped coffee beans into her grinder and cranked the handle with a vengeance. "I don't think I've ever been so frightened, but I will not allow this to govern my life, Sam."

He slammed the kettle down on the stove top. "What I want to know is how you managed to survive before I came along."

She stopped grinding and turned to pin him with a penetrating glare. "Of all the gall! I survived quite well, thank you very much."

"Who was your champion before me?"

"Pardon?"

"You know damned well what I'm talking about. You're an accident waiting to happen, Prairie. Who saved you from yourself before I came along?"

"You — you — arrogant, misbegotten fool!" she screeched, hurling the coffee grinder at him. Sam ducked and it hit the wall, splintering and scattering partially ground beans all over the floor. Before he could recover, she darted into the hall.

"That's right!" he called after her. "Go off and pout. That's what women do best!"

He waited a moment for her response. When none was forthcoming, he stepped across the hall and knocked on the bedroom door. "I'm sorry, Prairie. That was a stupid thing to say."

He paused, listening, then tried again. "All right. I'll clean up the mess you made while you cool off, and then we'll talk about it."

Sam halfway expected her to open the door and throw her arms around his neck and tell him she was sorry, too. When she didn't, he found her broom and dustpan and set about sweeping up the broken grinder and spilled beans. Still, she didn't come out of the bedroom.

He gave her a couple more minutes, then decided he'd had enough. "Prairie!" he called, his hand on the knob. "I'm coming in there."

He put his shoulder to the panel, expecting the door to be locked, but the knob turned easily in his palm. The door swung open on creaking hinges, revealing an empty room.

"What the hell—?"

A quick but thorough inspection convinced him she wasn't in the bedroom, nor did he find her in her study or the parlor. Where could she have gone in her robe? he wondered, opening the front door without truly expecting to see her. She wasn't outside.

Neither were Dolly and the surrey.

Sam sprinted down the walk and looked up and down the street, which was filling up with vendors hawking their goods: milk, eggs, coal oil, ice, bread, and meat. The wagons lumbered along, their massive wheels stirring up dust, the big draft horses snorting steam. Bells jingled and a chorus of male voices bade housewives to come out and select their purchases.

The red surrey was nowhere in sight.

"Damn her!" he fumed. "Damn her to hell and gone!"

Chapter Twenty-two

"Prairie, you need to eat something," Wynn said, her concern tinged with a hint of vexation.

Prairie sat on the window seat in her old room, staring out into a gray sky as dismal as her heart. "Leave it on the desk. I'm not hungry right now."

"You haven't been hungry since you arrived here in your robe five days ago," Wynn scolded. "When do you plan to regain your appetite?"

"I didn't *plan* this at all, Wynn."

The older woman moved some satin pillows out of the way, sat down on the bench beside Prairie, and placed a comforting arm across her shoulder. "No, I don't suppose you did," she agreed. "And you aren't handling it very well, either. You have to get hold of yourself, Prairie. It was just a spat. All lovers have quarrels from time to time. He'll be back when his well comes in, all full of himself but needing you to smile at him and pat him on his back and tell him what a great man he is anyway."

Prairie's voice was bitter. "He *knows* how great he is, Wynn. He doesn't need me for that."

"Yes, he does, dear. That's how men are. They have to think they're in control, and it's our job to assure them they are, whether it's true or not."

"Oh, Sam's definitely in control out at the rig. I can't believe he needs any reassurance from me."

Wynn sighed. "I'm not talking about his work. I'm

talking about Sam, period. Sure, he's confident enough at his job, but that doesn't mean he's confident about his relationship with you. You scare him half to death."

Prairie's eyes widened in disbelief. "Sam? Scared of me?" She shook her head in negation. "I don't think so."

"Well, you're wrong. He's terrified you won't think he's good enough for you."

"Did he tell you that?"

"No," Wynn said, smiling.

"Then how can you be so sure?"

"Do you think Michael was never a knothead? Do you think I was never so silly as to sit and stare out a window and pine for him to change?"

A tear escaped from Prairie's eye, and then another and another, until she found herself sobbing against Wynn's breast. When her tears subsided, she said, "We're never going to make it together, Wynn. We're too different."

"You may be right. But you're wrong about being different. The problem with you and Sam is that you're entirely too much alike."

Clarkston Number One hit the oil sand on Saturday while Sam was in town with Prairie. Ray Guidry stopped drilling and left only the pumps running while he waited for Sam to return or Clarkston to show up.

"I can't take responsibility for this well," Sam told him Saturday afternoon.

"I know you can't," Guidry said. "But I'm in one hell of a spot. If I don't use the screen, we'll lose this well. If I use it without Clarkston's permission and it doesn't work, he could ruin me. I might never find another job."

335

"There's always the possibility it will work, Ray, but I can understand your not wanting to take that sort of risk."

"It's not that I don't trust you, Sam."

"What are you planning to do?" Sam asked.

Guidry shook his head. "Send for Clarkston, I guess. See what he says. It's his well."

"Don't ask me to explain," Sam said, "but I can't be around that man right now. You'll have to do the persuading alone."

Clarkston didn't show up until early Monday afternoon. He didn't leave until almost dark. Sam waited until the motorcycle was out of sight before he walked over to see Raymond Guidry.

A broad grin wreathed the driller's face.

"He agreed?" Sam asked in amazement.

"Nope."

"I don't understand. Why are you smiling?"

" 'Cause I just remembered you offered me a job. Did you mean it?"

Sam smiled then. "I sure did. Are you thinking what I think you're thinking?"

"If that means am I going to use it anyway, the answer is yes."

"And if Clarkston fires you, you can come to work for me." Sam slapped him on the back. "Hell, you can come to work for me anyway!"

"I think I will, Sam. I think I will."

Early Wednesday morning, the well came in. King Clarkston had a gusher, though he was in town and therefore didn't know it.

Sam shut down drilling on Blackman Number Two, keeping only the pumps running. While oil spewed heavenward, the crews from both rigs spent the day feasting and celebrating and praying Sam's screen worked. By late afternoon, the earthen pits Clarkston's crew had dug were full of pure crude that didn't

336

bear a trace of sand. They had a producing field.

Sam wanted desperately to hitch up Dolly and drive into town to share his news with Prairie, but he was too close to bringing in his own well. Earlier that week, Wayne had brought out the screen they'd ordered from Henry Boudreaux, thus eliminating any excuse Sam might have had for going into town. Like it or not, he was stuck on the low hill in Jude Langley's rice field until Blackman Number Two came in.

He started drilling again Wednesday evening.

Word traveled fast. The minute King Clarkston learned his well had come in, he marched himself into Jonas Richardson's office and gave a statement to the press, claiming credit for the screen, as Sam figured he would. Proving it was his would have been easy enough, but Sam had other, more important matters on his mind, namely starting construction on the refinery as soon as possible.

On Friday, Wolfeschlegersteinhausenberger received a cable from Wayne. The German banker's heart soared. He buzzed his secretary.

"Yes, sir?" a young male voice crackled through the phone line.

"Make arrangements to have my private car hooked up to Sunday's westbound train. And call my house. Tell Armstead to pack enough clothes to last me for a week. Have you typed the Blackman Brothers contract yet?"

"Yes, sir. It's in a folder on your desk, sir."

"You're a good man, Chandler. Do I have anything pressing next week?"

"I'm checking your calendar, sir. No, sir, no business appointments at all, sir. It's, uh—Christmas is next week, sir. You have a number of social engagements. Shall I cancel them for you?"

337

"Yes. And call D.H. Holmes. Have them wrap a good selection of gifts for a young woman and four of something for men — it doesn't matter what, so long as it doesn't have a size. Also, gifts for three boys. Let me see" — he opened a folder and flipped through several pages until he located the information he needed — "ages eleven, fourteen, and sixteen. And a few things for an older, married couple."

"The young woman, sir. How old is she?" Chandler asked.

"In her early twenties."

"Women are difficult to please, sir. Do you have any idea what she likes?"

Wolfeschlegersteinhausenberger hummed, thinking. "Just regular feminine things — toilet water, handkerchiefs, parasols, that sort of thing. The clerk will know." He started to hang up the phone, then pulled the earpiece back to his head. "Oh, and Chandler, have them wrap a new typewriter and some wedding gifts, too. You know, linens and dishes and such."

He replaced the earpiece then and smiled at nothing — and at everything. For years, he had merely endured Christmas. This year he was going to enjoy it.

Wynn was right, Prairie decided. She had to get hold of herself.

Her writing had served her well as a catharsis, turning blue moods into sunny ones over the years. This particular blue mood, however, was such a deep shade she wasn't the least bit certain her writing could lighten it, but she supposed it was worth a try.

By the time Prairie heard the news about the success of Sam's screen, her writing had begun to purge some of the bitterness from her soul. Possessing two additional clues — the names Lucy and Wolf's Leg — had a heartening effect on her mood, but the most

338

important factor in her change of attitude was the knowledge that Sam had solved a problem that had seemed almost insurmountable to him not so very long ago. His solution was testimony that most problems have solutions.

It was time, she realized, to take her own advice and quit worrying about a solution, at least for the time being. If, by chance, things didn't work out for her and Sam, she had mailed the letters of application. In the meantime, she had a book to finish. There was nothing she and Sam could do to patch things up between them until his well was completed and he came home.

And he would come home. She had to believe that he would. She prayed he made it home before Christmas.

Sam wanted to go home.

He wondered if it could be possible. Could his wandering spirit have finally settled on a place to call home? If his present yearning were any indication, it must be so. But it wasn't a place, he realized, not in the geographic sense. Home was with Prairie, wherever that might be.

She was a constant in an ever-changing world, the sun he wanted to wake up to in the morning and go to bed with at night. His life with her might never run smooth, but he'd dodge all the coffee grinders she wanted to throw at him so long as he could have her in it.

Friday morning he hit the oil sand.

In just a few more days, maybe in a few more hours, he thought, *the well will come in and I can go home — home to Prairie.*

* * *

Prairie's typewriter keys were clanking away when Wynn stuck her head in the door Saturday afternoon. "How's it going?" she asked.

"Quite well," Prairie said, giving Wynn a wan smile. Since both Wynn and Michael had avoided discussing Prairie's writing with her, she could only surmise they were less than pleased.

"Michael and I are taking the boys Christmas shopping. We thought you might want to take a break and go with us."

Prairie shook her head. "Thanks, but I think I'll go by myself later. I want to finish this chapter first."

"All right, dear. We'll see you at supper."

Not long after Wynn left, Prairie turned from her typewriter to dig through a pile of research material stacked on her old desk. Several minutes spent looking convinced her it wasn't there. The only other place it could be was in her study — at her house — and she needed it to complete the chapter. Since she was going shopping anyway, she'd loop by her house and pick it up.

As she walked, she hummed Christmas carols, swinging a large, empty canvas bag in rhythm to the tunes, yet she felt uneasy. Prairie hummed louder, blaming the cloudy sky and close, humid atmosphere for her apprehension. The gray sky muted the gay colors of the decorations festooning fences, lamp posts, and the doors and windows of most of the houses. From time to time, she passed a yard where children played tag or a house where adults lounged on porches or verandas, enjoying the relative warmth of the afternoon. But for the most part, the residential streets she traversed were eerily quiet.

With Christmas only three days away, it was logical, she supposed, for folks to be out shopping. Logic, however, didn't prevent the shiver that danced down her spine. Prairie gave herself a good fussing at and turned toward her house.

But the feeling of foreboding refused to depart. Prairie's heart raced at the sight of the almost white branches of the leafless sycamores in the schoolyard, skeletons painted on the pewter sky, fearsome even to the birds, for not one perched on the stark limbs. The windows of both the school and her house gaped darkly at her. Never had this spot she loved so well seemed so forlorn.

This is ridiculous! she thought, fighting off the urge to turn and run. *I'm letting my imagination run wild.*

She fumbled with her keys, her hand trembling as she shoved the appropriate one into the lock on her front door. On creaking hinges, the heavy portal swung open. Behind it, her parlor loomed dusky and forbidding.

Prairie left the door standing open—for the meager light it permitted, she told herself and stepped into her house. Her gaze moved from the shadowy interior to the tall, massive hall tree blocking the door that connected the parlor with the room she used as a study. Never before had she regretted its position, which prevented intrusion into her private domain, but now she rued the day she'd had it put there.

One glance at the dark hallway persuaded her. She hung the canvas bag on one of the hooks, then placed her shoulder against the side of the piece and shoved. She might as well have been shoving on one of the sycamores, she decided, for all the good it did her. Still, she pushed at the hall tree, pushed with all the might she could gather, until beads of perspiration broke out on her forehead and upper lip and her bones ached from an effort that had gained her nothing.

Well, she decided, she wouldn't allow an unfounded fear to daunt her. She'd come to collect the research material, and collect it she would. If that meant having to traverse the dark hallway, then so be it.

Despite her determination, Prairie sorted through the contents of every drawer in the small chest by her chair, hoping to find a match. If one was hiding among the letters, ashtrays, and candle stubs, her probing fingers didn't find it.

There were matches aplenty in the kitchen, but the kitchen door was at the end of the hall. As Prairie stepped into the cavernous passageway, gooseflesh prickled her arms and a violent shiver racked her frame. She turned and fled.

For a moment, she stood in the thin rectangle of light just inside the front door, her palm flattened against her pounding chest. From whence, she wondered, had this unaccountable fear derived?

It was a Saturday, she recalled, when the James family had been butchered. A gray, cloudy Saturday, exactly four weeks ago. What were they doing when the murderer had entered their home? Had they felt this same presentiment?

Perhaps she was being ridiculous, but she decided she could manage without the research material until Michael could accompany her. Assuring herself that wisdom governed her cowardice, Prairie pulled her key out of the lock, then stepped back into the room to retrieve her canvas bag from the hall tree.

The door banged closed behind her, cloaking the room in utter darkness.

"Only a draft," she whispered, reaching into the gloom for the bag. For a moment, she heard only the thrum of her pulse and the huff of her short breaths. With the bag in one hand and the key in the other, she turned toward the door. Then she smelled whiskey, heard an unmistakable wheeze, and knew as clearly as she'd ever known anything that she'd never see Sam again.

* * *

All morning long, a terrible sense of foreboding plagued Sam. Something was wrong. Though he couldn't say what or why, he knew it as clearly as he'd ever known anything. Over and over, he checked the boiler and the pumps. Over and over, he examined the draw works and the cable. Over and over, he scrutinized the rotary and each piece of drill pipe as it was attached.

"What are you so jittery about?" Wayne asked. "Your screen works, Sam. Clarkston's well proved it."

Sam shook his head. "That's not it, Wayne. But something's not right. I just wish I knew what it was."

Shortly after one o'clock, Blackman Number Two came in. Amid all the spewing oil and shouting men, Sam pulled Wayne off to the side.

"I'm borrowing your horse. Drive the surrey back to town for me, okay?"

Wayne blinked in confusion. "Borrowing my horse? Where are you going?"

"To see Prairie."

"Can't you wait? What if you're right and something is wrong out here? We'll need you."

Sam pointed to the black stream. "There's no sand in that crude, Wayne. All Jake has to do is close the valves and start sending it through the pipeline. I'm convinced something *is* wrong, but it's not out here: it's in town."

Kevin McCormack pushed at the scrawny cat intent on licking the skin off his cheek. "Go 'way!" he whispered. "I can't see nothin' for you."

The cat meowed plaintively, then planted itself on top of Kevin's bent arm. The boy quickly raised his elbow, tossing the cat into a pier. When the cat stopped screeching, Kevin hissed, "Go 'way! I mean it!"

That time, the cat moved off a bit, but it didn't leave. Kevin glanced toward the animal, which was crouched low, close to the pier, its yellow eyes full of sorrow. "Quit lookin' at me like that," Kevin said. "I ain't got a bowl of milk on me. If I did, I'd give it to you."

Kevin turned his attention back to Miz Blackman's front porch. From his position under the schoolhouse, he had a clear view of both the front and one side of her house, but her back door was on that side. The man who'd gone in behind her had to come out one of the doors—unless he used a window on the back or opposite side.

Even then, Kevin would be able see the man's feet hit the ground—if the dadblasted cat would stay out of his way.

Kevin supposed Miz Blackman had come home while he was around on the far side of the school, chunking sycamore balls at a knothole in a tree. She hadn't made no noise, so he couldn't be sure, but he didn't recall noticing her front door standing open the last time he'd filled his pockets with sycamore balls from the school's front yard.

It was standing open, though, when he'd gone back for more. No light shone from her windows, and in the gray dimness, the house was just plain spooky-looking. Kevin leaned up against one of the syca-mores and regarded the open door. After a spell, Miz Blackman appeared in the doorway and acted like she was getting ready to leave.

That was when he saw the man sneaking around the far corner of Miz Blackman's house. He'd seen the man before around town, but Kevin couldn't place him. He might be Mr. Blackman. Kevin couldn't be sure. But whoever he was, the way he skulked around made Kevin think he was up to no good.

Kevin watched from behind the tree until the man

344

stepped over the threshold and closed the door. The boy's initial reaction had been to go in after him, but he got no further than Miz Blackman's steps before a little common sense and a lot of fear deflected his feet back to the schoolyard. He was certainly no match physically, he reasoned. If the man did mean to harm Miz Blackman, Kevin figured he could do a heap more for her by going for help than by getting himself walloped over the head — or worse.

But he wasn't leaving until he knew what was going on. He wiggled up under the schoolhouse where no one could see him and waited. He didn't know how long he ought to wait, but he figured he'd give it a few more minutes.

Wynn and Michael were drinking coffee in Louella's café when a boy came tearing in the door, so winded he couldn't speak clearly for a minute. Tears made trails on his dirty face and his eyes were round and glassy.

A woman wearing an apron and carrying an order pad detached herself from one of the tables and hurried toward the boy.

"Maw!" he gasped. "Somepin's wrong" — he wheezed — "over to Miz Blackman's."

"Don't panic," Michael said, laying a comforting palm on Wynn's shoulder as they got up. "We're Mrs. Blackman's parents," Michael told the boy. "Tell us what's wrong, son."

"Kevin," the waitress said. "His name's Kevin."

"What happened, Kevin?" Wynn asked.

"This man followed Miz Blackman in her house. I could see them from the schoolyard. They was in there a long time. Then I heard a bang, sorta like a firecracker makes, and the man came runnin' out." Kevin hiccupped. "I waited, but Miz Blackman, she

345

didn't come out, so I went to see 'bout her."

The boy burst into tears and buried his face in his mother's apron. Michael grasped him by the shoulders and turned him around.

"Can't you see the boy's upset?" the waitress snapped.

Michael shot a scornful glare her way, then returned his attention to the boy. "What did you see, Kevin? Was she hurt?"

Kevin nodded. "Real bad."

"When our boys get here," Wynn told Kevin's mother, "please send them home."

"Thank goodness we brought the carriage," Michael said as he helped Wynn onto the seat.

"I wish I had my medical bag. Michael, who could—" Her voice caught in her throat.

He shook his head. "I don't know. But we can't panic, Wynn. The boy may have misinterpreted what he saw."

Wynn didn't believe he had. Somehow, she was certain Kevin had been right. She closed her eyes, trying to erase a mental vision of the Jameses' twisted, blood-covered bodies. Although she hadn't seen them, she'd heard the descriptions from the doctors who had.

What manner of human being could shoot a man, his wife, and three boys, and then take an axe to their bodies? she wondered, sickened at the thought. Had the sheriff arrested the wrong man? Was there an axe murderer on the prowl in Jennings?

Lord, she prayed, *don't let my Prairie be one of his victims.*

Though the school was but a few blocks from the café, it seemed to take forever to get there. Michael drove the carriage right up into Prairie's yard.

"Prairie!" Wynn called, pushing open the front door and running into the house, Michael right behind her.

"Prairie!" she called again, her gaze searching the shadows in the parlor.

Wynn started toward the hall and stubbed her toe on an overturned chair. Michael helped her to her feet and stood the chair up.

"Let me go first," he said, moving to stand in front of her. "We don't know what we might encounter in the hall."

Or who, Wynn thought, glad to have him lead the way.

They found matches in the kitchen and lit a lamp. When they assured themselves Prairie wasn't in the kitchen, they moved across the hall into her bedroom.

Prairie was lying facedown on the bed, her feet and lower legs hanging off the side, her back covered in blood. She was unconscious.

"Oh, my lord, no!" Wynn cried. *"No-o-o-o!"*

Michael whirled around and grasped her upper arm with his free hand. "Wynnifred Donovan!" he barked. "Compose yourself. She needs your skill."

How could he ask her to separate the physician from the mother? She knew deep down that he was right, knowing this had to be as difficult for him as it was for her. Probably more difficult, considering his aversion to blood. Wynn closed her eyes and took a deep breath.

"Bring the lamp over here, by the bed."

She removed her gloves, lifted Prairie's limp wrist, and felt for a pulse. "Weak," she said. "I need some scissors to cut her shirtwaist off, and I could use some more light in here. Find a clean sheet and heat some water. See if you can find some kind of antiseptic. Dr. Tichenor's will do, or Listerine. Then go home and get my bag."

Michael was opening bureau drawers, looking for sheets. He found one and handed it to Wynn.

"I'm not leaving you here by yourself, Wynn."

"I need my bag, Michael, and I'm not leaving Prairie."

"We'll take her to our house."

With an edge of the sheet between her front teeth, Wynn shook her head. When she tore into it with her teeth, she pulled on it hard, ripping it all the way through. Then she folded the smaller strip she'd torn off and pressed it against Prairie's back.

"Look at this, Michael." She lifted the pad so he could see. "The bullet hit close to her spine. We don't know where it lodged. Moving her could kill her."

"Are you going to take it out?"

"I don't know. I wish we had electricity so I could use my X-ray machine!"

"I'll . . . find those other things, Wynn."

"Hurry, Michael! Please, hurry!"

Chapter Twenty-three

"She ain't here, Mr. Sam," Marmie said, grinning. "She went out shoppin' just a little while ago. I doan 'spect her back 'fore suppertime. Would you like to come in and wait?"

Sam smiled, relieved to hear she was all right. He couldn't wait to see her. "No, thanks, Marmalade. This town's not that big. I'll find her."

Sam turned away from the door to see Michael Donovan driving up in his carriage. Sam hailed him and started down the walk. Michael's pale, drawn face stopped him cold.

"Sam! Thank God you're back. Get over to Prairie's house — now."

Sam's heart felt as though it was going to jump right out of his chest. "What's wrong? What's happened to Prairie?"

"She's been shot."

"How did it happen?"

"We don't know. Wynn's with her. I just came to get some things." Michael frowned. "You on that horse?"

"Yes."

"On second thought, wait here while I get Wynn's bag. You can get there faster than I can."

A half hour later, Michael joined Sam in Prairie's kitchen. Between them, they had collected everything Wynn needed, and Michael had brought Doc and Ruth back with him. "There's tea on the stove," Sam said. "I couldn't make coffee. Prairie broke the grinder."

Michael nodded solemnly and poured himself a cup.

Sam rested his elbows on the table and drove his fingers into his hair. "She's not going to make it, is she, Michael?"

"Don't think that way, Sam. Wynn says we have to keep our hopes up."

"It's all my fault."

Michael's eyebrows rose to mid-forehead. "How do you figure that?"

"I should have been here for her."

"She's an adult, Sam, not a baby. Outside of locking her up, no one could watch her twenty-four hours a day. We told her not to come back here alone. Heaven only knows why she did. But none of us ever considered her life to be in danger."

"Who would have done this?" Sam cried. "Who would have shot her in the back?"

"Oh, my God!" Michael said, jumping up so fast he spilled his tea. "I have to go see about something."

Sam's head shot up. "What's wrong now?"

"There was an eyewitness. A little boy whose mother works for Louella. I've been so concerned about Prairie I forgot all about him. If the man who shot Prairie gets wind of it, that child's life could be in danger, too." Michael snatched his hat off the back of the chair and started for the door. "I have to find him and warn his mother."

"Try to get a description," Sam urged.

Michael left nodding.

A moment later, Ruth came in from the bedroom.

"How is she?" Sam asked.

Ruth shook her head sadly. "Not good. But those two doctors in there are the best for miles around. If anyone can pull her through, Enoch and Wynn can."

For a long time, they sat in silence, sipping tea, wrapped in their own private speculations.

"Does anyone know where King Clarkston was this afternoon?" Sam asked finally.

"I don't think any of us have thought about King at all. Why? Is there trouble at the rig?"

Sam rubbed his chin. "No. Both wells are producing."

"Then why? You don't think King had anything to do with shooting Prairie, do you?" Ruth asked skeptically.

"I don't know. Twice before, he tried to hurt her."

"But King wouldn't shoot anybody," Ruth argued. "I taught that boy the last couple of years he was in school. Let's see, he must have been eleven or twelve then. King's a good kid. Rotten to the core, but not homicidal."

Sam wasn't so sure, but he didn't want to quarrel with Ruth. He knew he didn't trust Clarkston. They'd know more when Michael came back with a description.

"Are you hungry?" Ruth asked.

"No."

"I suppose I ought to rustle up some food regardless. Someone's bound to be hungry eventually."

As Ruth moved around in the kitchen, Sam recalled the times he'd spent in this cozy room with Prairie. He gathered the memories around him like an old quilt, at once warmed and yet saddened at the realization that the coverlet wouldn't last forever.

Doc came out of the bedroom. "You got some coffee in here?"

"No, but there's tea," Ruth said.

"Prairie broke the grinder," Sam explained.

"How'd she do that?" Doc asked.

"She threw it at me."

Doc chuckled. "Sounds like something she'd do.

351

We're gonna need some coffee. One of you go somewhere and get a grinder."

"I brought one, Doc," Michael said, coming in the back door. He handed the grinder to Ruth and sat down at the table.

"Did you get a description?" Sam asked.

"Yeah. It sounds like King Clarkston."

"I'll kill him!" Sam avowed, his face mottled with rage. "I should have killed him when I had the chance!" He rose from his chair and started for the door.

Michael stopped him. "Calm down, Sam. Don't you think I'd like to kill him, too? But we have to be sure. Let's let the law handle it. I've already sent for Isaac Fontenot."

"It can't be King," Ruth said, stunned.

"Yes, it can. Kevin MacCormack's description matches him almost perfectly, so I asked around town about King. He was in the White Rabbit Saloon earlier, slugging down whiskey. The bartender says King left there sometime between one and one-thirty. Said he had some business to take care of. It was about two when Kevin got to Louella's. No one's seen King since. How's Prairie?"

"No change," Doc said. "I'd better get back in there and help Wynn. Ya'll let us know when the coffee's done."

Doc and Wynn didn't merely disagree on Prairie's treatment; they stood in diametrically opposing camps. Doc insisted the only way to save her was to probe for the bullet; Wynn said to do so would kill her. Civil War era medicine governed Doc's perspective; forty years of progress governed Wynn's.

Once they'd cleaned and sterilized the wound, applied an antiseptic dressing of cheesecloth saturated with iodoform, bandaged it, and made her as comfortable as they could, the two moved their dispute to Prairie's study. For one thing, they didn't know when she might regain consciousness, and neither of them thought it wise to disturb her with an argument that would upset her and thwart her possible recovery. For another, they didn't want Sam, Michael, and Ruth to know they disagreed.

The study provided as much privacy as they could manage and still remain close enough to Prairie to watch her. The two kept their voices low and their eyes on the bed.

"How many gunshot victims have you treated?" Doc asked Wynn.

"To be honest, less than a dozen."

"Well, I can't count the number of bullets I've removed," Doc declared smugly.

"How many of those patients survived?" Wynn countered.

Doc hiked a shoulder. "About half, I s'pose."

"So if we probe this wound, we automatically reduce Prairie's chances to fifty-fifty."

"Not reduce, Wynn. Increase."

"We've been through three presidential assassinations in our lives, Doc," Wynn said. "I was but a child when Lincoln was shot. I was *there* when McKinley was shot. But, perhaps more relevant to Prairie's case, I was in medical school when Garfield was shot."

Doc's brow beetled and his voice fell flat. "Garfield died, Wynn."

"Precisely. He died because the doctors probed the wound repeatedly in an attempt to remove a bullet they couldn't find."

"Where in the hell did you get that idea?" Doc's pitch was close to a bellow.

"*Sh-h-h!*" Wynn admonished with a finger pressed to her lips.

353

Doc lowered his voice again. "It was the bullet that killed him, not the probe. I've heard you say that McKinley might have been saved if the doctors had used that X-ray machine to pinpoint the bullet's location."

"McKinley's case doesn't apply here, Doc. His wound was abdominal. But Garfield was shot in the back. When they did find the bullet during autopsy, it was lodged in a muscle. He lived six weeks with that bullet in him. We studied his case in medical school. There was no infection around the bullet. The infection that killed him originated from the channels the surgeons had created with their probes—not from the bullet."

"But we can't be sure that the bullet in Prairie's back is lodged in a muscle. What if it punctured an internal organ?"

"If it did, there isn't just a whole lot we can do for her, is there? If we could only use my X-ray machine . . ."

"It'll be at least another month before the electrical lines are all up, Wynn," Doc reminded her. "She may not live that long. I still think we need to find that bullet."

Wynn worried her bottom lip for a moment, then said, "You remember Jamie MacDougall?"

Doc nodded. "Andrew's son. How could I forget? Michael and I worried about you for weeks while you were out at the MacDougall ranch. We thought you'd run off, when all the time, MacDougall was holding you hostage."

"And the price I had to pay for my freedom was saving Jamie's life. I probed his arm, looking for the bullet, but it had struck his humerus and shattered. His arm was broken and pieces of the bullet were scattered from his shoulder to his elbow. There was no way I could get all those pieces out. Then I had to

354

fight the infection from the probe. Jamie survived— miraculously. He's still alive—and he's still carrying those bullet fragments in his arm."

Doc sighed. "We could argue about this from now to eternity, Wynn. The answer, I'm afraid, lies in an X-ray picture we can't take."

Sam wanted to curl up somewhere and die. If Prairie didn't survive, that's what he was going to do, he decided. Perhaps not literally, but he'd never be alive without her.

He'd thought he'd known agony when she had her concussion, but that was nothing compared to this. He'd never felt so completely helpless.

There ought to be something he could do besides sit and wait. He didn't know what, but something . . .

There was something he could do if she lived. There were a multitude of things he could do if she lived. As he sat and waited, Sam mentally listed them.

Prairie had been right on target when she'd told him he allowed his work to interfere with their relationship. That wouldn't happen again. He could earn a living without letting his work consume him.

He'd drilled enough oil wells and spent enough nights in a tent to last him a lifetime. Sam recalled a time when he'd thought nothing could ever replace his wildcatting spirit, but that was before he fell in love with a wildcat. And he was in love with Prairie. Wholly. Unconditionally. Desperately in love with her.

He wanted their children. Perhaps, in time, she would want them, too. But more than anything, he wanted her. He needed her as he'd never needed before. His need for her humbled him, showed him how shallow, how incomplete he was without her. He vowed to spend the remainder of his days demonstrating his love for her.

Sam wasn't a praying man, but he prayed that day — prayed for Prairie, for himself and for the child she might even now be carrying.

Not long after dark, Prairie regained consciousness. At her moan, Wynn took her hand and squeezed it lightly.

"I know you're in pain, sweetheart," Wynn said, nodding at Doc, who quietly left the room. "I want you to drink some water. Can you lift your head and shoulders for me?"

Wynn was setting the water glass aside when Doc came back in with Michael and Sam. "Don't upset her," Wynn whispered, "and keep it brief."

Sam sat down on the bed and placed an open palm on Prairie's cheek. "Hello, darling," he said.

Her spice-colored eyes were glazed with tears and her voice was raspy. "Sam . . ." She closed her eyes and swallowed hard, then looked at him again. "The well —"

"Came in. We have a gusher. I'm so sorry I wasn't here, Prairie. I —" A firm hand on his shoulder quelled any further apology. Michael was right, Sam thought. An expression of regret would serve no purpose now. Everything they said to Prairie must be positive in nature.

But they also needed to know who was responsible for this heinous crime. Sam repressed his guilt and said, "Did you see who did this, Prairie?"

Prairie shuddered. Although the house had been quite dark, she had no doubts concerning the identity of the man who'd stuck a pistol in her ribs and forced her down the hall and into her bedroom.

She'd never forget the nauseating smell of stale whiskey on his breath or the insults he'd hurled at her. She'd never forget hearing King say that if he couldn't

356

ave her, no one could. She'd never forget the ugly things he'd said about Sam. She'd never forget the momentary triumph she felt when she slapped his face or his reaction, delayed by only the few seconds it took him to recover. The moment he did, he snatched her arm, turned her around, and pushed her toward the bed.

What a stupid thing to do! she thought, no longer pleased with herself. Only a fool would defy an armed man—a mentally unbalanced armed man. She stumbled, then simultaneously heard the report of the gun and felt the burning sting of the bullet in her back. Her last conscious thought had been, *Oh Sam! I did so want to see you again.*

Miraculously, the bullet hadn't killed her—not yet. She'd lived long enough to see Sam again, but Prairie figured her chances of survival were slim to nonexistent.

"I'm not quitting, Sam," she said.

Sam's heart soared at her assertion. It signified her intention to defy the odds and fight for her life. He smiled and brushed his hand over her hair. "Of course, you're not, darling. You're going to get well. I love you, Prairie."

"Are you sure?" she asked, afraid he said the words out of pity.

His clear blue eyes met her steady gaze with unmistakable honesty. "More sure than I've ever been about anything."

"I could die now and be happy," she said, pausing to moisten her lips with her tongue. "I want to live, Sam."

"And you will, sweetheart."

From behind him, Michael said, "Do you know who shot you, Prairie?"

"King," she said. "King Clarkston."

357

* * *

Late that night, Prairie took a turn for the worse.

Sam was with her, taking his shift at sitting up while the others rested. She moaned, loud and long, then passed out. When he couldn't revive her, he roused Wynn and Doc, then waited in the kitchen while they examined her.

After a while, Doc came out shaking his head.

"What happened?" Sam asked, his heart in his throat.

"She appears to be hemorrhaging internally."

"What can you do for her?"

Doc poured himself a glass of water and sat down heavily in one of the slat-bottomed chairs. "Nothing. Watch and wait. And hope we're wrong."

Sam swallowed hard. He didn't want to ask any more questions, but there was one more he had to ask. "And if you're right?"

"She probably won't survive the night."

For the remainder of the night and well into Sunday, Prairie's life hung by a gossamer thread. Never before had Sam realized how fragile a thing is life. He drowned himself in strong, black coffee — and waited. The more he thought about losing Prairie, the more important she became to him, until everything he'd ever had or ever hoped to have lost all significance.

Sometime in the early afternoon — time had become a measure of life rather than hours to Sam and the other watchers — Prairie rallied. Within a few hours she was doing so well Sam found it difficult to believe she'd ever hovered so close to death.

He offered a prayer of thanksgiving to the Almighty and stretched out on the sofa in the parlor, finally allowing his body and spirit the rest they sorely needed.

The Calcasieu Parish sheriffs' department staged an

ll-out manhunt for King Clarkston that lasted all that night and most of Sunday. He was apprehended while purchasing a train ticket at the Lake Charles station.

"We knew it was only a matter of time," Deputy Fontenot told Michael. "He was bound to show up eventually. But we have a problem."

"What's that?"

"Clarkston has an alibi. Says when he left the White Rabbit, he rode his motorcycle straight to Welsh to see his girlfriend."

"And you've talked to this so-called girlfriend?" Michael asked.

"Yep. She says he got there about two o'clock, which would mean he would have to have left the White Rabbit shortly after one. I talked to Panzica, the bartender, again, and he isn't the least bit certain what time Clarkston left. Said it could have been as early as one o'clock, but not before then. He remembers somebody inquiring about the time and Clarkston was the one who answered. It was right at one then."

"Maybe the girlfriend got the time confused."

"That's a possibility," Fontenot allowed. "But get this. The girl's name is Sybil James."

"So?"

"The one surviving member of the James family."

Michael considered that bit of information for a minute. "Do you think there might be some connection?"

"I think there's a strong possibility we have the wrong man in jail, if that's what you mean. Watson may be telling the truth."

"But you have two eye-witnesses to this shooting," Michael reminded the deputy.

"Yeah—an eight-year-old boy and a woman who couldn't see the man's face clearly in the dark."

"Prairie's known King most of her life, Fontenot. Don't you think she'd recognize him, even in dim light?"

"There was almost no light, Michael. All the shades and drapes were drawn and it was cloudy outside. It's not that I don't believe your daughter, but she was angry at Clarkston and admittedly afraid of him. A good lawyer can turn her anger and fear into an advantage for Clarkston, assuming she lives to testify."

"She'll live," Michael said with more confidence than he actually felt. "And you have her statement. In the meantime, you people work on building a strong case against Clarkston. Pursue the girlfriend angle. I'll bet you find she and Clarkston had something to do with those axe murders."

If he was right, Michael thought, he was damned glad Clarkston hadn't taken an axe to Prairie.

The Sunday train was more than two hours late. When Slim watched the long lines of disembarking passengers, he understood why. "I shoulda known we'd get another wave soon as those wells started producing," he mumbled to no one in particular.

What did surprise him was the private car being uncoupled and moved onto the spur. Why would anyone already rich want to come to Jennings? Slim had seen a few private railroad cars in his day, but they were always passing through—not stopping.

A tall, elegantly attired man approached him. "Pardon me, sir," he said, his voice as refined as his clothes. "I'm looking for a Mr. Slim Moreland. Might you be he?"

Slim bobbed his head. "How can I help you?"

"I'm Waldemar Wolfeschlegersteinhausenberger."

"Oh, yes, sir, Mr. Wolf—" Slim coughed uncomfortably. "I got your cable yesterday. I hope you're

360

happy with the arrangements I made for you, sir. Just follow me and I'll introduce you to your driver."

Minutes later, Wolfeschlegersteinhausenberger stood on the Donovans' front porch, trying to make sense out of the babble of a pre-pubescent boy.

"My sister's been hurt, mister, and my mama and my daddy are both over to her house. My mama's a doctor, you see, and she's trying to make Prairie all well again. We've been awful worried about her. Folks all over town have been praying since she was shot yesterday. They caught King today in Lake Charles. My daddy and Sam think King did it but the sheriff's not sure and Marmie says they'll prob'ly let him out 'cause he's so rich and then he'll shoot somebody else."

When the boy paused for breath, Wolf's Leg said quickly, "I need to see your father immediately. Where does your sister live?"

"Next to the schoolhouse."

On the way to Prairie's house, Wolf's Leg ran the child's story through his head again. His daughter— shot. His daughter, whom he'd never seen and now might not ever know. How? Why? Why did this have to happen now?

He was thinking selfishly, he knew, but he couldn't help it. For twenty-three years, his life had centered around finding Anna and their child. For twenty-three years, he'd dreamed of this moment, and he wouldn't have it snatched away now.

A loud banging on the front door startled Sam, who'd been dozing in one of the parlor chairs. He squelched the urge to yank the door open and lambast the perpetrator, but he didn't even attempt to hide his irritation, especially at the sight of the stranger standing there.

"Can't you read?" Sam snapped, pointing to a

hand-lettered sign tacked to the door.

"I believe it says 'No visitors please,'" the stranger said, his voice cultured and smooth though a bit husky. He stepped onto the threshold.

"Hey, you can't just barge in here!" Sam hissed. "You have no right. My wife is very ill."

"So I understand. At least, she's alive. And you're wrong. I do have a right, Mr. Blackman. You *are* Sam Blackman?"

"Yes."

"As I said, I do have a right. Your wife, you see, is my daughter."

Sam gave the man a skeptical perusal. "Yeah, and I'm the King of England." He started to close the door, but the stranger put his palm against it.

"No need to be sarcastic, Mr. Blackman. If your wife is Prairie Rose Jernigan Blackman, I truly am her father—her real father."

"And who might you be?"

The stranger smiled. "I believe you've heard of me through your brother Wayne. I am Waldemar Paxton Wolfeschlegersteinhausenberger."

Chapter Twenty-four

Sam blinked a couple of times, then felt his jaw drop clean to his knees. Wolf's Leg was his father-in-law? Unbelievable!

Once Sam recovered from the initial shock, he opened the door wider and grinned self-consciously.

"Do come in, Mr. Wolf's—" Sam caught himself in the nick of time. It wouldn't do at all to call this man by the nickname he'd devised. Not to his face. No, not ever again, he mentally corrected. Recalling his quip about the law firm, he started over, verbally dividing the banker's name into its five separate parts.

"Call me Val. Not only is it easier to remember, it also takes a lot less time to vocalize."

As Sam took Val's hat and cane, he pondered this unexpected turn of events. There was one question he felt compelled to ask. "Please understand, Mr. . . . Val." Sam felt uncomfortable with the name. He also felt uncomfortable with his question, but he had to know. "How do you know Prairie is your daughter?"

"Suffice it to say, I *know*. At present, I want to see her."

Sam shook his head. "She's resting, and rest for her is a rare commodity."

"Well, son," Val said, offering Sam his hand, "I suppose we both have a score of questions for each other and an abundance of catching up to do. I want to know what happened to my daughter, and then I'll tell you my story. But first, please let me take a peek at her. I promise not to disturb her rest, but I've waited over twenty years for this moment."

"Very well," Sam said, shaking Val's hand firmly. "There's a fresh pot of coffee on the stove—and there are some people in the kitchen who'll want to meet you."

Wynn and Doc shot questioning looks at Sam, who assured them *sotto voce* that he'd explain later. Val moved quietly to Prairie's bedside and stood stock still, staring down at her for a long time. When they moved into the kitchen's stronger light, Sam could see a gathering of tears in his father-in-law's eyes and the man's voice was husky when he said, "She looks so much like her mother."

Sam wasn't exactly sure what he'd expected from this wealthy financier, but it wasn't congeniality. He supposed he'd thought that anyone with that much money, and therefore that much power, would hold himself above commonfolk. But not Wolf's Leg. He greeted Ruth and Michael with genuine warmth and accepted their hospitality as though he sat down at a kitchen table every day of his life. No matter how hard Sam tried, he couldn't imagine this man ever choosing to sit in a slat-bottom chair at an enamel-topped table or drinking coffee from a stoneware mug by design.

Together, Sam and Michael told Val about the shooting and the events that had led up to it, then Ruth offered to sit with Prairie while Doc and Wynn talked to him.

When Sam had introduced Val as Prairie's father, he took a great deal of pleasure from watching Michael's and Ruth's reactions—profound astonishment mixed with a degree of disbelief, much as he himself had responded to the announcement. Though Doc's reaction followed the same course, Wynn's lack of surprise caught everyone unawares.

"Well," she said in a huff, planting her hands on her hips, "it took you long enough to show up."

"You knew about me?" Val asked in total bewilderment.

"Not about you specifically," she explained, "only that Prairie had a father somewhere. You have a lot to answer for, mister."

Her veiled accusation drew a tentative smile from Val Wolfeschlegersteinhausenberger. "I will be most happy to oblige you, madam, at a more propitious time. At present, I think it best you fill me in on my daughter's condition."

Sam could see the wheels turning in Val's head as his father-in-law listened to Doc's and Wynn's discourse. When they had finished, Val drew his hands together and rested his steepled fingers under his chin. "So you both agree that Prairie needs an X-ray. Can she be moved?"

"Not in a wagon," Wynn said.

"I was thinking about my private railroad car."

"Where do you want to take her?" Doc asked.

"New Orleans."

"We'll have to exercise every caution," Wynn commented, "but I'm not sure we have a choice anymore."

After a moment of private deliberation, Doc and Wynn agreed—on the condition they both be allowed to accompany her.

"I can't guarantee either of you will be allowed to perform the surgery, should Prairie require it," Val cautioned them.

"Neither of us truly wants to," Wynn assured him. "We're both too close to her. But we do want to be consulted."

"I'm certain that can easily be arranged," Val said.

"Excuse me," Ruth said, coming into the kitchen. "She's awake."

When Val started to rise, Wynn said, "Let me

365

change her dressing and prepare her to meet you. It should only take a few minutes."

After all these years, Prairie thought, *after all the hopes and dreams, after all the hard work and disappointments, the search is over.*

During all those years and all her searching, she'd often imagined that finding a relative would bring her peace. Now that it had finally happened, she didn't feel peaceful; she felt excited—alive and sentient. She discovered the feeling was far more wonderful than anything she could ever have conceived.

Prairie wished she could see everyone's face so that she could photograph their reactions and paste them in a mental scrapbook. And later, perhaps in her old age should she live, she could turn the pages and relive this night.

"This was the day my father found me," she would think. "We'd been looking for each other for a long time. Here's Sam, sitting on the other side of my bed. And there are Wynn and Michael standing by the window, and Doc and Ruth sitting in chairs they'd brought from the kitchen. And all the while my father talked no one said a word or asked a question. From time to time, Doc would pull his ear or Wynn's eyes would widen in wonder, but all the while Sam sat with his elbows on his knees and his chin in his hand, as fascinated by it all as I was."

However, the necessity of her prone position prevented her from seeing anyone except her father. As Prairie watched him, she memorized every detail of his face, every aspect of his appearance. She had no difficulty understanding how Anna had fallen in love with this man whose very being exuded strength and vitality and a lust for life.

"It was my lust for wealth that destroyed our relationship," he admitted candidly, "but by the time I realized what I was doing, it was too late. Anna was gone." He laughed then, a short, self-deprecating laugh that brought a tear of sorrow to Prairie's eyes. Had Anna ever realized she'd separated two halves of one soul?

"Life is so strange," he continued. "Once I stopped pursuing wealth, it started pursuing me. Everything I touched turned to gold, but all that money never brought me happiness. It couldn't even bring me you, Prairie. You did that, with your stories. Had you not written them, I would still be searching for you."

When she would have asked him some questions, he took her hand and squeezed it. "There will be ample time later," he promised her, "after you are well. You must conserve your strength. I must go now and make arrangements for an engine to pull my car back to New Orleans. Dr. Donovan will explain." He patted her hand, then rose to leave.

"Papa," she called, warming at the sweet sound of the word in her ears. "Could I kiss you goodbye?"

He knelt down by her bed and kissed her on the cheek. "This isn't goodbye, my daughter. It's only good night. You won't be rid of me quite so easily."

"I don't want to be rid of you, Papa," she whispered. "I'm so happy you found me."

Long after he had left and everyone but Wynn had returned to the kitchen, Prairie lay on her stomach and cried softly into her pillow. Now that she'd had time to think about everything, to put it all into perspective and review her behavior over the years, she found herself woefully deficient in life's most valuable commodity: the ability to love unconditionally.

Wynn sat down on the bed and put her arm around Prairie's shoulders. "Don't cry," she soothed. "You must keep your spirits up, Prairie. Your chances of survival are good—even better since we're taking you to New Orleans."

"It's not that," Prairie murmured. "I'm so angry at myself, Wynn. All these years, I've held myself aloof from you because you weren't my mother. I love you and Michael and the boys. I'm glad I found my father—or rather, that he found me, but I realize now that no one could ever take your place in my heart."

"I'm guilty too, Prairie. Let's not look back. Let's look forward. We have a number of good years ahead of us to straighten out this mess we've made."

Prairie sniffled and blew her nose on the handkerchief Wynn provided. "Could I have a glass of water?"

"Of course, dear."

After she took a few sips, she handed the glass back to Wynn and said, "I need to talk to Sam. Do you think he could sleep with me tonight?"

Wynn chuckled. "Only if you promise to behave."

"Do I have a choice?" Prairie quipped.

"Are you sure you don't want a dose of laudanum to ease the pain and help you rest?" Wynn asked.

"No. The pain isn't so bad, so long as I don't move. I don't want my senses dulled. If my hours are numbered, I want to count them as they go by."

"Faith, Prairie, faith," Wynn said, "but I understand. I'll get Sam."

He came in and stretched out beside her on top of the covers. "No, Sam," Prairie said. "I want to feel you beside me. I want to feel your arm around me and your breath on my cheek."

"Are you sure it's all right?" he asked. "Maybe I should ask Wynn."

"It's fine," Prairie assured him.

He stripped down to his union suit and climbed in beside her, his every tender movement an expression of his love.

"I want to apologize, Sam," she began.

"You have nothing to apologize for."

"Yes, I do. I accused you with being obsessed when I was the one with an obsession. I thought you had to let go of your work to love me, but I wasn't willing to let go of my work to love you."

"Loving each other doesn't require us to let go of anything," Sam said.

Prairie sighed. "I know that now. I wish my mother had known that. I think she did know it before she died. I can remember so much more about her now — how sad she was all the time, and yet how bitter. I had thought she blamed my father for her misery, but I realize now that she blamed herself. When she told me not to make the same mistake she did, she was talking about leaving my father, not marrying him."

"But if she hadn't left your father, Prairie, you wouldn't have come to Jennings and we would never have met."

"I've brought you nothing but misery, Sam."

"That isn't true!" he staunchly denied. "I'm not the least bit miserable."

"Yes, you are. You're just too good to say so."

"And why, pray tell, do you think I'm so miserable?"

"You were forced to marry me."

Sam chuckled. "Do you honestly think I would have married you if I hadn't wanted to?"

"Maybe not."

"Definitely not. It was *you* who didn't want me, if I remember correctly. Have you, perhaps, changed your mind?"

"Oh, Sam!" Prairie cried. "I've always wanted you."

For a moment, they were silent. Then Sam said, "There is one thing I wish you'd explain to me, though."

"What's that?"

"Why you don't want my children."

Prairie winced inwardly at the evident pain in his voice. "I do want your children, Sam."

"But you fear childbirth."

"No, that's not it at all. I feared bringing a child into the world who never knew her father. I was afraid history would repeat itself."

"Are you still afraid?"

"Not anymore, Sam."

She went to sleep with Sam combing his fingers through her hair, but Sam lay awake for hours. Prairie might not be afraid anymore, but he was terrified she'd never live long enough to bear a child.

Sam had always supposed if you had enough money, you could accomplish almost anything. Val's money and influence got Prairie to New Orleans and into a private hospital with facilities as modern and doctors as well-trained and competent as any in the South.

When the X-ray showed the bullet to be lodged in a muscle, Wynn waged a one-woman war against all the other physicians who examined Prairie. "Surgery should never be undertaken if it can be avoided," she insisted, but to no avail.

Convincing the other doctors was not her major battle, however. It was convincing Sam. The doctors would not remove the bullet without his approval.

For days, he vacillated between camps, not in complete agreement with either. While he postponed a decision, Prairie made slow but steady improvement. This was to be expected, the doctors said. Gunshot victims usually rallied, once the body readjusted itself. But later, they warned, infection would set in. That wasn't necessarily true, Wynn argued.

Sam didn't know who to believe. One day, he posed the question to Prairie.

"I trust your judgment, Sam."

"I don't know anything about medicine, Prairie," he reminded her.

"You're thinking too hard again, Sam."

"There is no easy solution this time," he argued. "At the moment, surgery doesn't appear necessary. But the doctors say that if we delay too long, then surgery may not help. They're certain you can't live with that bullet in you."

"Well, I'm certain I can. Jamie MacDougall is living proof."

"So Wynn tells me. I still think we're taking a big risk."

Prairie smiled. "That's nothing new for either of us."

Sam wanted to tell her this was different, that her life was at stake, but she knew those things. Rehashing them now would serve no purpose.

"Promise me something, Sam."

"Anything."

"Promise me you'll write to Beadle and Adams and tell them who Pampas J. Rose really is."

"Why?" he asked, perplexed. "Don't you want to continue to write for them?"

"I'm tired of the deception, Sam. I don't want to live a lie ever again."

"You can write to them, Prairie, when you get home."

"Promise me, Sam," she said again, and this time he couldn't ignore the hidden plea of a woman determined to tie up all the loose ends of her life.

Sam stood at the window, staring out at the thick pine forest which covered the rolling hills of North Louisiana, seeing little more than a blur of green but watching closely for the occasional relief of a flowering white dogwood. The delicate flowers signaled the onset of a spring Sam had thought never to notice, for without Prairie, nothing would ever be new again.

And that was what spring was: a rebirth, not only of the earth, but of hope and beauty, of faith and love, of life rejuvenating itself after a long, hard winter.

There had never been a winter so long or so hard as this past one had been for Sam. He would gladly choose to weather bitter cold and blinding blizzards over enduring the frigid bite of death's specter again.

Prairie's phenomenal progress had fostered false hopes. No one had seen the hand writing on the wall, least of all Sam, who'd sent Wynn and Doc home to welcome in the new year with their families. There were ample doctors available, he argued, to care for her, and he was there around the clock to massage and exercise her legs and arms and help her keep her spirits up. Additionally, her father visited her daily. The three had a relationship to build almost from scratch.

And then, a week into January, Prairie developed a chill and her temperature shot up to 104 degrees. "This is the infection we warned you about," the doctors said, shaking their heads. They recommended emergency surgery to remove the bullet.

Sam stalled them long enough to wire Wynn. Her reply: "Make them trace the infection. Hold off on surgery if you can. I'm on my way."

The doctors balked at being given orders by an oil-man and a country doctor who was a woman to boot, but Val intervened on Sam's behalf. Privately, Val confided to Sam. "I hope Wynn Donovan knows what she's talking about."

Sam agreed. "I'll feel much better when she gets here in the morning. At least it's Wednesday. She can catch the train tonight."

Sam and Val sat with Prairie throughout the night,

packing her in ice when she was hot, wrapping her in warm blankets when she was chilled, and holding her arms and legs when she tried to thrash about.

Not long before daylight, Sam said, "She isn't going to make it, Val, and it's all my fault. I should have let them remove the bullet."

"You don't know that, Sam," Val consoled. "She could have died on the operating table. We all look back and wish we'd done things differently, but if we had, our entire lives would have taken a different course. Who can say that we would have been happier? Who can say that the other decisions would have been the right ones? You did what you thought was best for Prairie and I, for one, will never hold you responsible, regardless of what happens now."

"There was one thing I could have done — *should* have done that would have made everything better," Sam said bitterly. "I should have killed Clarkston when I had the chance — before he shot Prairie."

Val thought about that a minute. "If you had, do you think you and Prairie would still be together?" At Sam's raised eyebrow, he said, "She told me about the premarital agreement. You don't have to answer. Maybe you would. Maybe you wouldn't. The truth is you'll both be stronger after this, and your love for each other will be stronger, too."

Wynn arrived at seven-thirty. They heard her before they saw her.

"Hey, you! Lady! You can't go in there!" a male voice harped.

"Oh, yes, I can!" Wynn snapped right back. "My daughter's in there."

The orderly followed her into the room, continuing his tirade, though he lowered his voice. Val took the young man by his shoulders and ushered him out of the room. "I'm calling Dr. Abrahms," the orderly threatened.

373

"Please do," Val said, and he closed the door.

"What did they say about the infection?" Wynn asked.

"They didn't," Sam replied, "outside of insisting it originated with the bullet."

Wynn checked Prairie's vital signs, then listened to her chest. "Take a deep breath for me, Prairie," Wynn instructed, then nodded and removed her stethoscope.

"Just as I thought. Pneumonia. Have they given her any medication?"

"No," Sam said.

"Good. What about purging? Did they try that?"

"No."

"No blood-letting either?"

"No. I wouldn't let them touch her."

Wynn patted Sam's arm. "You did the right thing. What have you and Val done for her?"

"Tried to cool her when she was feverish and warm her when she was chilled. How did she get pneumonia?"

Wynn shrugged as she tucked her stethoscope into her medical bag. "Probably picked up a germ. Hospitals are full of them."

Sam found himself indebted to Val once again, for the man used his wealth and his influence to persuade the chief of staff to allow the three of them total control over Prairie's care. They worked over her day and night, administering cool compresses and ice bags alternately with hot fomentations, following a schedule Wynn decreed. Although Wynn assured Sam and Val that pneumonia was seldom fatal, Prairie seemed to hover on the verge of death, and occasionally Wynn would mumble something about her father dying from a simple case of pneumonia.

By the grace of God and the vigilance of husband, father, and foster mother, Prairie pulled through. As soon as she was well enough, Val had her transported by ambulance to his house in the Garden District. Her complete recovery required another six weeks.

Sam had already made arrangements for their return to Jennings when Val burst in the door one afternoon with a smile so wide it almost obliterated his eyes.

"What is it?" Prairie asked, catching her father's excitement.

"This!" he said, thrusting a letter into her hands.

She pulled the single sheet out of the slitted top of the envelope, but as her gaze drifted down the page, she began to tremble. And when she finished reading the letter, her eyes were awash with tears.

Val's excitement coupled with Prairie's distress confused Sam. He glanced from one to the other, silently begging for an explanation.

"I've been writing to her for years," Val said, "but she would never respond. I couldn't be certain she was still alive, although I've had one of my operatives check on her at least annually."

"Who are you talking about?" Sam asked.

"Annie," Prairie whispered, almost reverently. "My grandmother. She wants to meet me."

"I suppose we could take a detour on the way home," Sam had said.

"Rather a long one," she had quipped. "Thank you, Sam."

Sam felt Prairie's arm slip around his waist as she joined him at the window in her father's private railroad car. Sam saw his love for her reflected in her ginger-colored eyes. "Did you have a good nap?" he asked.

She nodded, setting her dangling earbobs ajingle. "I could get spoiled with Daddy's private car."

Sam gave her an indulgent smile. "According to Wayne, we have a small fortune waiting for us in Jennings, Mrs. Blackman. I suppose we can afford to buy our own."

"I don't think so," she said.

"And why not?" Sam asked, feigning injury.

"Because once we get back home, mister, we're not going anywhere else for some time."

"And why not?" Sam asked again, this time out of obvious curiosity.

Her eyes sparkled with barely suppressed glee. "Because, Mr. Blackman, we're going to have a baby."

"We are?"

She nodded.

"We are!" He threw his arms around her waist, lifted her off the floor, and whirled her around until she giggled and begged for mercy.

"I'll give you mercy," he teased, falling with her onto the bed. "I'll give you more mercy that you can handle."

"Show me," she said.

And he did.

Epilogue

April 16, 1903

Prairie giggled as Sam turned her round and round.

"What are you doing, blindfolding me and then turning me around like this?" she said.

"You'll see." Sam chuckled and steered her toward the dining room.

"You're making me dizzy."

"That's the point."

"You're going to be disappointed," she teased. "I never was good at pinning the tail on the donkey."

"Oh, shoot!" he said. "I wish I'd thought of that game. Maybe next year."

"Next year? Whatever are you doing?"

"Patience, Mrs. Blackman, patience."

Sam could remember a time not so very long ago when he'd given himself the same advice. Humph! He could remember *many* a time over the past year when he'd told himself to be patient.

First, there had been Annie O'Malley's reluctance to accept Prairie as her grandchild. He'd hated seeing the crushed look on Prairie's face when the grizzled old woman had given her a cursory glance and then flicked a shooing hand toward the door.

"You've seen me now, youngun," Annie had said. "I

never needed to see you atall. You look just like my Anna and it hurts me to look at you. Reminds me of things I'd just as soon forget."

"Then why did you ask to see me?" Prairie questioned, attempting to mask the hurt she was feeling, though it was written all over her face.

"To make Wolf's Leg quit pesterin' me."

They'd stayed in St. Louis for two weeks. Though Prairie had visited her grandmother daily, the old woman never opened her heart to her long lost granddaughter.

"I had so many things wrong," Prairie said on their way back to Louisiana. "It's a wonder my darn fool silly notion ever worked. Big Spring wasn't a town; it was a ranch. Wolf's Leg wasn't a half-breed; he was a German with an impossible name. And the name Susie apparently didn't mean anything to anyone except me. I thought all along it would be an aunt or a grandmother who would recognize the clues. I wasn't completely wrong there. At least I know now that Lucy Byers is my great aunt, and that Martha was probably Jernigan's sister and not my aunt at all."

"Would you like to take a little detour to Texarkana on our way home," Sam asked, "and see your Aunt Lucy?"

Lucy Byers bore no resemblance—either in looks or personality—to her sister Annie. Once she'd heard their story, she received Prairie with open arms, and the two spent the better part of two days talking and poring over scrapbooks, boxes of photographs, and the family Bible. They parted with the promise to correspond regularly.

Shortly after their return to Jennings, they were forced to endure King Clarkston's trial, during which every grueling detail of the shooting had been exposed then rehashed repeatedly. It had looked as though King would be acquitted, despite Prairie's and Kevin's testimonies, on which King's lawyer capably cast doubt, just as Fontenot had said he would.

But at the last minute, Sybil James asked to be recalled to the stand. The young woman admitted she'd perjured herself by providing an alibi for King. He had threatened her life, she said, if she refused to cover for him. Since she was reasonably certain he had killed her family, she had succumbed to his intimidation. She had felt certain the evidence against him was too strong for the alibi to matter, but when it looked as though he might go free, she had realized she had to tell the truth.

King shot out of his chair and screamed obscenities at her. His face was that of a madman.

The jury found King Clarkston guilty of attempted murder and sentenced him to fifty years at hard labor. Unfortunately, Watson, the hired hand, had already been tried, convicted, and hanged for the axe murders of the James family.

Sam and Prairie had breathed easier after the trial, though it wasn't too long afterward that Sam's patience was tested again. He'd never imagined there could be so many decisions to make concerning a house—or so many arguments raised over a shade of paint or a pattern for wallpaper. For weeks, he divided his time among construction sites: the Blackman Brothers office building, the refinery, and the house.

They'd barely settled into their new home before the baby was born. Throughout the long hours of labor, Sam paced the sitting room, listening to Prairie's screams, terrified that she had been delivered to him only to be snatched away during childbirth.

In the end, she bore him a beautiful daughter, whom they named Anna—and then she shocked him to his toes with the announcement that she wanted to have another child next year.

"I don't think I could stand this that often!" he said.

"You get used to it," Michael assured him.

There were a slew of things going on that were going to take some getting used to. Jennings had almost doubled in size since the boom, and with the new prosperity had come change—major change. As the residents had planned following the fire, the town now had its own water system and fire department. The electrical and telephone lines had also been completed and service installed in all the new buildings and many of the old ones.

But the biggest change was the face of the town itself. Sturdy brick buildings rose from the ashes, among them Wynn's hospital, an opera hall, and a new hundred-room hotel which attracted travelers by the droves. Seldom did the hotel have a vacancy.

"I used to write to create excitement," Prairie said. "Now, I have more excitement than I can manage."

Following her recuperation, Prairie wrote to Beadle and Adams. Not only did she reveal her identity, but she also told them in no uncertain terms that Pampas J. Rose had retired—at least temporarily. At first, the firm ignored her claim. When they received no further manuscripts from David, they wrote to him. His reply convinced them of the truth.

Thus ensued a lengthy apology to Prairie—and an assurance that the publishing firm of Beadle and Adams would be more than happy to consider forthcoming manuscripts from her whenever she should choose to send them. Recently, she'd dragged out the Cherokee Sally story and decided to try out the typewriter Val had given her—belatedly—for Christmas over a year ago.

Sam didn't like to recall the first Christmas he and Prairie had shared, but this past one had been an extraordinary occasion for him. He discovered that he truly enjoyed shopping for Prairie and creating surprises for his wife.

It was this enjoyment that prompted his surprise for her that day. Sam stopped steering Prairie and fumbled with the knot he'd made in the handkerchief he'd tied around her eyes.

"All right. You can look now."

Prairie's ginger-colored eyes widened and her pouty lips fell open at the sight before her. Guests packed the dining room, which had been gaily decorated with balloons and ribbon streamers. A large banner declaring "Happy Birthday" had been tacked above the opposite doorway and a huge, candle-laden cake graced the table. Everyone burst into song.

When she'd had a moment to recover, Prairie nudged Sam. "How did you know it was my birthday?" she asked.

"I didn't — or rather, I don't know. Is it?"

"I don't know either. I've never known when my birthday was. Why did you choose today?"

He grinned. "Because, according to Wynn, it was on April sixteenth that Jernigan brought you to her house. We figured today was as good a day as any."

Her eyes glistened with unshed tears. "Better than any other," she whispered. "What a wonderful way to commemorate one of the most important days of my life."

LET ARCHER AND CLEARY
AWAKEN AND CAPTURE YOUR HEART!

CAPTIVE DESIRE   (2612, $3.75)
by Jane Archer

Victoria Malone fancied herself a great adventuress and student of life, but being kidnapped by handsome Cord Cordova was too much excitement for even her! Convincing her kidnapper that she had been an innocent bystander when the stagecoach was robbed was futile when he was kissing her until she was senseless!

REBEL SEDUCTION   (3249, $4.25)
by Jane Archer

"Stop that train!" came Lacey Whitmore's terrified warning as she rushed toward the locomotive that carried wounded Confederates and her own beloved father. But no one paid heed, least of all the Union spy Clint McCullough, who pinned her to the ground as the train suddenly exploded into flames.

DREAM'S DESIRE   (3093, $4.50)
by Gwen Cleary

Desperate to escape an arranged marriage, Antonia Winston y Ortega fled her father's hacienda to the arms of the arrogant Captain Domino. She would spend the night with him and would be free for no gentleman wants a ruined bride. And ruined she would be, for Tonia would never forget his searing kisses!

VICTORIA'S ECSTASY   (2906, $4.25)
by Gwen Cleary

Proud Victoria Torrington was short of cash to run her shipping empire, so she traveled to America to meet her partner for the first time. Expecting a withered, ancient cowhand, Victoria didn't know what to do when she met virile, muscular Judge Colston and her body budded with desire.

Available wherever paperbacks are sold, or order direct from the Publisher. Send cover price plus 50¢ per copy for mailing and handling to Zebra Books, Dept. 4172, 475 Park Avenue South, New York, N.Y. 10016. Residents of New York and Tennessee must include sales tax. DO NOT SEND CASH. For a free Zebra/ Pinnacle catalog please write to the above address.

PASSION BLAZES IN A ZEBRA HEARTFIRE!

COLORADO MOONFIRE (3730, $4.25/$5.50)
by Charlotte Hubbard

Lila O'Riley left Ireland, determined to make her own way in America. Finding work and saving pennies presented no problem for the independent lass; locating love was another story. Then one hot night, Lila meets Marshal Barry Thompson. Sparks fly between the fiery beauty and the lawman. Lila learns that America is the promised land, indeed!

MIDNIGHT LOVESTORM (3705, $4.25/$5.50)
by Linda Windsor

Dr. Catalina McCulloch was eager to begin her practice in Los Reyes, California. On her trip from East Texas, the train is robbed by the notorious, masked bandit known as Archangel. Before making his escape, the thief grabs Cat, kisses her fervently, and steals her heart. Even at the risk of losing her standing in the community, Cat must find her mysterious lover once again. No matter what the future might bring . . .

MOUNTAIN ECSTASY (3729, $4.25/$5.50)
by Linda Sandifer

As a divorced woman, Hattie Longmore knew that she faced prejudice. Hoping to escape wagging tongues, she traveled to her brother's Idaho ranch, only to learn of his murder from long, lean Jim Rider. Hattie seeks comfort in Rider's powerful arms, but she soon discovers that this strong cowboy has one weakness . . . marriage. Trying to lasso this wandering man's heart is a challenge that Hattie enthusiastically undertakes.

RENEGADE BRIDE (3813, $4.25/$5.50)
by Barbara Ankrum

In her heart, Mariah Parsons always believed that she would marry the man who had given her her first kiss at age sixteen. Four years later, she is actually on her way West to begin her life with him . . . and she meets Creed Deveraux. Creed is a rough-and-tumble bounty hunter with a masculine swagger and a powerful magnetism. Mariah finds herself drawn to this bold wilderness man, and their passion is as unbridled as the Montana landscape.

ROYAL ECSTASY (3861, $4.25/$5.50)
by Robin Gideon

The name Princess Jade Crosse has become hated throughout the kingdom. After her husband's death, her "advisors" have punished and taxed the commoners with relentless glee. Sir Lyon Beauchane has sworn to stop this evil tyrant and her cruel ways. Scaling the castle wall, he meets this "wicked" woman face to face . . . and is overpowered by love. Beauchane learns the truth behind Jade's imprisonment. Together they struggle to free Jade from her jailors and from her inhibitions.

Available wherever paperbacks are sold, or order direct from the Publisher. Send cover price plus 50¢ per copy for mailing and handling to Zebra Books, Dept. 4172, 475 Park Avenue South, New York, N.Y. 10016. Residents of New York and Tennessee must include sales tax. DO NOT SEND CASH. For a free Zebra/ Pinnacle catalog please write to the above address.